PENGUIN ⓟ CLASSICS

DADDY-LONG-LEGS *and* DEAR ENEMY

JEAN WEBSTER was born Alice Jane Chandler Webster in 1876 and grew up in Fredonia, New York, and in New York City. A grand-niece of Mark Twain, Webster attended Vassar College, where she developed an interest in orphanages and social welfare and began to pursue a literary career. Her interest in both continued after her graduation in 1901, especially when she moved to New York's Greenwich Village. She published stories and articles in news-papers and in magazines, including *McClure's*. Her first novel, *When Patty Went to College,* came out in 1903, and was followed by *The Wheat Princess* (1905), *Jerry Junior* (1907), *The Four Pools Mystery* (1908), *Much Ado About Peter* (1909), and *Just Patty* (1911). In 1912 Webster published *Daddy-Long-Legs,* the novel that brought her great popular acclaim as well as financial security when she adapted it into a stage play in 1914. It later be-came the basis for several movies. The novel's sequel, *Dear Enemy,* appeared in 1915. Also in 1915, Jean Webster married lawyer and Standard Oil Company heir Glenn Ford McKinney, some seven years after they began their affair (and a few months after his di-vorce was final). She died the following year, shortly after giving birth to their daughter, who survived.

ELAINE SHOWALTER is the author of the groundbreaking *A Litera-ture of Their Own* and other books including *Teaching Litera-ture, Inventing Herself, Hystories, Sexual Anarchy,* and *The Female Malady,* and the editor of volumes including the Penguin Classics editions of Louisa May Alcott's *Little Women* and George Gissing's *The Odd Women.* Her articles have appeared in an array of publications, including the *Times Literary Supple-ment* and *People.* She is professor emerita of English at Princeton University and now lives in Washington, D.C., and London.

JEAN WEBSTER
Daddy-Long-Legs

and

Dear Enemy

Edited with an Introduction and
Notes by ELAINE SHOWALTER

PENGUIN BOOKS

PENGUIN BOOKS

Published by the Penguin Group
Penguin Group (USA) Inc., 375 Hudson Street,
New York, New York 10014, U.S.A.
Penguin Books Ltd, 80 Strand,
London, WC2R 0RL, England
Penguin Books Australia Ltd, 250 Camberwell Road, Camberwell,
Victoria 3124, Australia
Penguin Books Canada Ltd, 10 Alcorn Avenue,
Toronto, Ontario, Canada M4V 3B2
Penguin Books India (P) Ltd, 11 Community Centre, Panchsheel Park,
New Delhi – 110 017, India
Penguin Books (NZ), Cnr Airborne and Rosedale Roads, Albany,
Auckland 1310, New Zealand
Penguin Books (South Africa) (Pty) Ltd, 24 Sturdee Avenue,
Rosebank, Johannesburg 2196, South Africa

Penguin Books Ltd, Registered Offices:
80 Strand, London, WC2R 0RL, England

Daddy-Long-Legs first published in the United States of America by The Century Co. 1912
Dear Enemy first published in the United States of America by The Century Co. 1915
This edition with an introduction and notes by Elaine Showalter published in Penguin Books 2004

1 3 5 7 9 10 8 6 4 2

Introduction and notes copyright © Elaine Showalter, 2004
All rights reserved

LIBRARY OF CONGRESS CATALOGING-IN-PUBLICATION DATA

Webster, Jean, 1876–1916.
Daddy Long Legs ; and, Dear enemy / Jean Webster ; edited with an introduction
and notes by Elaine Showalter.
p. cm.
Includes bibliographical references.
ISBN 0-14-303906-7
1. Women college students—Fiction. 2. Philanthropists—Fiction. 3. Women authors—Fiction.
4. Young women—Fiction. 5. Orphans—Fiction. I. Showalter, Elaine.
II. Webster, Jean, 1876–1916. Dear enemy. III. Title: Dear enemy. IV. Title.

PS3545.E365D3 2004
813'.52—dc22   2004048210

Printed in the United States of America
Set in Adobe Sabon

Contents

Introduction

Jean Webster's *Daddy-Long-Legs* (1912) and its sequel, *Dear Enemy* (1915), come from a literary era in which best-selling American woman writers like Kate Douglas Wiggin (*Rebecca of Sunnybrook Farm*), Eleanor H. Porter (*Pollyanna*), and Gene Stratton-Porter (*A Girl of the Limberlost*) created sentimental girl heroines. In contrast, one of the truly modern qualities of Webster's writing is its lack of sentimentality and preachiness. Although her heroines Judy and Sallie are idealistic reformers, they are also irreverent and irrepressible; although they are staunch feminists, they also take great pleasure in kid gloves, new dresses, and male company. The epistolary format of these two novels allows the liveliness of women's letter-writing to cloak the radical notions of women's limitless strength and capability.

In many respects, Webster's novels are in the great American tradition of Louisa May Alcott's fiction. Like Jo March in *Little Women,* which Judy mentions among the books she is reading in *Daddy-Long-Legs,* Judy aspires to be a writer, and must discard both the patriarchal models of her education and the sensational stories of her imagination before she realizes that her own experience is her best material, and finds her own voice. Like Jo in the sequels, *Little Men* and *Jo's Boys,* Sallie McBride in *Dear Enemy* discovers that running a model institution for children is more interesting than romance; "I see marriage as a man must," writes Sallie, "a good, sensible workaday institution; but awfully curbing to one's liberty."

Finally, like Jo, both Judy and Sallie find happiness with men who will accept and support their yearning to work. Although each novel ends with a predictable love scene, these seem almost an afterthought, for the action of these novels comes not from Judy Abbott's and Sallie McBride's search for a strong man, but from their discoveries of their own strength. They are unconventional New Women, as well as independent American girls; indeed, Sallie muses, "one man doesn't seem quite enough for me."

Daddy-Long-Legs, the most popular of Jean Webster's books, is both a love story and a Künstlerroman—an autobiographical account of an artist's development. Rescued from the dreary wasteland of the John Grier Home for orphans by an anonymous philanthropist, Jerusha Abbott (whose solemn name the director of the Home has selected from the phone book and the cemetery) is sent to college with her benefactor's express intent that she should be educated "to become a writer." A John Grier Trustee, he has read her essay "Blue Wednesday," describing the "Perfectly Awful Day" of the month, the first Wednesday, on which the trustees and their ladies come to hear reports and to inspect their charges. "Blue Wednesday" is satiric and "impertinent," but luckily the Trustee has a sense of humor and finds it original. We can judge it a bit ourselves, because "Blue Wednesday" is also the first chapter of the novel, and the only one written in the third person.

The trustee wishes to be anonymous, and insists only that Jerusha send him monthly letters of her progress, addressed to "Mr. John Smith," because "he thinks nothing so fosters facility in literary expression as letter-writing." But he will never reply, because he himself detests writing letters, and does not care for girls. Thereafter, the story is told through the lively letters of the heroine, and illustrated with her cartoons and drawings. She begins by renaming herself "Judy" and giving her benefactor the nickname "Daddy-Long-Legs" because she has caught a glimpse of his shadow, with "grotesquely elongated legs and arms." (Webster glosses over Judy's lack of initiative in figuring out who he is—surely the John Grier Home cannot have anonymous trustees.) But by the novel's end, after her graduation from college, not only has Judy discovered Daddy-Long-Legs' identity and found her true love, but she has also sold her first novel. Finally, she reflects upon a Blue Wednesday from the vantage point of her last semester of college, and concludes that being an orphan was "a very unusual adventure" that has given her "a perspective on the world, that other people, who have been brought up in the thick of things, entirely lack."

Webster weaves Judy's road to authorship through her letters to Daddy-Long-Legs. She buys five hundred sheets of yellow manuscript paper with his first Christmas present, and regularly wins literary prizes and publications in college; a poem, "From My Tower," as a freshman; the short-story competition as a sophomore; another story and a scholarship for "marked proficiency in English" the same year. As a junior, she tries writing a novel based on her two-week holiday trip to New York, but it is rejected as "improbable" and "unnatural." She burns it, and dreams that she is holding a book called "The Life and Letters of Judy Abbott," with a picture of the John Grier Home on the cover. By her senior year, she realizes that her own life is her true subject. "I'm a realist now," she explains. "I've abandoned romanticism; I shall go back to it later though, when my own adventurous future begins." And when she decides to marry, she realizes that she can keep on being a writer: "the two professions are not necessarily exclusive."

How much of a realist was Jean Webster? Many of the themes and details of the two novels are autobiographical, but Webster's life was much more privileged and cosmopolitan. Born in 1876 to Charles Luther and Annie (Moffet) Webster, Alice Jane Chandler Webster enjoyed a comfortable childhood in Fredonia, New York. In 1884, her father became the business partner and publisher of Mark Twain, his wife's uncle, and moved the family to Manhattan, where he directed the Charles L. Webster Publishing Company. Publishing such best-sellers as *The Adventures of Huckleberry Finn* and General Ulysses S. Grant's overwhelmingly successful *Personal Memoirs,* Charles Webster met both great success and stressful responsibility. He developed severe headaches, a form of nervous breakdown, and had to move back to the country. After his recovery, Twain refused to take him back, charged him with poor management, and bought him out for less than his shares were worth. Charles

Webster committed suicide in 1891, when his daughter was fifteen. According to Karen Alkalay-Gut, "the rest of [Jean Webster's] life, in many ways, exhibited a protest against patriarchal authority, authoritative systems, and authoritative individuals, and an examination of alternatives to destructive authoritative systems is her constant concern in almost every aspect of her life and writing."[1]

From 1894 to 1896, she attended a boarding school—The Lady Jane Grey School at Binghamton—where she renamed herself Jean because her roommate's name was Alice as well. But the education offered by a finishing school was not enough to satisfy her intellectual curiosity and her nascent spirit of social reform. In 1897, she entered Vassar College with the class of 1901 to study English and economics. She wrote a number of stories for the Vassar literary magazine, *Vassar Miscellany*. In her sophomore year, Webster roomed with the future poet Adelaide Crapsey (with whom she carried the socialist banner in a campus parade), and the class president, Margaret Jackson. She also spent a semester of her junior year abroad in Greece, England, and Italy, researching a paper on poverty in Italy. Meanwhile, she wrote a column for the *Poughkeepsie Sunday Courier*, for which she earned $3 per week. As the paper later noted, "Miss Webster was the correspondent for The Courier while a student at the college and her letters will be remembered by our readers for the atmosphere of cheerfulness that characterized them. No humorous incident at the college ever escaped Miss Webster's attention. At the same time there was no lack of dignity when serious subjects were under consideration. In addition to her correspondence Miss Webster also contributed a series of articles to The Courier covering her experiences while travelling in Europe."[2]

There are many elements of her Vassar experience in *Daddy-Long-Legs*. During her four years as an undergraduate, Vassar was a college of six hundred women, predominantly Republican in their leanings, while Webster was already a socialist. The college did not support women's suffrage or allow the students to participate in suffrage activism. But Vassar was already becoming known as a literary center; Edna St. Vincent Millay chose it over Smith when she entered as a scholarship student in 1913 (with a monthly allowance of $20, compared to the munificent $35 Judy Abbott receives from her patron). In her English class, Judy is expected to comment on a poem by Emily Dickinson (she is baffled)—an indication of how sophisticated the syllabus was for the period. She also participates in the Field Day athletic competitions between the classes, instituted at Vassar in 1895; and she describes the construction of a new dormitory and the infirmary. Most important, she describes herself as a Fabian socialist, one who is willing to wait while "instituting industrial, educational and orphan asylum reforms." In 1898, Sidney and Beatrice Webb, two of the founders of the British Fabian Society, had spoken at Vassar about "The Scope of Democracy in England."[3]

After her 1901 graduation, Webster energetically pursued a literary career. She published her first piece, an article and photographs about Monte Carlo, in 1902 in the *Buffalo Express,* under the pseudonym "Carly Ward." For the next several years, Webster regularly submitted stories to various magazines, persisting despite frequent rejection, and within a few years she was selling to *McClure's* and other periodicals. Her first book, *When Patty Went to College,* came out in 1903. Mark Twain read it and congratulated her mother: "It is limpid, bright, sometimes brilliant; it is easy, flowing, effortless, and brimming with girlish spirits."[4] In November 1903, Webster took off again for Rome, where she visited the graves of Keats and Shelley, and stayed at a convent. She continued to publish stories and novels—*The Wheat Princess* (1905) and *Jerry Junior* (1907).

In November 1907, Webster embarked on a year-long journey around the world with her friends Ethelyn McKinney, daughter of the president of the Standard Oil Company of Pennsylvania, and Lena Weinstein, a New York art critic. They visited Egypt, India, China, Japan, Burma, and Ceylon; in a society clipping in her files, the reporter notes that "She is planning, evidently, for very warm weather, for the main portion of her wardrobe consists of twenty-five white dresses."[5] Such a trip and such a wardrobe were hardly the hallmarks of the bohemian, but Jean was much more daring than she may have appeared. In the summer of 1908, she fell in love with a married man—Ethelyn's brother, the lawyer and Standard Oil Company heir Glenn Ford McKinney. A graduate of Princeton, class of 1891, McKinney was married and had a son; his wife, Annette, had suffered periodic attacks of manic depression. In July 1908, Webster and McKinney began a long-term secret affair. According to Anne Bower, Webster's almost daily letters to him "were a study of good cheer, chattiness, and constancy as she encouraged him to fight alcoholism and the frustration of work he did not enjoy." In July 1913 she wrote to him: "Our salvation is work and work and *more* work. Fortunately we both have some ready to our hands. Set to work with all promptitude and cheerfulness at your farm and accomplish as much as possible against the time when I can look at it with you."[6] Louisa May Alcott could not have put the case for work and duty better.

But Webster was not just a workaholic stoic. On her return from Europe, she settled in Greenwich Village, on West 10th Street. The path from Vassar to the Village was well-trod by feminists, including the suffragists Crystal Eastman and Inez Mulholland. Randolph Bourne aptly described the feminist bohemians of the period to a friend thinking of moving to Greenwich Village: "They are all social workers, or magazine writers in a small way. They are decidedly emancipated and advanced, and so thoroughly healthy and zestful, or at least so it seems to my unsophisticated masculine sense. They shock you constantly. . . . They have an amazing combination of wisdom and youthfulness, of humor and ability, and innocence and self-reliance, which absolutely belies everything you will read in the storybooks or any other description of womankind. They are, of course, all self-supporting and independent; and they enjoy the adventure of life."[7]

Webster was part of this generation. While living in New York and writing, she also became more involved with aiding the unfortunate, continuing an interest that had begun in college when she visited institutions for the destitute and delinquent as part of an economics course. She served on committees for prison reform and worked with Sing-Sing convicts. She defined herself as a socialist and marched in the Women's Suffrage May Day parade, but her tactics were usually playful rather than militant. In the spring of 1909, for example, she received a notice demanding that "Jean Webster, Author" appear for jury duty. Of course, women were not allowed to serve on juries in New York or most states, a form of legal discrimination which elicited protest from feminist writers such as Susan Glaspell, in her story "A Jury of Her Peers." Suffragist friends urged Webster to try to be seated on a jury. Instead, she wrote back on her most feminine stationery ("pale tinted paper, scented with violets"):

> Dear Sir. If you really wish it I shall be delighted to serve on the jury. I have always thought that it would be an interesting experience, but I had never hoped to be invited. The opportunity is very apropos, as I am thinking of having a courtroom scene in my next story, and it will be an excellent opportunity to study local color. Thank you so much for asking me. I am going to the country in June, so that I should not be able to serve then, but any time in May would be convenient, except for Saturday, which is my day at home.
>   Sincerely,
>   Jean Webster
>
> P.S.—I am sure I shall make an intelligent juror. I never read the papers. J. W.

She received a letter in response reiterating that she had to appear for jury duty or face a $250 fine. After asking ten lawyers for legal advice, Webster went to court on the appointed day, and was excused.[8]

Meanwhile, her literary career continued, with the publication of *The Four Pools Mystery* (1908), *Much Ado About Peter* (1909), and *Just Patty* (1911). But *Daddy-Long-Legs*, published in 1912, became the major triumph of her career, an instant and overwhelming success both in the United States and abroad in translation. In one sense, it was about her affair with McKinney; dedicated "To You," it celebrates the epistolary romance. In another sense, one critic argues, it is "the ideal love story" of a feminist: "a girl is brought by a distinguished man to absolute independence and is then in a position to have an equal relationship with him."[9]

In 1914, Webster turned the novel into a stage play starring Ruth Chatterton. It was "the biggest dramatic hit in the country," and after an extensive run at New York's Gaiety Theatre, played in Minneapolis, Atlantic City, Chicago, and Washington, as well as touring California and London.[10] In Chicago, it ran for twenty-five weeks to full houses, and it was performed at the Opera House in Poughkeepsie at the special request of Vassar students.

Webster's papers at Vassar College contain her descriptions of each act and her summaries of the main characters. Without the confines of the first-person epistolary mode, Webster is more explicit and didactic about her intentions. In particular, she stresses Judy's innate and perhaps genetic gifts. While the "orphans as a body represent a dead level of mediocrity, the result of bad environment and in some cases bad heredity . . . Judy stands out in striking contrast." She "rises out of the mass, original, resourceful, courageous. . . . She emerges from her dark background, throws off the trammels that have bound her down and daringly faces life. . . . There is an element of revolt in her nature, a spirit of *fight* which makes her a fierce little rebel against injustice."[11]

Daddy-Long-Legs inspired much interest in the plight of orphans. In 1915 *Woman's World* reported,

> The book has aroused public interest in the lot of the lonely and homeless children of the asylums, and many well to do people, inspired by the example of Daddy Longlegs [sic] of the story, have come forward to adopt or bear the burden of the expense of educating one or more orphans. It is said a wealthy New York bachelor has thus adopted forty children. The New York State Charities Aid Society found so many requests for orphans for adoption coming in after the publication of the book that they appointed a special committee to look after the applications.

Webster encouraged this interest in orphans with the production of thousands of *Daddy-Long-Legs* dolls, each carrying a message about the needs of children in institutions, which were sold in 150 cities of forty states. Webster was among the most highly paid women writers in the United States. As the author of five best sellers in addition to *Daddy-Long-Legs,* she earned book royalties averaging more than $10,000 a year. Royalties from the productions of *Daddy-Long-Legs,* averaging almost $2,000 per week, vaulted her into a whole different league of earnings.

At the height of her celebrity, Webster published her sequel to *Daddy-Long-Legs,* another novel-in-letters called *Dear Enemy.* In her letters, Judy Abbott returns frequently to her dreams of an ideal orphan asylum: "Wait till you see the orphan asylum that I'm going to be the head of! It's my favorite play at night before I go to sleep. I plan it out to the littlest detail—the meals and clothes and study and amusements and punishments; for even my superior orphans are sometimes bad." Judy becomes a writer and a mother instead, but she persuades her college roommate Sallie McBride to take over the John Grier Home. Sallie brings her experience as a social and settlement worker to John Grier, and has to contend with the resident doctor Sandy MacRae, a dour Scot who believes in heredity defects and genetics above environment.

Dear Enemy shows the evolution in Webster's thinking about these issues, and addresses questions of heredity in a more sophisticated fashion than does *Daddy-Long-Legs,* with its tributes to Judy's uniqueness. MacRae and his cohorts are eugenicists who ask whether children's destinies have been set from birth by bad heredity. Could even those children, if brought up in a good, loving family, turn out all right in the end? What could be done about alcoholism, retardation, even crime? He makes Sallie read the studies of inbreeding popular in the period, horror tales of the degenerate and feeble-minded inbred Jukes and Kallikaks, and starts her thinking about weeding out defectives.

But Sallie has her own ideas about child care. As she declares, "Orphan-asylums have gone out of style. What I am going to develop is a boarding-school for the physical, moral, and mental growth of children whose parents have not been able to provide for their care." She emphasizes environment—colorful surroundings, fresh air, appetizing food, pretty clothes for the girls, an Indian-style Adirondack camp for the boys, and self-esteem, private property, and vocational training for all. Sadie Kate Kilcoyne, a feisty orphan, emerges in *Dear Enemy* as a leader in the next generation of intelligent women. She is, like Judy and Sallie, imaginative, playful, and, perhaps most importantly, a good letter writer. With Sadie Kate's help, Sallie succeeds in converting the doctor, as well as the children and the Trustees to her methods.

There are elements of *Dear Enemy* that are also disguised autobiography. Dr. MacRae is married to a woman who "went insane" and had to be institutionalized, as did their little girl. His wife conveniently dies in time for him to court Sallie. Real life was harsher. In June 1915, McKinney's wife divorced him on the grounds of desertion. Although divorce was no scandal in Greenwich Village, Webster chose to keep the wedding modest and small. She asked her friend Mrs. Joseph W. Lewis of St. Louis to plan the small September 7, 1915, ceremony. Her only attendants were Lewis's little son and daughter. After the wedding the McKinneys lived in Manhattan, and at his farm in Dutchess County, New York, where they raised ducks and pheasants.

Tragically, this idyll did not last long. Webster died from complications of childbirth less than a year after her marriage, only a few hours after the birth of her daughter, Jean Webster McKinney, who survived. Uterine fibroids were cited as the cause in some reports; certainly having a first child at the age of forty carried more risk in 1916 than it does today. Webster's obituary and birth announcement for her daughter appeared side by side in the newspaper.

Following her death, Webster's reputation waned; but *Daddy-Long-Legs* has been made into three film versions. Despite Webster's emphasis on Judy's rebellious spirit, these films make her less central as a character and allow her less agency in changing people and institutions. In the popular 1919 silent film, starring Mary Pickford, more than half the time is given to Judy's childhood in the orphanage. According to *Variety*, "The punch of the picture is not in the love story of Judy growing up, falling in love with her guardian, and eventually marrying him, but in the pathos of the wistful little Judy, with her heart full of love, being constantly misunderstood—extracting joy through the instructive 'mothering' of the other little orphans."[12] The 1931 version, starring Janet Gaynor, is also more of a Cinderella story, with Judy as the poor orphan girl who marries a rich man. The best-known movie treatment is the 1955 musical, with Leslie Caron and Fred Astaire. Caron, as a sweet, passive French version of Judy named Julie André, seems bizarrely out of place at Walston, an American women's college of the 1950s with the students in beanies and tight-waisted dresses. Astaire is the rogue scion of the Pendleton family, who plays the drums when he is taking a break from advising the French government on its economy. In his New York mansion/family museum, we see his grandfather, Jervis Pendleton, painted by Whistler; his father, Jervis Pendleton II, painted by Sargent; and his own portrait by Picasso. Johnny Mercer wrote one of his best songs, "Something's Gotta Give," for the screen romance of Judy and Jervis; but the description of Judy as an "irresistible force" seems peculiar in light of Caron's kittenish and saccharine performance.

But Judy Abbott and Sallie McBride were indeed irresistible forces who bowled over both their suitors and their antagonists with their intelligence, imagination, high spirits, determination, and grit. They were part of a new wave of American heroines in the twentieth century, feisty and fast-talking dames whose refusal to kowtow to men marked their independence and charm rather than hostility or prudishness. This kind of heroine flourished particularly in the movies; as Karen Alkalay-Gut suggests, "the concept of playful, combative, and productive partnerships between a man and a woman in American novels and film . . . from Katharine Hepburn and Spencer Tracy to the present, . . . was first . . . fixed by Webster."[13] With their colloquial language, cartoon-like illustrations, and frank descriptions of their lives, problems, and feelings, Judy and Sallie can be seen as precursors of today's endearing singletons and bachelorettes, from Cathy Guisewaite's popular comic-strip heroine, to Helen Fielding's Bridget Jones, with her diary, and her hordes of scribbling sisters and imitators. Webster contributed a mixture of seriousness of purpose and playfulness of expression to the portrait of the New Woman that is as fresh and modern as it was a century ago, and should delight a new generation of readers.

NOTES TO INTRODUCTION

1. Karen Alkalay-Gut, "Jean Webster," http://karenalkalay-gut.com/web.html.
2. Jean Webster McKinney Papers, Vassar College, Box 25, Folder 1.
3. Elizabeth Daniels, "Vassar History," http://vassun,vassar.edu/~daniels/1891_1904.html.
4. Quoted in Karen Alkalay-Gut, *Alone in the Dawn: The Life of Adelaide Crapsey*, Athens and London: University of Georgia Press, 1988, 119.
5. Jean Webster McKinney Papers, Vassar College, Box 25, Folder 1; unidentified clipping from 1907.
6. Anne Bower, *Epistolary Responses: The Letter in 20th-Century American Fiction and Criticism*, Tuscaloosa and London: University of Alabama Press, 1987, 99.
7. Quoted in Christine Stansell, *American Moderns: Bohemian New York and the Creation of a New Century*, New York: Henry Holt, 2000, 231.
8. "Girl Writer as a Juror—Help," *New York Times*, May 11, 1909.
9. Alkalay-Gut, *Alone in the Dawn*, 249.
10. Alan Simpson, with Mary Simpson, *Jean Webster: Storyteller*, New York: Tymor Associates, 1984, 81.
11. Jean Webster McKinney Papers, Vassar College, Box 12, Folder 5.
12. *Variety*, May 16, 1919:54, quoted in Bower, 104–105.
13. Alkalay-Gut, "Jean Webster."

Suggestions for Further Reading

BOOKS BY JEAN WEBSTER

When Patty Went to College. New York: Century, 1903.

The Wheat Princess. New York: Century, 1905.

Jerry Junior. New York: Century, 1907.

The Four Pools Mystery. New York: Century, 1908.

Much Ado About Peter. New York: Century, 1909.

Just Patty. New York: Century, 1911.

Daddy-Long-Legs. New York: Century, 1912.

Dear Enemy. New York: Century, 1915.

ABOUT JEAN WEBSTER

Alkalay-Gut, Karen. "Jean Webster," http://karenalkalay-gut.com/web.html.

Salisbury, Rachel. "Jean Webster," *Notable American Women,* Vol. III. Cambridge, Mass.: Belknap Press of Harvard University Press, 1971, 555–556.

Simpson, Alan and Mary, with Ralph Connor. *Jean Webster: Storyteller.* Poughkeepsie, N.Y.: Tymor Associates, 1984.

Papers, letters, manuscripts, and clippings are in the Jean Webster McKinney Collection at Vassar College.

ON *DADDY-LONG-LEGS*

Alkalay-Gut, Karen. " 'If Mark Twain Had a Sister': Gender-Specific Values and Structures in Jean Webster's *Daddy-Long-Legs*." *Journal of American Culture,* 16 (Winter 1993): 91–99.

Bower, Ann. "Delettering: Responses to Agencies in Jean Webster's *Daddy-Long-Legs*," in *Epistolary Responses: The Letter in Twentieth-Century American Fiction and Criticism.* Tuscaloosa: University of Alabama Press, 1997.

BACKGROUND READING

Adickes, Sandra L. *To Be Young Was Very Heaven: Women in New York Before the First World War.* New York: St. Martin's Press, 1997.

Alkalay-Gut, Karen. *Alone in the Dawn: The Life of Adelaide Crapsey.* Athens and London: University of Georgia Press, 1988.

Horowitz, Helen Lefkowitz. *Alma Mater: Design and Experience in the Women's Colleges from Their Nineteenth-Century Beginnings to the 1920s.* Amherst: University of Massachusetts Press, 1985.

Stansell, Christine. *American Moderns: Bohemian New York and the Creation of a New Century.* New York: Henry Holt and Company, 2000.

A Note on the Texts

The texts of *Daddy-Long-Legs* and *Dear Enemy* have been re-set from the original editions, published by The Century Co. in 1912 and 1915 respectively. Jean Webster's drawings, which are integral to the novels, are reproduced here.

A Note on the Texts

DADDY-LONG-LEGS

BY
JEAN WEBSTER

With Illustrations
by The Author

NEW YORK
THE CENTURY CO.
1912

TO YOU

"BLUE WEDNESDAY"

The first Wednesday in every month was a Perfectly Awful Day—a day to be awaited with dread, endured with courage and forgotten with haste. Every floor must be spotless, every chair dustless, and every bed without a wrinkle. Ninety-seven squirming little orphans must be scrubbed and combed and buttoned into freshly starched ginghams; and all ninety-seven reminded of their manners, and told to say, "Yes, sir," "No, sir," whenever a Trustee spoke.

It was a distressing time; and poor Jerusha Abbott, being the oldest orphan, had to bear the brunt of it. But this particular first Wednesday, like its predecessors, finally dragged itself to a close. Jerusha escaped from the pantry where she had been making sandwiches for the asylum's guests, and turned upstairs to accomplish her regular work. Her special care was room F, where eleven little tots, from four to seven, occupied eleven little cots set in a row. Jerusha assembled her charges, straightened their rumpled frocks, wiped their noses, and started them in an orderly and willing line toward the dining-room to engage themselves for a blessed half hour with bread and milk and prune pudding.

Then she dropped down on the window seat and leaned throbbing temples against the cool glass. She had been on her feet since five that morning, doing everybody's bidding, scolded and hurried by a nervous matron. Mrs. Lippett, behind the scenes, did not always maintain that calm and pompous dignity with which she faced an audience of Trustees and lady visitors. Jerusha gazed out across a broad stretch of frozen lawn, beyond the tall iron paling that marked the confines of the asylum, down undulating ridges sprinkled with country estates, to the spires of the village rising from the midst of bare trees.

The day was ended—quite successfully, so far as she knew. The Trustees and the visiting committee had made their rounds, and read their reports, and drunk their tea, and now were hurrying home to their own cheerful firesides, to forget their bothersome little charges for another month. Jerusha leaned forward watching with curiosity—and a touch of wistfulness—the stream of carriages and automobiles that rolled out of the asylum gates. In imagination she followed first one equipage then another to the big houses dotted along the hillside. She pictured herself in a fur coat and a velvet hat trimmed with feathers leaning back in the seat and nonchalantly murmuring "Home" to the driver. But on the door-sill of her home the picture grew blurred.

Jerusha had an imagination—an imagination, Mrs. Lippett told her, that would get her into trouble if she didn't take care—but keen as it was, it could not carry her beyond the front porch of the houses she would enter. Poor, eager, adventurous little Jerusha, in all her seventeen years, had never stepped inside an ordinary house; she could not picture the daily routine of those other human beings who carried on their lives undiscommoded by orphans.

> Je-ru-sha Ab-bott
> You are wan-ted
> In the of-fice,
> And I think you'd
> Better hurry up!

Tommy Dillon who had joined the choir, came singing up the stairs and down the corridor, his chant growing louder as he approached room F. Jerusha wrenched herself from the window and refaced the troubles of life.

"Who wants me?" she cut into Tommy's chant with a note of sharp anxiety.

> Mrs. Lippett in the office,
> And I think she's mad.
> Ah-a-men!

Tommy piously intoned, but his accent was not entirely malicious. Even the most hardened little orphan felt sympathy for an erring sister who was summoned to the office to face an annoyed matron; and Tommy liked Jerusha even if she did sometimes jerk him by the arm and nearly scrub his nose off.

Jerusha went without comment, but with two parallel lines on her brow. What could have gone wrong, she wondered. Were the sandwiches not thin enough? Were there shells in the nut cakes? Had a lady visitor seen the hole in Susie Hawthorn's stocking? Had—O horrors!—one of the cherubic little babes in her own room F "sassed" a Trustee?

The long lower hall had not been lighted, and as she came downstairs, a last Trustee stood, on the point of departure, in the open door that led to the porte-cochère. Jerusha caught only a fleeting impression of the man—and the impression consisted entirely of tallness. He was waving his arm toward an automobile waiting in the curved drive. As it sprang into motion and approached, head on for an instant, the glaring headlights threw his shadow sharply against the wall inside. The shadow pictured grotesquely elongated legs and arms that ran along the floor and up the wall of the corridor. It looked, for all the world, like a huge, wavering daddy-long-legs.

Jerusha's anxious frown gave place to quick laughter. She was by nature a sunny soul, and had always snatched the tiniest excuse to be amused. If one could derive any sort of entertainment out of the oppressive fact of a Trustee, it was something unexpected to the good. She advanced to the office quite cheered by the tiny episode, and presented a smiling face to Mrs. Lippett. To her surprise the matron was also, if not exactly smiling, at least appreciably affable; she wore an expression almost as pleasant as the one she donned for visitors.

"Sit down, Jerusha, I have something to say to you."

Jerusha dropped into the nearest chair and waited with a touch of breathlessness. An automobile flashed past the window; Mrs. Lippett glanced after it.

"Did you notice the gentleman who has just gone?"

"I saw his back."

"He is one of our most affluential Trustees, and has given large sums of money toward the asylum's support. I am not at liberty to mention his name; he expressly stipulated that he was to remain unknown."

Jerusha's eyes widened slightly; she was not accustomed to being summoned to the office to discuss the eccentricities of Trustees with the matron.

"This gentleman has taken an interest in several of our boys. You remember Charles Benton and Henry Freize? They were both sent through college by Mr.—er—this Trustee, and both have repaid with hard work and success the money that was so generously expended. Other payment the gentleman does not wish. Heretofore his philanthropies have been directed solely toward the boys; I have never been able to interest him in the slightest degree in any of the girls in the institution, no matter how deserving. He does not, I may tell you, care for girls."

"No, ma'am," Jerusha murmured, since some reply seemed to be expected at this point.

"To-day at the regular meeting, the question of your future was brought up."

Mrs. Lippett allowed a moment of silence to fall, then resumed in a slow, placid manner extremely trying to her hearer's suddenly tightened nerves.

"Usually, as you know, the children are not kept after they are sixteen, but an exception was made in your case. You had finished our school at fourteen, and having done so well in your studies—not always, I must say, in your conduct—it was determined to let you go on in the village high school. Now you are finishing that, and of course the asylum cannot be responsible any longer for your support. As it is, you have had two years more than most."

Mrs. Lippett overlooked the fact that Jerusha had worked hard for her board during those two years, that the convenience of the asylum had come first and her education second; that on days like the present she was kept at home to scrub.

"As I say, the question of your future was brought up and your record was discussed—thoroughly discussed."

Mrs. Lippett brought accusing eyes to bear upon the prisoner in the dock, and the prisoner looked guilty because it seemed to be expected—not because she could remember any strikingly black pages in her record.

"Of course the usual disposition of one in your place would be to put you in a position where you could begin to work, but you have done well in school in certain branches; it seems that your work in English has even been brilliant. Miss Pritchard who is on our visiting committee is also on the school board; she has been talking with your rhetoric teacher, and made a speech in your favor. She also read aloud an essay that you had written entitled, 'Blue Wednesday.'"

Jerusha's guilty expression this time was not assumed.

"It seemed to me that you showed little gratitude in holding up to ridicule the institution that has done so much for you. Had you not managed to be funny I doubt if you would have been forgiven. But fortunately for you, Mr. ——, that is, the gentleman who has just gone—appears to have an immoderate sense of humor. On the strength of that impertinent paper, he has offered to send you to college."

"To college?" Jerusha's eyes grew big.

Mrs. Lippett nodded.

"He waited to discuss the terms with me. They are unusual. The gentleman, I may say, is erratic. He believes that you have originality, and he is planning to educate you to become a writer."

"A writer?" Jerusha's mind was numbed. She could only repeat Mrs. Lippett's words.

"That is his wish. Whether anything will come of it, the future will show. He is giving you a very liberal allowance, almost, for a girl who has never had any experience in taking care of money, too liberal. But he planned the matter in detail, and I did not feel free to make any suggestions. You are to remain here through the summer, and Miss Pritchard has kindly offered to superintend your outfit. Your board and tuition will be paid directly to the college, and you will receive in addition during the four years you are there, an allowance of thirty-five dollars a month. This will enable you to enter on the same standing as the other students. The money will be sent to you by the gentleman's private secretary once a month, and in return, you will write a letter of acknowledgment once a month. That is—you are not to thank him for the money; he doesn't care to have that mentioned, but you are to write a letter telling of the progress in your studies and the details of your daily life. Just such a letter as you would write to your parents if they were living.

"These letters will be addressed to Mr. John Smith and will be sent in care of the secretary. The gentleman's name is not John Smith, but he prefers to remain unknown. To you he will never be anything but John Smith. His reason in requiring the letters is that he thinks nothing so fosters facility in literary expression as letter-writing. Since you have no family with whom to correspond, he desires you to write in this way; also, he wishes to keep track of your progress. He will never answer your letters, nor in the slightest particular take any notice of them. He detests letter-writing, and does not wish you to become a burden. If any point should ever arise where an answer would seem to be imperative—such as in the event of your being expelled, which I trust will not occur—you may correspond with Mr. Griggs, his secretary. These monthly letters are absolutely obligatory on your part; they are the only payment that Mr. Smith requires, so you must be as punctilious in sending them as though it were a bill that you were paying. I hope that they will always be respectful in tone and will reflect credit on your training. You must remember that you are writing to a Trustee of the John Grier Home."

Jerusha's eyes longingly sought the door. Her head was in a whirl of excitement, and she wished only to escape from Mrs. Lippett's platitudes, and think. She rose and took a tentative step backwards. Mrs. Lippett detained her with a gesture; it was an oratorical opportunity not to be slighted.

"I trust that you are properly grateful for this very rare good fortune that has befallen you? Not many girls in your position ever have such an opportunity to rise in the world. You must always remember—"

"I—yes, ma'am, thank you. I think, if that's all, I must go and sew a patch on Freddie Perkins's trousers."

The door closed behind her, and Mrs. Lippett watched it with dropped jaw, her peroration in mid-air.

THE LETTERS OF
MISS JERUSHA ABBOTT
to
MR. DADDY-LONG-LEGS SMITH

Dear Kind-Trustee-Who-Sends-Orphans-to-College,

Here I am! I traveled yesterday for four hours in a train. It's a funny sensation isn't it? I never rode in one before.

College is the biggest, most bewildering place—I get lost whenever I leave my room. I will write you a description later when I'm feeling less muddled; also I will tell you about my lessons. Classes don't begin until Monday morning, and this is Saturday night. But I wanted to write a letter first just to get acquainted.

It seems queer to be writing letters to somebody you don't know. It seems queer for me to be writing letters at all—I've never written more than three or four in my life, so please overlook it if these are not a model kind.

Before leaving yesterday morning, Mrs. Lippett and I had a very serious talk. She told me how to behave all the rest of my life, and especially how to behave toward the kind gentleman who is doing so much for me. I must take care to be Very Respectful.

But how can one be very respectful to a person who wishes to be called John Smith? Why couldn't you have picked out a name with a little personality? I might as well write letters to Dear Hitching-Post or Dear Clothes-Pole.

I have been thinking about you a great deal this summer; having somebody take an interest in me after all these years, makes me feel as though I had found a sort of family. It seems as though I belonged to somebody now, and it's a very comfortable sensation. I must say, however, that when I think about you, my imagination has very little to work upon. There are just three things that I know:

    I. You are tall.
   II. You are rich.
  III. You hate girls.

I suppose I might call you Dear Mr. Girl-Hater. Only that's sort of insulting to me. Or Dear Mr. Rich-Man, but that's insulting to you, as though money were the only important thing about you. Besides, being rich is such a very external quality. Maybe you won't stay rich all your life; lots of very clever men get smashed up in Wall Street. But at least you will stay tall all your life! So I've decided to call you Dear Daddy-Long-Legs. I hope you won't mind. It's just a private pet name—we won't tell Mrs. Lippett.

The ten o'clock bell is going to ring in two minutes. Our day is divided into sections by bells. We eat and sleep and study by bells. It's very enlivening; I feel like a fire horse all of the time. There it goes! Lights out. Good night.

Observe with what precision I obey rules—due to my training in the John Grier Home.

> Yours most respectfully,
> JERUSHA ABBOTT.

To Mr. Daddy-Long-Legs Smith.

                                                            October 1st.

Dear Daddy-Long-Legs,

I love college and I love you for sending me—I'm very, *very* happy, and so excited every moment of the time that I can scarcely sleep. You can't imagine how different it is from the John Grier Home. I never dreamed there was such a place in the world. I'm feeling sorry for everybody who isn't a girl and who can't come here; I am sure the college you attended when you were a boy couldn't have been so nice.

My room is up in a tower that used to be the contagious ward before they built the new infirmary. There are three other girls on the same floor of the tower—a Senior who wears spectacles and is always asking us please to be a little more quiet, and two Freshmen named Sallie McBride and Julia Rutledge Pendleton. Sallie has red hair and a turned-up nose and is quite friendly; Julia comes from one of the first families in New York and hasn't noticed me yet. They room together and the Senior and I have singles. Usually Freshmen can't get singles; they are very scarce, but I got one without even asking. I suppose the registrar didn't think it would be right to ask a properly brought-up girl to room with a foundling. You see there are advantages!

My room is on the northwest corner with two windows and a view. After you've lived in a ward for eighteen years with twenty room-mates, it is restful to be alone. This is the first chance I've ever had to get acquainted with Jerusha Abbott. I think I'm going to like her.

Do you think you are?

Tuesday.

They are organizing the Freshman basket-ball team and there's just a chance that I shall make it. I'm little of course, but terribly quick and wiry and tough. While the others are hopping about in the air, I can dodge under their feet and grab the ball. It's loads of fun practising—out in the athletic field in the afternoon with the trees all red and yellow and the air full of the smell of burning leaves, and everybody laughing and shouting. These are the happiest girls I ever saw—and I am the happiest of all!

I meant to write a long letter and tell you all the things I'm learning (Mrs. Lippett said you wanted to know) but 7th hour has just rung, and in ten minutes I'm due at the athletic field in gymnasium clothes. Don't you hope I'll make the team?

Yours always,
JERUSHA ABBOTT.

P.S. (9 o'clock)

Sallie McBride just poked her head in at my door. This is what she said:

"I'm so homesick that I simply can't stand it. Do you feel that way?"

I smiled a little and said no, I thought I could pull through. At least homesickness is one disease that I've escaped! I never heard of anybody being asylumsick, did you?

October 10th.

Dear Daddy-Long-Legs,

Did you ever hear of Michael Angelo?[1]

He was a famous artist who lived in Italy in the Middle Ages. Everybody in English Literature seemed to know about him and the whole class laughed because I thought he was an archangel. He sounds like an archangel, doesn't he? The trouble with college is that you are expected to know such a lot of things you've never learned. It's very embarrassing at times. But now, when the girls talk about things that I never heard of, I just keep still and look them up in the encyclopedia.

I made an awful mistake the first day. Somebody mentioned Maurice Maeterlinck,[2] and I asked if she was a Freshman. That joke has gone all over college. But anyway, I'm just as bright in class as any of the others—and brighter than some of them!

Do you care to know how I've furnished my room? It's a symphony in brown and yellow. The wall was tinted buff, and I've bought yellow denim curtains and cushions and a mahogany desk (second hand for three dollars) and a rattan chair and a brown rug with an ink spot in the middle. I stand the chair over the spot.

The windows are up high; you can't look out from an ordinary seat. But I unscrewed the looking-glass from the back of the bureau, upholstered the top, and moved it up against the window. It's just the right height for a window seat. You pull out the drawers like steps and walk up. Very comfortable!

Sallie McBride helped me choose the things at the Senior auction. She has lived in a house all her life and knows about furnishing. You can't imagine what fun it is to shop and pay with a real five-dollar bill and get some change—when you've never had more than a nickel in your life. I assure you, Daddy dear, I do appreciate that allowance.

Sallie is the most entertaining person in the world—and Julia Rutledge Pendleton the least so. It's queer what a mixture the registrar can make in the matter of room-mates. Sallie thinks everything is funny—even flunking—and Julia is bored at everything. She never makes the slightest effort to be amiable. She believes that if you are a Pendleton, that fact alone admits you to heaven without any further examination. Julia and I were born to be enemies.

And now I suppose you've been waiting very impatiently to hear what I'm learning?

I. *Latin: Second Punic war.*[3] Hannibal and his forces pitched camp at Lake Trasimenus last night. They prepared an ambuscade for the Romans, and a battle took place at the fourth watch this morning. Romans in retreat.

II. *French:* 24 pages of the "Three Musketeers"[4] and third conjugation, irregular verbs.

III. *Geometry:* Finished cylinders; now doing cones.

IV. *English:* Studying exposition. My style improves daily in clearness and brevity.

V. *Physiology:* Reached the digestive system. Bile and the pancreas next time.

> Yours, on the way
> to being educated,
> JERUSHA ABBOTT.

P.S. I hope you never touch alcohol, Daddy?
It does dreadful things to your liver.

Wednesday

Dear Daddy-Long-Legs,

I've changed my name.

I'm still "Jerusha" in the catalogue, but I'm "Judy" every place else. It's sort of too bad, isn't it, to have to give yourself the only pet name you ever had? I didn't quite make up the Judy though. That's what Freddie Perkins used to call me before he could talk plain.

I wish Mrs. Lippett would use a little more ingenuity about choosing babies' names. She gets the last names out of the telephone book—you'll find Abbott on the first page—and she picks the Christian names up anywhere; she got Jerusha from a tombstone. I've always hated it; but I rather like Judy. It's such a silly name. It belongs to the kind of girl I'm not—a sweet little blue-eyed thing, petted and spoiled by all the family, who romps her way through life without any cares. Wouldn't it be nice to be like that? Whatever faults I may have, no one can ever accuse me of having been spoiled by my family! But it's sort of fun to pretend I've been. In the future please always address me as Judy.

Do you want to know something? I have three pairs of kid gloves. I've had kid mittens before from the Christmas tree, but never real kid gloves with five fingers. I take them out and try them on every little while. It's all I can do not to wear them to classes.

(Dinner bell. Good-by.)

                                                            Friday.

What do you think, Daddy? The English instructor said that my last paper shows an unusual amount of originality. She did, truly. Those were her words. It doesn't seem possible, does it, considering the eighteen years of training that I've had? The aim of the John Grier Home (as you doubtless know and heartily approve of) is to turn the ninety-seven orphans into ninety-seven twins.

The unusual artistic ability which I exhibit, was developed at an early age through drawing chalk pictures of Mrs. Lippett on the woodshed door.

I hope that I don't hurt your feelings when I criticize the home of my youth? But you have the upper hand, you know, for if I become too impertinent, you can always stop payment on your checks. That isn't a very polite thing to say—but you can't expect me to have any manners; a foundling asylum isn't a young ladies' finishing school.

ANY ORPHAN

Rear Elevation   Front Elevation

You know, Daddy, it isn't the work that is going to be hard in college. It's the play. Half the time I don't know what the girls are talking about; their jokes seem to relate to a past that every one but me has shared. I'm a foreigner in the world and I don't understand the language. It's a miserable feeling. I've had it all my life. At the high school the girls would stand in groups and just look at me. I was queer and different and everybody knew it. I could *feel* "John Grier Home" written on my face. And then a few charitable ones would make a point of coming up and saying something polite. *I hated every one of them*—the charitable ones most of all.

Nobody here knows that I was brought up in an asylum. I told Sallie McBride that my mother and father were dead, and that a kind old gentleman was sending me to college—which is entirely true so far as it goes. I don't want you to think I am a coward, but I do want to be like the other girls, and that Dreadful Home looming over my childhood is the one great big difference. If I can turn my back on that and shut out the remembrance, I think I might be just as desirable as any other girl. I don't believe there's any real, underneath difference, do you?

Anyway, Sallie McBride likes me!

Yours ever,
JUDY ABBOTT.
(NÉE JERUSHA.)

Saturday morning.

I've just been reading this letter over and it sounds pretty uncheerful. But can't you guess that I have a special topic due Monday morning and a review in geometry and a very sneezy cold?

Sunday.

I forgot to mail this yesterday so I will add an indignant postscript. We had a bishop this morning, and *what do you think he said?*

"The most beneficent promise made us in the Bible is this, 'The poor ye have always with you.' They were put here in order to keep us charitable."

The poor, please observe, being a sort of useful domestic animal. If I hadn't grown into such a perfect lady, I should have gone up after service and told him what I thought.

October 25th.

Dear Daddy-Long-Legs,

I've made the basket-ball team and you ought to see the bruise on my left shoulder. It's blue and mahogany with little streaks of orange. Julia Pendleton tried for the team, but she didn't make it. Hooray!

You see what a mean disposition I have.

College gets nicer and nicer. I like the girls and the teachers and the classes and the campus and the things to eat. We have ice-cream twice a week and we never have corn-meal mush.

You only wanted to hear from me once a month, didn't you? And I've been peppering you with letters every few days! But I've been so excited about all these new adventures that I *must* talk to somebody; and you're the only one I know. Please excuse my exuberance; I'll settle pretty soon. If my letters bore you, you can always toss them into the waste-basket. I promise not to write another till the middle of November.

Yours most loquaciously,

JUDY ABBOTT.

Judy at
Basket Ball

November 15th.

Dear Daddy-Long-Legs,

Listen to what I've learned to-day:

The area of the convex surface of the frustum of a regular pyramid is half the product of the sum of the perimeters of its bases by the altitude of either of its trapezoids.

It doesn't sound true, but it is—I can prove it!

You've never heard about my clothes, have you, Daddy? Six dresses, all new and beautiful and bought for me—not handed down from somebody bigger. Perhaps you don't realize what a climax that marks in the career of an orphan? You gave them to me, and I am very, very, *very* much obliged. It's a fine thing to be educated—but nothing compared to the dizzying experience of owning six new dresses. Miss Pritchard who is on the visiting committee picked them out—not Mrs. Lippett, thank goodness. I have an evening dress, pink mull over silk (I'm perfectly beautiful in that), and a blue church dress, and a dinner dress of red veiling with Oriental trimming (makes me look like a Gipsy) and another of rose-colored challis, and a gray street suit, and an every-day dress for classes. That wouldn't be an awfully big wardrobe for Julia Rutledge Pendleton, perhaps, but for Jerusha Abbott—Oh, my!

I suppose you're thinking now what a frivolous, shallow, little beast she is, and what a waste of money to educate a girl?

But Daddy, if you'd been dressed in check ginghams all your life, you'd appreciate how I feel. And when I started to the high school, I entered upon another period even worse than the checked ginghams.

The poor box.

You can't know how I dreaded appearing in school in those miserable poor-box dresses. I was perfectly sure to be put down in class next to the girl who first owned my dress, and she would whisper and giggle and point it out to the others. The bitterness of wearing your enemies' cast-off clothes eats into your soul. If I wore silk stockings for the rest of my life, I don't believe I could obliterate the scar.

LATEST WAR BULLETIN!
News from the Scene of Action.

At the fourth watch on Thursday the 13th of November, Hannibal routed the advance guard of the Romans and led the Carthaginian forces over the mountains into the plains of Casilinum. A cohort of light armed Numidians engaged the infantry of Quintus Fabius Maximus. Two battles and light skirmishing. Romans repulsed with heavy losses.

I have the honor of being,
Your special correspondent from the front

                                            J. Abbott.

P.S. I know I'm not to expect any letters in return, and I've
been warned not to bother you with questions, but tell me,
Daddy, just this once—are you awfully old or just a little
old? And are you perfectly bald or just a little bald? It is very
difficult thinking about you in the abstract like a theorem in
geometry.

Given a tall rich man who hates girls, but is very generous to
one quite impertinent girl, what does he look like?

R.S.V.P.

                                            December 19th.

Dear Daddy-Long-Legs,

You never answered my question
and it was very important.

ARE YOU BALD?

I have it planned exactly what you
look like—very satisfactorily—until
I reach the top of your head, and then
I *am* stuck. I can't decide whether you
have white hair or black hair or sort
of sprinkly gray hair or maybe none
at all.

Here is your portrait:

But the problem is, shall I add
some hair?

Would you like to know what
color your eyes are? They're gray,
and your eyebrows stick out like a
porch roof (beetling, they're called
in novels) and your mouth is a
straight line with a tendency to turn

down at the corners. Oh, you see, I know! You're a snappy old
thing with a temper.

(Chapel bell.)

9.45 P.M.

I have a new unbreakable rule: never, never to study at night
no matter how many written reviews are coming in the morning. Instead, I read just plain books—I have to, you know, because there are eighteen blank years behind me. You wouldn't
believe, Daddy, what an abyss of ignorance my mind is; I am
just realizing the depths myself. The things that most girls with
a properly assorted family and a home and friends and a library know by absorption, I have never heard of. For example:

I never read "Mother Goose" or "David Copperfield" or
"Ivanhoe" or "Cinderella" or "Blue Beard" or "Robinson
Crusoe" or "Jane Eyre" or "Alice in Wonderland" or a word of
Rudyard Kipling.[5] I didn't know that Henry the Eighth[6] was
married more than once or that Shelley[7] was a poet. I didn't
know that people used to be monkeys and that the Garden of
Eden was a beautiful myth. I didn't know that R.L.S. stood for
Robert Louis Stevenson[8] or that George Eliot[9] was a lady. I had
never seen a picture of the "Mona Lisa"[10] and (it's true but you
won't believe it) I had never heard of Sherlock Holmes.[11]

Now, I know all of these things and a lot of others besides,
but you can see how much I need to catch up. And oh, but it's
fun! I look forward all day to evening, and then I put an "engaged" on the door and get into my nice red bath robe and
furry slippers and pile all the cushions behind me on the couch
and light the brass student lamp at my elbow, and read and
read and read. One book isn't enough. I have four going at
once. Just now, they're Tennyson's poems[12] and "Vanity Fair"[13]
and Kipling's "Plain Tales"[14] and—don't laugh—"Little
Women."[15] I find that I am the only girl in college who wasn't
brought up on "Little Women." I haven't told anybody though
(that *would* stamp me as queer). I just quietly went and bought
it with $1.12 of my last month's allowance; and the next time
somebody mentions pickled limes,[16] I'll know what she is talking about!

(Ten o'clock bell. This is a very interrupted letter.)

Saturday.

Sir,

I have the honor to report fresh explorations in the field of geometry. On Friday last we abandoned our former works in parallelopipeds and proceeded to truncated prisms. We are finding the road rough and very uphill.

Sunday.

The Christmas holidays begin next week and the trunks are up. The corridors are so cluttered that you can hardly get through, and everybody is so bubbling over with excitement that studying is getting left out. I'm going to have a beautiful time in vacation; there's another Freshman who lives in Texas staying behind, and we are planning to take long walks and— if there's any ice—learn to skate. Then there is still the whole library to be read—and three empty weeks to do it in!

Good-by, Daddy, I hope that you are feeling as happy as I am.

Yours ever,

JUDY.

P.S. Don't forget to answer my question. If you don't want the trouble of writing, have your secretary telegraph. He can just say:

Mr. Smith is quite bald,

or

Mr. Smith is not bald,

or

Mr. Smith has white hair.

And you can deduct the twenty-five cents out of my allowance.

Good-by till January—and a merry Christmas!

> Toward the end of
> the Christmas vacation.
>
> Exact date unknown.

Dear Daddy-Long-Legs,

Is it snowing where you are? All the world that I see from my tower is draped in white and the flakes are coming down as big as pop-corn. It's late afternoon—the sun is just setting (a cold yellow color) behind some colder violet hills, and I am up in my window seat using the last light to write to you.

Your five gold pieces were a surprise! I'm not used to receiving Christmas presents. You have already given me such lots of things—everything I have, you know—that I don't quite feel that I deserve extras. But I like them just the same. Do you want to know what I bought with my money?

I. A silver watch in a leather case to wear on my wrist and get me to recitations on time.

II. Matthew Arnold's poems.[17]

III. A hot water bottle.

IV. A steamer rug. (My tower is cold.)

V. Five hundred sheets of yellow manuscript paper. (I'm going to commence being an author pretty soon.)

VI. A dictionary of synonyms. (To enlarge the author's vocabulary.)

VII. (I don't much like to confess this last item, but I will.) A pair of silk stockings.

And now, Daddy, never say I don't tell all!

It was a very low motive, if you must know it, that prompted the silk stockings. Julia Pendleton comes into my room to do geometry, and she sits cross legged on the couch and wears silk stockings every night. But just wait—as soon as she gets back from vacation I shall go in and sit on her couch in my silk stockings. You see, Daddy, the miserable creature that I am—but at least I'm honest; and you knew already, from my asylum record, that I wasn't perfect, didn't you?

To recapitulate (that's the way the English instructor begins every other sentence), I am *very* much obliged for my seven presents. I'm pretending to myself that they came in a box from my family in California. The watch is from father, the rug from mother, the hot water bottle from grandmother—who is always worrying for fear I shall catch cold in this climate—and the yellow paper from my little brother Harry. My sister Isobel gave me the silk stockings, and Aunt Susan the Matthew Arnold poems; Uncle Harry (little Harry is named for him) gave me the dictionary. He wanted to send chocolates, but I insisted on synonyms.

You don't object do you, to playing the part of a composite family?

And now, shall I tell you about my vacation, or are you only interested in my education as such? I hope you appreciate the delicate shade of meaning in "as such." It is the latest addition to my vocabulary.

The girl from Texas is named Leonora Fenton. (Almost as funny as Jerusha, isn't it?) I like her, but not so much as Sallie McBride; I shall never like any one so much as Sallie—except you. I must always like you the best of all, because you're my whole family rolled into one. Leonora and I and two Sophomores have walked 'cross country every pleasant day and explored the whole neighborhood, dressed in short skirts and knit jackets and caps, and carrying shinny sticks to whack things with. Once we walked into town—four miles—and stopped at a restaurant where the college girls go for dinner. Broiled lobster (35 cents) and for dessert, buckwheat cakes and maple syrup (15 cents). Nourishing and cheap.

It was such a lark! Especially for me, because it was so awfully different from the asylum—I feel like an escaped convict every time I leave the campus. Before I thought, I started to tell the others what an experience I was having. The cat was almost out of the bag when I grabbed it by its tail and pulled it back. It's awfully hard for me not to tell everything I know. I'm a very confiding soul by nature; if I didn't have you to tell things to, I'd burst.

We had a molasses candy pull last Friday evening, given by the house matron of Fergussen to the left-behinds in the other halls. Freshmen and Sophomores and Juniors and Seniors all united in amicable accord. The kitchen is huge, with copper pots and kettles hanging in rows on the stone wall—the littlest casserole among them about the size of a wash boiler. Four hundred girls live in Fergussen. The chef, in a white cap and apron, fetched out twenty-two other white caps and aprons—I can't imagine where he got so many—and we all turned ourselves into cooks.

It was great fun, though I have seen better candy. When it was finally finished, and ourselves and the kitchen and the doorknobs all thoroughly sticky, we organized a procession and still in our caps and aprons, each carrying a big fork or spoon or frying pan, we marched through the empty corridors to the officers' parlor where half-a-dozen professors and instructors were passing a tranquil evening. We serenaded them with college songs and offered refreshments. They accepted politely but dubiously. We left them sucking chunks of molasses candy, sticky and speechless.

So you see, Daddy, my education progresses!

Don't you really think that I ought to be an artist instead of an author?

Vacation will be over in two days and I shall be glad to see the girls again. My tower is just a trifle lonely; when nine people occupy a house that was built for four hundred, they do rattle around a bit.

Eleven pages—poor Daddy, you must be tired! I meant this to be just a short little thank-you note—but when I get started I seem to have a ready pen.

Good-by, and thank you for thinking of me—I should be perfectly happy except for one little threatening cloud on the horizon. Examinations come in February.

                                    Yours with love,
                                        JUDY.

P.S. Maybe it isn't proper to send love? If it isn't, please excuse. But I must love somebody and there's only you and Mrs. Lippett to choose between, so you see—you'll *have* to put up with it, Daddy dear, because I can't love her.

On the Eve.

Dear Daddy-Long-Legs,

You should see the way this college is studying! We've forgotten we ever had a vacation. Fifty-seven irregular verbs have I introduced to my brain in the past four days—I'm only hoping they'll stay till after examinations.

Some of the girls sell their text-books when they're through with them, but I intend to keep mine. Then after I've graduated I shall have my whole education in a row in the bookcase, and when I need to use any detail, I can turn to it without the slightest hesitation. So much easier and more accurate than trying to keep it in your head.

Julia Pendleton dropped in this evening to pay a social call, and stayed a solid hour. She got started on the subject of family, and I *couldn't* switch her off. She wanted to know what my mother's maiden name was—did you ever hear such an impertinent question to ask of a person from a foundling asylum? I didn't have the courage to say I didn't know, so I just miserably plumped on the first name I could think of, and that was Montgomery. Then she wanted to know whether I belonged to the Massachusetts Montgomerys or the Virginia Montgomerys.

Her mother was a Rutherford. The family came over in the ark, and were connected by marriage with Henry the VIII. On her father's side they date back further than Adam. On the topmost branches of her family tree there's a superior breed of monkeys, with very fine silky hair and extra long tails.

I meant to write you a nice, cheerful, entertaining letter tonight, but I'm too sleepy—and scared. The Freshman's lot is not a happy one.

Yours, about to be examined,
JUDY ABBOTT.

Sunday.

Dearest Daddy-Long-Legs,

I have some awful, awful, awful news to tell you, but I won't begin with it; I'll try to get you in a good humor first.

Jerusha Abbott has commenced to be an author. A poem entitled, "From my Tower," appears in the February *Monthly*— on the first page, which is a very great honor for a Freshman. My English instructor stopped me on the way out from chapel last night, and said it was a charming piece of work except for the sixth line, which had too many feet. I will send you a copy in case you care to read it.

Let me see if I can't think of something else pleasant—Oh, yes! I'm learning to skate, and can glide about quite respectably all by myself. Also I've learned how to slide down a rope from the roof of the gymnasium, and I can vault a bar three feet and six inches high—I hope shortly to pull up to four feet.

We had a very inspiring sermon this morning preached by the Bishop of Alabama. His text was: "Judge not that ye be not judged."[18] It was about the necessity of overlooking mistakes in others, and not discouraging people by harsh judgments. I wish you might have heard it.

This is the sunniest, most blinding winter afternoon, with icicles dripping from the fir trees and all the world bending under a weight of snow—except me, and I'm bending under a weight of sorrow.

Now for the news—courage, Judy!—you must tell.

Are you *surely* in a good humor? I flunked mathematics and Latin prose. I am tutoring in them, and will take another examination next month. I'm sorry if you're disappointed, but otherwise I don't care a bit because I've learned such a lot of things not mentioned in the catalogue. I've read seventeen novels and *bushels* of poetry—really necessary novels like "Vanity Fair" and "Richard Feverel"[19] and "Alice in Wonderland." Also Emerson's "Essays"[20] and Lockhart's "Life of Scott"[21]

and the first volume of Gibbon's "Roman Empire"[22] and half of Benvenuto Cellini's "Life"[23]—wasn't he entertaining? He used to saunter out and casually kill a man before breakfast.

So you see, Daddy, I'm much more intelligent than if I'd stuck to Latin. Will you forgive me this once if I promise never to flunk again?

Yours in sackcloth,

JUDY.

Dear Daddy-Long-Legs,

This is an extra letter in the middle of the month because I'm sort of lonely tonight. It's awfully stormy; the snow is beating

against my tower. All the lights are out on the campus, but I
drank black coffee and I can't go to sleep.

I had a supper party this evening consisting of Sallie and Julia and Leonora Fenton—and sardines and toasted muffins and
salad and fudge and coffee. Julia said she'd had a good time,
but Sallie stayed to help wash the dishes.

I might, very usefully, put some time on Latin to-night—but,
there's no doubt about it, I'm a very languid Latin scholar.
We've finished Livy[24] and De Senectute and are now engaged
with De Amicitia[25] (pronounced Damn Icitia).

Should you mind, just for a little while, pretending you are
my grandmother? Sallie has one and Julia and Leonora each
two, and they were all comparing them to-night. I can't think
of anything I'd rather have; it's such a respectable relationship.
So, if you really don't object—When I went into town yesterday, I saw the sweetest cap of Cluny lace trimmed with lavender ribbons. I am going to make you a present of it on your
eighty-third birthday.

!!!!!!!!!!!!

That's the clock in the chapel tower striking twelve. I believe
I am sleepy after all.

Good night, Granny.
I love you dearly.
JUDY.

The Ides of March.

Dear D. L. L.,

I am studying Latin prose composition. I have been studying
it. I shall be studying it. I shall be about to have been studying it.
My reëxamination comes the 7th hour next Tuesday, and I am
going to pass or BUST. So you may expect to hear from me next,
whole and happy and free from conditions, or in fragments.

I will write a respectable letter when it's over. To-night I have
a pressing engagement with the Ablative Absolute.

Yours—in evident haste,
J. A.

March 26th.

Dear D. L. L. Smith.

SIR: You never answer any questions; you never show the slightest interest in anything I do. You are probably the horridest one of all those horrid Trustees, and the reason you are educating me is, not because you care a bit about me, but from a sense of Duty.

I don't know a single thing about you. I don't even know your name. It is very uninspiring writing to a Thing. I haven't a doubt but that you throw my letters into the waste-basket without reading them. Hereafter I shall write only about work.

My reëxaminations in Latin and geometry came last week. I passed them both and am now free from conditions.

Yours truly,
JERUSHA ABBOTT.

April 2d.

Dear Daddy-Long-Legs,

I am a BEAST.

Please forget about that dreadful letter I sent you last week— I was feeling terribly lonely and miserable and sore-throaty the night I wrote. I didn't know it, but I was just coming down with tonsilitis and grippe and lots of things mixed. I'm in the infirmary now, and have been here for six days; this is the first time they would let me sit up and have a pen and paper. The head nurse is *very bossy.* But I've been thinking about it all the time and I shan't get well until you forgive me.

Here is a picture of the way I look, with a bandage tied around my head in rabbit's ears.

Doesn't that arouse your sympathy? I am having sublingual gland swelling. And I've been studying physiology all the year without ever hearing of sublingual glands. How futile a thing is education!

I can't write any more; I get sort of shaky when I sit up too
long. Please forgive me for being impertinent and ungrateful. I
was badly brought up.

Yours with love,

JUDY ABBOTT.

THE INFIRMARY.

April 4th.

Dearest Daddy-Long-Legs,

Yesterday evening just toward dark, when I was sitting up in
bed looking out at the rain and feeling awfully bored with life
in a great institution, the nurse appeared with a long white box
addressed to me, and filled with the *loveliest* pink rosebuds.
And much nicer still, it contained a card with a very polite message written in a funny little uphill back hand (but one which
shows a great deal of character). Thank you, Daddy, a thousand times. Your flowers make the first real, true present I ever
received in my life. If you want to know what a baby I am, I lay
down and cried because I was so happy.

Now that I am sure you read my letters, I'll make them much
more interesting, so they'll be worth keeping in a safe with red
tape around them—only please take out that dreadful one and
burn it up. I'd hate to think that you ever read it over.

Thank you for making a very sick, cross, miserable Freshman cheerful. Probably you have lots of loving family and

friends, and you don't know what it feels like to be alone. But I do.

Good-by—I'll promise never to be horrid again, because now I know you're a real person; also I'll promise never to bother you with more questions.

Do you still hate girls?

Yours forever,
JUDY.

8th hour, Monday.

Dear Daddy-Long-Legs,

I hope you aren't the Trustee who sat on the toad? It went off—I was told—with quite a pop, so probably he was a fatter Trustee.

Do you remember the little dugout places with gratings over them by the laundry windows in the John Grier Home? Every spring when the hoptoad season opened we used to form a collection of toads and keep them in those window holes; and occasionally they would spill over into the laundry, causing a very pleasurable commotion on wash days. We were severely punished for our activities in this direction, but in spite of all discouragement the toads would collect.

And one day—well, I won't bore you with particulars—but somehow, one of the fattest, biggest, *juiciest* toads got into one of those big leather arm chairs in the Trustees' room and that afternoon at the Trustees' meeting— But I dare say you were there and recall the rest?

Looking back dispassionately after a period of time, I will say that punishment was merited, and—if I remember rightly—adequate.

I don't know why I am in such a reminiscent mood except that spring and the reappearance of toads always awakens the old acquisitive instinct. The only thing that keeps me from starting a collection is the fact that no rule exists against it.

After chapel, Thursday.

What do you think is my favorite book? Just now, I mean; I change every three days. "Wuthering Heights."[26] Emily Brontë was quite young when she wrote it, and had never been outside of Haworth churchyard. She had never known any men in her life; how *could* she imagine a man like Heathcliffe?[27]

I couldn't do it, and I'm quite young and never outside the John Grier Asylum—I've had every chance in the world. Sometimes a dreadful fear comes over me that I'm not a genius. Will you be awfully disappointed, Daddy, if I don't turn out to be a great author? In the spring when everything is so beautiful and green and budding, I feel like turning my back on lessons, and running away to play with the weather. There are such lots of adventures out in the fields! It's much more entertaining to live books than to write them.

Ow ! ! ! ! ! !

That was a shriek which brought Sallie and Julia and (for a disgusted moment) the Senior from across the hall. It was caused by a centipede like this:

only worse. Just as I had finished the last sentence and was thinking what to say next—plump!—it fell off the ceiling and landed at my side. I tipped two cups off the tea table in trying to get away. Sallie whacked it with the back of my hair brush—which I shall never be able to use again—and killed the front end, but the rear fifty feet ran under the bureau and escaped.

This dormitory, owing to its age and ivy-covered walls, is full of centipedes. They are dreadful creatures. I'd rather find a tiger under the bed.

Friday, 9.30 P.M.

Such a lot of troubles! I didn't hear the rising bell this morning, then I broke my shoe-string while I was hurrying to dress

and dropped my collar button down my neck. I was late for
breakfast and also the first-hour recitation. I forgot to take any
blotting paper and my fountain pen leaked. In trigonometry
the Professor and I had a disagreement touching a little matter
of logarithms. On looking it up, I find that she was right. We
had mutton stew and pie-plant[28] for lunch—hate 'em both;
they taste like the asylum. Nothing but bills in my mail (though
I must say that I never do get anything else; my family are not
the kind that write). In English class this afternoon we had an
unexpected writing lesson. This was it:

> I asked no other thing,
> No other was denied.
> I offered Being for it;
> The mighty merchant smiled.

> Brazil? He twirled a button
> Without a glance my way:
> But, madam, is there nothing else
> That we can show to-day?[29]

That is a poem. I don't know who wrote it or what it means. It
was simply printed out on the blackboard when we arrived and
we were ordered to comment upon it. When I read the first verse
I thought I had an idea—The Mighty Merchant was a divinity
who distributes blessings in return for virtuous deeds—but when
I got to the second verse and found him twirling a button, it
seemed a blasphemous supposition, and I hastily changed my
mind. The rest of the class was in the same predicament; and there
we sat for three quarters of an hour with blank paper and equally
blank minds. Getting an education is an awfully wearing process!

But this didn't end the day. There's worse to come.

It rained so we couldn't play golf, but had to go to gymnasium
instead. The girl next to me banged my elbow with an Indian
club. I got home to find that the box with my new blue spring
dress had come, and the skirt was so tight that I couldn't sit down.
Friday is sweeping day, and the maid had mixed all the papers on
my desk. We had tombstone for dessert (milk and gelatin flavored
with vanilla). We were kept in chapel twenty minutes later than

usual to listen to a speech about womanly women. And then—
just as I was settling down with a sigh of well-earned relief to
"The Portrait of a Lady,"[30] a girl named Ackerly, a dough-faced,
deadly, unintermittently stupid girl, who sits next to me in Latin
because her name begins with A (I wish Mrs. Lippett had named
me Zabriski), came to ask if Monday's lesson commenced at
paragraph 69 or 70, and stayed ONE HOUR. She has just gone.

Did you ever hear of such a discouraging series of events? It
isn't the big troubles in life that require character. Anybody can
rise to a crisis and face a crushing tragedy with courage, but to
meet the petty hazards of the day with a laugh—I really think
that requires *spirit*.

It's the kind of character that I am going to develop. I am going to pretend that all life is just a game which I must play as
skilfully and fairly as I can. If I lose, I am going to shrug my
shoulders and laugh—also if I win.

Anyway, I am going to be a sport. You will never hear me
complain again, Daddy dear, because Julia wears silk stockings
and centipedes drop off the wall.

Yours ever,
JUDY.

Answer soon.

May 27th.

Daddy-Long-Legs, Esq.

DEAR SIR: I am in receipt of a letter from Mrs. Lippett. She
hopes that I am doing well in deportment and studies. Since I
probably have no place to go this summer, she will let me come
back to the asylum and work for my board until college opens.
I HATE THE JOHN GRIER HOME.
I'd rather die than go back.

Yours most truthfully,
JERUSHA ABBOTT.

Cher Daddy-Jambes-Longes,

    Vous etes un brick!

    Je suis tres heureuse about the farm, *parsque je n'ai jamais* been on a farm *dans ma vie* and I'd hate to *retourner chez* John Grier, *et* wash dishes *tout l'été.* There would be danger of *quelque chose affreuse* happening, *parsque j'ai perdue ma humilité d'autre fois et j'ai peur* that I would just break out *quelque jour et* smash every cup and saucer *dans la maison.*

    Pardon brièveté et paper. *Je ne peux pas* send *des mes nouvelles parseque je suis dans* French class *et j'ai peur que Monsieur le Professeur* is going to call on me *tout de suite.*

    He did!

Au revoir,
Je vous aime beaucoup.

JUDY.[31]

May 30th.

Dear Daddy-Long-Legs,

    Did you ever see this campus? (That is merely a rhetorical question. Don't let it annoy you.) It is a heavenly spot in May. All the shrubs are in blossom and the trees are the loveliest young green—even the old pines look fresh and new. The grass is dotted with yellow dandelions and hundreds of girls in blue and white and pink dresses. Everybody is joyous and carefree, for vacation's coming, and with that to look forward to, examinations don't count.

    Isn't that a happy frame of mind to be in? And oh, Daddy! I'm the happiest of all! Because I'm not in the asylum any more; and I'm not anybody's nurse-maid or typewriter or bookkeeper (I should have been, you know, except for you).

    I'm sorry now for all my past badnesses.

I'm sorry I was ever impertinent to Mrs. Lippett.

I'm sorry I ever slapped Freddie Perkins.

I'm sorry I ever filled the sugar bowl with salt.

I'm sorry I ever made faces behind the Trustees' backs.

I'm going to be good and sweet and kind to everybody because I'm so happy. And this summer I'm going to write and write and write and begin to be a great author. Isn't that an exalted stand to take? Oh, I'm developing a beautiful character! It droops a bit under cold and frost, but it does grow fast when the sun shines.

That's the way with everybody. I don't agree with the theory that adversity and sorrow and disappointment develop moral strength. The happy people are the ones who are bubbling over with kindliness. I have no faith in misanthropes. (Fine word! Just learned it.) You are not a misanthrope are you, Daddy?

I started to tell you about the campus. I wish you'd come for a little visit and let me walk you about and say:

"That is the library. This is the gas plant, Daddy dear. The Gothic building on your left is the gymnasium, and the Tudor Romanesque beside it is the new infirmary."

Oh, I'm fine at showing people about, I've done it all my life at the asylum, and I've been doing it all day here. I have honestly.

And a Man, too!

That's a great experience. I never talked to a man before (except occasional Trustees, and they don't count). Pardon, Daddy. I don't mean to hurt your feelings when I abuse Trustees. I don't consider that you really belong among them. You just tumbled onto the Board by chance. The Trustee, as such, is fat and pompous and benevolent. He pats one on the head and wears a gold watch chain.

That looks like a June bug, but is meant to be a portrait of any Trustee except you.

However—to resume:

I have been walking and talking and having tea with a man. And with a very superior man—with Mr. Jervis Pendleton of the House of Julia; her uncle, in short (in long, perhaps I ought to say; he's as tall as you). Being in town on business, he decided to run out to the college and call on his niece. He's her

father's youngest brother, but she doesn't know him very intimately. It seems he glanced at her when she was a baby, decided he didn't like her, and has never noticed her since.

Anyway, there he was, sitting in the reception room very proper with his hat and stick and gloves beside him; and Julia and Sallie with seventh-hour recitations that they couldn't cut. So Julia dashed into my room and begged me to walk him about the campus and then deliver him to her when the seventh hour was over. I said I would, obligingly but unenthusiastically, because I don't care much for Pendletons.

But he turned out to be a sweet lamb. He's a real human being—not a Pendleton at all. We had a beautiful time; I've longed for an uncle ever since. Do you mind pretending you're my uncle? I believe they're superior to grandmothers.

Mr. Pendleton reminded me a little of you, Daddy, as you were twenty years ago. You see I know you intimately, even if we haven't ever met!

He's tall and thinnish with a dark face all over lines, and the funniest underneath smile that never quite comes through but just wrinkles up the corners of his mouth. And he has a way of making you feel right off as though you'd known him a long time. He's very companionable.

We walked all over the campus from the quadrangle to the athletic grounds; then he said he felt weak and must have some tea. He proposed that we go to College Inn—it's just off the campus by the pine walk. I said we ought to go back for Julia and Sallie, but he said he didn't like to have his nieces drink too much tea; it made them nervous. So we just ran away and had tea and muffins and marmalade and ice-cream and cake at a nice little table out on the balcony. The inn was quite conveniently empty, this being the end of the month and allowances low.

We had the jolliest time! But he had to run for his train the minute he got back and he barely saw Julia at all. She was furious with me for taking him off; it seems he's an unusually rich and desirable uncle. It relieved my mind to find he was rich, for the tea and things cost sixty cents apiece.

This morning (it's Monday now) three boxes of chocolates came by express for Julia and Sallie and me. What do you think of that? To be getting candy from a man!

I begin to feel like a girl instead of a foundling.

I wish you'd come and take tea some day and let me see if I like you. But wouldn't it be dreadful if I didn't? However, I know I should.

Bien! I make you my compliments.

"Jamais je ne t'oublierai."[32]

JUDY.

P.S. I looked in the glass this morning and found a perfectly new dimple that I'd never seen before. It's very curious. Where do you suppose it came from?

June 9th.

Dear Daddy-Long-Legs,

Happy day! I've just finished my last examination—Physiology. And now:

Three months on a farm!

I don't know what kind of a thing a farm is. I've never been on one in my life. I've never even looked at one (except from the car window), but I know I'm going to love it, and I'm going to love being *free*.

I am not used even yet to being outside the John Grier Home. Whenever I think of it excited little thrills chase up and down my back. I feel as though I must run faster and faster and keep looking over my shoulder to make sure that Mrs. Lippett isn't after me with her arm stretched out to grab me back.

I don't have to mind any one this summer, do I?

Your nominal authority doesn't annoy me in the least; you are too far away to do any harm. Mrs. Lippett is dead forever, so far as I am concerned, and the Semples aren't expected to overlook my moral welfare, are they? No, I am sure not. I am entirely grown up. Hooray!

I leave you now to pack a trunk, and three boxes of tea-kettles and dishes and sofa cushions and books.

Yours ever,

JUDY.

P.S. Here is my physiology exam. Do you think you could have passed?

LOCK WILLOW FARM,
Saturday night.

Dearest Daddy-Long-Legs,

I've only just come and I'm not unpacked, but I can't wait to tell you how much I like farms. This is a heavenly, heavenly, *heavenly* spot! The house is square like this:

And *old*. A hundred years or so. It has a veranda on the side which I can't draw and a sweet porch in front. The picture really doesn't do it justice—those things that look like feather dusters are maple trees, and the prickly ones that border the drive are murmuring pines and hemlocks. It stands on the top of a hill and looks way off over miles of green meadows to another line of hills.

That is the way Connecticut goes, in a series of Marcelle waves;[33] and Lock Willow Farm is just on the crest of one wave. The barns used to be across the road where they obstructed the view, but a kind flash of lightning came from heaven and burnt them down.

The people are Mr. and Mrs. Semple and a hired girl and two hired men. The hired people eat in the kitchen, and the Semples and Judy in the dining-room. We had ham and eggs and biscuits and honey and jelly-cake and pie and pickles and cheese and tea for supper—and a great deal of conversation. I have never been so entertaining in my life; everything I say appears to be funny. I suppose it is, because I've never been in the country before, and my questions are backed by an all-inclusive ignorance.

The room marked with a cross is not where the murder was committed, but the one that I occupy. It's big and square and empty, with adorable old-fashioned furniture and windows that have to be propped up on sticks and green shades trimmed with gold that fall down if you touch them. And a big square mahogany table—I'm going to spend the summer with my elbows spread out on it, writing a novel.

Oh, Daddy, I'm so excited! I can't wait till daylight to explore. It's 8.30 now, and I am about to blow out my candle and try to go to sleep. We rise at five. Did you ever know such fun? I can't believe this is really Judy. You and the Good Lord give me more than I deserve. I must be a very, very, *very* good person to pay. I'm going to be. You'll see.

Good night,
JUDY.

P.S. You should hear the frogs sing and the little pigs squeal—and you should see the new moon! I saw it over my right shoulder.

LOCK WILLOW,
July 12th.

Dear Daddy-Long-Legs,

How did your secretary come to know about Lock Willow? (That isn't a rhetorical question. I am awfully curious to know.) For listen to this: Mr. Jervis Pendleton used to own this farm, but now he has given it to Mrs. Semple who was his old nurse. Did you ever hear of such a funny coincidence? She still calls him "Master Jervie" and talks about what a sweet little boy he used to be. She has one of his baby curls put away in a box, and it's red—or at least reddish!

Since she discovered that I know him, I have risen very much in her opinion. Knowing a member of the Pendleton family is the best introduction one can have at Lock Willow. And the cream of the whole family is Master Jervie—I am pleased to say that Julia belongs to an inferior branch.

The farm gets more and more entertaining. I rode on a hay wagon yesterday. We have three big pigs and nine little piglets, and you should see them eat. They *are* pigs! We've oceans of little baby chickens and ducks and turkeys and guinea fowls. You must be mad to live in a city when you might live on a farm.

It is my daily business to hunt the eggs. I fell off a beam in the barn loft yesterday, while I was trying to crawl over to a nest that the black hen has stolen. And when I came in with a scratched knee, Mrs. Semple bound it up with witch-hazel, murmuring all the time, "Dear! Dear! It seems only yesterday that Master Jervie fell off that very same beam and scratched this very same knee."

The scenery around here is perfectly beautiful. There's a valley and a river and a lot of wooded hills, and way in the distance, a tall blue mountain that simply melts in your mouth.

We churn twice a week; and we keep the cream in the spring house which is made of stone with the brook running underneath. Some of the farmers around here have a separator, but we don't care for these new-fashioned ideas. It may be a little harder to take care of cream raised in pans, but it's enough better to pay. We have six calves; and I've chosen the names for all of them.

1. Sylvia, because she was born in the woods.
2. Lesbia, after the Lesbia in Catullus.[34]
3. Sallie.
4. Julia—a spotted, nondescript animal.
5. Judy, after me.
6. Daddy-Long-Legs. You don't mind, do you, Daddy? He's pure Jersey and has a sweet disposition. He looks like this—you can see how appropriate the name is.

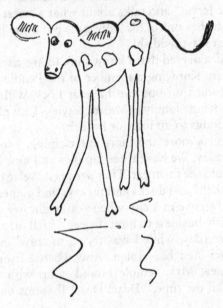

I haven't had time yet to begin my immortal novel; the farm keeps me too busy.

Yours always,
JUDY.

P.S. I've learned to make doughnuts.

P.S. (2) If you are thinking of raising chickens, let me recommend Buff Orpingtons. They haven't any pin feathers.

P.S. (3) I wish I could send you a pat of the nice, fresh butter I churned yesterday. I'm a fine dairy-maid!

P.S. (4) This is a picture of Miss Jerusha Abbott, the future great author, driving home the cows.

Sunday.

Dear Daddy-Long-Legs,

Isn't it funny? I started to write to you yesterday afternoon, but as far as I got was the heading, "Dear Daddy-Long-Legs," and then I remembered I'd promised to pick some blackberries for supper, so I went off and left the sheet lying on the table,

and when I came back to-day, what do you think I found sitting
in the middle of the page? A real true Daddy-Long-Legs!

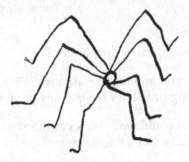

I picked him up very gently by one leg, and dropped him out
of the window. I wouldn't hurt one of them for the world. They
always remind me of you.

We hitched up the spring wagon this morning and drove to
the Center to church. It's a sweet little white frame church with
a spire and three Doric columns in front (or maybe Ionic[35]—I
always get them mixed).

A nice, sleepy sermon with everybody drowsily waving palm-
leaf fans, and the only sound aside from the minister, the buzzing of
locusts in the trees outside. I didn't wake up till I found myself on
my feet singing the hymn, and then I was awfully sorry I hadn't
listened to the sermon; I should like to know more of the psychology of a man who would pick out such a hymn. This was it:

> Come, leave your sports and earthly toys
> And join me in celestial joys.
> Or else, dear friend, a long farewell.
> I leave you now to sink to hell.

I find that it isn't safe to discuss religion with the Semples.
Their God (whom they have inherited intact from their remote
Puritan ancestors) is a narrow, irrational, unjust, mean, re-
vengeful, bigoted Person. Thank heaven I don't inherit any
God from anybody! I am free to make mine up as I wish Him.
He's kind and sympathetic and imaginative and forgiving and
understanding—and He has a sense of humor.

I like the Semples immensely; their practice is so superior to their theory. They are better than their own God. I told them so—and they are horribly troubled. They think I am blasphemous—and I think they are! We've dropped theology from our conversation.

This is Sunday afternoon.

Amasai (hired man) in a purple tie and some bright yellow buckskin gloves, very red and shaved, has just driven off with Carrie (hired girl) in a big hat trimmed with red roses and a blue muslin dress and her hair curled as tight as it will curl. Amasai spent all the morning washing the buggy; and Carrie stayed home from church ostensibly to cook the dinner, but really to iron the muslin dress.

In two minutes more when this letter is finished I am going to settle down to a book which I found in the attic. It's entitled, "On the Trail," and sprawled across the front page in a funny little-boy hand:

> Jervis Pendleton
> If this book should ever roam,
> Box its ears and send it home.

He spent the summer here once after he had been ill, when he was about eleven years old; and he left "On the Trail" behind. It looks well read—the marks of his grimy little hands are frequent! Also in a corner of the attic there is a water wheel and a windmill and some bows and arrows. Mrs. Semple talks so constantly about him that I begin to believe he really lives—not a grown man with a silk hat and walking stick, but a nice, dirty, tousle-headed boy who clatters up the stairs with an awful racket, and leaves the screen doors open, and is always asking for cookies. (And getting them, too, if I know Mrs. Semple!) He seems to have been an adventurous little soul—and brave and truthful. I'm sorry to think he is a Pendleton; he was meant for something better.

We're going to begin threshing oats tomorrow; a steam engine is coming and three extra men.

It grieves me to tell you that Buttercup (the spotted cow with one horn, Mother of Lesbia) has done a disgraceful thing. She got into the orchard Friday evening and ate apples under the trees, and ate and ate until they went to her head. For two days she has been perfectly dead drunk! That is the truth I am telling. Did you ever hear anything so scandalous?

>   Sir,
>   I remain,
>   Your affectionate orphan,
>   JUDY ABBOTT.

P.S. Indians in the first chapter and highwaymen in the second. I hold my breath. What *can* the third contain? "Red Hawk leapt twenty feet in the air and bit the dust." That is the subject of the frontispiece. Aren't Judy and Jervie having fun?

>   September 15th.

Dear Daddy,

I was weighed yesterday on the flour scales in the general store at the Corners. I've gained nine pounds! Let me recommend Lock Willow as a health resort.

>   Yours ever,
>   JUDY.

September 25th.

Dear Daddy-Long-Legs,

Behold me—a Sophomore! I came up last Friday, sorry to leave Lock Willow, but glad to see the campus again. It *is* a pleasant sensation to come back to something familiar. I am beginning to feel at home in college, and in command of the situation; I am beginning, in fact, to feel at home in the world—as though I really belonged in it and had not just crept in on sufferance.

I don't suppose you understand in the least what I am trying to say. A person important enough to be a Trustee can't appreciate the feelings of a person unimportant enough to be a foundling.

And now, Daddy, listen to this. Whom do you think I am rooming with? Sallie McBride and Julia Rutledge Pendleton. It's the truth. We have a study and three little bedrooms—*voila!*

Sallie and I decided last spring that we should like to room together, and Julia made up her mind to stay with Sallie—why, I can't imagine, for they are not a bit alike; but the Pendletons are naturally conservative and inimical (fine word!) to change. Anyway, here we are. Think of Jerusha Abbott, late of the John Grier Home for Orphans, rooming with a Pendleton. This is a democratic country.

Sallie is running for class president, and unless all signs fails, she is going to be elected. Such an atmosphere of intrigue—you should see what politicians we are! Oh, I tell you, Daddy, when we women get our rights, you men will have to look alive in order to keep yours. Election comes next Saturday, and we're going to have a torchlight procession in the evening, no matter who wins.

I am beginning chemistry, a most unusual study. I've never seen anything like it before. Molecules and Atoms are the material employed, but I'll be in a position to discuss them more definitely next month.

I am also taking argumentation and logic.

Also history of the whole world.

Also plays of William Shakespeare.[36]

Also French.

If this keeps up many years longer, I shall become quite intelligent.

I should rather have elected economics than French, but I didn't dare, because I was afraid that unless I reëlected French, the Professor would not let me pass—as it was, I just managed to squeeze through the June examination. But I will say that my high-school preparation was not very adequate.

There's one girl in the class who chatters away in French as fast as she does in English. She went abroad with her parents when she was a child, and spent three years in a convent school. You can imagine how bright she is compared with the rest of us—irregular verbs are mere playthings. I wish my parents had chucked me into a French convent when I was little instead of a foundling asylum. Oh, no, I don't either! Because then maybe I should never have known you. I'd rather know you than French.

Good-by, Daddy. I must call on Harriet Martin now, and, having discussed the chemical situation, casually drop a few thoughts on the subject of our next president.

Yours in politics,
J. ABBOTT.

October 17th.

Dear Daddy-Long-Legs,

Supposing the swimming tank in the gymnasium were filled full of lemon jelly, could a person trying to swim manage to keep on top or would he sink?

We were having lemon jelly for dessert when the question came up. We discussed it heatedly for half an hour and it's still unsettled. Sallie thinks that she could swim in it, but I am perfectly sure that the best swimmer in the world would sink. Wouldn't it be funny to be drowned in lemon jelly?

Two other problems are engaging the attention of our table.

1ST. What shape are the rooms in an octagon house? Some of the girls insist that they're square; but I think they'd have to be shaped like a piece of pie. Don't you?

2nd. Suppose there were a great big hollow sphere made of looking-glass and you were sitting inside. Where would it stop reflecting your face and begin reflecting your back? The more one thinks about this problem, the more puzzling it becomes. You can see with what deep philosophical reflection we engage our leisure!

Did I ever tell you about the election? It happened three weeks ago, but so fast do we live, that three weeks is ancient history. Sallie was elected, and we had a torchlight parade with transparencies saying, "McBride Forever," and a band consisting of fourteen pieces (three mouth organs and eleven combs).

We're very important persons now in "258." Julia and I come in for a great deal of reflected glory. It's quite a social strain to be living in the same house with a president.

Bonne nuit, cher Daddy.

> *Acceptez mes compliments,*
> *Très respectueux.*
> *Je suis,*
> *Votre* JUDY.

November 12th.

Dear Daddy-Long-Legs,

We beat the Freshmen at basket ball yesterday. Of course we're pleased—but oh, if we could only beat the Juniors! I'd be willing to be black and blue all over and stay in bed a week in a witch-hazel compress.

Sallie has invited me to spend the Christmas vacation with her. She lives in Worcester, Massachusetts. Wasn't it nice of her? I shall love to go. I've never been in a private family in my life, except at Lock Willow, and the Semples were grown-up and old and don't count. But the McBrides have a houseful of children (anyway two or three) and a mother and father and grandmother, and an Angora cat. It's a perfectly complete family! Packing your trunk and going away *is* more fun than staying behind. I am terribly excited at the prospect.

Seventh hour—I must run to rehearsal. I'm to be in the

Thanksgiving theatricals. A prince in a tower with a velvet tunic and yellow curls. Isn't that a lark?

Yours,

J. A.

Saturday.

Do you want to know what I look like? Here's a photograph of all three that Leonora Fenton took.

The light one who is laughing is Sallie, and the tall one with her nose in the air is Julia, and the little one with the hair blowing across her face is Judy—she is really more beautiful than that, but the sun was in her eyes.

"STONE GATE,"
WORCESTER, MASS.,
December 31st.

Dear Daddy-Long-Legs,

I meant to write to you before and thank you for your Christmas check, but life in the McBride household is very absorbing, and I don't seem able to find two consecutive minutes to spend at a desk.

I bought a new gown—one that I didn't need, but just wanted. My Christmas present this year is from Daddy-Long-Legs; my family just sent love.

I've been having the most beautiful vacation visiting Sallie. She lives in a big old-fashioned brick house with white trimmings set back from the street—exactly the kind of house that I used to look at so curiously when I was in the John Grier Home, and wonder what it could be like inside. I never expected to see with my own eyes—but here I am! Everything is so comfortable and restful and homelike; I walk from room to room and drink in the furnishings.

It is the most perfect house for children to be brought up in; with shadowy nooks for hide and seek, and open fireplaces for pop-corn, and an attic to romp in on rainy days, and slippery banisters with a comfortable flat knob at the bottom, and a great big sunny kitchen, and a nice fat, sunny cook who has lived in the family thirteen years and always saves out a piece of dough for the children to bake. Just the sight of such a house makes you want to be a child all over again.

And as for families! I never dreamed they could be so nice. Sallie has a father and mother and grandmother, and the sweetest three-year-old baby sister all over curls, and a medium-sized brother who always forgets to wipe his feet, and a big, good-looking brother named Jimmie, who is a junior at Princeton.

We have the jolliest times at the table—everybody laughs and jokes and talks at once, and we don't have to say grace beforehand. It's a relief not having to thank Somebody for every mouthful you eat. (I dare say I'm blasphemous; but you'd be, too, if you'd offered as much obligatory thanks as I have.)

Such a lot of things we've done—I can't begin to tell you about them. Mr. McBride owns a factory, and Christmas eve he had a tree for the employees' children. It was in the long packing-room which was decorated with evergreens and holly. Jimmie McBride was dressed as Santa Claus, and Sallie and I helped him distribute the presents.

Dear me, Daddy, but it was a funny sensation! I felt as benevolent as a Trustee of the John Grier Home. I kissed one sweet, sticky little boy—but I don't think I patted any of them on the head!

And two days after Christmas, they gave a dance at their own house for ME.

It was the first really true ball I ever attended—college doesn't count where we dance with girls. I had a new white evening gown (your Christmas present—many thanks) and long white gloves and white satin slippers. The only drawback to my perfect, utter, absolute happiness was the fact that Mrs. Lippett couldn't see me leading the cotillion with Jimmie McBride. Tell her about it, please, the next time you visit the J. G. H.

                              Yours ever,
                              JUDY ABBOTT.

P.S. Would you be terribly displeased, Daddy, if I didn't turn
out to be a Great Author after all, but just a Plain Girl?

6.30, Saturday.

Dear Daddy,

We started to walk to town to-day, but mercy! how it
poured. I like winter to be winter with snow instead of rain.

Julia's desirable uncle called again this afternoon—and
brought a five-pound box of chocolates. There are advantages
you see about rooming with Julia.

Our innocent prattle appeared to amuse him and he waited
over a train in order to take tea in the study. And an awful lot
of trouble we had getting permission. It's hard enough entertaining fathers and grandfathers, but uncles are a step worse;
and as for brothers and cousins, they are next to impossible.
Julia had to swear that he was her uncle before a notary public
and then have the county clerk's certificate attached. (Don't I
know a lot of law?) And even then I doubt if we could have had
our tea if the Dean had chanced to see how youngish and good-
looking Uncle Jervis is.

Anyway, we had it, with brown bread Swiss cheese sandwiches. He helped make them and then ate four. I told him that
I had spent last summer at Lock Willow, and we had a beautiful gossipy time about the Semples, and the horses and cows
and chickens. All the horses that he used to know are dead, except Grover, who was a baby colt at the time of his last visit—
and poor Grove now is so old he can just limp about the
pasture.

He asked if they still kept doughnuts in a yellow crock with
a blue plate over it on the bottom shelf of the pantry—and they
do! He wanted to know if there was still a woodchuck's hole
under the pile of rocks in the night pasture—and there is! Amasai caught a big, fat, gray one there this summer, the twenty-
fifth great-grandson of the one Master Jervie caught when he
was a little boy.

I called him "Master Jervie" to his face, but he didn't appear to be insulted. Julia says that she has never seen him so amiable; he's usually pretty unapproachable. But Julia hasn't a bit of tact; and men, I find, require a great deal. They purr if you rub them the right way and spit if you don't. (That isn't a very elegant metaphor. I mean it figuratively.)

We're reading Marie Bashkirtseff's journal.[37] Isn't it amazing? Listen to this: "Last night I was seized by a fit of despair that found utterance in moans, and that finally drove me to throw the dining-room clock into the sea."

It makes me almost hope I'm not a genius; they must be very wearing to have about—and awfully destructive to the furniture.

Mercy! how it keeps pouring. We shall have to swim to chapel to-night.

Yours ever,

JUDY.

Jan. 20th.

Dear Daddy-Long-Legs,

Did you ever have a sweet baby girl who was stolen from the cradle in infancy?

Maybe I am she! If we were in a novel, that would be the dénouement, wouldn't it?

It's really awfully queer not to know what one is—sort of

exciting and romantic. There are such a lot of possibilities. Maybe I'm not American; lots of people aren't. I may be straight descended from the ancient Romans, or I may be a Viking's daughter, or I may be the child of a Russian exile and belong by rights in a Siberian prison, or maybe I'm a Gipsy—I think perhaps I am. I have a very *wandering* spirit, though I haven't as yet had much chance to develop it.

Do you know about the one scandalous blot in my career—the time I ran away from the asylum because they punished me for stealing cookies? It's down in the books free for any Trustee to read. But really, Daddy, what could you expect? When you put a hungry little nine-year girl in the pantry scouring knives, with the cookie jar at her elbow, and go off and leave her alone; and then suddenly pop in again, wouldn't you expect to find her a bit crumby? And then when you jerk her by the elbow and box her ears, and make her leave the table when the pudding comes, and tell all the other children that it's because she's a thief, wouldn't you expect her to run away?

I only ran four miles. They caught me and brought me back; and every day for a week I was tied, like a naughty puppy, to a stake in the back yard while the other children were out at recess.

Oh, dear! There's the chapel bell, and after chapel I have a committee meeting. I'm sorry because I meant to write you a *very* entertaining letter this time.

>   *Auf wiedersehen*
>   *Cher* Daddy
>   *Pax tibi!*
>   JUDY.

P.S. There's one thing I'm perfectly sure of. I'm *not* a Chinaman.

February 4th.

Dear Daddy-Long-Legs,

Jimmie McBride has sent me a Princeton banner as big as one end of the room; I am very grateful to him for remember-

ing me, but I don't know what on earth to do with it. Sallie and
Julia won't let me hang it up; our room this year is furnished in
red, and you can imagine what an effect we'd have if I added
orange and black. But it's such nice, warm, thick felt, I hate to
waste it. Would it be very improper to have it made into a bath
robe? My old one shrank when it was washed.

6.A.M.

It's the early bird
that catches the tub.

I've entirely omitted of late telling you what I am learning,
but though you might not imagine it from my letters, my time
is exclusively occupied with study. It's a very bewildering matter to get educated in five branches at once.

"The test of true scholarship," says Chemistry Professor, "is
a painstaking passion for detail."

"Be careful not to keep your eyes glued to detail," says History Professor. "Stand far enough away to get a perspective on
the whole."

You can see with what nicety we have to trim our sails between chemistry and history. I like the historical method best.
If I say that William the Conqueror came over in 1492, and
Columbus discovered America in 1100 or 1066[38] or whenever
it was, that's a mere detail that the Professor overlooks. It gives
a feeling of security and restfulness to the history recitation,
that is entirely lacking in chemistry.

Sixth-hour bell—I must go to the laboratory and look into a little matter of acids and salts and alkalis. I've burned a hole as big as a plate in the front of my chemistry apron, with hydrochloric acid. If the theory worked, I ought to be able to neutralize that hole with good strong ammonia, oughtn't I?

Examinations next week, but who's afraid?

Yours ever,
JUDY.

March 5th.

Dear Daddy-Long-Legs,

There is a March wind blowing, and the sky is filled with heavy, black moving clouds. The crows in the pine trees are making such a clamor! It's an intoxicating, exhilarating, *calling* noise. You want to close your books and be off over the hills to race with the wind.

We had a paper chase last Saturday over five miles of squashy 'cross country. The fox (composed of three girls and a bushel or so of confetti) started half an hour before the twenty-seven hunters. I was one of the twenty-seven; eight dropped by the wayside; we ended nineteen. The trail led over a hill, through a cornfield, and into a swamp where we had to leap lightly from hummock to hummock. Of course half of us went in ankle deep. We kept losing the trail, and wasted twenty-five minutes over that swamp. Then up a hill through some woods and in at the barn window! The barn doors were all locked and the window was up high and pretty small. I don't call that fair, do you?

But we didn't go through; we circumnavigated the barn and picked up the trail where it issued by way of a low shed roof onto the top of a fence. The fox thought he had us there, but we fooled him. Then straight away over two miles of rolling meadow; and awfully hard to follow, for the confetti was getting sparse. The rule is that it must be at the most six feet apart, but they were the longest six feet I ever saw. Finally, after two hours of steady trotting, we tracked Monsieur Fox into the kitchen of Crystal Spring (that's a farm where the girls go in bob sleighs and hay wagons for chicken and waffle suppers) and we found the three foxes placidly eating milk and honey and biscuits. They hadn't thought we would get that far; they were expecting us to stick in the barn window.

Both sides insist that they won. I think we did, don't you? Because we caught them before they got back to the campus. Anyway, all nineteen of us settled like locusts over the furniture and clamored for honey. There wasn't enough to go round, but Mrs. Crystal Spring (that's our pet name for her; she's by rights a Johnson) brought up a jar of strawberry jam and a can of maple syrup—just made last week—and three loaves of brown bread.

We didn't get back to college till half-past six—half an hour late for dinner—and we went straight in without dressing, and with perfectly unimpaired appetites! Then we all cut evening chapel, the state of our boots being enough of an excuse.

I never told you about examinations. I passed everything with the utmost ease—I know the secret now, and am never going to flunk again. I shan't be able to graduate with honors though, because of that beastly Latin prose and geometry Freshman year. But I don't care. Wot's the hodds so long as you're 'appy? (That's a quotation. I've been reading the English classics.)

Speaking of classics, have you ever read "Hamlet"?[39] If you haven't, do it right off. It's *perfectly corking*. I've been hearing about Shakespeare all my life, but I had no idea he really wrote so well; I always suspected him of going largely on his reputation.

I have a beautiful play that I invented a long time ago when I first learned to read. I put myself to sleep every night by pretending I'm the person (the most important person) in the book I'm reading at the moment.

At present I'm Ophelia—and such a sensible Ophelia! I keep Hamlet amused all the time, and pet him and scold him and make him wrap up his throat when he has a cold. I've entirely cured him of being melancholy. The King and Queen are both dead—an accident at sea; no funeral necessary—so Hamlet and I are ruling Denmark without any bother. We have the kingdom working beautifully. He takes care of the governing, and I

look after the charities. I have just founded some first-class orphan asylums. If you or any of the other Trustees would like to
visit them, I shall be pleased to show you through. I think you
might find a great many helpful suggestions.

I remain, sir,

Yours most graciously,

OPHELIA,

QUEEN OF DENMARK.

March 24th

maybe the 25th.

Dear Daddy-Long-Legs,

I don't believe I can be going to Heaven—I am getting such a
lot of good things here; it wouldn't be fair to get them hereafter,
too. Listen to what has happened.

Jerusha Abbott has won the short-story contest (a twenty-
five dollar prize) that the *Monthly* holds every year. And she a
Sophomore! The contestants are mostly Seniors. When I saw
my name posted, I couldn't quite believe it was true. Maybe I
am going to be an author after all. I wish Mrs. Lippett hadn't
given me such a silly name—it sounds like an author-ess,
doesn't it?

Also I have been chosen for the spring dramatics—"As You
Like It"[40] out of doors. I am going to be Celia, own cousin to
Rosalind.

And lastly: Julia and Sallie and I are going to New York next
Friday to do some spring shopping and stay all night and go to
the theater the next day with "Master Jervie." He invited us.
Julia is going to stay at home with her family, but Sallie and I
are going to stop at the Martha Washington Hotel. Did you
ever hear of anything so exciting? I've never been in a hotel in
my life, nor in a theater; except once when the Catholic Church
had a festival and invited the orphans, but that wasn't a real
play and it doesn't count.

And what do you think we're going to see? "Hamlet." Think

of that! We studied it for four weeks in Shakespeare class and I
know it by heart.

I am so excited over all these prospects that I can scarcely
sleep.

Good-by, Daddy.

This is a very entertaining world.

Yours ever,

JUDY.

P.S. I've just looked at the calendar. It's the 28th.

Another postscript.

I saw a street car conductor to-day with one brown eye and
one blue. Wouldn't he make a nice villain for a detective story?

April 7th.

Dear Daddy-Long-Legs,

Mercy! Isn't New York big? Worcester is nothing to it. Do
you mean to tell me that you actually live in all that confusion?
I don't believe that I shall recover for months from the bewildering effect of two days of it. I can't begin to tell you all the
amazing things I've seen; I suppose you know, though, since
you live there yourself.

But aren't the streets entertaining? And the people? And the
shops? I never saw such lovely things as there are in the windows. It makes you want to devote your life to wearing clothes.

Sallie and Julia and I went shopping together Saturday
morning. Julia went into the very most gorgeous place I ever
saw, white and gold walls and blue carpets and blue silk curtains and gilt chairs. A perfectly beautiful lady with yellow hair
and a long black silk trailing gown came to meet us with a welcoming smile. I thought we were paying a social call, and started
to shake hands, but it seems we were only buying hats—at least
Julia was. She sat down in front of a mirror and tried on a

dozen, each lovelier than the last, and bought the two loveliest of all.

I can't imagine any joy in life greater than sitting down in front of a mirror and buying any hat you choose without having first to consider the price! There's no doubt about it, Daddy; New York would rapidly undermine this fine, stoical character which the John Grier Home so patiently built up.

And after we'd finished our shopping, we met Master Jervie at Sherry's. I suppose you've been in Sherry's? Picture that, then picture the dining-room of the John Grier Home with its oilcloth-covered tables, and white crockery that you *can't* break, and wooden-handled knives and forks; and fancy the way I felt!

I ate my fish with the wrong fork, but the waiter very kindly gave me another so that nobody noticed.

And after luncheon, we went to the theater—it was dazzling, marvelous, unbelievable—I dream about it every night.

Isn't Shakespeare wonderful?

"Hamlet" is so much better on the stage than when we analyze it in class; I appreciated it before, but now, dear me!

I think, if you don't mind, that I'd rather be an actress than a writer. Wouldn't you like me to leave college and go into a dramatic school? And then I'll send you a box for all my performances, and smile at you across the footlights. Only wear a red rose in your buttonhole, please, so I'll surely smile at the right man. It would be an awfully embarrassing mistake if I picked out the wrong one.

We came back Saturday night and had our dinner in the train, at little tables with pink lamps and negro waiters. I never heard of meals being served in trains before, and I inadvertently said so.

"Where on earth were you brought up?" said Julia to me.

"In a village," said I, meekly to Julia.

"But didn't you ever travel?" said she to me.

"Not till I came to college, and then it was only a hundred and sixty miles and we didn't eat," said I to her.

She's getting quite interested in me, because I say such funny things. I try hard not to, but they do pop out when I'm surprised—and I'm surprised most of the time. It's a dizzying ex-

perience, Daddy, to pass eighteen years in the John Grier
Home, and then suddenly to be plunged into the WORLD.

But I'm getting acclimated. I don't make such awful mistakes
as I did; and I don't feel uncomfortable any more with the other
girls. I used to squirm whenever people looked at me. I felt as
though they saw right through my sham new clothes to the
checked ginghams underneath. But I'm not letting the ginghams bother me any more. Sufficient unto yesterday is the evil
thereof.

I forgot to tell you about our flowers. Master Jervie gave us
each a big bunch of violets and lilies-of-the-valley. Wasn't that
sweet of him? I never used to care much for men—judging by
Trustees—but I'm changing my mind.

Eleven pages—this *is* a letter! Have courage. I'm going to
stop.

Yours always,
JUDY.

April 10th.

Dear Mr. Rich-Man,

Here's your check for fifty dollars. Thank you very much,
but I do not feel that I can keep it. My allowance is sufficient to
afford all of the hats that I need. I am sorry that I wrote all that
silly stuff about the millinery shop; it's just that I had never seen
anything like it before.

However, I wasn't begging! And I would rather not accept
any more charity than I have to.

Sincerely yours,
JERUSHA ABBOTT.

April 11th.

Dearest Daddy,

Will you please forgive me for the letter I wrote you yesterday? After I posted it I was sorry, and tried to get it back, but that beastly mail clerk wouldn't give it to me.

It's the middle of the night now; I've been awake for hours thinking what a Worm I am—what a Thousand-legged Worm—and that's the worst I can say! I've closed the door very softly into the study so as not to wake Julia and Sallie, and am sitting up in bed writing to you on paper torn out of my history note-book.

I just wanted to tell you that I am sorry I was so impolite about your check. I know you meant it kindly, and I think you're an old dear to take so much trouble for such a silly thing as a hat. I ought to have returned it very much more graciously.

But in any case, I had to return it. It's different with me than with other girls. They can take things naturally from people. They have fathers and brothers and aunts and uncles; but I can't be on any such relations with any one. I like to pretend that you belong to me, just to play with the idea, but of course I know you don't. I'm alone, really—with my back to the wall fighting the world—and I get sort of gaspy when I think about it. I put it out of my mind, and keep on pretending; but don't you see, Daddy? I can't accept any more money than I have to, because some day I shall be wanting to pay it back, and even as great an author as I intend to be, won't be able to face a *perfectly tremendous* debt.

I'd love pretty hats and things, but I mustn't mortgage the future to pay for them.

You'll forgive me, won't you, for being so rude? I have an awful habit of writing impulsively when I first think things, and then posting the letter beyond recall. But if I sometimes seem thoughtless and ungrateful, I never mean it. In my heart I thank you always for the life and freedom and independence that you

have given me. My childhood was just a long, sullen stretch of
revolt, and now I am so happy every moment of the day that I
can't believe it's true. I feel like a made-up heroine in a story-
book.

It's a quarter past two. I'm going to tiptoe out to the mail
chute and get this off now. You'll receive it in the next mail after the other; so you won't have a very long time to think bad
of me.

Good night, Daddy,
I love you always,

JUDY.

May 4th.

Dear Daddy-Long-Legs,

Field Day last Saturday. It was a very spectacular occasion.
First we had a parade of all the classes, with everybody dressed
in white linen, the Seniors carrying blue and gold Japanese um-
brellas, and the Juniors white and yellow banners. Our class
had crimson balloons—very fetching, especially as they were
always getting loose and floating off—and the Freshmen wore
green tissue-paper hats with long streamers. Also we had a
band in blue uniforms hired from town. Also about a dozen
funny people, like clowns in a circus, to keep the spectators entertained between events.

Julia was dressed as a fat country man with a linen duster and
whiskers and baggy umbrella. Patsy Moriarty (Patricia, really.
Did you ever hear such a name? Mrs. Lippett couldn't have done
better.) who is tall and thin was Julia's wife in an absurd green
bonnet over one ear. Waves of laughter followed them the whole
length of the course. Julia played the part extremely well. I never
dreamed that a Pendleton could display so much comedy spirit—
begging Master Jervie's pardon; I don't consider him a true
Pendleton though, any more than I consider you a true Trustee.

Sallie and I weren't in the parade because we were entered
for the events. And what do you think? We both won! At least

in something. We tried for the running broad jump and lost;
but Sallie won the pole-vaulting (seven feet three inches) and I
won the fifty-yard dash (eight seconds).

I was pretty panting at the end, but it was great fun, with the
whole class waving balloons and cheering and yelling:

> What's the matter with Judy Abbott?
> She's all right.
> Who's all right?
> Judy Ab-bott!

Judy Wins the
Fifty Yard Dash

That, Daddy, is true fame. Then trotting back to the dressing
tent and being rubbed down with alcohol and having a lemon
to suck. You see we're very professional. It's a fine thing to win
an event for your class, because the class that wins the most
gets the athletic cup for the year. The Seniors won it this year,
with seven events to their credit. The athletic association gave
a dinner in the gymnasium to all of the winners. We had fried
soft-shell crabs, and chocolate ice-cream molded in the shape
of basket balls.

I sat up half of last night reading "Jane Eyre."[41] Are you old
enough, Daddy, to remember sixty years ago? And if so, did
people talk that way?

The haughty Lady Blanche says to the footman, "Stop your
chattering, knave, and do my bidding." Mr. Rochester talks

about the metal welkin when he means the sky; and as for the
mad woman who laughs like a hyena and sets fire to bed curtains and tears up wedding veils and *bites*—it's melodrama of
the purest, but just the same, you read and read and read. I
can't see how any girl could have written such a book, especially any girl who was brought up in a churchyard. There's
something about those Brontës that fascinates me. Their
books, their lives, their spirit. Where did they get it? When I
was reading about little Jane's troubles in the charity school, I
got so angry that I had to go out and take a walk. I understood
exactly how she felt. Having known Mrs. Lippett, I could see
Mr. Brocklehurst.

Don't be outraged, Daddy. I am not intimating that the John
Grier Home was like the Lowood Institute.[42] We had plenty to
eat and plenty to wear, sufficient water to wash in, and a furnace in the cellar. But there was one deadly likeness. Our lives
were absolutely monotonous and uneventful. Nothing nice
ever happened, except ice-cream on Sundays, and even that
was regular. In all the eighteen years I was there I only had one
adventure—when the woodshed burned. We had to get up in
the night and dress so as to be ready in case the house should
catch. But it didn't catch and we went back to bed.

Everybody likes a few surprises; it's a perfectly natural human craving. But I never had one until Mrs. Lippett called me
to the office to tell me that Mr. John Smith was going to send
me to college. And then she broke the news so gradually that it
just barely shocked me.

You know, Daddy, I think that the most necessary quality for
any person to have is imagination. It makes people able to put
themselves in other people's places. It makes them kind and
sympathetic and understanding. It ought to be cultivated in
children. But the John Grier Home instantly stamped out the
slightest flicker that appeared. Duty was the one quality that
was encouraged. I don't think children ought to know the
meaning of the word; it's odious, detestable. They ought to do
everything from love.

Wait until you see the orphan asylum that I am going to be
the head of! It's my favorite play at night before I go to sleep. I

plan it out to the littlest detail—the meals and clothes and study and amusements and punishments; for even my superior orphans are sometimes bad.

But anyway, they are going to be happy. I think that every one, no matter how many troubles he may have when he grows up, ought to have a happy childhood to look back upon. And if I ever have any children of my own, no matter how unhappy I may be, I am not going to let them have any cares until they grow up.

(There goes the chapel bell—I'll finish this letter sometime.)

Thursday.

When I came in from laboratory this afternoon, I found a squirrel sitting on the tea table helping himself to almonds. These are the kind of callers we entertain now that warm weather has come and the window stays open—

"My dear Mrs. Centipede, will you have one lump or two?"

Saturday morning.

Perhaps you think, last night being Friday, with no classes to-day, that I passed a nice quiet, readable evening with the set of Stevenson[43] that I bought with my prize money? But if so, you've never attended a girls' college, Daddy dear. Six friends dropped in to make fudge, and one of them dropped the fudge—while it was still liquid—right in the middle of our best rug. We shall never be able to clean up the mess.

I haven't mentioned any lessons of late; but we are still hav-

ing them every day. It's sort of a relief though, to get away from
them and discuss life in the large—rather one-sided discussions
that you and I hold, but that's your own fault. You are welcome to answer back any time you choose.

I've been writing this letter off and on for three days, and I
fear by now *vous êtes bien* bored!

Good-by, nice Mr. Man,

JUDY.

Mr. Daddy-Long-Legs Smith.

SIR: Having completed the study of argumentation and the
science of dividing a thesis into heads, I have decided to adopt
the following form for letter-writing. It contains all the necessary facts, but no unnecessary verbiage.

I. We had written examinations this week in:
    A. Chemistry.
    B. History.
II. A new dormitory is being built.
    A. Its material is:
        (a) red brick.
        (b) gray stone.
    B. Its capacity will be:
        (a) one dean, five instructors.
        (b) two hundred girls.
        (c) one housekeeper, three cooks, twenty waitresses,
           twenty chambermaids.
III. We had junket for dessert to-night.
IV. I am writing a special topic upon the Sources of Shake-
speare's Plays.
V. Lou McMahon slipped and fell this afternoon at basket
ball, and she:
    A. Dislocated her shoulder.
    B. Bruised her knee.
VI. I have a new hat trimmed with:
    A. Blue velvet ribbon.
    B. Two blue quills.

C. Three red pompons.
VII. It is half-past nine.
VIII. Good night.

JUDY.

June 2d.

Dear Daddy-Long-Legs,

You will never guess the nice thing that has happened.

The McBrides have asked me to spend the summer at their camp in the Adirondacks! They belong to a sort of club on a lovely little lake in the middle of the woods. The different members have houses made of logs dotted about among the trees, and they go canoeing on the lake, and take long walks through trails to other camps, and have dances once a week in the club house—Jimmie McBride is going to have a college friend visiting him part of the summer, so you see we shall have plenty of men to dance with.

Wasn't it sweet of Mrs. McBride to ask me? It appears that she liked me when I was there for Christmas.

Please excuse this being short. It isn't a real letter; it's just to let you know that I'm disposed of for the summer.

Yours,
In a *very* contented frame of mind.

JUDY.

June 5th.

Dear Daddy-Long-Legs,

Your secretary man has just written to me saying that Mr. Smith prefers that I should not accept Mrs. McBride's invitation, but should return to Lock Willow the same as last summer.

Why, why, *why*, Daddy?

You don't understand about it. Mrs. McBride does want me, really and truly. I'm not the least bit of trouble in the house. I'm a help. They don't take up many servants, and Sallie and I can do lots of useful things. It's a fine chance for me to learn house-keeping. Every woman ought to understand it, and I only know asylum-keeping.

There aren't any girls our age at the camp, and Mrs. McBride wants me for a companion for Sallie. We are planning to do a lot of reading together. We are going to read all of the books for next year's English and sociology. The Professor said it would be a great help if we would get our reading finished in the summer; and it's so much easier to remember it, if we read together and talk it over.

Just to live in the same house with Sallie's mother is an educa-tion. She's the most interesting, entertaining, companionable, charming woman in the world; she knows everything. Think how many summers I've spent with Mrs. Lippett and how I'll appreci-ate the contrast. You needn't be afraid that I'll be crowding them, for their house is made of rubber. When they have a lot of com-pany, they just sprinkle tents about in the woods and turn the boys outside. It's going to be such a nice, healthy summer exercis-ing out of doors every minute. Jimmie McBride is going to teach me how to ride horseback and paddle a canoe, and how to shoot and—oh, lots of things I ought to know. It's the kind of nice, jolly, care-free time that I've never had; and I think every girl deserves it once in her life. Of course I'll do exactly as you say, but please, *please* let me go, Daddy. I've never wanted anything so much.

This isn't Jerusha Abbott, the future great author, writing to you. It's just Judy—a girl.

June 9th.

Mr. John Smith.

SIR: Yours of the 7th inst. at hand. In compliance with the in-structions received through your secretary, I leave on Friday next to spend the summer at Lock Willow Farm.

I hope always to remain,

(MISS) JERUSHA ABBOTT.

LOCK WILLOW FARM,
August Third.

Dear Daddy-Long-Legs,

It has been nearly two months since I wrote, which wasn't nice of me, I know, but I haven't loved you much this summer—you see I'm being frank!

You can't imagine how disappointed I was at having to give up the McBrides' camp. Of course I know that you're my guardian, and that I have to regard your wishes in all matters, but I couldn't see any *reason*. It was so distinctly the best thing that could have happened to me. If I had been Daddy, and you had been Judy, I should have said, "Bless you, my child, run along and have a good time; see lots of new people and learn lots of new things; live out of doors, and get strong and well and rested for a year of hard work."

But not at all! Just a curt line from your secretary ordering me to Lock Willow.

It's the impersonality of your commands that hurts my feelings. It seems as though, if you felt the tiniest little bit for me the way I feel for you, you'd sometimes send me a message that you'd written with your own hand, instead of those beastly typewritten secretary's notes. If there were the slightest hint that you cared, I'd do anything on earth to please you.

I know that I was to write nice, long, detailed letters without ever expecting any answer. You're living up to your side of the bargain—I'm being educated—and I suppose you're thinking I'm not living up to mine!

But, Daddy, it is a hard bargain. It is, really. I'm so awfully lonely. You are the only person I have to care for, and you are so shadowy. You're just an imaginary man that I've made up—and probably the real *you* isn't a bit like my imaginary *you*. But you did once, when I was ill in the infirmary, send me a message, and now, when I am feeling awfully forgotten, I get out your card and read it over.

I don't think I am telling you at all what I started to say, which was this:

Although my feelings are still hurt, for it is very humiliating to be picked up and moved about by an arbitrary, peremptory, unreasonable, omnipotent, invisible Providence, still, when a man has been as kind and generous and thoughtful as you have heretofore been toward me, I suppose he has a right to be an arbitrary, peremptory, unreasonable, invisible Providence if he chooses, and so—I'll forgive you and be cheerful again. But I still don't enjoy getting Sallie's letters about the good times they are having in camp!

However—we will draw a veil over that and begin again.

I've been writing and writing this summer; four short stories finished and sent to four different magazines. So you see I'm trying to be an author. I have a workroom fixed in a corner of the attic where Master Jervie used to have his rainy-day playroom. It's in a cool, breezy corner with two dormer windows, and shaded by a maple tree with a family of red squirrels living in a hole.

I'll write a nicer letter in a few days and tell you all the farm news.

We need rain.

Yours as ever,
JUDY.

August 10th.

Mr. Daddy-Long-Legs,

SIR: I address you from the second crotch in the willow tree by the pool in the pasture. There's a frog croaking underneath, a locust singing overhead and two little "devil down-heads" darting up and down the trunk. I've been here for an hour; it's a very comfortable crotch, especially after being upholstered with two sofa cushions. I came up with a pen and tablet hoping to write an immortal short story, but I've been having a dreadful time with my heroine—I *can't* make her behave as I want her to behave; so I've abandoned her for the moment, and am writing to you. (Not much relief though, for I can't make you behave as I want you to, either.)

If you are in that dreadful New York, I wish I could send you some of this lovely, breezy, sunshiny outlook. The country is Heaven after a week of rain.

Speaking of Heaven—do you remember Mr. Kellogg that I told you about last summer?—the minister of the little white church at the Corners. Well, the poor old soul is dead—last winter of pneumonia. I went half-a-dozen times to hear him preach and got very well acquainted with his theology. He believed to the end, exactly the same things he started with. It seems to me that a man who can think straight along for forty-seven years without changing a single idea ought to be kept in a cabinet as a curiosity. I hope he is enjoying his harp and golden crown; he was so perfectly sure of finding them! There's a new young man, very up and coming, in his place. The congregation is pretty dubious, especially the faction led by Deacon Cummings. It looks as though there was going to be an awful split in the church. We don't care for innovations in religion in this neighborhood.

During our week of rain I sat up in the attic and had an orgie of reading—Stevenson, mostly. He himself is more entertaining than any of the characters in his books; I dare say he made himself into the kind of hero that would look well in print. Don't you think it was perfect of him to spend all the ten thousand dollars his father left, for a yacht, and go sailing off to the South Seas?[44] He lived up to his adventurous creed. If my father had left me ten thousand dollars, I'd do it, too. The thought of Vailima makes me wild. I want to see the tropics. I want to see the whole world. I am going to some day—I am, really, Daddy, when I get to be a great author, or artist, or actress, or playwright—or whatever sort of a great person I turn out to be. I have a terrible wanderthirst; the very sight of a map makes me want to put on my hat and take an umbrella and start. "I shall see before I die the palms and temples of the South."

Thursday evening at twilight, sitting on the doorstep.

Very hard to get any news into this letter! Judy is becoming so philosophical of late, that she wishes to discourse largely of

the world in general, instead of descending to the trivial details
of daily life. But if you *must* have news, here it is:

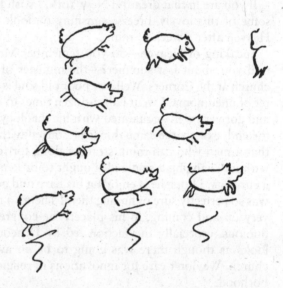

Our nine young pigs waded across the brook and ran away
last Tuesday, and only eight came back. We don't want to accuse any one unjustly, but we suspect that Widow Dowd has
one more than she ought to have.

Mr. Weaver has painted his barn and his two silos a bright
pumpkin yellow—a very ugly color, but he says it will wear.

The Brewers have company this week; Mrs. Brewer's sister
and two nieces from Ohio.

One of our Rhode Island Reds only brought off three chicks
out of fifteen eggs. We can't imagine what was the trouble.
Rhode Island Reds, in my opinion, are a very inferior breed. I
prefer Buff Orpingtons.

The new clerk in the post-office at Bonnyrigg Four Corners drank every drop of Jamaica ginger they had in stock—seven dollars' worth—before he was discovered.

Old Ira Hatch has rheumatism and can't work any more; he never saved his money when he was earning good wages, so now he has to live on the town.

There's to be an ice-cream social at the schoolhouse next Saturday evening. Come and bring your families.

I have a new hat that I bought for twenty-five cents at the post-office. This is my latest portrait, on my way to rake the hay.

It's getting too dark to see; anyway, the news is all used up.

Good night,
JUDY.

Friday.

Good morning! Here *is* some news! What do you think? You'd never, never, never guess who's coming to Lock Willow. A letter to Mrs. Semple from Mr. Pendleton. He's motoring through the Berkshires, and is tired and wants to rest on a nice quiet farm—if he climbs out at her doorstep some night will she have a room ready for him? Maybe he'll stay one week, or maybe two, or maybe three; he'll see how restful it is when he gets here.

Such a flutter as we are in! The whole house is being cleaned and all the curtains washed. I am driving to the Corners this morning to get some new oilcloth for the entry, and two cans of brown floor paint for the hall and back stairs. Mrs. Dowd is engaged to come to-morrow to wash the windows (in the exigency of the moment, we waive our suspicions in regard to the piglet). You might think, from this account of our activities, that the house was not already immaculate; but I assure you it was! Whatever Mrs. Semple's limitations, she is a HOUSE-KEEPER.

But isn't it just like a man, Daddy? He doesn't give the remotest hint as to whether he will land on the doorstep to-day, or two weeks from to-day. We shall live in a perpetual breathlessness until he comes—and if he doesn't hurry, the cleaning may all have to be done over again.

There's Amasai waiting below with the buckboard and Grover. I drive alone—but if you could see old Grove, you wouldn't be worried as to my safety.

Old Grove is perfectly safe.

With my hand on my heart—farewell.

JUDY.

P.S. Isn't that a nice ending? I got it out of Stevenson's letters.

Saturday.

Good morning again! I didn't get this *enveloped* yesterday before the postman came, so I'll add some more. We have one mail a day at twelve o'clock. Rural delivery is a blessing to the farmers! Our postman not only delivers letters, but he runs errands for us in town, at five cents an errand. Yesterday he brought me some shoe-strings and a jar of cold cream (I sunburned all the skin off my nose before I got my new hat) and a blue Windsor tie and a bottle of blacking all for ten cents. That was an unusual bargain, owing to the largeness of my order.

Also he tells us what is happening in the Great World. Several people on the route take daily papers, and he reads them as he jogs along, and repeats the news to the ones who don't subscribe. So in case war breaks out between the United States and Japan, or the president is assassinated, or Mr. Rockefeller leaves a million dollars to the John Grier Home, you needn't bother to write; I'll hear it anyway.

No sign yet of Master Jervie. But you should see how clean our house is—and with what anxiety we wipe our feet before we step in!

I hope he'll come soon; I am longing for some one to talk to. Mrs. Semple, to tell you the truth, gets sort of monotonous. She never lets ideas interrupt the easy flow of her conversation. It's a funny thing about the people here. Their world is just this single hilltop. They are not a bit universal, if you know what I mean. It's exactly the same as at the John Grier Home. Our ideas there were bounded by the four sides of the iron fence, only I didn't mind it so much because I was younger and was so awfully busy. By the time I'd got all my beds made and my babies' faces washed and had gone to school and come home and had washed their faces again and darned their stockings and mended Freddie Perkins's trousers (he tore them every day of his life) and learned my lessons in between—I was ready to go to bed, and I didn't notice any lack of social intercourse. But after two years in a conversational college, I do miss it; and I shall be glad to see somebody who speaks my language.

I really believe I've finished, Daddy. Nothing else occurs to me at the moment—I'll try to write a longer letter next time.

Yours always,

JUDY.

P.S. The lettuce hasn't done at all well this year. It was so dry early in the season.

August 25th.

Well, Daddy, Master Jervie's here. And such a nice time we're having! At least I am, and I think he is, too—he has been here ten days and he doesn't show any signs of going. The way Mrs. Semple pampers that man is scandalous. If she indulged him as much when he was a baby, I don't know how he ever turned out so well.

He and I eat at a little table set on the side porch, or sometimes under the trees, or—when it rains or is cold—in the best parlor. He just picks out the spot he wants to eat in and Carrie trots after him with the table. Then if it has been an awful nuisance, and she has had to carry the dishes very far, she finds a dollar under the sugar bowl.

He is an awfully companionable sort of man, though you would never believe it to see him casually; he looks at first glance like a true Pendleton, but he isn't in the least. He is just as simple and unaffected and sweet as he can be—that seems a funny way to describe a man, but it's true. He's extremely nice with the farmers around here; he meets them in a sort of man-to-man fashion that disarms them immediately. They were very suspicious at first. They didn't care for his clothes! And I will say that his clothes are rather amazing. He wears knickerbockers and pleated jackets and white flannels and riding clothes with puffed trousers. Whenever he comes down in anything new, Mrs. Semple, beaming with pride, walks around and views him from every angle, and urges him to be careful when he sits down; she is so afraid he will pick up some dust. It bores him dreadfully. He's always saying to her:

"Run along, Lizzie, and tend to your work. You can't boss me any longer. I've grown up."

It's awfully funny to think of that great, big, long-legged man (he's nearly as long-legged as you, Daddy) ever sitting in Mrs. Semple's lap and having his face washed. Particularly funny when you see her lap! She has two laps now, and three chins. But he says that once she was thin and wiry and spry and could run faster than he.

Such a lot of adventures we're having! We've explored the country for miles, and I've learned to fish with funny little flies made of feathers. Also to shoot with a rifle and a revolver. Also to ride horseback—there's an astonishing amount of life in old Grove. We fed him on oats for three days, and he shied at a calf and almost ran away with me.

Wednesday.

We climbed Sky Hill Monday afternoon. That's a mountain near here; not an awfully high mountain, perhaps—no snow on the summit—but at least you are pretty breathless when you reach the top. The lower slopes are covered with woods, but the top is just piled rocks and open moor. We stayed up for the sunset and built a fire and cooked our supper. Master Jervie did the cooking; he said he knew how better than me—and he did, too, because he's used to camping. Then we came down by moonlight, and, when we reached the wood trail where it was dark, by the light of an electric bulb that he had in his pocket. It was such fun! He laughed and joked all the way and talked about interesting things. He's read all the books I've ever read, and a lot of others besides. It's astonishing how many different things he knows.

We went for a long tramp this morning and got caught in a storm. Our clothes were drenched before we reached home—but our spirits not even damp. You should have seen Mrs. Semple's face when we dripped into her kitchen.

"Oh, Master Jervie—Miss Judy! You are soaked through. Dear! Dear! What shall I do? That nice new coat is perfectly ruined."

She was awfully funny; you would have thought that we were ten years old, and she a distracted mother. I was afraid for a while that we weren't going to get any jam for tea.

Saturday.

I started this letter ages ago, but I haven't had a second to finish it.

Isn't this a nice thought from Stevenson?

> The world is so full of a number of things,
> I am sure we should all be as happy as kings.

It's true, you know. The world is full of happiness, and plenty to go round, if you are only willing to take the kind that comes your way. The whole secret is in being *pliable*. In the country, especially, there are such a lot of entertaining things. I can walk over everybody's land, and look at everybody's view, and dabble in everybody's brook; and enjoy it just as much as though I owned the land—and with no taxes to pay!

. . . . . .

It's Sunday night now, about eleven o'clock, and I am supposed to be getting some beauty sleep, but I had black coffee for dinner, so—no beauty sleep for me!

This morning, said Mrs. Semple to Mr. Pendleton, with a very determined accent:

"We have to leave here at a quarter past ten in order to get to church by eleven."

"Very well, Lizzie," said Master Jervie, "you have the surrey ready, and if I'm not dressed, just go on without waiting."

"We'll wait," said she.

"As you please," said he, "only don't keep the horses standing too long."

Then while she was dressing, he told Carrie to pack up a lunch, and he told me to scramble into my walking clothes; and we slipped out the back way and went fishing.

It discommoded the household dreadfully, because Lock Willow of a Sunday dines at two. But he ordered dinner at seven—he orders meals whenever he chooses; you would think the place

were a restaurant—and that kept Carrie and Amasai from going driving. But he said it was all the better because it wasn't
proper for them to go driving without a chaperon; and anyway,
he wanted the horses himself to take me driving. Did you ever
hear anything so funny?

And poor Mrs. Semple believes that people who go fishing
on Sundays, go afterwards to a sizzling hot hell! She is awfully
troubled to think that she didn't train him better when he was
small and helpless and she had the chance. Besides—she wished
to show him off in church.

Anyway, we had our fishing (he caught four little ones) and
we cooked them on a camp-fire for lunch. They kept falling off
our spiked sticks into the fire, so they tasted a little ashy, but we
ate them. We got home at four and went driving at five and had
dinner at seven, and at ten I was sent to bed—and here I am,
writing to you.

I am getting a little sleepy though.

Good night.

Here is a picture of the one fish I caught.

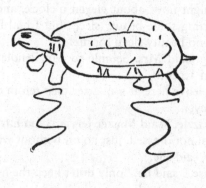

Ship ahoy, Cap'n Long-Legs!

Avast! Belay! Yo, ho, ho, and a bottle of rum. Guess what I'm
reading? Our conversation these past two days has been nauti-
cal and piratical. Isn't "Treasure Island"⁴⁵ fun? Did you ever
read it, or wasn't it written when you were a boy? Stevenson

only got thirty pounds for the serial rights—I don't believe it pays to be a great author. Maybe I'll teach school.

Excuse me for filling my letters so full of Stevenson; my mind is very much engaged with him at present. He comprises Lock Willow's library.

I've been writing this letter for two weeks, and I think it's about long enough. Never say, Daddy, that I don't give details. I wish you were here, too; we'd all have such a jolly time together. I like my different friends to know each other. I wanted to ask Mr. Pendleton if he knew you in New York—I should think he might; you must move in about the same exalted social circles, and you are both interested in reforms and things—but I couldn't, for I don't know your real name.

It's the silliest thing I ever heard of, not to know your name. Mrs. Lippett warned me that you were eccentric. I should think so!

Affectionately,
JUDY.

P.S. On reading this over, I find that it isn't all Stevenson. There are one or two glancing references to Master Jervie.

September 10th.

Dear Daddy,

He has gone, and we are missing him! When you get accustomed to people or places or ways of living, and then have them

suddenly snatched away, it does leave an awfully empty, gnawing sort of sensation. I'm finding Mrs. Semple's conversation
pretty unseasoned food.

College opens in two weeks and I shall be glad to begin work
again. I have worked quite a lot this summer though—six short
stories and seven poems. Those I sent to the magazines all came
back with the most courteous promptitude. But I don't mind.
It's good practice. Master Jervie read them—he brought in the
mail, so I couldn't help his knowing—and he said they were
dreadful. They showed that I didn't have the slightest idea of
what I was talking about. (Master Jervie doesn't let politeness
interfere with truth.) But the last one I did—just a little sketch
laid in college—he said wasn't bad; and he had it typewritten,
and I sent it to a magazine. They've had it two weeks; maybe
they're thinking it over.

You should see the sky! There's the queerest orange-colored
light over everything. We're going to have a storm.

· · · · · ·

It commenced just that moment with drops as big as quarters
and all the shutters banging. I had to run to close windows,
while Carrie flew to the attic with an armful of milk pans to put
under the places where the roof leaks—and then, just as I was
resuming my pen, I remembered that I'd left a cushion and rug
and hat and Matthew Arnold's poems under a tree in the orchard, so I dashed out to get them, all quite soaked. The red
cover of the poems had run into the inside; "Dover Beach" in
the future will be washed by pink waves.

A storm is awfully disturbing in the country. You are always
having to think of so many things that are out of doors and getting spoiled.

Thursday.

Daddy! Daddy! What do you think? The postman has just
come with two letters.

1st.—My story is accepted. $50.

Alors! I'm an AUTHOR.

2d.—A letter from the college secretary. I'm to have a scholarship for two years that will cover board and tuition. It was founded by an alumna for "marked proficiency in English with general excellency in other lines." And I've won it! I applied for it before I left, but I didn't have an idea I'd get it, on account of my Freshman bad work in math. and Latin. But it seems I've made it up. I am awfully glad, Daddy, because now I won't be such a burden to you. The monthly allowance will be all I'll need, and maybe I can earn that with writing or tutoring or something.

I'm *crazy* to go back and begin work.

> Yours ever,
>
> JERUSHA ABBOTT,
> AUTHOR OF, "WHEN THE
> SOPHOMORES WON THE GAME."
> FOR SALE AT ALL NEWS
> STANDS, PRICE TEN CENTS.

> September 26th.

Dear Daddy-Long-Legs,

Back at college again and an upper classman. Our study is better than ever this year—faces the South with two huge windows—and oh! so furnished. Julia, with an unlimited allowance, arrived two days early and was attacked with a fever of settling.

We have new wall paper and Oriental rugs and mahogany chairs—not painted mahogany which made us sufficiently happy last year, but real. It's very gorgeous, but I don't feel as though I belonged in it; I'm nervous all the time for fear I'll get an ink spot in the wrong place.

And, Daddy, I found your letter waiting for me—pardon—I mean your secretary's.

Will you kindly convey to me a comprehensible reason why I should not accept that scholarship? I don't understand your objection in the least. But anyway, it won't do the slightest good for you to object, for I've already accepted it—and I am not going to change! That sounds a little impertinent, but I don't mean it so.

I suppose you feel that when you set out to educate me, you'd like to finish the work, and put a neat period, in the shape of a diploma, at the end.

But look at it just a second from my point of view. I shall owe my education to you just as much as though I let you pay for the whole of it, but I won't be quite so much indebted. I know that you don't want me to return the money, but nevertheless, I am going to want to do it, if I possibly can; and winning this scholarship makes it so much easier. I was expecting to spend the rest of my life in paying my debts, but now I shall only have to spend one-half of the rest of it.

I hope you understand my position and won't be cross. The allowance I shall still most gratefully accept. It requires an allowance to live up to Julia and her furniture! I wish that she had been reared to simpler tastes, or else that she were not my room-mate.

This isn't much of a letter; I meant to have written a lot—but I've been hemming four window curtains and three portières (I'm glad you can't see the length of the stitches) and polishing a brass desk set with tooth powder (very uphill work) and sawing off picture wire with manicure scissors, and unpacking four boxes of books, and putting away two trunkfuls of clothes (it doesn't seem believable that Jerusha Abbott owns two trunks full of clothes, but she does!) and welcoming back fifty dear friends in between.

Opening day is a joyous occasion!

Good night, Daddy dear, and don't be annoyed because your chick is wanting to scratch for herself. She's growing up into an awfully energetic little hen—with a very determined cluck and lots of beautiful feathers (all due to you).

Affectionately,

JUDY.

                                        September 30th.

Dear Daddy,

Are you still harping on that scholarship? I never knew a
man so obstinate and stubborn and unreasonable, and tenacious,
and bull-doggish, and unable-to-see-other-people's-points-of-
view as you.

You prefer that I should not be accepting favors from strangers.
Strangers!—And what are you, pray?

Is there any one in the world that I know less? I shouldn't
recognize you if I met you on the street. Now, you see, if you
had been a sane, sensible person and had written nice, cheering, fatherly letters to your little Judy, and had come occasionally and patted her on the head, and had said you were glad she
was such a good girl—Then, perhaps, she wouldn't have flouted
you in your old age, but would have obeyed your slightest wish
like the dutiful daughter she was meant to be.

Strangers indeed! You live in a glass house, Mr. Smith.

And besides, this isn't a favor; it's like a prize—I earned it by
hard work. If nobody had been good enough in English, the
committee wouldn't have awarded the scholarship; some years
they don't. Also—But what's the use of arguing with a man?
You belong, Mr. Smith, to a sex devoid of a sense of logic. To
bring a man into line, there are just two methods: one must either coax or be disagreeable. I scorn to coax men for what I
wish. Therefore, I must be disagreeable.

I refuse, sir, to give up the scholarship; and if you make any
more fuss, I won't accept the monthly allowance either, but will
wear myself into a nervous wreck tutoring stupid Freshmen.

That is my ultimatum!

And listen—I have a further thought. Since you are so afraid
that by taking this scholarship, I am depriving some one else of
an education, I know a way out. You can apply the money that
you would have spent for me, toward educating some other little girl from the John Grier Home. Don't you think that's a nice

idea? Only, Daddy, *educate* the new girl as much as you choose, but please don't *like* her any better than me.

I trust that your secretary won't be hurt because I pay so little attention to the suggestions offered in his letter, but I can't help it if he is. He's a spoiled child, Daddy. I've meekly given in to his whims heretofore, but this time I intend to be FIRM.

Yours,
With a Mind,
Completely and Irrevocably and
World-without-End Made-up.

JERUSHA ABBOTT.

November 9th.

Dear Daddy-Long-Legs,

I started down to-day to buy a bottle of shoe blacking and some collars and the material for a new blouse and a jar of violet cream[46] and a cake of Castile soap—all very necessary; I couldn't be happy another day without them—and when I tried to pay the car fare, I found that I had left my purse in the pocket of my other coat. So I had to get out and take the next car, and was late for gymnasium.

It's a dreadful thing to have no memory and two coats!

Julia Pendleton has invited me to visit her for the Christmas holidays. How does that strike you, Mr. Smith? Fancy Jerusha Abbott, of the John Grier Home, sitting at the tables of the rich. I don't know why Julia wants me—she seems to be getting quite attached to me of late. I should, to tell the truth, very much prefer going to Sallie's, but Julia asked me first, so if I go anywhere, it must be to New York instead of to Worcester. I'm rather awed at the prospect of meeting Pendletons *en masse,* and also I'd have to get a lot of new clothes—so, Daddy dear, if you write that you would prefer having me remain quietly at college, I will bow to your wishes with my usual sweet docility.

I'm engaged at odd moments with the "Life and Letters of Thomas Huxley"[47]—it makes nice, light reading to pick up between times. Do you know what an archæopteryx[48] is? It's a bird. And a stereognathus?[49] I'm not sure myself but I think it's a missing link, like a bird with teeth or a lizard with wings. No, it isn't either; I've just looked in the book. It's a mesozoic mammal.

This is the only picture extant of a stereognathus.

He has a head like a snake and ears, like a dog and feet like a cow and a tail like a lizard and wings like a swan and is covered with nice soft fur like a sweet little pussy cat.

I've elected economics this year—very illuminating subject. When I finish that I'm going to take Charity and Reform; then, Mr. Trustee, I'll know just how an orphan asylum ought to be run. Don't you think I'd make an admirable voter if I had my rights? I was twenty-one last week. This is an awfully wasteful country to throw away such an honest, educated, conscientious, intelligent citizen as I would be.

Yours always,

JUDY.

December 7th.

Dear Daddy-Long-Legs,

Thank you for permission to visit Julia—I take it that silence means consent.

Such a social whirl as we've been having! The Founder's dance came last week—this was the first year that any of us could attend; only upper classmen being allowed.

I invited Jimmie McBride, and Sallie invited his room-mate at Princeton, who visited them last summer at their camp—an awfully nice man with red hair—and Julia invited a man from New York, not very exciting, but socially irreproachable. He is connected with the De la Mater Chichesters. Perhaps that means something to you? It doesn't illuminate me to any extent.

However—our guests came Friday afternoon in time for tea in the senior corridor, and then dashed down to the hotel for dinner. The hotel was so full that they slept in rows on the billiard tables, they say. Jimmie McBride says that the next time he is bidden to a social event in this college, he is going to bring one of their Adirondack tents and pitch it on the campus.

At seven-thirty they came back for the President's reception and dance. Our functions commence early! We had the men's cards all made out ahead of time, and after every dance, we'd leave them in groups under the letter that stood for their names, so that they could be readily found by their next partners. Jimmie McBride, for example, would stand patiently under "M" until he was claimed. (At least, he ought to have stood patiently, but he kept wandering off and getting mixed with "R's" and "S's" and all sorts of letters.) I found him a very difficult guest; he was sulky because he had only three dances with me. He said he was bashful about dancing with girls he didn't know!

The next morning we had a glee club concert—and who do you think wrote the funny new song composed for the occasion? It's the truth. She did. Oh, I tell you, Daddy, your little foundling is getting to be quite a prominent person!

Anyway, our gay two days were great fun, and I think the men enjoyed it. Some of them were awfully perturbed at first at the prospect of facing one thousand girls; but they got acclimated very quickly. Our two Princeton men had a beautiful time—at least they politely said they had, and they've invited us to their dance next spring. We've accepted, so please don't object, Daddy dear.

Julia and Sallie and I all had new dresses. Do you want to hear about them? Julia's was cream satin and gold embroidery, and she wore purple orchids. It was a *dream* and came from Paris, and cost a million dollars.

Sallie's was pale blue trimmed with Persian embroidery, and

went beautifully with red hair. It didn't cost quite a million, but was just as effective as Julia's.

Mine was pale pink crêpe de chine trimmed with écru lace and rose satin. And I carried crimson roses which J. McB. sent (Sallie having told him what color to get). And we all had satin slippers and silk stockings and chiffon scarfs to match.

You must be deeply impressed by these millinery details!

One can't help thinking, Daddy, what a colorless life a man is forced to lead, when one reflects that chiffon and Venetian point and hand embroidery and Irish crochet are to him mere empty words. Whereas a woman, whether she is interested in babies or microbes or husbands or poetry or servants or parallelograms or gardens or Plato[50] or bridge—is fundamentally and always interested in clothes.

It's the one touch of nature that makes the whole world kin.[51] (That isn't original. I got it out of one of Shakespeare's plays.)

However, to resume. Do you want me to tell you a secret that I've lately discovered? And will you promise not to think me vain? Then listen:

I'm pretty.

I am, really. I'd be an awful idiot not to know it with three looking-glasses in the room.

                                        A FRIEND.

P.S. This is one of those wicked anonymous letters you read about in novels.

                                        December 20th.

Dear Daddy-Long-Legs,

I've just a moment, because I must attend two classes, pack a trunk and a suitcase, and catch the four-o'clock train—but I couldn't go without sending a word to let you know how much I appreciate my Christmas box.

I love the furs and the necklace and the liberty scarf and the gloves and handkerchiefs and books and purse—and most of all I love you! But Daddy, you have no *business* to spoil me this way. I'm only human—and a girl at that. How can I keep my mind sternly fixed on a studious career, when you deflect me with such worldly frivolities?

I have strong suspicions now as to which one of the John Grier Trustees used to give the Christmas tree and the Sunday ice-cream. He was nameless, but by his works I know him! You deserve to be happy for all the good things you do.

Good-by, and a very merry Christmas.

Yours always,
JUDY.

P.S. I am sending a slight token, too. Do you think you would like her if you knew her?

January 11th.

I meant to write to you from the city, Daddy, but New York is an engrossing place.

I had an interesting—and illuminating—time, but I'm glad I don't belong in such a family! I should truly rather have the John Grier Home for a background. Whatever the drawbacks of my bringing up, there was at least no pretense about it. I know now what people mean when they say they are weighed down by Things. The material atmosphere of that house was crushing; I didn't draw a deep breath until I was on an express train coming back. All the furniture was carved and upholstered and gorgeous; the people I met were beautifully dressed and low-voiced and well-bred, but it's the truth, Daddy, I never heard one word of real talk from the time we arrived until we left. I don't think an idea ever entered the front door.

Mrs. Pendleton never thinks of anything but jewels and dressmakers and social engagements. She did seem a different kind of mother from Mrs. McBride! If I ever marry and have a family, I'm going to make them as exactly like the McBrides as I can. Not for all the money in the world would I ever let any children of mine develop into Pendletons. Maybe it isn't polite to criticize people you've been visiting? If it isn't, please excuse. This is very confidential, between you and me.

I only saw Master Jervie once when he called at tea time, and then I didn't have a chance to speak to him alone. It was sort of disappointing after our nice time last summer. I don't think he cares much for his relatives—and I am sure they don't care much for him! Julia's mother says he's unbalanced. He's a Socialist— except, thank Heaven, he doesn't let his hair grow and wear red ties. She can't imagine where he picked up his queer ideas; the family have been Church of England for generations. He throws away his money on every sort of crazy reform, instead of spending it on such sensible things as yachts and automobiles and polo ponies. He does buy candy with it though! He sent Julia and me each a box for Christmas.

You know, I think I'll be a Socialist, too. You wouldn't mind, would you, Daddy? They're quite different from Anarchists; they don't believe in blowing people up. Probably I am one by rights; I belong to the proletariat. I haven't determined yet just which kind I am going to be. I will look into the subject over Sunday, and declare my principles in my next.

I've seen loads of theaters and hotels and beautiful houses. My mind is a confused jumble of onyx and gilding and mosaic floors and palms. I'm still pretty breathless but I am glad to get back to college and my books—I believe that I really am a student; this atmosphere of academic calm I find more bracing than New York. College is a very satisfying sort of life; the books and study and regular classes keep you alive mentally, and then when your mind gets tired, you have the gymnasium and outdoor athletics, and always plenty of congenial friends who are thinking about the same things you are. We spend a whole evening in nothing but talk—talk—talk—and go to bed with a very uplifted feeling, as though we had settled permanently some pressing world problems. And filling in every crevice, there is always such a lot of nonsense—just silly jokes about the little things that come up—but very satisfying. We do appreciate our own witticisms!

It isn't the great big pleasures that count the most; it's making a great deal out of the little ones—I've discovered the true secret of happiness, Daddy, and that is to live in the *now*. Not to be forever regretting the past, or anticipating the future; but to get the most that you can out of this very instant. It's like farming. You can have extensive farming and intensive farming; well, I am going to have intensive living after this. I'm going to enjoy every second, and I'm going to *know* I'm enjoying it while I'm enjoying it. Most people don't live; they just race. They are trying to reach some goal far away on the horizon, and in the heat of the going they get so breathless and panting that they lose all sight of the beautiful, tranquil country they are passing through; and then the first thing they know, they are old and worn out, and it doesn't make any difference whether they've reached the goal or not. I've decided to sit down by the way and pile up a lot of little happinesses, even if I never become a Great Author. Did you ever know such a philosopheress as I am developing into?

Yours ever,
JUDY.

P.S. It's raining cats and dogs tonight. Two puppies and a kitten have just landed on the window-sill.

Dear Comrade,

Hooray! I'm a Fabian.[52]

That's a Socialist who's willing to wait. We don't want the social revolution to come to-morrow morning; it would be too upsetting. We want it to come very gradually in the distant future, when we shall all be prepared and able to sustain the shock.

In the meantime we must be getting ready, by instituting industrial, educational and orphan asylum reforms.

Yours, with fraternal love,
JUDY.
MONDAY, 3D HOUR.

February 11th.

Dear D. L. L.,

Don't be insulted because this is so short. It isn't a letter; it's just a *line* to say that I'm going to write a letter pretty soon when examinations are over. It is not only necessary that I pass, but pass W E L L. I have a scholarship to live up to.

Yours, studying hard,

J. A.

March 5th.

Dear Daddy-Long-Legs,

President Cuyler made a speech this evening about the modern generation being flippant and superficial. He says that we are losing the old ideals of earnest endeavor and true scholarship; and particularly is this falling-off noticeable in our disrespectful attitude toward organized authority. We no longer pay a seemly deference to our superiors.

I came away from chapel very sober.

Am I too familiar, Daddy? Ought I to treat you with more dignity and aloofness?—Yes, I'm sure I ought. I'll begin again.

• • • • •

My dear Mr. Smith,

You will be pleased to hear that I passed successfully my mid-year examinations, and am now commencing work in the new semester. I am leaving chemistry—having completed the course in qualitative analysis—and am entering upon the study of biology. I approach this subject with some hesitation, as I understand that we dissect angleworms and frogs.

An extremely interesting and valuable lecture was given in the chapel last week upon Roman Remains in Southern France.

I have never listened to a more illuminating exposition of the subject.

We are reading Wordsworth's "Tinturn Abbey"[53] in connection with our course in English Literature. What an exquisite work it is, and how adequately it embodies his conception of Pantheism! The Romantic movement of the early part of the last century, exemplified in the works of such poets as Shelley, Byron, Keats,[54] and Wordsworth, appeals to me very much more than the Classical period that preceded it. Speaking of poetry, have you ever read that charming little thing of Tennyson's called "Locksley Hall"?[55]

I am attending gymnasium very regularly of late. A proctor system has been devised, and failure to comply with the rules causes a great deal of inconvenience. The gymnasium is equipped with a very beautiful swimming tank of cement and marble, the gift of a former graduate. My room-mate, Miss McBride, has given me her bathing-suit (it shrank so that she can no longer wear it) and I am about to begin swimming lessons.

We had delicious pink ice-cream for dessert last night. Only vegetable dyes are used in coloring the food. The college is very much opposed, both from esthetic and hygienic motives, to the use of aniline dyes.[56]

The weather of late has been ideal—bright sunshine and clouds interspersed with a few welcome snow-storms. I and my companions have enjoyed our walks to and from classes—particularly from.

Trusting, my dear Mr. Smith, that this will find you in your usual good health,

> I remain,
> Most cordially yours,
>   JERUSHA ABBOTT.

April 24th.

Dear Daddy,

Spring has come again! You should see how lovely the campus is. I think you might come and look at it for yourself. Master Jervie dropped in again last Friday—but he chose a most unpropitious time, for Sallie and Julia and I were just running to catch a train. And where do you think we were going? To Princeton, to attend a dance and a ball game, if you please! I didn't ask you if I might go, because I had a feeling that your secretary would say no. But it was entirely regular; we had leave-of-absence from college, and Mrs. McBride chaperoned us. We had a charming time—but I shall have to omit details; they are too many and complicated.

                                        Saturday.

Up before dawn! The night watchman called us—six of us— and we made coffee in a chafing dish (you never saw so many grounds!) and walked two miles to the top of One Tree Hill to see the sun rise. We had to scramble up the last slope! The sun almost beat us! And perhaps you think we didn't bring back appetites to breakfast!

Dear me, Daddy, I seem to have a very ejaculatory style to-day; this page is peppered with exclamations.

I meant to have written a lot about the budding trees and the

new cinder path in the athletic field, and the awful lesson we
have in biology for to-morrow, and the new canoes on the lake,
and Catherine Prentiss who has pneumonia, and Prexy's Angora kitten that strayed from home and has been boarding in
Fergussen Hall for two weeks until a chambermaid reported it,
and about my three new dresses—white and pink and blue polka
dots with a hat to match—but I am too sleepy. I am always
making this excuse, am I not? But a girl's college is a busy place
and we do get tired by the end of the day! Particularly when the
day begins at dawn.

Affectionately,

JUDY.

This is Prexy's
kitten. You can see.
From the picture how
Angora he is.

May 15th.

Dear Daddy-Long-Legs,

Is it good manners when you get into a car just to stare straight
ahead and not see anybody else?

A very beautiful lady in a very beautiful velvet dress got into
the car to-day, and without the slightest expression sat for fifteen
minutes and looked at a sign advertising suspenders. It doesn't
seem polite to ignore everybody else as though you were the only
important person present. Anyway, you miss a lot. While she
was absorbing that silly sign, I was studying a whole car full of
interesting human beings.

The accompanying illustration is hereby reproduced for the
first time. It looks like a spider on the end of string, but it isn't
at all; it's a picture of me learning to swim in the tank in the
gymnasium.

The instructor hooks a rope into a ring in the back of my belt, and runs it through a pulley in the ceiling. It would be a beautiful system if one had perfect confidence in the probity of one's instructor. I'm always afraid, though, that she will let the rope get slack, so I keep one anxious eye on her and swim with the other, and with this divided interest I do not make the progress that I otherwise might.

Very miscellaneous weather we're having of late. It was raining when I commenced and now the sun is shining. Sallie and I are going out to play tennis—thereby gaining exemption from Gym.

A week later.

I should have finished this letter long ago, but I didn't. You don't mind, do you, Daddy, if I'm not very regular? I really do love to write to you; it gives me such a respectable feeling of having some family. Would you like me to tell you something? You are not the only man to whom I write letters. There are two others! I have been receiving beautiful long letters this winter from Master Jervie (with typewritten envelopes so Julia won't recognize the writing). Did you ever hear anything so shocking? And every week or so a very scrawly epistle, usually on yellow tablet paper, arrives from Princeton. All of which I answer with businesslike promptness. So you see—I am not so different from other girls—I get mail, too.

Did I tell you that I have been elected a member of the Senior

Dramatic Club? Very *recherché*[57] organization. Only seventy-five members out of one thousand. Do you think as a consistent Socialist that I ought to belong?

What do you suppose is at present engaging my attention in sociology? I am writing (*figurez vous!*)[58] a paper on the Care of Dependent Children. The Professor shuffled up his subjects and dealt them out promiscuously, and that fell to me. *C'est drôle ça n'est pas?*[59]

There goes the gong for dinner. I'll mail this as I pass the chute.

Affectionately,

J.

June 4th.

Dear Daddy,

Very busy time—commencement in ten days, examinations to-morrow; lots of studying, lots of packing, and the outdoors world so lovely that it hurts you to stay inside.

But never mind, vacation's coming. Julia is going abroad this summer—it makes the fourth time. No doubt about it, Daddy, goods are not distributed evenly. Sallie, as usual, goes to the Adirondacks. And what do you think I am going to do? You may have three guesses. Lock Willow? Wrong. The Adirondacks with Sallie? Wrong. (I'll never attempt that again; I was discouraged last year.) Can't you guess anything else? You're not very inventive. I'll tell you, Daddy, if you'll promise not to make a lot of objections. I warn your secretary ahead of time that my mind is made up.

I am going to spend the summer at the seaside with a Mrs. Charles Paterson and tutor her daughter who is to enter college in the autumn. I met her through the McBrides, and she is a very charming woman. I am to give lessons in English and Latin to the younger daughter, too, but I shall have a little time to myself, and I shall be earning fifty dollars a month! Doesn't that impress you as a perfectly exorbitant amount? She offered it; I should have blushed to ask more than twenty-five.

I finish at Magnolia (that's where she lives) the first of September and shall probably spend the remaining three weeks at Lock Willow—I should like to see the Semples again and all the friendly animals.

How does my program strike you, Daddy? I am getting quite independent, you see. You have put me on my feet and I think I can almost walk alone by now.

Princeton commencement and our examinations exactly coincide—which is an awful blow. Sallie and I did so want to get away in time for it, but of course that is utterly impossible.

Good-by, Daddy. Have a nice summer and come back in the autumn rested and ready for another year of work. (That's what you ought to be writing to me!) I haven't an idea what you do in the summer, or how you amuse yourself. I can't visualize your surroundings. Do you play golf or hunt or ride horseback or just sit in the sun and meditate?

Anyway, whatever it is, have a good time and don't forget Judy.

June Tenth.

Dear Daddy,

This is the hardest letter I ever wrote, but I have decided what I must do, and there isn't going to be any turning back. It is very sweet and generous and dear of you to wish to send me to Europe this summer—for the moment I was intoxicated by the idea; but sober second thoughts said no. It would be rather illogical of me to refuse to take your money for college, and then use it instead just for amusement! You mustn't get me used to too many luxuries. One doesn't miss what one has never had; but it is awfully hard going without things after one has commenced thinking they are his—hers (English language needs another pronoun) by natural right. Living with Sallie and Julia is an awful strain on my stoical philosophy. They have both had things from the time they were babies; they accept happiness as a matter of course. The World, they think, owes them

everything they want. Maybe the World does—in any case, it
seems to acknowledge the debt and pay up. But as for me, it
owes me nothing, and distinctly told me so in the beginning. I
have no right to borrow on credit, for there will come a time
when the World will repudiate my claim.

I seem to be floundering in a sea of metaphor—but I hope
you grasp my meaning? Anyway, I have a very strong feeling
that the only honest thing for me to do is to teach this summer
and begin to support myself.

• • • • •

MAGNOLIA,
Four days later.

I'd got just that much written, when—what do you think
happened? The maid arrived with Master Jervie's card. He is
going abroad too this summer; not with Julia and her family
but entirely by himself. I told him that you had invited me to go
with a lady who is chaperoning a party of girls. He knows
about you, Daddy. That is, he knows that my father and
mother are dead, and that a kind gentleman is sending me to
college; I simply didn't have the courage to tell him about the
John Grier Home and all the rest. He thinks that you are my
guardian and a perfectly legitimate old family friend. I have
never told him that I didn't know you—that would seem too
queer!

Anyway, he insisted on my going to Europe. He said that it
was a necessary part of my education and that I mustn't think
of refusing. Also, that he would be in Paris at the same time,
and that we would run away from the chaperon occasionally
and have dinner together at nice, funny, foreign restaurants.

Well, Daddy, it did appeal to me! I almost weakened; if he
hadn't been so dictatorial, maybe I should have entirely weakened. I can be enticed step by step, but I *won't* be forced. He
said I was a silly, foolish, irrational, quixotic, idiotic, stubborn
child (those are a few of his abusive adjectives; the rest escape
me) and that I didn't know what was good for me; I ought to
let older people judge. We almost quarreled—I am not sure but
that we entirely did!

In any case, I packed my trunk fast and came up here. I thought I'd better see my bridges in flames behind me before I finished writing to you. They are entirely reduced to ashes now. Here I am at Cliff Top (the name of Mrs. Paterson's cottage) with my trunk unpacked and Florence (the little one) already struggling with first declension nouns. And it bids fair to be a struggle! She is a most uncommonly spoiled child; I shall have to teach her first how to study—she has never in her life concentrated on anything more difficult than ice-cream soda water.

We use a quiet corner of the cliffs for a schoolroom—Mrs. Paterson wishes me to keep them out of doors—and I will say that *I* find it difficult to concentrate with the blue sea before me and ships a-sailing by! And when I think I might be on one, sailing off to foreign lands—but I *won't* let myself think of anything but Latin Grammar.

> The prepositions a or ab, absque, coram, cum, de, e or ex, prae, pro, sine, tenus, in, subter, sub and super govern the ablative.

So you see, Daddy, I am already plunged into work with my eyes persistently set against temptation. Don't be cross with me, please, and don't think that I do not appreciate your kindness, for I do—always—always. The only way I can ever repay you is by turning out a Very Useful Citizen (Are women citizens? I don't suppose they are).[60] Anyway, a Very Useful Person. And when you look at me you can say, "I gave that Very Useful Person to the world."

That sounds well, doesn't it, Daddy? But I don't wish to mislead you. The feeling often comes over me that I am not at all remarkable; it is fun to plan a career, but in all probability, I shan't turn out a bit different from any other ordinary person. I may end by marrying an undertaker and being an inspiration to him in his work.

Yours ever,

JUDY.

August 19th.

Dear Daddy-Long-Legs,

My window looks out on the loveliest landscape—ocean-scape rather—nothing but water and rocks.

The summer goes. I spend the morning with Latin and English and algebra and my two stupid girls. I don't know how Marion is ever going to get into college, or stay in after she gets there. And as for Florence, she is hopeless—but oh! such a little beauty. I don't suppose it matters in the least whether they are stupid or not so long as they are pretty? One can't help thinking though, how their conversation will bore their husbands, unless they are fortunate enough to obtain stupid husbands. I suppose that's quite possible; the world seems to be filled with stupid men; I've met a number this summer.

In the afternoon we take a walk on the cliffs, or swim, if the tide is right. I can swim in salt water with the utmost ease—you see my education is already being put to use!

A letter comes from Mr. Jervis Pendleton in Paris, rather a short, concise letter; I'm not quite forgiven yet for refusing to follow his advice. However, if he gets back in time, he will see me for a few days at Lock Willow before college opens, and if I am very nice and sweet and docile, I shall (I am led to infer) be received into favor again.

Also a letter from Sallie. She wants me to come to their camp for two weeks in September. Must I ask your permission, or haven't I yet arrived at the place where I can do as I please? Yes, I am sure I have—I'm a Senior, you know. Having worked all summer, I feel like taking a little healthful recreation; I want to see the Adirondacks; I want to see Sallie; I want to see Sallie's brother—he's going to teach me to canoe—and (we come to my chief motive, which is mean) I want Master Jervie to arrive at Lock Willow and find me not there.

I *must* show him that he can't dictate to me. No one can dictate to me but you, Daddy—and you can't always! I'm off for the woods.

JUDY.

CAMP MCBRIDE,
September 6th.

Dear Daddy,

Your letter didn't come in time (I am pleased to say). If you wish your instructions to be obeyed, you must have your secretary transmit them in less than two weeks. As you observe, I am here, and have been for five days.

The woods are fine, and so is the camp, and so is the weather, and so are the McBrides, and so is the whole world. I'm very happy!

There's Jimmie calling for me to come canoeing. Good-by— sorry to have disobeyed, but why are you so persistent about not wanting me to play a little? When I've worked all summer I deserve two weeks. You are awfully dog-in-the-mangerish.

However—I love you still, Daddy, in spite of all your faults.

JUDY.

October 3rd.

Dear Daddy-Long-Legs,

Back at college and a Senior—also editor of the *Monthly*. It doesn't seem possible, does it, that so sophisticated a person, just four years ago, was an inmate of the John Grier Home? We do arrive fast in America!

What do you think of this? A note from Master Jervie directed to Lock Willow and forwarded here. He's sorry but he finds that he can't get up there this autumn; he has accepted an invitation to go yachting with some friends. Hopes I've had a nice summer and am enjoying the country.

And he knew all the time that I was with the McBrides, for

Julia told him so! You men ought to leave intrigue to women; you haven't a light enough touch.

Julia has a trunkful of the most ravishing new clothes—an evening gown of rainbow Liberty crêpe that would be fitting raiment for the angels in Paradise. And I thought that my own clothes this year were unprecedentedly (is there such a word?) beautiful. I copied Mrs. Paterson's wardrobe with the aid of a cheap dressmaker, and though the gowns didn't turn out quite twins of the originals, I was entirely happy until Julia unpacked. But now—I live to see Paris!

Dear Daddy, aren't you glad you're not a girl? I suppose you think that the fuss we make over clothes is too absolutely silly? It is. No doubt about it. But it's entirely your fault.

Did you ever hear about the learned Herr Professor who regarded unnecessary adornment with contempt, and favored sensible, utilitarian clothes for women? His wife, who was an obliging creature, adopted "dress reform." And what do you think he did? He eloped with a chorus girl.

> Yours ever,
> JUDY.

P.S. The chamber-maid on our corridor wears blue checked gingham aprons. I am going to get her some brown ones instead, and sink the blue ones in the bottom of the lake. I have a reminiscent chill every time I look at them.

November 17th.

Dear Daddy-Long-Legs,

Such a blight has fallen over my literary career. I don't know whether to tell you or not, but I would like some sympathy— silent sympathy, please; don't reopen the wound by referring to it in your next letter.

I've been writing a book, all last winter in the evenings, and all summer when I wasn't teaching Latin to my two stupid children. I just finished it before college opened and sent it to a publisher. He kept it two months, and I was certain he was going to take it; but yesterday morning an express parcel came (thirty cents due) and there it was back again with a letter from the publisher, a very nice, fatherly letter—but frank! He said he saw from the address that I was still in college, and if I would accept some advice, he would suggest that I put all of my energy into my lessons and wait until I graduated before beginning to write. He enclosed his reader's opinion. Here it is:

"Plot highly improbable. Characterization exaggerated. Conversation unnatural. A good deal of humor but not always in the best of taste. Tell her to keep on trying, and in time she may produce a real book."

Not on the whole flattering, is it, Daddy? And I thought I was making a notable addition to American literature, I did truly. I was planning to surprise you by writing a great novel before I graduated. I collected the material for it while I was at Julia's last Christmas. But I dare say the editor is right. Probably two weeks was not enough in which to observe the manners and customs of a great city.

I took it walking with me yesterday afternoon, and when I came to the gas house, I went in and asked the engineer if I might borrow his furnace. He politely opened the door, and with my own hands I chucked it in. I felt as though I had cremated my own child!

I went to bed last night utterly dejected; I thought I was never going to amount to anything, and that you had thrown away your money for nothing. But what do you think? I woke up this morning with a beautiful new plot in my head, and I've been going about all day planning my characters, just as happy as I could be. No one can ever accuse me of being a pessimist! If I had a husband and twelve children swallowed by an earthquake one day, I'd bob up smilingly the next morning and commence to look for another set.

Affectionately,

JUDY.

December 14th.

Dear Daddy-Long-Legs,

I dreamed the funniest dream last night. I thought I went into
a book store and the clerk brought me a new book named "The
Life and Letters of Judy Abbott." I could see it perfectly plainly—
red cloth binding with a picture of the John Grier Home on the
cover, and my portrait for a frontispiece with, "Very truly yours,
Judy Abbott," written below. But just as I was turning to the
end to read the inscription on my tombstone, I woke up. It was
very annoying! I almost found out who I'm going to marry and
when I'm going to die.

Don't you think it would be interesting if you really could
read the story of your life—written perfectly truthfully by an
omniscient author? And suppose you could only read it on this
condition: that you would never forget it, but would have to go
through life knowing ahead of time exactly how everything you
did would turn out, and foreseeing to the exact hour the time
when you would die. How many people do you suppose would
have the courage to read it then? Or how many could suppress
their curiosity sufficiently to escape from reading it, even at the
price of having to live without hope and without surprises?

Life is monotonous enough at best; you have to eat and sleep
about so often. But imagine how *deadly* monotonous it would
be if nothing unexpected could happen between meals. Mercy!
Daddy, there's a blot, but I'm on the third page and I can't begin a new sheet.

I'm going on with biology again this year—very interesting
subject; we're studying the alimentary system at present. You
should see how sweet a cross-section of the duodenum of a cat
is under the microscope.

Also we've arrived at philosophy—interesting but evanescent.
I prefer biology where you can pin the subject under discussion
to a board. There's another! And another! This pen is weeping
copiously. Please excuse its tears.

Do you believe in free will? I do—unreservedly. I don't agree at all with the philosophers who think that every action is the absolutely inevitable and automatic resultant of an aggregation of remote causes. That's the most immoral doctrine I ever heard—nobody would be to blame for anything. If a man believed in fatalism, he would naturally just sit down and say, "The Lord's will be done," and continue to sit until he fell over dead.

I believe absolutely in my own free will and my own power to accomplish—and that is the belief that moves mountains. You watch me become a great author! I have four chapters of my new book finished and five more drafted.

This is a very abstruse letter—does your head ache, Daddy? I think we'll stop now and make some fudge. I'm sorry I can't send you a piece; it will be unusually good, for we're going to make it with real cream and three butter balls.

Yours affectionately,
JUDY.

P.S. We're having fancy dancing in gymnasium class. You can see by the accompanying picture how much we look like a real ballet. The one on the end accomplishing a graceful pirouette is me—I mean I.

December 26th.

My dear, dear Daddy,

Haven't you any sense? Don't you *know* that you mustn't give one girl seventeen Christmas presents? I'm a Socialist, please remember; do you wish to turn me into a Plutocrat?

Think how embarrassing it would be if we should ever quarrel! I should have to engage a moving van to return your gifts.

I am sorry that the necktie I sent was so wobbly; I knit it with my own hands (as you doubtless discovered from internal evidence). You will have to wear it on cold days and keep your coat buttoned up tight.

Thank you, Daddy, a thousand times. I think you're the sweetest man that ever lived—and the foolishest!

JUDY.

Here's a four-leaf clover from Camp McBride to bring you good luck for the New Year.

January 9th.

Do you wish to do something, Daddy, that will insure your eternal salvation? There is a family here who are in awfully desperate straits. A mother and father and four visible children—the two older boys have disappeared into the world to make their fortune and have not sent any of it back. The father worked in a glass factory and got consumption—it's awfully unhealthy work—and now has been sent away to a hospital. That took all of their savings, and the support of the family falls upon the oldest daughter who is twenty-four. She dressmakes for $1.50 a day (when she can get it) and embroiders centerpieces in the evening. The mother isn't very strong and is extremely ineffectual and pious. She sits with her hands folded, a picture of patient resignation, while the daughter kills herself with overwork and responsibility and worry; she doesn't see how they are going to get through the rest of the winter—and I don't either. One hundred dollars would buy some coal and some shoes for the three children so that they could go to school, and give a little margin so that she needn't worry herself to death when a few days pass and she doesn't get work.

You are the richest man I know. Don't you suppose you could spare one hundred dollars? That girl deserves help a lot more than I ever did. I wouldn't ask it except for the girl; I don't care much what happens to the mother—she is such a jellyfish.

The way people are forever rolling their eyes to heaven and saying, "Perhaps it's all for the best," when they are perfectly dead sure it's not, makes me enraged. Humility or resignation or whatever you choose to call it, is simply impotent inertia. I'm for a more militant religion!

We are getting the most dreadful lessons in philosophy—all of Schopenhauer[61] for to-morrow. The professor doesn't seem to realize that we are taking any other subject. He's a queer old duck; he goes about with his head in the clouds and blinks dazedly when occasionally he strikes solid earth. He tries to lighten his lectures with an occasional witticism—and we do our best to smile, but I assure you his jokes are no laughing matter. He spends his entire time between classes in trying to figure out whether matter really exists or whether he only thinks it exists.

I'm sure my sewing girl hasn't any doubt that it exists!

Where do you think my new novel is? In the waste basket. I can see myself that it's no good on earth, and when a loving author realizes that, what *would* be the judgment of a critical public?

Later.

I address you, Daddy, from a bed of pain. For two days I've been laid up with swollen tonsils; I can just swallow hot milk, and that is all. "What were your parents thinking of not to have those tonsils out when you were a baby?" the doctor wished to

know. I'm sure I haven't an idea, but I doubt if they were thinking much about me.

Yours,

J.A.

Next morning.

I just read this over before sealing it. I don't know *why* I cast
such a misty atmosphere over life. I hasten to assure you that I am
young and happy and exuberant; and I trust you are the same.
Youth has nothing to do with birthdays, only with *alivedness* of
spirit, so even if your hair is gray, Daddy, you can still be a boy.

Affectionately,

JUDY.

Jan. 12th.

Dear Mr. Philanthropist,

Your check for my family came yesterday. Thank you so
much! I cut gymnasium and took it down to them right after
luncheon, and you should have seen the girl's face! She was so
surprised and happy and relieved that she looked almost young;
and she's only twenty-four. Isn't it pitiful?

Anyway, she feels now as though all the good things were
coming together. She has steady work ahead for two months—
some one's getting married, and there's a trousseau to make.

"Thank the good Lord!" cried the mother, when she grasped
the fact that the small piece of paper was one hundred dollars.

"It wasn't the good Lord at all," said I, "it was Daddy-Long-
Legs." (Mr. Smith, I called you.)

"But it was the good Lord who put it in his mind," said she.

"Not at all! I put it in his mind myself," said I.

But anyway, Daddy, I trust the good Lord will reward you
suitably. You deserve ten thousand years out of purgatory.

Yours most gratefully,

JUDY ABBOTT.

Feb. 15th.

May it please Your Most Excellent Majesty:

This morning I did eat my breakfast upon a cold turkey pie
and a goose, and I did send for a cup of tee (a china drink) of
which I had never drank before.

Don't be nervous, Daddy—I haven't lost my mind; I'm merely
quoting Sam'l Pepys.[62] We're reading him in connection with
English History, original sources. Sallie and Julia and I converse
now in the language of 1660. Listen to this:

"I went to Charing Cross to see Major Harrison hanged,
drawn and quartered: he looking as cheerful as any man could
do in that condition." And this: "Dined with my lady who is in
handsome mourning for her brother who died yesterday of spotted fever."

Seems a little early to commence entertaining, doesn't it? A
friend of Pepys devised a very cunning manner whereby the
king might pay his debts out of the sale to poor people of old
decayed provisions. What do you, a reformer, think of that? I
don't believe we're so bad to-day as the newspapers make out.

Samuel was as excited about his clothes as any girl; he spent
five times as much on dress as his wife—that appears to have
been the Golden Age of husbands. Isn't this a touching entry?
You see he really was honest. "To-day came home my fine Cam-
lett cloak with gold buttons, which cost me much money, and I
pray God to make me able to pay for it."

Excuse me for being so full of Pepys; I'm writing a special
topic on him.

What do you think, Daddy? The Self-Government Association has abolished the ten-o'clock rule. We can keep our lights
all night if we choose, the only requirement being that we do
not disturb others—we are not supposed to entertain on a large
scale. The result is a beautiful commentary on human nature.
Now that we may stay up as long as we choose, we no longer
choose. Our heads begin to nod at nine o'clock, and by nine-

thirty the pen drops from our nerveless grasp. It's nine-thirty now. Good night.

> Sunday.

Just back from church—preacher from Georgia. We must take care, he says, not to develop our intellects at the expense of our emotional natures—but methought it was a poor, dry sermon (Pepys again). It doesn't matter what part of the United States or Canada they come from, or what denomination they are, we always get the same sermon. Why on earth don't they go to men's colleges and urge the students not to allow their manly natures to be crushed out by too much mental application?

It's a beautiful day—frozen and icy and clear. As soon as dinner is over, Sallie and Julia and Marty Keene and Eleanor Pratt (friends of mine, but you don't know them) and I are going to put on short skirts and walk 'cross country to Crystal Spring Farm and have a fried chicken and waffle supper, and then have Mr. Crystal Spring drive us home in his buckboard. We are supposed to be inside the campus at seven, but we are going to stretch a point to-night and make it eight.

Farewell, kind Sir.

I have the honour of subscribing myself,
> Your most loyall, dutifull, faithfull
> and obedient servant,
>> J. ABBOTT.

> March Fifth.

Dear Mr. Trustee,

To-morrow is the first Wednesday in the month—a weary day for the John Grier Home. How relieved they'll be when five o'clock comes and you pat them on the head and take yourselves off! Did you (individually) ever pat me on the head, Daddy? I don't believe so—my memory seems to be concerned only with fat Trustees.

Give the Home my love, please—my *truly* love. I have quite a feeling of tenderness for it as I look back through a haze of four years. When I first came to college I felt quite resentful because I'd been robbed of the normal kind of childhood that the other girls had had; but now, I don't feel that way in the least. I regard it as a very unusual adventure. It gives me a sort of vantage point from which to stand aside and look at life. Emerging full grown, I get a perspective on the world, that other people who have been brought up in the thick of things, entirely lack.

I know lots of girls (Julia, for instance) who never know that they are happy. They are so accustomed to the feeling that their senses are deadened to it, but as for me—I am perfectly sure every moment of my life that I am happy. And I'm going to keep on being, no matter what unpleasant things turn up. I'm going to regard them (even toothaches) as interesting experiences, and be glad to know what they feel like. "Whatever sky's above me, I've a heart for any fate."

However, Daddy, don't take this new affection for the J. G. H. too literally. If I have five children, like Rousseau,[63] I shan't leave them on the steps of a foundling asylum in order to insure their being brought up simply.

Give my kindest regards to Mrs. Lippett (that, I think, is truthful; love would be a little strong) and don't forget to tell her what a beautiful nature I've developed.

Affectionately,
JUDY.

LOCK WILLOW,
April 4th.

Dear Daddy,

Do you observe the postmark? Sallie and I are embellishing Lock Willow with our presence during the Easter vacation. We decided that the best thing we could do with our ten days was to come where it is quiet. Our nerves had got to the point where they wouldn't stand another meal in Fergussen. Dining in a room

with four hundred girls is an ordeal when you are tired. There
is so much noise that you can't hear the girls across the table
speak unless they make their hands into a megaphone and shout.
That is the truth.

We are tramping over the hills and reading and writing, and
having a nice, restful time. We climbed to the top of "Sky Hill"
this morning where Master Jervie and I once cooked supper—
it doesn't seem possible that it was nearly two years ago. I
could still see the place where the smoke of our fire blackened
the rock. It is funny how certain places get connected with certain people, and you never go back without thinking of them. I
was quite lonely without him—for two minutes.

What do you think is my latest activity, Daddy? You will begin to believe that I am incorrigible—I am writing a book. I
started it three weeks ago and am eating it up in chunks. I've
caught the secret. Master Jervie and that editor man were right;
you are most convincing when you write about the things you
know. And this time it is about something that I do know—
exhaustively. Guess where it's laid? In the John Grier Home!
And it's good, Daddy, I actually believe it is—just about the
tiny little things that happened every day. I'm a realist now. I've
abandoned romanticism; I shall go back to it later though,
when my own adventurous future begins.

This new book is going to get itself finished—and published!
You see if it doesn't. If you just want a thing hard enough
and keep on trying, you do get it in the end. I've been trying
for four years to get a letter from you—and I haven't given up
hope yet.

Good-by, Daddy dear,

(I like to call you Daddy dear; it's so alliterative.)

Affectionately,

JUDY.

P.S. I forgot to tell you the farm news, but it's very distressing. Skip this postscript if you don't want your sensibilities all
wrought up.

Poor old Grove is dead. He got so he couldn't chew and they
had to shoot him.

Nine chickens were killed by a weasel or a skunk or a rat last week.

One of the cows is sick, and we had to have the veterinary surgeon out from Bonnyrigg Four Corners. Amasai stayed up all night to give her linseed oil and whisky. But we have an awful suspicion that the poor sick cow got nothing but linseed oil.

Sentimental Tommy (the tortoise-shell cat) has disappeared; we are afraid he has been caught in a trap.

There are lots of troubles in the world!

May 17th.

Dear Daddy-Long-Legs,

This is going to be extremely short because my shoulder aches at the sight of a pen. Lecture notes all day, immortal novel all evening makes too much writing.

Commencement three weeks from next Wednesday. I think you might come and make my acquaintance—I shall hate you if you don't! Julia's inviting Master Jervie, he being her family, and Sallie's inviting Jimmie McB., he being her family, but who is there for me to invite? Just you and Mrs. Lippett, and I don't want her. Please come.

Yours, with love and writer's cramp.
JUDY.

LOCK WILLOW.
June 19th.

Dear Daddy-Long-Legs,

I'm educated! My diploma is in the bottom bureau drawer with my two best dresses. Commencement was as usual, with a few showers at vital moments. Thank you for your rosebuds. They were lovely. Master Jervie and Master Jimmie both gave me roses, too, but I left theirs in the bath tub and carried yours in the class procession.

Here I am at Lock Willow for the summer—forever maybe. The board is cheap; the surroundings quiet and conducive to a literary life. What more does a struggling author wish? I am mad about my book. I think of it every waking moment, and dream of it at night. All I want is peace and quiet and lots of time to work (interspersed with nourishing meals).

Master Jervie is coming up for a week or so in August, and Jimmie McBride is going to drop in sometime through the summer. He's connected with a bond house now, and goes about the country selling bonds to banks. He's going to combine the "Farmers' National" at the Corners and me on the same trip.

You see that Lock Willow isn't entirely lacking in society. I'd be expecting to have you come motoring through—only I know now that that is hopeless. When you wouldn't come to my commencement, I tore you from my heart and buried you forever.

JUDY ABBOTT, A.B.

July 24th.

Dearest Daddy-Long-Legs,

Isn't it fun to work—or don't you ever do it? It's especially fun when your kind of work is the thing you'd rather do more than anything else in the world. I've been writing as fast as my pen would go every day this summer, and my only quarrel with life is that the days aren't long enough to write all the beautiful and valuable and entertaining thoughts I'm thinking.

I've finished the second draft of my book and am going to begin the third to-morrow morning at half-past seven. It's the sweetest book you ever saw—it is, truly. I think of nothing else. I can barely wait in the morning to dress and eat before beginning; then I write and write and write till suddenly I'm so tired that I'm limp all over. Then I go out with Colin (the new sheep dog) and romp through the fields and get a fresh supply of ideas

for the next day. It's the most beautiful book you ever saw—
Oh, pardon—I said that before.

You don't think me conceited, do you, Daddy dear?

I'm not, really, only just now I'm in the enthusiastic stage.
Maybe later on I'll get cold and critical and sniffy. No, I'm sure
I won't! This time I've written a real book. Just wait till you
see it.

I'll try for a minute to talk about something else. I never told
you, did I, that Amasai and Carrie got married last May? They
are still working here, but so far as I can see it has spoiled them
both. She used just to laugh when he tramped in mud or
dropped ashes on the floor, but now—you should hear her
scold! And she doesn't curl her hair any longer. Amasai, who
used to be so obliging about beating rugs and carrying wood,
grumbles if you suggest such a thing. Also his neckties are quite
dingy—black and brown, where they used to be scarlet and purple. I've determined never to marry. It's a deteriorating process,
evidently.

There isn't much of any farm news. The animals are all in the
best of health. The pigs are unusually fat, the cows seem contented and the hens are laying well. Are you interested in poul-
try? If so, let me recommend that invaluable little work, "200
Eggs per Hen per Year." I am thinking of starting an incubator
next spring and raising broilers. You see I'm settled at Lock
Willow permanently. I have decided to stay until I've written
114 novels like Anthony Trollope's mother.[64] Then I shall have
completed my life work and can retire and travel.

Mr. James McBride spent last Sunday with us. Fried chicken
and ice-cream for dinner, both of which he appeared to appreciate. I was awfully glad to see him; he brought a momentary
reminder that the world at large exists. Poor Jimmie is having a
hard time peddling his bonds. The Farmers' National at the
Corners wouldn't have anything to do with them in spite of the
fact that they pay six per cent. interest and sometimes seven. I
think he'll end by going home to Worcester and taking a job in
his father's factory. He's too open and confiding and kind-hearted
ever to make a successful financier. But to be the manager of a
flourishing overall factory is a very desirable position, don't you

think? Just now he turns up his nose at overalls, but he'll come to them.

I hope you appreciate the fact that this is a long letter from a person with writer's cramp. But I still love you, Daddy dear, and I'm very happy. With beautiful scenery all about, and lots to eat and a comfortable four-post bed and a ream of blank paper and a pint of ink—what more does one want in the world?

Yours, as always,

JUDY.

P.S. The postman arrives with some more news. We are to expect Master Jervie on Friday next to spend a week. That's a very pleasant prospect—only I am afraid my poor book will suffer. Master Jervie is very demanding.

August 27th.

Dear Daddy-Long-Legs,

Where are you, I wonder?

I never know what part of the world you are in, but I hope you're not in New York during his awful weather. I hope you're on a mountain peak (but not in Switzerland; somewhere nearer) looking at the snow and thinking about me. Please be thinking about me. I'm quite lonely and I want to be thought about. Oh, Daddy, I wish I knew you! Then when we were unhappy we could cheer each other up.

I don't think I can stand much more of Lock Willow. I'm thinking of moving. Sallie is going to do settlement work in Boston next winter. Don't you think it would be nice for me to go with her, then we could have a studio together? I could write while she *settled* and we could be together in the evenings. Evenings are very long when there's no one but the Semples and Carrie and Amasai to talk to. I know ahead of time that you won't like my studio idea. I can read your secretary's letter now:

"*Miss Jerusha Abbott.*
   "DEAR MADAM,
   "Mr. Smith prefers that you remain at Lock Willow.
                           "Yours truly,
                                "ELMER H. GRIGGS."

I hate your secretary. I am certain that a man named Elmer H.
Griggs must be horrid. But truly, Daddy, I think I shall have to go
to Boston. I can't stay here. If something doesn't happen soon, I
shall throw myself into the silo pit out of sheer desperation.

Mercy! but it's hot. All the grass is burnt up and the brooks are
dry and the roads are dusty. It hasn't rained for weeks and weeks.

This letter sounds as though I had hydrophobia, but I haven't.
I just want some family.

Good-by, my dearest Daddy.

                           I wish I knew you.
                                         JUDY.

                                   LOCK WILLOW,
                                   September 19th.

Dear Daddy,

Something has happened and I need advice. I need it from
you, and from nobody else in the world. Wouldn't it be possible for me to see you? It's so much easier to talk than to write;
and I'm afraid your secretary might open the letter.
                                         JUDY.

P.S. I'm very unhappy.

LOCK WILLOW,
October 3d.

Dear Daddy-Long-Legs,

Your note written in your own hand—and a pretty wobbly hand!—came this morning. I am so sorry that you have been ill; I wouldn't have bothered you with my affairs if I had known. Yes, I will tell you the trouble, but it's sort of complicated to write, and *very private*. Please don't keep this letter, but burn it.

Before I begin—here's a check for one thousand dollars. It seems funny, doesn't it, for me to be sending a check to you? Where do you think I got it?

I've sold my story, Daddy. It's going to be published serially in seven parts, and then in a book! You might think I'd be wild with joy, but I'm not. I'm entirely apathetic. Of course I'm glad to begin paying you—I owe you over two thousand more. It's coming in instalments. Now don't be horrid, please, about taking it, because it makes me happy to return it. I owe you a great deal more than the mere money, and the rest I will continue to pay all my life in gratitude and affection.

And now, Daddy, about the other thing; please give me your most worldly advice, whether you think I'll like it or not.

You know that I've always had a very special feeling toward you; you sort of represented my whole family; but you won't mind, will you, if I tell you that I have a very much more special feeling for another man? You can probably guess without much trouble who he is. I suspect that my letters have been very full of Master Jervie for a very long time.

I wish I could make you understand what he is like and how entirely companionable we are. We think the same about everything—I am afraid I have a tendency to make over my ideas to match his! But he is almost always right; he ought to be, you know, for he has fourteen years' start of me. In other ways, though, he's just an overgrown boy, and he does need looking after—he hasn't any sense about wearing rubbers when it rains.

He and I always think the same things are funny, and that is such a lot; it's dreadful when two people's senses of humor are antagonistic. I don't believe there's any bridging that gulf!

And he is—Oh, well! He is just himself, and I miss him, and miss him, and miss him. The whole world seems empty and aching. I hate the moonlight because it's beautiful and he isn't here to see it with me. But maybe you've loved somebody, too, and you know? If you have, I don't need to explain; if you haven't, I can't explain.

Anyway, that's the way I feel—and I've refused to marry him. I didn't tell him why; I was just dumb and miserable. I couldn't think of anything to say. And now he has gone away imagining that I want to marry Jimmie McBride—I don't in the least, I wouldn't think of marrying Jimmie; he isn't grown up enough. But Master Jervie and I got into a dreadful muddle of misunderstanding, and we both hurt each other's feelings. The reason I sent him away was not because I didn't care for him, but because I cared for him so much. I was afraid he would regret it in the future—and I couldn't stand that! It didn't seem right for a person of my lack of antecedents to marry into any such family as his. I never told him about the orphan asylum, and I hated to explain that I didn't know who I was. I may be *dreadful*, you know. And his family are proud—and I'm proud, too!

Also, I felt sort of bound to you. After having been educated to be a writer, I must at least try to be one; it would scarcely be fair to accept your education and then go off and not use it. But now that I am going to be able to pay back the money, I feel that I have partially discharged that debt—besides, I suppose I could keep on being a writer even if I did marry. The two professions are not necessarily exclusive.

I've been thinking very hard about it. Of course he is a Socialist, and he has unconventional ideas; maybe he wouldn't mind marrying into the proletariat so much as some men might. Perhaps when two people are exactly in accord, and always happy when together and lonely when apart, they ought not to let anything in the world stand between them. Of course I *want* to believe that! But I'd like to get your unemotional opinion. You probably belong to a Family also, and will look at it from a worldly point of view and not just a sympathetic, human point of view—so you see how brave I am to lay it before you.

Suppose I go to him and explain that the trouble isn't Jimmie, but is the John Grier Home—would that be a dreadful thing for me to do? It would take a great deal of courage. I'd almost rather be miserable for the rest of my life.

This happened nearly two months ago; I haven't heard a word from him since he was here. I was just getting sort of acclimated to the feeling of a broken heart, when a letter came from Julia that stirred me all up again. She said—very casually—that "Uncle Jervis" had been caught out all night in a storm when he was hunting in Canada, and had been ill ever since with pneumonia. And I never knew it. I was feeling hurt because he had just disappeared into blankness without a word. I think he's pretty unhappy, and I know I am!

What seems to you the right thing for me to do?

JUDY.

October 6th.

Dearest Daddy-Long-Legs,

Yes, certainly I'll come—at half-past four next Wednesday afternoon. Of *course* I can find the way. I've been in New York three times and am not quite a baby. I can't believe that I am really going to see you—I've been just *thinking* you so long that it hardly seems as though you are a tangible flesh-and-blood person.

You are awfully good, Daddy, to bother yourself with me, when you're not strong. Take care and don't catch cold. These fall rains are very damp.

Affectionately,

JUDY.

P.S. I've just had an awful thought. Have you a butler? I'm afraid of butlers, and if one opens the door I shall faint upon the step. What can I say to him? You didn't tell me your name. Shall I ask for Mr. Smith?

Thursday Morning.

My very dearest Master-Jervie-Daddy-Long-Legs-
Pendleton-Smith,

Did you sleep last night? I didn't. Not a single wink. I was too amazed and excited and bewildered and happy. I don't believe I ever shall sleep again—or eat either. But I hope you slept; you must, you know, because then you will get well faster and can come to me.

Dear Man, I can't bear to think how ill you've been—and all the time I never knew it. When the doctor came down yesterday to put me in the cab, he told me that for three days they gave you up. Oh, dearest, if that had happened, the light would have gone out of the world for me. I suppose that some day—in the far future—one of us must leave the other; but at least we shall have had our happiness and there will be memories to live with.

I meant to cheer you up—and instead I have to cheer myself. For in spite of being happier than I ever dreamed I could be, I'm also soberer. The fear that something may happen to you rests like a shadow on my heart. Always before I could be frivolous and care-free and unconcerned, because I had nothing precious to lose. But now—I shall have a Great Big Worry all the rest of my life. Whenever you are away from me I shall be thinking of all the automobiles that can run over you, or the sign-boards that can fall on your head or the dreadful, squirmy germs that you may be swallowing. My peace of mind is gone forever—but anyway, I never cared much for just plain peace.

Please get well—fast—fast—fast. I want to have you close by where I can touch you and make sure you are tangible. Such a little half hour we had together! I'm afraid maybe I dreamed it. If I were only a member of your family (a very distant fourth

cousin) then I could come and visit you every day, and read
aloud and plump up your pillow and smooth out those two little wrinkles in your forehead and make the corners of your
mouth turn up in a nice cheerful smile. But you are cheerful
again, aren't you? You were yesterday before I left. The doctor said I must be a good nurse, that you looked ten years
younger. I hope that being in love doesn't make every one ten
years younger. Will you still care for me, darling, if I turn out
to be only eleven?

Yesterday was the most wonderful day that could ever happen. If I live to be ninety-nine I shall never forget the tiniest detail. The girl that left Lock Willow at dawn was a very different
person from the one who came back at night. Mrs. Semple
called me at half-past four. I started wide awake in the darkness
and the first thought that popped into my head was, "I am going to see Daddy-Long-Legs!" I ate breakfast in the kitchen by
candle-light, and then drove the five miles to the station through
the most glorious October coloring. The sun came up on the
way, and the swamp maples and dogwood glowed crimson and
orange and the stone walls and cornfields sparkled with hoar
frost; the air was keen and clear and full of promise. I *knew*
something was going to happen. All the way in the train the
rails kept singing, "You're going to see Daddy-Long-Legs." It
made me feel secure. I had such faith in Daddy's ability to set
things right. And I knew that somewhere another man—dearer
than Daddy—was wanting to see me, and somehow I had a
feeling that before the journey ended I should meet him, too.
And you see!

When I came to the house on Madison Avenue it looked so
big and brown and forbidding that I didn't dare go in, so I
walked around the block to get up my courage. But I needn't
have been a bit afraid; your butler is such a nice, fatherly old
man that he made me feel at home at once. "Is this Miss Abbott?" he said to me, and I said, "Yes," so I didn't have to ask
for Mr. Smith after all. He told me to wait in the drawing-
room. It was a very somber, magnificent, man's sort of room. I
sat down on the edge of a big upholstered chair and kept saying to myself:

"I'm going to see Daddy-Long-Legs! I'm going to see Daddy-Long-Legs!"

Then presently the man came back and asked me please to step up to the library. I was so excited that really and truly my feet would hardly take me up. Outside the door he turned and whispered, "He's been very ill, Miss. This is the first day he's been allowed to sit up. You'll not stay long enough to excite him?" I knew from the way he said it that he loved you—and I think he's an old dear!

Then he knocked and said, "Miss Abbott," and I went in and the door closed behind me.

It was so dim coming in from the brightly lighted hall that for a moment I could scarcely make out anything; then I saw a big easy chair before the fire and a shining tea table with a smaller chair beside it. And I realized that a man was sitting in the big chair propped up by pillows with a rug over his knees. Before I could stop him he rose—sort of shakily—and steadied himself by the back of the chair and just looked at me without a word. And then—and then—I saw it was you! But even with that I didn't understand. I thought Daddy had had you come there to meet me for a surprise.

Then you laughed and held out your hand and said, "Dear little Judy, couldn't you guess that I was Daddy-Long-Legs?"

In an instant it flashed over me. Oh, but I have been stupid! A hundred little things might have told me, if I had had any wits. I wouldn't make a very good detective, would I, Daddy?—Jervie? What must I call you? Just plain Jervie sounds disrespectful, and I can't be disrespectful to you!

It was a very sweet half hour before your doctor came and sent me away. I was so dazed when I got to the station that I almost took a train for St. Louis. And you were pretty dazed, too. You forgot to give me any tea. But we're both very, very happy, aren't we? I drove back to Lock Willow in the dark—but oh, how the stars were shining! And this morning I've been out with Colin visiting all the places that you and I went to together, and remembering what you said and how you looked. The woods to-day are burnished bronze and the air is full of frost. It's *climbing* weather. I wish you were here to climb the hills with me. I am missing you dreadfully, Jervie dear, but it's a happy kind of missing; we'll be together soon. We belong to each other now really and truly, no make-believe. Doesn't it seem queer for me to belong to some one at last? It seems very, very sweet.

And I shall never let you be sorry for a single instant.

Yours, forever and ever,

JUDY.

P.S. This is the first love letter I ever wrote. Isn't it funny that I know how?

THE END

DEAR ENEMY

By

JEAN WEBSTER

Author of "When Patty Went to College," "Daddy
Long-Legs," etc.

ILLUSTRATED
BY THE AUTHOR

NEW YORK
THE CENTURY CO.
1915

STONE GATE, WORCESTER,
MASSACHUSETTS,
December 27.

Dear Judy:

Your letter is here. I have read it twice, and with amazement.
Do I understand that Jervis has given you, for a Christmas
present, the making over of the John Grier Home into a
model institution, and that you have chosen me to disburse
the money? Me—I, Sallie McBride, the head of an orphan-
asylum!—My poor people, have you lost your senses, or have
you become addicted to the use of opium, and is this the rav-
ing of two fevered imaginations? I am exactly as well fitted to
take care of one hundred children as to become the curator of
a zoo.

And you offer as bait an interesting Scotch doctor? My dear
Judy—likewise my dear Jervis,—I see through you! I know ex-
actly the kind of family conference that has been held about the
Pendleton fireside.

"Isn't it a pity that Sallie hasn't amounted to more since she
left college? She ought to be doing something useful instead
of frittering her time away in the petty social life of Worcester. Also [Jervis speaks] she is getting interested in that con-
founded young Hallock, too good-looking and fascinating and
erratic; I never did like politicians. We must deflect her mind
with some uplifting and absorbing occupation until the danger
is past. Ha! I have it! We will put her in charge of the John
Grier Home."

Oh, I can hear him as clearly as if I were there! On the occasion of my last visit in your delectable household Jervis and I
had a very solemn conversation in regard to (1) marriage, (2)

the low ideals of politicians, (3) the frivolous, useless lives that
society women lead.

Please tell your moral husband that I took his words deeply
to heart, and that ever since my return to Worcester I have been
spending one afternoon a week reading poetry with the inmates of the Female Inebriate Asylum. My life is not so pur-
poseless as it appears.

Also let me assure you that the politician is not dangerously
imminent; and that, anyway, he is a very desirable politician, even
though his views on tariff and single tax[1] and trade-unionism do
not exactly coincide with Jervis's.

Your desire to dedicate my life to the public good is very sweet,
but you should look at it from the asylum's point of view. Have
you no pity for those poor defenseless little orphan children?

I have, if you haven't, and I respectfully decline the position
which you offer.

I shall be charmed, however, to accept your invitation to visit
you in New York, though I must acknowledge that I am not
very excited over the list of gaieties you have planned.

Please substitute for the New York Orphanage and the
Foundling Hospital a few theaters and operas and a dinner or
so. I have two new evening gowns and a blue and gold coat
with a white fur collar.

I dash to pack them; so telegraph fast if you don't wish to see
me for myself alone, but only as a successor to Mrs. Lippett.

> Yours as ever,
> Entirely frivolous,
> And intending to remain so,
> SALLIE MCBRIDE.

P.S. Your invitation is especially seasonable. A charming young
politician named Gordon Hallock is to be in New York next
week. I am sure you will like him when you know him better.

P.S. (2) Sallie taking her afternoon walk as Judy would like
to see her:

50 sweet little boys   S.Mᶜ B.   50 dear little girls

I ask you again, have you both gone mad?

THE JOHN GRIER HOME,
February 15.

Dear Judy:

We arrived in a snow-storm at eleven last night, Singapore
and Jane and I. It does not appear to be customary for superin-
tendents of orphan-asylums to bring with them personal maids
and Chinese chows. The night-watchman and house-keeper,
who had waited up to receive me, were thrown into an awful
flutter. They had never seen the like of Sing, and thought that I
was introducing a wolf into the fold. I reassured them as to his
dogginess; and the watchman, after studying his black tongue,

ventured a witticism. He wanted to know if I fed him on huckleberry pie.

It was difficult to find accommodations for my family. Poor Sing was dragged off whimpering to a strange woodshed, and given a piece of burlap. Jane did not fare much better. There was not an extra bed in the building, barring a five-foot crib in the hospital room. She, as you know, approaches six. We tucked her in, and she spent the night folded up like a jackknife. She has limped about to-day, looking like a decrepit letter S, openly deploring this latest escapade on the part of her flighty mistress, and longing for the time when we shall come to our senses, and return to the parental fireside in Worcester.

I know that she is going to spoil all my chances of being popular with the rest of the staff. Having her here is the silliest idea that was ever conceived; but you know my family. I fought their objections step by step, but they made their last stand on Jane. If I brought her along to see that I ate nourishing food and didn't stay up all night, I might come—temporarily; but if I refused to bring her—oh, dear me, I am not sure that I was ever again to cross the threshold of Stone Gate! So here we are, and neither of us very welcome, I am afraid.

I woke by a gong at six this morning, and lay for a time, listening to the racket that twenty-five little girls made in the lavatory over my head. It appears that they do not get baths,—just face-washes,—but they make as much splashing as twenty-five puppies in a pool. I rose and dressed and explored a bit. You were wise in not having me come to look the place over before I engaged.

While my little charges were at breakfast, it seemed a happy time to introduce myself; so I sought the dining-room. Horror piled on horror—those bare drab walls and oil-cloth-covered tables with tin cups and plates and wooden benches, and, by way of decoration, that one illuminated text, "The Lord Will Provide"! The trustee who added that last touch must possess a grim sense of humor.

Really, Judy, I never knew there was any spot in the world so entirely ugly; and when I saw those rows and rows of pale, listless, blue-uniformed children, the whole dismal business suddenly struck me with such a shock that I almost collapsed. It seemed like an unachievable goal for one person to bring sunshine to one hundred little faces when what they need is a mother apiece.

I plunged into this thing lightly enough, partly because you were too persuasive, and mostly, I honestly think, because that scurrilous Gordon Hallock laughed so uproariously at the idea of my being able to manage an asylum. Between you all you hypnotized me. And then of course, after I began reading up on the subject and visiting all those seventeen institutions, I got excited over orphans, and wanted to put my own ideas into practice. But now I'm aghast at finding myself here; it's such a stupendous undertaking. The future health and happiness of a hundred human beings lie in my hands, to say nothing of their three or four hundred children and thousand grandchildren. The thing's geometrically progressive. It's awful. Who am I to undertake this job? Look, oh, look for another superintendent!

Jane says dinner's ready. Having eaten two of your institution meals, the thought of another doesn't excite me.

Later.

The staff had mutton hash and spinach, with tapioca pudding for dessert; what the children had I hate to consider.

I started to tell you about my first official speech at breakfast this morning. It dealt with all the wonderful new changes that are to come to the John Grier Home through the generosity of Mr. Jervis Pendleton, the president of our board of trustees, and of Mrs. Pendleton, the dear "Aunt Judy" of every little boy and girl here.

Please don't object to my featuring the Pendleton family so prominently. I did it for political reasons. As the entire working-staff of the institution was present, I thought it a good opportunity to emphasize the fact that all of these upsetting innovations come straight from headquarters, and not out of my excitable brain.

The children stopped eating and stared. The conspicuous color of my hair and the frivolous tilt of my nose are evidently

new attributes in a superintendent. My colleagues also showed
plainly that they consider me too young and too inexperienced
to be set in authority. I haven't seen Jervis's wonderful Scotch
doctor yet, but I assure you that he will have to be *very* wonderful to make up for the rest of these people, especially the
kindergarten teacher. Miss Snaith and I clashed early on the
subject of fresh air; but I intend to get rid of this dreadful institution smell, if I freeze every child into a little ice statue.

This being a sunny, sparkling, snowy afternoon, I ordered that
dungeon of a playroom closed and the children out of doors.

"She's chasin' us out," I heard one small urchin grumbling as
he struggled into a two-years-too-small overcoat.

They simply stood about the yard, all humped in their
clothes, waiting patiently to be allowed to come back in. No
running or shouting or coasting or snowballs. Think of it!
These children don't know how to play.

Still Later.

I have already begun the congenial task of spending your
money. I bought eleven hot-water bottles this afternoon (every
one that the village drug store contained) likewise some woolen
blankets and padded quilts. And the windows are wide open in
the babies' dormitory. Those poor little tots are going to enjoy
the perfectly new sensation of being able to breathe at night.

There are a million things I want to grumble about, but it's
half-past ten, and Jane says I *must* go to bed.

Yours in command,
SALLIE MCBRIDE.

P.S. Before turning in, I tiptoed through the corridor to make
sure that all was right, and what do you think I found? Miss
Snaith softly closing the windows in the babies' dormitory! Just
as soon as I can find a suitable position for her in an old ladies'
home, I am going to discharge that woman.

Jane takes the pen from my hand.

Good night.

THE JOHN GRIER HOME,
February 20.

Dear Judy:

Dr. Robin MacRae called this afternoon to make the acquaintance of the new superintendent. Please invite him to dinner upon the occasion of his next visit to New York, and see for yourself what your husband has done. Jervis grossly misrepresented the facts when he led me to believe that one of the chief advantages of my position would be the daily intercourse with a man of Dr. MacRae's polish and brilliancy and scholarliness and charm.

He is tall and thinnish, with sandy hair and cold gray eyes. During the hour he spent in my society (and I was very sprightly) no shadow of a smile so much as lightened the straight line of his mouth. Can a shadow lighten? Maybe not; but, anyway, what *is* the matter with the man? Has he committed some remorseful crime, or is his taciturnity due merely to his natural Scotchness? He's as companionable as a granite tombstone!

Incidentally, our doctor didn't like me any more than I liked him. He thinks I'm frivolous and inconsequential, and totally unfitted for this position of trust. I dare say Jervis has had a letter from him by now asking to have me removed.

In the matter of conversation we didn't hit it off in the least. He discussed broadly and philosophically the evils of institutional care for dependent children, while I lightly deplored the unbecoming coiffure that prevails among our girls.

To prove my point, I had in Sadie Kate, my special errand orphan. Her hair is strained back as tightly as though it had been done with a monkey-wrench, and is braided behind into two wiry little pigtails. Decidedly, orphans' ears need to be softened. But Dr. Robin MacRae doesn't give a hang whether their ears are becoming or not; what he cares about is their stomachs. We also split upon the subject of red petticoats. I don't see how any little girl can preserve any self-respect when dressed in a red flannel petticoat an irregular inch longer than her blue checked gingham dress; but he thinks that red petticoats are cheerful and warm and hygienic. I foresee a warlike reign for the new superintendent.

In regard to the doctor, there is just one detail to be thankful for: he is almost as new as I am, and he cannot instruct me in the traditions of the asylum. I don't believe I *could* have worked with the old doctor, who, judging from the specimens of his art that he left behind, knew as much about babies as a veterinary surgeon.

In the matter of asylum etiquette, the entire staff has undertaken my education. Even the cook this morning told me firmly that the John Grier Home has corn-meal mush on Wednesday nights.

Are you searching hard for another superintendent? I'll stay until she comes, but please find her fast.

Yours,
With my mind made up,
SALLIE McBRIDE.

SUP'T'S OFFICE,
JOHN GRIER HOME,
February 27.

Dear Gordon:

Are you still insulted because I wouldn't take your advice? Don't you know that a reddish-haired person of Irish forebears, with a dash of Scotch, can't be driven, but must be gently led? Had you been less obnoxiously insistent, I should have listened sweetly, and been saved. As it is, I frankly confess that I have spent the last five days in repenting our quarrel. You were right, and I was wrong, and, as you see, I handsomely acknowledge it. If I ever emerge from this present predicament, I shall in the future be guided (almost always) by your judgment. Could any woman make a more sweeping retraction than that?

U.S. CAPITOL

JOHN GRIER HOME

Red Hair →

"Oh Willow Woe is me
Alack & Well a day
If I were only free
I'd hie me far away"

The romantic glamour which Judy cast over this orphan-
asylum exists only in her poetic imagination. The place is *awful*. Words can't tell you how dreary and dismal and smelly it
is: long corridors, bare walls; blue-uniformed, dough-faced little inmates that haven't the slightest resemblance to human

children. And, oh, the dreadful institution smell! A mingling of
wet scrubbed floors, unaired rooms, and food for a hundred
people always steaming on the stove.

The asylum not only has to be made over, but every child as
well, and it's too herculean a task for such a selfish, luxurious,
and lazy person as Sallie McBride ever to have undertaken. I'm
resigning the very first moment that Judy can find a suitable
successor; but that, I fear, will not be immediately. She has gone
off South, leaving me stranded; and of course, after having
promised, I can't simply abandon her asylum. But in the meantime I assure you that I'm homesick.

Write me a cheering letter, and send a flower to brighten my
private drawing-room. I inherited it, furnished, from Mrs. Lippett. The wall is covered with a tapestry paper in brown and
red; the furniture is electric-blue plush, except the center-table,
which is gilt. Green predominates in the carpet. If you presented
some pink rosebuds, they would complete the color scheme.

I really was obnoxious that last evening, but you are avenged.

Remorsefully yours,
SALLIE McBRIDE.

P.S. You needn't have been so grumpy about the Scotch doctor. The man is everything dour that the word "Scotch" im-
plies. I detest him on sight, and he detests me. Oh, we're going
to have a sweet time working together!

THE JOHN GRIER HOME,
February 22.

My dear Gordon:

Your vigorous and expensive message is here. I know that
you have plenty of money, but that is no reason why you
should waste it so frivolously. When you feel so bursting with
talk that only a hundred-word telegram will relieve an explosion, at least turn it into a night lettergram. My orphans can
use the money if you don't need it.

Also, my dear sir, please use a trifle of common sense. Of course I can't chuck the asylum in the casual manner you suggest. It wouldn't be fair to Judy and Jervis. If you will pardon the statement, they have been my friends for many more years than you, and I have no intention of letting them go hang. I came up here in a spirit of—well, say adventure, and I must see the venture through. You wouldn't like me if I were a short sport. This doesn't mean, however, that I am sentencing myself for life; I am intending to resign just as soon as the opportunity comes. But really I ought to feel somewhat gratified that the Pendletons were willing to trust me with such a responsible post. Though you, my dear sir, do not suspect it, I possess considerable executive ability, and more common sense than is visible on the surface. If I chose to put my whole soul into this enterprise, I could make the rippingest superintendent that any 111 orphans ever had.

I suppose you think that's funny? It's true. Judy and Jervis know it, and that's why they asked me to come. So you see, when they have shown so much confidence in me, I can't throw them over in quite the unceremonious fashion you suggest. So long as I am here, I am going to accomplish just as much as it is given one person to accomplish every twenty-four hours. I am going to turn the place over to my successor with things moving fast in the right direction.

But in the meantime please don't wash your hands of me under the belief that I'm too busy to be homesick; for I'm not. I wake up every morning and stare at Mrs. Lippett's wall-paper in a sort of daze, feeling as though it's some bad dream, and I'm not really here. What on earth was I thinking of to turn my back upon my nice cheerful own home and the good times that by rights are mine? I frequently agree with your opinion of my sanity.

But why, may I ask, should you be making such a fuss? You wouldn't be seeing me in any case. Worcester is quite as far from Washington as the John Grier Home. And I will add, for your further comfort, that whereas there is no man in the neighborhood of this asylum who admires red hair, in Worcester there are several. Therefore, most difficult of men, please be appeased. I didn't come entirely to spite you. I wanted an adventure in life, and, oh dear! oh dear! I'm having it!

Please write soon, and cheer me up.

Yours in sackcloth,

SALLIE.

THE JOHN GRIER HOME,

February 24.

Dear Judy:

You tell Jervis that I am not hasty at forming judgments. I have a sweet, sunny, unsuspicious nature, and I like everybody, almost. But no one could like that Scotch doctor. He *never* smiles.

He paid me another visit this afternoon. I invited him to accommodate himself in one of Mrs. Lippett's electric-blue chairs, and then sat down opposite to enjoy the harmony. He was dressed in a mustard-colored homespun, with a dash of green and a glint of yellow in the weave, a "heather mixture" calculated to add life to a dull Scotch moor. Purple socks and a red tie, with an amethyst pin, completed the picture. Clearly, your paragon of a doctor is not going to be of much assistance in pulling up the esthetic tone of this establishment.

During the fifteen minutes of his call he succinctly outlined all the changes he wishes to see accomplished in this institution. *He* forsooth! And what, may I ask, are the duties of a superintendent? Is she merely a figurehead to take orders from the visiting physician?

It's up wi' the bonnets o' McBride and MacRae![2]

I am,

Indignantly yours,

SALLIE.

THE JOHN GRIER HOME,
Monday.

Dear Dr. MacRae:

I am sending this note by Sadie Kate, as it seems impossible
to reach you by telephone. Is the person who calls herself Mrs.
McGur-rk and hangs up in the middle of a sentence your
housekeeper? If she answers the telephone often, I don't see
how your patients have any patience left.

As you did not come this morning, per agreement, and the
painters did come, I was fain to choose a cheerful corn color to
be placed upon the walls of your new laboratory room. I trust
there is nothing unhygienic about corn color.

Also, if you can spare a moment this afternoon, kindly motor yourself to Dr. Brice's on Water Street and look at the dentist's chair and appurtenances which are to be had at half-price.
If all of the pleasant paraphernalia of his profession were
here,—in a corner of your laboratory,—Dr. Brice could finish
his 111 new patients with much more despatch than if we had
to transport them separately to Water Street. Don't you think
that's a useful idea? It came to me in the middle of the night,
but as I never happened to buy a dentist's chair before, I'd appreciate some professional advice.

Yours truly,
S. McBRIDE.

THE JOHN GRIER HOME,
March 1.

Dear Judy:

Do stop sending me telegrams!

Of course I know that you want to know everything that is
happening, and I would send you a daily bulletin, but I truly

don't find a minute. I am so tired when night comes that if it weren't for Jane's strict discipline, I should go to bed with my clothes on.

Later, when we slip a little more into routine, and I can be sure that my assistants are all running off their respective jobs, I shall be the regularest correspondent you ever had.

It was five days ago, wasn't it, that I wrote? Things have been happening in those five days. The MacRae and I have mapped out a plan of campaign, and are stirring up this place to its sluggish depths. I like him less and less, but we have declared a sort of working truce. And the man *is* a worker. I always thought I had sufficient energy myself, but when an improvement is to be introduced, I toil along panting in his wake. He is as stubborn and tenacious and bull-doggish as a Scotchman can be, but he does understand babies; that is, he understands their physiological aspects. He hasn't any more feeling for them personally than for so many frogs that he might happen to be dissecting.

Do you remember Jervis's holding forth one evening for an hour or so about our doctor's beautiful humanitarian ideals? *C'est à rire!*[3] The man merely regards the J. G. H. as his own private laboratory, where he can try out scientific experiments with no loving parents to object. I shouldn't be surprised any day to find him introducing scarlet fever cultures into the babies' porridge in order to test a newly invented serum.

Of the house staff, the only two who strike me as really efficient are the primary teacher and the furnace-man. You should see how the children run to meet Miss Matthews and beg for caresses, and how painstakingly polite they are to the other teachers. Children are quick to size up character. I shall be very embarrassed if they are too polite to me.

Just as soon as I get my bearings a little, and know exactly what we need, I am going to accomplish some wide-spread discharging. I should like to begin with Miss Snaith; but I discover that she is the niece of one of our most generous trustees, and isn't exactly dischargeable. She's a vague, chinless, pale-eyed creature, who talks through her nose and breathes through her mouth. She can't say anything decisively and then stop; her sentences all trail off into incoherent murmurings. Every time I see the woman I feel an almost uncontrollable desire to take her by the shoulders and shake some decision into her. And Miss Snaith is the one who has had entire supervision of the seventeen little tots aged from two to five! But, anyway, even if I can't discharge her, I have reduced her to a subordinate position without her being aware of the fact.

The doctor has found for me a charming girl who lives a few miles from here and comes in every day to manage the kindergarten. She has big, gentle, brown eyes, like a cow's, and motherly manners (she is just nineteen), and the babies love her. At the head of the nursery I have placed a jolly, comfortable middle-aged woman who has reared five of her own and has a hand with bairns. Our doctor also found her; you see, he is useful. She is technically under Miss Snaith, but is usurping dictatorship in a satisfactory fashion. I can now sleep at night without being afraid that my babies are being inefficiently murdered.

You see, our reforms are getting started; and while I acquiesce with all the intelligence at my command to our doctor's basic scientific upheavals, still, they sometimes leave me cold. The problem that keeps churning and churning in my mind is, How can I ever instil enough love and warmth and sunshine into those bleak little lives? And I am not sure that the doctor's science will accomplish that.

One of our most pressing *intelligent* needs just now is to get our records into coherent form. The books have been most outrageously unkept. Mrs. Lippett had a big black account-book into which she jumbled any facts that happened to drift her way as to the children's family, their conduct, and their health; but for weeks at a time she didn't trouble to make an entry. If any adopting family wants to know a child's parentage, half the time we can't even tell where we got the child!

> "Where did you come from, baby dear?"
> "The blue sky opened, and I am here,"[4]

is an exact description of their arrival.

We need a field worker to travel about the country and pick up all the hereditary statistics she can about our chicks. It will be an easy matter, as most of them have relatives. What do you think of Janet Ware for the job? You remember what a shark she was in economics; she simply battened on tables and charts and surveys.

I have also to inform you that the John Grier Home is undergoing a very searching physical examination, and it is the shocking truth that out of the twenty-eight poor little rats so far examined only five are up to specification. And the five have not been here long.

Do you remember the ugly green reception-room on the first floor? I have removed as much of its greenness as possible, and fitted it up as the doctor's laboratory. It contains scales and drugs and, most professional touch of all, a dentist's chair and one of those sweet grinding-machines. (Bought them second-hand from Doctor Brice in the village, who is putting in, for the gratification of his own patients, white enamel and nickel-plate.) That drilling-machine is looked upon as an infernal engine, and I as an infernal monster for instituting it. But every little victim who is discharged *filled* may come to my room every day for a week and receive two pieces of chocolate. Though our children are not conspicuously brave, they are, we discover, fighters. Young Thomas Kehoe nearly bit the doctor's thumb in two after kicking over a tableful of instruments. It requires physical strength as well as skill to be dental adviser to the J. G. H.

·   ·   ·   ·   ·   ·   ·

Interrupted here to show a benevolent lady over the institution. She asked fifty irrelevant questions, took up an hour of my time, then finally wiped away a tear and left a dollar for my "poor little charges."

So far, my poor little charges are not enthusiastic about these new reforms. They don't care much for the sudden draft of fresh air that has blown in upon them, or the deluge of water. I am shoving in two baths a week, and as soon as we collect tubs enough and a few extra faucets, they are going to get *seven*.

But at least I have started one most popular reform. Our daily bill of fare has been increased, a change deplored by the cook as causing trouble, and deplored by the rest of the staff

BATH MAT

SEVEN BATHS A WEEK!!

Unprecedented Cruelty on the part of an Orphan Asylum Superintendent

as causing an immoral increase in expense. ECONOMY spelt in capitals has been the guiding principle of this institution for so many years that it has become a religion. I assure my timid co-workers twenty times a day that, owing to the generosity of our president, the endowment has been exactly doubled, and that I have vast sums besides from Mrs. Pendleton for necessary purposes like ice-cream. But they simply *can't* get over the feeling that it is a wicked extravagance to feed these children.

The doctor and I have been studying with care the menus of the past, and we are filled with amazement at the mind that could have devised them. Here is one of her frequently recurring dinners:

> Boiled potatoes
> Boiled rice
> Blanc mange

It's a wonder to me that the children are anything more than one hundred and eleven little lumps of starch.

Looking about this institution, one is moved to misquote Robert Browning.

> "There may be heaven; there must be hell;
> Meanwhile, there is the John Grier—well!"[5]

S. McB.

THE JOHN GRIER HOME,
Saturday.

Dear Judy:

Dr. Robin MacRae and I fought another battle yesterday over a very trivial matter (in which I was right), and since then I have adopted for our doctor a special pet name. "Good morning, Enemy!" was my greeting to-day, at which he was quite solemnly annoyed. He says he does not wish to be regarded as an enemy. He is not in the least antagonistic—so long as I mold my policy upon his wishes!

We have two new children, Isador Gutschneider and Max Yog, given to us by the Baptist Ladies' Aid Society. Where on earth do you suppose those children picked up such a religion? I didn't want to take them, but the poor ladies were very persuasive, and they pay the princely sum of four dollars and fifty cents per week per child. This makes 113, which makes us very crowded. I have half a dozen babies to give away. Find me some kind families who want to adopt.

You know it's very embarrassing not to be able to remember offhand how large your family is, but mine seems to vary from day to day, like the stock market. I should like to keep it at about par. When a woman has more than a hundred children, she can't give them the individual attention they ought to have.

Monday.

This letter has been lying two days on my desk, and I haven't found the time to stick on a stamp. But now I seem to have a free evening ahead, so I will add a page or two more before starting it on a pleasant journey to Florida.

I am just beginning to pick out individual faces among the children; it seemed at first as though I could never learn them, they looked so hopelessly cut out of one pattern, with those unspeakably ugly uniforms. Now please don't write back that you want the children put into new clothes immediately. I know you do; you've already told me five times. In about a month I shall be ready to consider the question, but just now their insides are more important than their outsides.

There is no doubt about it—orphans in the mass do not appeal to me. I am beginning to be afraid that this famous mother instinct which we hear so much about was left out of my character. Children as children are dirty, spitty little things, and their noses all need wiping. Here and there I pick out a naughty, mischievous little one that awakens a flicker of interest; but for the most part they are just a composite blur of white face and blue check.

With one exception, though. Sadie Kate Kilcoyne emerged from the mass the first day, and bids fair to stay out for all time. She is my special little errand girl, and she furnishes me with all my daily amusement. No piece of mischief has been launched in this institution for the last eight years that did not originate in her abnormal brain. This young person has, to me, a most unusual history, though I understand it's common enough in foundling circles. She was discovered eleven years ago on the bottom step of a Thirty-ninth Street house, asleep in a pasteboard box labeled, "Altman & Co."[6]

"Sadie Kate Kilcoyne, aged five weeks. Be kind to her," was neatly printed on the cover.

The policeman who picked her up took her to Bellevue, where the foundlings are pronounced, in the order of their arrival. "Catholic, Protestant, Catholic, Protestant, with perfect impartiality. Our Sadie Kate, despite her name and blue Irish eyes, was made a Protestant. And here she is growing Irisher and Irisher every day, but, true to her christening, protesting loudly against every detail of life.

Her two little black braids point in opposite directions; her little monkey face is all screwed up with mischief; she is as active as a terrier, and you have to keep her busy every moment. Her record of badnesses occupies pages in the Doomsday Book. The last item reads:

"For stumping Maggie Geer to get a door-knob into her mouth—punishment, the afternoon spent in bed, and crackers for supper."

It seems that Maggie Geer, fitted with a mouth of unusual stretching capacity, got the door-knob in, but couldn't get it out. The doctor was called, and cannily solved the problem with a buttered shoe-horn. "Muckle-mouthed Meg,"[7] he has dubbed the patient ever since.

You can understand that my thoughts are anxiously occupied in filling every crevice of Sadie Kate's existence.

There are a million subjects that I ought to consult with the president about. I think it was very unkind of you and him to saddle me with your orphan-asylum and run off South to play. It would serve you right if I did everything wrong. While you

are traveling about in private cars, and strolling in the moonlight on palm beaches, please think of me in the drizzle of a
New York March, taking care of 113 babies that by rights are
yours—and be grateful.

I remain (for a limited time),

SALLIE McBRIDE,

SUP'T JOHN GRIER HOME.

Dear Enemy:

I am sending herewith (under separate cover) Sammy Speir,
who got mislaid when you paid your morning visit. Miss Snaith
brought him to light after you had gone. Please scrutinize his
thumb. I never saw a felon,[8] but I have diagnosed it as such.

Yours truly,

S. McBRIDE.

SUP'T JOHN GRIER HOME,
March 6.

Dear Judy:

I don't know yet whether the children are going to love me or not, but they *do* love my dog. No creature so popular as Singapore ever entered these gates. Every afternoon three boys who have been perfect in deportment are allowed to brush and comb him, while three other good boys may serve him with food and drink. But every Saturday morning the climax of the week is reached, when three superlatively good boys give him a nice lathery bath with hot water and flea soap. The privilege of serving as Singapore's valet is going to be the only incentive I shall need for maintaining discipline.

But isn't it pathetically unnatural for these youngsters to be living in the country and never owning a pet? Especially when they, of all children, do so need something to love. I am going to manage pets for them somehow, if I have to spend our new endowment for a menagerie. Couldn't you bring back some baby alligators and a pelican? Anything alive will be gratefully received.

This should by rights be my first "Trustees' Day." I am deeply grateful to Jervis for arranging a simple business meeting in New York, as we are not yet on dress parade up here; but we are hoping by the first Wednesday in April to have something visible to show. If all of the doctor's ideas, and a few of my own, get themselves materialized, our trustees will open their eyes a bit when we show them about.

I have just made a chart for next week's meals, and posted it in the kitchen in the sight of an aggrieved cook. Variety is a word hitherto not found in the lexicon of the J. G. H. You would never dream all of the delightful surprises we are going to have: brown bread, corn pone, graham muffins, samp,[9] rice pudding with *lots* of raisins, thick vegetable soup, macaroni Italian fashion, polenta cakes with molasses, apple-dumplings, ginger-bread—oh, an endless list! After our biggest girls have assisted in the manufacture of such appetizing dainties, they will almost be capable of keeping future husbands in love with them.

Oh, dear me! Here I am babbling these silly nothings when I have some real news up my sleeve. We have a new worker, a gem of a worker.

Do you remember Betsy Kindred, 1910? She led the glee club and was president of dramatics. I remember her perfectly; she always had lovely clothes. Well, if you please, she lives only twelve miles from here. I ran across her by chance yesterday morning as she was motoring through the village; or, rather, she just escaped running across me.

I never spoke to her in my life, but we greeted each other like the oldest friends. It pays to have conspicuous hair; she recognized me instantly. I hopped upon the running-board of her car and said:

"Betsy Kindred, 1910, you've got to come back to my orphan-asylum and help me catalogue my orphans."

And it astonished her so that she came. She's to be here four or five days a week as temporary secretary, and somehow I must manage to keep her permanently. She's the most useful person I ever saw. I am hoping that orphans will become such a habit with her that she won't be able to give them up. I think she might stay if we pay her a big enough salary. She likes to be independent of her family, as do all of us in these degenerate times.

In my growing zeal for cataloguing people, I should like to get our doctor tabulated. If Jervis knows any gossip about him, write it to me, please; the worse, the better. He called yesterday to lance a felon on Sammy Speir's thumb, then ascended to my electric-blue parlor to give instructions as to the dressing of thumbs. The duties of a superintendent are manifold.

It was just tea-time, so I casually asked him to stay, and he did! Not for the pleasure of my society,—no, indeed,—but because Jane appeared at the moment with a plate of toasted muffins. He hadn't had any luncheon, it seems, and dinner was a long way ahead. Between muffins (he ate the whole plateful) he saw fit to interrogate me as to my preparedness for this po-

sition. Had I studied biology in college? How far had I gone in
chemistry? What did I know of sociology? Had I visited that
model institution at Hastings?[10]

To all of which I responded affably and openly. Then I per-
mitted myself a question or two: just what sort of youthful
training had been required to produce such a model of logic,
accuracy, dignity, and common sense as I saw sitting before
me? Through persistent prodding I elicited a few forlorn facts,
but all quite respectable. You'd think, from his reticence,
there'd been a hanging in the family. The MacRae *père* was
born in Scotland, and came to the States to occupy a chair at
Johns Hopkins; son Robin was shipped back to Auld Reekie
for his education. His grandmother was a M'Lachlan of Strath-
lachan (I am sure she sounds respectable), and his vacations
were spent in the Hielands a-chasing the deer.

So much could I gather; so much, and no more. Tell me, I
beg, some gossip about my enemy—something scandalous by
preference.

Why, if he is such an awfully efficient person does he bury
himself in this remote locality? You would think an up-and-
coming scientific man would want a hospital at one elbow and
a morgue at the other. Are you sure that he didn't commit a
crime and isn't hiding from the law?

I seem to have covered a lot of paper without telling you
much. *Vive la bagatelle!*[11]

                              Yours as usual,
                                   SALLIE.

P.S. I am relieved on one point. Dr. MacRae does not pick
out his own clothes. He leaves all such unessential trifles to his
housekeeper, Mrs. Maggie McGurk.

                    Again, and irrevocably, good-by!

The John Grier Home,
Wednesday.

Dear Gordon:

Your roses and your letter cheered me for an entire morning, and it's the first time I've approached cheerfulness since the fourteenth of February, when I waved good-by to Worcester.

Words can't tell you how monotonously oppressive the daily round of institution life gets to be. The only glimmer in the whole dull affair is the fact that Betsy Kindred spends four days a week with us. Betsy and I were in college together, and we do occasionally find something funny to laugh about.

Yesterday we were having tea in my *hideous* parlor when we suddenly determined to revolt against so much unnecessary ugliness. We called in six sturdy and destructive orphans, a step-ladder, and a bucket of hot water, and in two hours had every vestige of that tapestry paper off those walls. You can't imagine what fun it is ripping paper off walls.

Two paper-hangers are at work this moment hanging the best that our village affords, while a German upholsterer is on his knees measuring my chairs for chintz slip-covers that will hide every inch of their plush upholstery.

Please don't get nervous. This doesn't mean that I'm preparing to spend my life in the asylum. It means only that I'm preparing a cheerful welcome for my successor. I haven't dared tell Judy how dismal I find it, because I don't want to cloud Florida; but when she returns to New York she will find my official resignation waiting to meet her in the front hall.

I would write you a long letter in grateful payment for seven pages, but two of my little dears are holding a fight under the window. I dash to separate them.

Yours as ever,
S. McB.

THE JOHN GRIER HOME,
March 8.
My dear Judy:

I myself have bestowed a little present upon the John Grier Home—the refurnishing of the superintendent's private parlor. I saw the first night here that neither I nor any future occupant could be happy with Mrs. Lippett's electric plush. You see, I am planning to make my successor contented and willing to stay.

Betsy Kindred assisted in the rehabilitation of the Lippett's chamber of horrors, and between us we have created a symphony in dull blue and gold. Really and truly, it's one of the loveliest rooms you've ever seen; the sight of it will be an artistic education to any orphan. New paper on the wall, new rugs on the floor (my own prized Persians expressed from Worcester by an expostulating family). New casement curtains at my three windows, revealing a wide and charming view, hitherto hidden by Nottingham lace. A new big table, some lamps and books and a picture or so, and a real open fire. She had closed the fireplace because it let in air.

I never realized what a difference artistic surroundings make in the peace of one's soul. I sat last night and watched my fire throw nice high lights on my new old fender, and purred with contentment. And I assure you it's the first purr that has come from this cat since she entered the gates of the John Grier Home.

But the refurnishing of the superintendent's parlor is the slightest of our needs. The children's private apartments demand so much basic attention that I can't decide where to begin. That dark north playroom is a shocking scandal, but no more shocking than our hideous dining-room or our unventilated dormitories or our tubless lavatories.

If the institution is very saving, do you think it can ever afford to burn down this smelly old original building, and put up instead some nice, ventilated modern cottages? I cannot contemplate that wonderful institution at Hastings without being filled with envy. It would be some fun to run an asylum if you had a plant like that to work with. But, anyway, when you get back to New York and are ready to consult the architect about remodeling, please apply to me for suggestions. Among other little details I want two hundred feet of sleeping-porch running along the outside of our dormitories.

You see, it's this way: our physical examination reveals the fact that about half of our children are ænemic—aneamic—anæmic (Mercy! what a word!), and a lot of them have tubercular ancestors, and more have alcoholic. Their first need is oxygen rather than education. And if the sickly ones need it, why wouldn't it be good for the well ones? I should like to have every child, winter and summer, sleeping in the open air; but I know that if I let fall such a bomb on the board of trustees, the whole body would explode.

Speaking of trustees, I have met up with the Hon. Cyrus Wykoff, and I really believe that I dislike him more than Dr. Robin MacRae or the kindergarten teacher or the cook. I seem to have a genius for discovering enemies!

Mr. Wykoff called on Wednesday last to look over the new superintendent.

Having lowered himself into my most comfortable armchair, he proceeded to spend the day. He asked my father's business, and whether or not he was well-to-do. I told him that my father manufactured overalls, and that, even in these hard times, the demand for overalls was pretty steady.

He seemed relieved; he approves of the utilitarian aspect of overalls. He had been afraid that I had come from the family of a minister or professor or writer, a lot of high thinking and no common sense. Cyrus believes in common sense.

And what had been my training for this position?

That, as you know, is a slightly embarrassing question. But I produced my college education and a few lectures at the School of Philanthropy, also a short residence in the college settlement (I didn't tell him that all I had done there was to paint the back hall and stairs). Then I submitted some social work among my father's employees and a few friendly visits to the Home for Female Inebriates.

To all of which he grunted.

I added that I had lately made a study of the care of dependent children, and casually mentioned my seventeen institutions.

He grunted again, and said he didn't take much stock in this new-fangled scientific charity.

At this point Jane entered with a box of roses from the florist's. That blessed Gordon Hallock sends me roses twice a week to brighten the rigors of institution life.

Our trustee began an indignant investigation. He wished to know where I got those flowers, and was visibly relieved when he learned that I had not spent the institution's money for them. He next wished to know who Jane might be. I had foreseen that question and decided to brazen it out.

"My maid," said I.

"Your what?" he bellowed, quite red in the face.

"My maid."

"What is she doing here?"

I amiably went into details. "She mends my clothes, blacks my boots, keeps my bureau drawers in order, washes my hair."

I really thought the man would choke, so I charitably added that I paid her wages out of my own private income, and paid five dollars and fifty cents a week to the institution for her board; and that, though she was big, she didn't eat much.

He allowed that I might make use of one of the orphans for all legitimate service.

I explained—still polite, but growing bored—that Jane had been in my service for many years, and was indispensable.

He finally took himself off, after telling me that he, for one, had never found any fault with Mrs. Lippett. She was a common-sense Christian woman, without many fancy ideas, but with plenty of good solid work in her. He hoped that I would be wise enough to model my policy upon hers!

And what, my dear Judy, do you think of that?

The doctor dropped in a few minutes later, and I repeated the Hon. Cyrus's conversation in detail. For the first time in the history of our intercourse the doctor and I agreed.

"Mrs. Lippett indeed!" he growled. "The blethering auld gomerel! May the Lord send him mair sense!"

When our doctor really becomes aroused, he drops into Scotch. My latest pet name for him (behind his back) is Sandy.

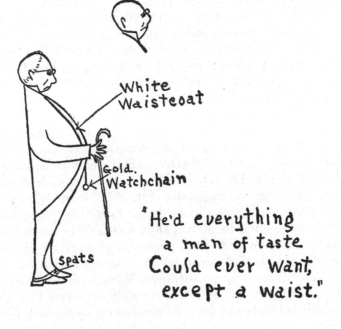

The Honorable Cyrus Wykoff

White Waistcoat

Gold Watchchain

spats

"He'd everything a man of taste Could ever want, except a waist."

Sadie Kate is sitting on the floor as I write, untangling sewing-silks and winding them neatly for Jane, who is becoming quite attached to the little imp.

"I am writing to your Aunt Judy," say I to Sadie Kate. "What message shall I send from you?"

"I never heard of no Aunt Judy."

"She is the aunt of every good little girl in this school."

"Tell her to come and visit me and bring some candy," says Sadie Kate.

I say so, too.

My love to the president,

SALLIE.

March 13.

MRS. JUDY ABBOTT PENDLETON,

Dear Madam:

Your four letters, two telegrams, and three checks are at hand, and your instructions shall be obeyed just as quickly as this overworked superintendent can manage it.

I delegated the dining-room job to Betsy Kindred. One hundred dollars did I allow her for the rehabilitation of that dreary apartment. She accepted the trust, picked out five likely orphans to assist in the mechanical details, and closed the door. For three days the children have been eating from the desks in the school-room. I haven't an idea what Betsy is doing; but she has a lot better taste than I, so there isn't much use in interfering.

It is such a heaven-sent relief to be able to leave something to somebody else, and be sure it will be carried out! With all due respect to the age and experience of the staff I found here, they are not very open to new ideas. As the John Grier Home was planned by its noble founder in 1875, so shall it be run to-day.

Incidentally, my dear Judy, your idea of a private dining-room for the superintendent, which I, being a social soul, at first scorned, has been my salvation. When I am dead tired I dine alone, but in my live intervals I invite an officer to share the meal; and in the expansive intimacy of the dinner-table I get in my most effective strokes. When it becomes desirable to plant the seeds of fresh air in the soul of Miss Snaith, I invite her to dinner, and tactfully sandwich in a little oxygen between her slices of pressed veal.

Pressed veal is our cook's idea of an acceptable *pièce de résistance* for a dinner party. In another month I am going to face the subject of suitable nourishment for the executive staff; meanwhile there are so many things more important than our own comfort that we shall have to worry along on veal.

A terrible bumping has just occurred outside my door. One little cherub seems to be kicking another little cherub downstairs. But I write on undisturbed. If I am to spend my days among orphans, I must cultivate a cheerful detachment.

Did you get Leonora Fenton's cards? She's marrying a medical missionary and going to Siam to live! Did you ever hear of anything so absurd as Leonora presiding over a missionary's menage? Do you suppose she will entertain the heathen with skirt dances?

It isn't any absurder, though, than me in an orphan-asylum, or you as a conservative settled matron, or Marty Keene a social butterfly in Paris. Do you suppose she goes to embassy balls in riding-clothes, and what on earth does she do about hair? It couldn't have grown so soon; she must wear a wig. Isn't our class turning out some hilarious surprises?

The mail arrives. Excuse me while I read a nice fat letter from Washington.

Not so nice; quite impertinent. Gordon can't get over the idea that it is a joke, S. McB. in conjunction with one hundred and thirteen orphans. But he wouldn't think it such a joke if he could try it for a few days. He says he is going to drop off here on his next trip North and watch the struggle. How would it be if I left him in charge while I dashed to New York to accomplish some shopping? Our sheets are all worn out, and we haven't more than two hundred and eleven blankets in the house.

Singapore, sole puppy of my heart and home, sends his respectful love.

I also,

S. McB.

THE JOHN GRIER HOME,
Friday.

My dearest Judy:

You should see what your hundred dollars and Betsy Kindred did to that dining-room!

It's a dazzling dream of yellow paint. Being a north room, she thought to brighten it; and she has. The walls are kalsomined buff, with a frieze of little molly cottontails skurrying around the top. All of the woodwork—tables and benches included—is a cheerful chrome yellow. Instead of table-cloths, which we can't afford, we have linen runners, with stenciled rabbits hopping along their length. Also yellow bowls, filled at present with pussy-willows, but looking forward to dandelions and cowslips and buttercups. And new dishes, my dear—white, with yellow jonquils (we think), though they may be roses; there is no botany expert in the house. Most wonderful touch of all, we have *napkins,* the first we have seen in our whole lives. The children thought they were handkerchiefs, and ecstatically wiped their noses.

To honor the opening of the new room, we had ice-cream and cake for dessert. It is such a pleasure to see these children anything but cowed and apathetic, that I am offering prizes for boisterousness—to every one but Sadie Kate. She drummed on the table with her knife and fork and sang, "Welcome to dem golden halls."

You remember that illuminated text over the dining-room door—"The Lord Will Provide." We've painted it out, and covered the spot with rabbits. It's all very well to teach so easy a belief to normal children, who have a proper family and roof behind them; but a person whose only refuge in distress will be a park bench must learn a more militant creed than that.

"The Lord has given you two hands and a brain and a big world to use them in. Use them well, and you will be provided for; use them ill, and you will want," is our motto, and that with reservations.

Betsey and five
husky Orphans decorate
the dining-room

In the sorting process that has been going on I have got rid of eleven children. That blessed State Charities Aid Association helped me dispose of three little girls, all placed in very nice homes, and one to be adopted legally if the family likes her. And the family will like her; I saw to that. She was the prize child of the institution, obedient and polite, with curly hair and affectionate ways, exactly the little girl that every family needs. When a couple of adopting parents are choosing a daughter, I stand by with my heart in my mouth, feeling as though I were assisting in the inscrutable designs of Fate. Such a little thing turns the balance! The child smiles, and a loving home is hers for life; she sneezes, and it passes her by forever.

Three of our biggest boys have gone to work on farms, one of them out West to a RANCH! Report has it that he is to become a cow-boy and Indian fighter and grizzly-bear hunter, though I believe in reality he is to engage in the pastoral work of harvesting wheat. He marched off, a hero of romance, followed by the wistful eyes of twenty-five adventurous lads, who turned back with a sigh to the safely monotonous life of the J. G. H.

Five other children have been sent to their proper institutions. One of them is deaf, one an epileptic, and the other three approaching idiocy. None of them ought ever to have been accepted here. This is an educational institution, and we can't waste our valuable plant in caring for defectives.

Orphan-asylums have gone out of style. What I am going to develop is a boarding-school for the physical, moral, and mental growth of children whose parents have not been able to provide for their care.

"Orphans" is merely my generic term for the children; a good many of them are not orphans in the least. They have one troublesome and tenacious parent left who won't sign a surrender, so I can't place them out for adoption. But those that are available would be far better off in loving foster-homes than in the best institution that I can ever make. So I am fitting them for adoption as quickly as possible, and searching for the homes.

You ought to run across a lot of pleasant families in your travels; can't you bully some of them into adopting children? Boys by preference. We've got an awful lot of extra boys, and

nobody wants them. Talk about anti-feminism! It's nothing to the anti-masculism that exists in the breasts of adopting parents. I could place out a thousand dimpled little girls with yellow hair, but a good live boy from nine to thirteen is a drug on the market. There seems to be a general feeling that they track in dirt and scratch up mahogany furniture.

Shouldn't you think that men's clubs might like to adopt boys, as a sort of mascot? The boy could be boarded in a nice respectable family, and drawn out by the different members on Saturday afternoons. They could take him to ball-games and the circus, and then return him when they had had enough, just as you do with a library book. It would be very valuable training for bachelors. People are forever talking about the desirability of training girls for motherhood. Why not institute a course of training in fatherhood, and get the best men's clubs to take it up? Will you please have Jervis agitate the matter at his various clubs, and I'll have Gordon start the idea in Washington. They both belong to such a lot of clubs that we ought to dispose of at least a dozen boys.

> I remain,
>
> The ever-distracted mother of 113.
>
> S. McB.

THE JOHN GRIER HOME,
March 18.

Dear Judy:

I have been having a pleasant respite from the 113 cares of motherhood.

Yesterday who should drop down upon our peaceful village but Mr. Gordon Hallock, on his way back to Washington to resume the cares of the nation. At least he said it was on his way, but I notice from the map in the primary room that it was one hundred miles out of his way.

And dear, but I was glad to see him! He is the first glimpse of the outside world I have had since I was incarcerated in this asylum. And such a lot of entertaining businesses he had to talk about! He knows the inside of all of the outside things you read in the newspapers; so far as I can make out, he is the social center about which Washington revolves. I always knew he would get on in politics, for he has a way with him; there's no doubt about it.

You can't imagine how exhilarated and set-up I feel, as though I'd come into my own again after a period of social ostracism. I must confess that I get lonely for some one who talks my kind of nonsensical talk. Betsy trots off home every weekend, and the doctor is conversational enough, but, oh, so horribly logical! Gordon somehow seems to stand for the life I belong to,—of country clubs and motors and dancing and sport and politeness,—a poor, foolish, silly life, if you will, but mine own. And I have missed it. This serving-society business is theoretically admirable and compelling and interesting, but deadly stupid in its working details. I am afraid I was never born to set the crooked straight.

I tried to show Gordon about and make him take an interest
in the babies, but he wouldn't glance at them. He thinks I came
just to spite him, which, of course, I did. Your siren call would
never have lured me from the path of frivolity had Gordon not
been so unpleasantly hilarious at the idea of my being able to
manage an orphan-asylum. I came here to show him that I
could; and now, when I *can* show him, the beast refuses to
look.

I invited him to dinner, with a warning about the pressed
veal; but he said no, thanks, that I needed a change. So we went
to Brantwood Inn and had broiled lobster. I had positively forgotten that the creatures were edible.

This morning at seven o'clock I was wakened by the furious
ringing of the telephone bell. It was Gordon at the station, about
to resume his journey to Washington. He was in quite a contrite mood about the asylum, and apologized largely for refusing to look at my children. It was not that he didn't like orphans,
he said; it was just that he didn't like them in juxtaposition to
me. And to prove his good intentions, he would send them a bag
of peanuts.

I feel as fresh and revivified after my little fling as though I'd
had a real vacation. There's no doubt about it, an hour or so of
exciting talk is more of a tonic to me than a pint of iron and
strychnine pills.

You owe me two letters, dear Madam. Pay them *tout de
suite*, or I lay down my pen forever.

Yours, as usual,

S. McB.

Tuesday, 5 P.M.

My dear Enemy:

I am told that during my absence this afternoon you paid us
a call and dug up a scandal. You claim that the children under
Miss Snaith are not receiving their due in the matter of cod-liver
oil.

I am sorry if your medicinal orders have not been carried

out, but you must know that it is a difficult matter to introduce
that abominably smelling stuff into the inside of a squirming
child. And poor Miss Snaith is a very much overworked person. She has ten more children to care for than should rightly
fall to the lot of any single woman, and until we find her another assistant, she has very little time for the fancy touches you
demand.

Also, my dear Enemy, she is very susceptible to abuse. When
you feel in a fighting mood, I wish you would expend your bel-
ligerence upon me. I don't mind it; quite the contrary. But that
poor lady has retired to her room in a state of hysterics, leaving
nine babies to be tucked into bed by whomever it may concern.

If you have any powders that would be settling to her nerves,
please send them back by Sadie Kate.

Yours truly,

S. McBRIDE.

Wednesday morning.

Dear Dr. MacRae:

I am not taking an unintelligent stand in the least; I am simply asking that you come to me with all complaints, and not stir
up my staff in any such volcanic fashion as that of yesterday.

I endeavor to carry out all of your orders—of a medical
nature—with scrupulous care. In the present case there seems
to have been some negligence; I don't know what did become
of those fourteen unadministered bottles of cod-liver oil that
you have made such a fuss about, but I shall investigate.

And I cannot, for various reasons, pack off Miss Snaith in
the summary fashion you demand. She may be, in certain respects, inefficient; but she is kind to the children, and with supervision will answer temporarily.

Yours truly,

S. McBRIDE.

Thursday.

Dear Enemy:

Soyez tranquille.[12] I have issued orders, and in the future the children shall receive all of the cod-liver oil that by rights is theirs. A wilfu' man maun hae his way.

S. McB.

March 22.

Dear Judy:

Asylum life has looked up a trifle during the past few days— since the great Cod-Liver Oil War has been raging. The first skirmish occurred on Tuesday, and I unfortunately missed it, having accompanied four of my children on a shopping trip to the village. I returned to find the asylum teeming with hysterics. Our explosive doctor had paid us a visit.

Sandy has two passions in life: one is for cod-liver oil and the other for spinach, neither popular in our nursery. Some time ago—before I came, in fact—he had ordered cod-liver oil for all of the { ænemic / aneamic }—Heavens! there's that word again!—children, and had given instructions as to its application to Miss Snaith. Yesterday, in his suspicious Scotch fashion, he began nosing about to find out why the poor little rats weren't fattening up as fast as he thought they ought, and he unearthed a hideous scandal. They haven't received a whiff of cod-liver oil for three whole weeks! At that point he exploded, and all was joy and excitement and hysterics.

Betsy says that she had to send Sadie Kate to the laundry on an improvised errand, as his language was not fit for orphan ears. By the time I got home he had gone, and Miss Snaith had retired, weeping, to her room, and the whereabouts of fourteen bottles of cod-liver oil was still unexplained. He had accused her at the top of his voice of taking them herself. Imagine Miss Snaith,—she who looks so innocent and chinless and inoffensive—stealing cod-liver oil from these poor helpless little orphans and guzzling it in private!

Her defense consisted in hysterical assertions that she loved the children, and had done her duty as she saw it. She did not believe in giving medicine to babies; she thought drugs bad for their poor little stomachs. You can imagine Sandy! Oh, dear! oh, dear! To think I missed it!

Well, the tempest raged for three days, and Sadie Kate nearly ran her little legs off carrying peppery messages back and forth between us and the doctor. It is only under stress that I communicate with him by telephone, as he has an interfering old termagant of a housekeeper who "listens in" on the down-stairs switch; I don't wish the scandalous secrets of the John Grier spread abroad. The doctor demanded Miss Snaith's instant dismissal, and I refused. Of course she is a vague, unfocused, inefficient old thing, but she does love the children, and with proper supervision is fairly useful.

At least, in the light of her exalted family connections, I can't pack her off in disgrace like a drunken cook. I am hoping in time to eliminate her by a process of delicate suggestion; perhaps I can make her feel that her health requires a winter in

California. And also, no matter what the doctor wants, so positive and dictatorial is his manner that just out of self-respect one must take the other side. When he states that the world is round, I instantly assert it to be triangular.

Finally, after three pleasantly exhilarating days, the whole business settled itself. An apology (a very dilute one) was extracted from him for being so unkind to the poor lady, and full confession, with promises for the future, was drawn from her. It seems that she couldn't bear to make the little dears take the stuff, but, for obvious reasons, she couldn't bear to cross Dr. MacRae, so she hid the last fourteen bottles in a dark corner of the cellar. Just how she was planning to dispose of her loot I don't know. Can you pawn cod-liver oil?

Later.

Peace negotiations had just ended this afternoon, and Sandy had made a dignified exit, when the Hon. Cyrus Wykoff was announced. Two enemies in the course of an hour are really too much!

The Hon. Cy was awfully impressed with the new dining-room, especially when he heard that Betsy had put on those rabbits with her own lily-white hands. Stenciling rabbits on walls, he allows, is a fitting pursuit for a woman, but an executive position like mine is a trifle out of her sphere. He thinks it would be far wiser if Mr. Pendleton did not give me such free scope in the spending of his money.

While we were still contemplating Betsy's mural flight, an awful crash came from the pantry, and we found Gladiola Murphy weeping among the ruins of five yellow plates. It is sufficiently shattering to my nerves to hear these crashes when I am alone, but it is peculiarly shattering when receiving a call from an unsympathetic trustee.

I shall cherish that set of dishes to the best of my ability, but if you wish to see your gift in all its uncracked beauty, I should advise you to hurry North, and visit the John Grier Home without delay.

Yours as ever,
SALLIE.

March 26.

My dear Judy:

I have just been holding an interview with a woman who wants to take a baby home to surprise her husband. I had a hard time convincing her that, since he is to support the child, it might be a delicate attention to consult him about its adoption. She argued stubbornly that it was none of his business, seeing that the onerous work of washing and dressing and training would fall upon her. I am really beginning to feel sorry for men. Some of them seem to have very few rights.

Even our pugnacious doctor I suspect of being a victim of domestic tyranny, and his housekeeper's at that. It is scandalous the way Maggie McGurk neglects the poor man. I have had to put him in charge of an orphan. Sadie Kate, with a very housewifely air, is this moment sitting cross-legged on the hearth rug sewing buttons on his overcoat while he is upstairs tending babies.

You would never believe it, but Sandy and I are growing quite confidential in a dour Scotch fashion. It has become his habit, when homeward bound after his professional calls, to chug up to our door about four in the afternoon, and make the rounds of the house to make sure that we are not developing cholera morbus or infanticide or anything catching, and then present himself at four-thirty at my library door to talk over our mutual problems.

Does he come to see me? Oh, no, indeed; he comes to get tea and toast and marmalade. The man hath a lean and hungry look. His housekeeper doesn't feed him enough. As soon as I get the upper hand of him a little more, I am going to urge him on to revolt.

Meanwhile he is very grateful for something to eat, but oh, so funny in his attempts at social grace! At first he would hold a cup of tea in one hand, a plate of muffins in the other, and then search blankly for a third hand to eat them with. Now he has solved the problem. He turns in his toes and brings his knees together; then he folds his napkin into a long, narrow wedge that fills the crack between them, thus forming a very workable pseudo-lap; after that he sits with tense muscles until the tea is drunk. I suppose I ought to provide a table, but the spectacle of Sandy with his toes turned in is the one gleam of amusement that my day affords.

The postman is just driving in with, I trust, a letter from you. Letters make a very interesting break in the monotony of asylum life. If you wish to keep this superintendent contented, you'd better write often.

· · · · ·

Mail received and contents noted.

Kindly convey my thanks to Jervis for three alligators in a swamp. He shows rare artistic taste in the selection of his postcards. Your seven-page illustrated letter from Miami arrives at the same time. I should have known Jervis from the palm-tree perfectly, even without the label, as the tree has so much the more hair of the two. Also, I have a polite bread-and-butter letter from my nice young man in Washington, and a book from him, likewise a box of candy. The bag of peanuts for the kiddies he has shipped by express. Did you ever know such assiduity?

Jimmie favors me with the news that he is coming to visit me as soon as father can spare him from the factory. The poor boy does hate that factory so! It isn't that he is lazy; he just simply isn't interested in overalls. But father can't understand such a lack of taste. Having built up the factory, he of course has developed a passion for overalls, which should have been inherited by his eldest son. I find it awfully convenient to have been born a daughter; I am not asked to like overalls, but am left free to follow any morbid career I may choose, such as this.

To return to my mail: There arrives an advertisement from a wholesale grocer, saying that he has exceptionally economical brands of oatmeal, rice, flour, prunes, and dried apples that he packs specially for prisons and charitable institutions. Sounds nutritious, doesn't it?

I also have letters from a couple of farmers, each of whom would like to have a strong, husky boy of fourteen who is not afraid of work, their object being to give him a good home. These good homes appear with great frequency just as the spring

planting is coming on. When we investigated one of them last
week, the village minister, in answer to our usual question, "Does
he own any property?" replied in a very guarded manner, "I
think he must own a corkscrew."

You would hardly credit some of the homes that we have investigated. We found a very prosperous country family the other
day, who lived huddled together in three rooms in order to keep
the rest of their handsome house clean. The fourteen-year-old
girl they wished to adopt, by way of a cheap servant, was to
sleep in the same tiny room with their own three children. Their
kitchen-dining-parlor apartment was more cluttered up and unaired than any city tenement I ever saw, and the thermometer at
eighty-four. One could scarcely say they were *living* there; they
were rather *cooking*. You may be sure they got no girl from us!

I have made one invariable rule—every other is flexible. No
child is to be placed out unless the proposed family can offer
better advantages than we can give. I mean than we are going
to be able to give in the course of a few months, when we get
ourselves made over into a model institution. I shall have to
confess that at present we are still pretty bad.

But anyway, I am very *choosey* in regard to homes, and I re-
ject three-fourths of those that offer.

                                                              Later.

Gordon has made honorable amends to my children. His bag
of peanuts is here, made of burlap and three feet high.

Do you remember the dessert of peanuts and maple sugar
they used to give us at college? We turned up our noses, but ate.
I am instituting it here, and I assure you we don't turn up our
noses. It is a pleasure to feed children who have graduated
from a course of Mrs. Lippett; they are pathetically grateful for
small blessings.

You can't complain that this letter is too short.

                              Yours,
                                   On the verge of writer's cramp,
                                          S. McB.

Dear Judy:

You will be interested to hear that I have encountered another enemy—the doctor's housekeeper. I had talked to the creature several times over the telephone, and had noted that her voice was not distinguished by the soft, low accents that mark the caste of "Vere de Vere";[13] but now I have seen her. This morning, while returning from the village, I made a slight detour, and passed our doctor's house. Sandy is evidently the result of environment—olive green, with a mansard roof and the shades pulled down. You would think he had just been holding a funeral. I don't wonder that the amenities of life have somewhat escaped the poor man. After studying the outside of his house, I was filled with curiosity to see if the inside matched.

Having sneezed five times before breakfast this morning, I decided to go in and consult him professionally. To be sure, he is a children's specialist, but sneezes are common to all ages. So I boldly marched up the steps and rang the bell.

Hark! What sound is that that breaks upon our revelry? The

Hon. Cy's voice, as I live, approaching up the stairs. I've letters
to write, and I can't be tormented by his blether, so I am rushing Jane to the door with orders to look him firmly in the eye
and tell him I am out.

*   *   *   *   *   *   *   *

On with the dance! Let joy be unconfined. He's gone.

But those eight stars represent eight agonizing minutes spent
in the dark of my library closet. The Hon. Cy received Jane's
communication with the affable statement that he would sit
down and wait. Whereupon he entered and sat. But did Jane
leave me to languish in the closet? No; she enticed him to the
nursery to see the *awful* thing that Sadie Kate had done. The
Hon. Cy loves to see awful things, particularly when done by
Sadie Kate. I haven't an idea what scandal Jane is about to dis-
close; but no matter, he has gone.

Where was I? Oh, yes; I had rung the doctor's bell.

The door was opened by a large, husky person with her
sleeves rolled up. She looked very businesslike, with a hawk's
nose and cold gray eyes.

"Well?" said she, her tone implying that I was a vacuum-
cleaning agent.

"Good morning." I smiled affably, and stepped inside. "Is
this Mrs. McGurk?"

"It is," said she. "An' ye'll be the new young woman in the
orphan-asylum?"

"I am that," said I. "Is himself at home?"

"He is not," said she.

"But this is his office hour."

"He don't keep it regular'."

"He ought," said I, sternly. "Kindly tell him that Miss McBride
called to consult him, and ask him to look in at the John Grier
Home this afternoon."

"Ump'!" grunted Mrs. McGurk, and closed the door so
promptly that she shut in the hem of my skirt.

When I told the doctor this afternoon, he shrugged his shoulders, and observed that that was Maggie's gracious way.

"And why do you put up with Maggie?" said I.

"And where would I find any one better?" said he. "Doing

the work for a lone man who comes as irregularly to meals as
a twenty-four-hour day will permit is no sinecure. She furnishes
little sunshine in the home, but she does manage to produce a
hot dinner at nine o'clock at night."

Just the same, I am willing to wager that her hot dinners are
neither delicious nor well served. She's an inefficient, lazy old
termagant, and I know why she doesn't like me. She imagines
that I want to steal away the doctor and oust her from a comfortable position, something of a joke, considering. But I am
not undeceiving her; it will do the old thing good to worry a little. She may cook him better dinners, and fatten him a trifle. I
understand that fat men are good-natured.

Ten o'clock.

I don't know what silly stuff I have been writing to you
off and on all day, between interruptions. It has got to be
night at last, and I am too tired to do so much as hold up my
head. Your song tells the sad truth, "There is no joy in life but
sleep."

I bid you good night.

S. McB.

Isn't the English language absurd? Look at those forty mono-
syllables in a row!

J. G. H.
April 1.

Dear Judy:

I have placed out Isador Gutschneider. His new mother is a Swedish woman, fat and smiling, with blue eyes and yellow hair. She chose him out of the whole nurseryful of children because he was the brunettest baby there. She has always loved brunettes, but in her most ambitious dreams has never hoped to have one of her own. His name is going to be changed to Oscar Carlson, after his new dead uncle.

My first trustees' meeting is to occur next Wednesday. I confess that I am not looking forward to it with impatience—especially as an inaugural address by me will be its chief feature. I wish our president were here to back me up! But at least I am sure of one thing. I am never going to adopt the Uriah Heepish[14] attitude toward trustees that characterized Mrs. Lippett's manners. I shall treat "first Wednesdays" as a pleasant social diversion, my day at home, when the friends of the asylum gather for discussion and relaxation; and I shall endeavor not to let our pleasures discommode the orphans. You see how I have taken to heart the unhappy experiences of that little Jerusha.

Your last letter has arrived, and no suggestion in it of traveling North. Isn't it about time that you were turning your faces back toward Fifth Avenue? Hame is hame, be 't ever sae hamely. Don't you marvel at the Scotch that flows so readily from my pen? Since being acquent' wi' Sandy, I hae gathered a muckle new vocabulary.

The dinner gong! I leave you, to devote a revivifying half-hour to mutton hash. We eat to live in the John Grier Home.

Six o'clock.

The Hon. Cy has been calling again; he drops in with great frequency, hoping to catch me *in delictu*. How I do not like that man! He is a pink, fat, puffy old thing, with a pink, fat, puffy soul.

I was in a very cheery, optimistic frame of mind before his arrival, but now I shall do nothing but grumble for the rest of the day.

He deplores all of the useless innovations that I am endeavoring to introduce, such as a cheerful playroom, prettier clothes, baths, and better food and fresh air and play and fun and ice-cream and kisses. He says that I will unfit these children to occupy the position in life that God has called them to occupy.

At that my Irish blood came to the surface, and I told him that if God had planned to make all of these 113 little children into useless, ignorant, unhappy citizens, I was going to fool God! That we weren't educating them out of their class in the least. We were educating them *into* their natural class much more effectually than is done in the average family. We weren't trying to force them into college if they hadn't any brains, as happens with rich men's sons; and we weren't putting them to work at fourteen if they were naturally ambitious, as happens with poor men's sons. We were watching them closely and individually and discovering their level. If our children showed an aptitude to become farm laborers and nurse-maids, we were going to teach them to be the best possible farm laborers and nurse-maids; and if they showed a tendency to become lawyers, we would turn them into honest, intelligent, open-minded lawyers. (He's a lawyer himself, but certainly not an open-minded one.)

He grunted when I had finished my remarks, and stirred his tea vigorously. Whereupon I suggested that perhaps he needed another lump of sugar, and dropped it in, and left him to absorb it.

The only way to deal with trustees is with a firm and steady hand. You have to keep them in their places.

Oh, my dear! that smudge in the corner was caused by Singapore's black tongue. He is trying to send you an affectionate kiss. Poor Sing thinks he's a lap dog—isn't it a tragedy when people mistake their vocations? I myself am not always certain that I was born an orphan asylum superintendent.

Yours, til deth,

S. McB.

SUPERINTENDENT'S OFFICE,
JOHN GRIER HOME,
April 4.

THE PENDLETON FAMILY,
PALM BEACH, FLORIDA.

Dear Sir and Madam:

I have weathered my first visitors' day, and made the trustees
a beautiful speech. Everybody said it was a beautiful speech—
even my enemies.

Mr. Gordon Hallock's recent visit was exceptionally oppor-
tune; I gleaned from him many suggestions as to how to carry
an audience.

"Be funny."—I told about Sadie Kate and a few other cherubs
that you don't know.

"Keep it concrete and fitted to the intelligence of your audience."—I watched the Hon. Cy, and never said a thing that he
couldn't understand.

"Flatter your hearers."—I hinted delicately that all of these
new reforms were due to the wisdom and initiative of our peer-
less trustees.

"Give it a high moral tone, with a dash of pathos."—I
dwelt upon the parentless condition of these little wards of
Society. And it was very affecting—my enemy wiped away a
tear!

Then I fed them up on chocolate and whipped cream and
lemonade and tartar sandwiches, and sent them home, expansive and beaming, but without any appetite for dinner.

I dwell thus at length upon our triumph, in order to create in
you a happy frame of mind, before passing to the hideous
calamity that so nearly wrecked the occasion.

> "Now follows the dim horror of my tale,
> And I feel I'm growing gradually pale,
>   For, even at this day,

> Though its smell has passed away,
> When I venture to remember it, I quail!"[15]

You never heard of our little Tammas Kehoe, did you? I simply haven't featured Tammas because he requires so much ink and time and vocabulary. He's a spirited lad, and he follows his dad, a mighty hunter of old—that sounds like more *Bab Ballads,* but it isn't; I made it up as I went along.

We can't break Tammas of his inherited predatory instincts. He shoots the chickens with bows and arrows and lassoes the pigs and plays bull-fight with the cows—and oh, is very destructive! But his crowning villainy occurred an hour before the trustees' meeting, when we wanted to be so clean and sweet and engaging.

It seems that he had stolen the rat-trap from the oat-bin, and had set it up in the wood lot, and yesterday was so fortunate as to catch a fine big skunk.

Singapore was the first to report the discovery. He returned to the house and rolled on the rugs in a frenzy of remorse over his part of the business. While our attention was occupied with Sing, Tammas was busily skinning his prey in the seclusion of the wood-shed. He buttoned the pelt inside his jacket, conveyed it by a devious route through the length of this building, and concealed it under his bed where he thought it wouldn't be found. Then he went—per schedule—to the basement to help freeze the ice-cream for our guests. You notice that we omitted ice-cream from the menu.

In the short time that remained we created all the counter-irritation that was possible. Noah (negro furnace man) started smudge fires at intervals about the grounds. Cook waved a shovelful of burning coffee through the house. Betsy sprinkled the corridors with ammonia. Miss Snaith daintily treated the rugs with violet water. I sent an emergency call to the doctor, who came and mixed a gigantic solution of chlorid of lime. But still, above and beneath and through every other odor, the unlaid ghost of Tammas's victim cried for vengeance.

The first business that came up at the meeting, was whether we should dig a hole and bury, not only Tammas, but the whole main building. You can see with what finesse I carried off the shocking event, when I tell you that the Hon. Cy went home chuckling over a funny story, instead of grumbling at the new superintendent's inability to manage boys.

We've our ain bit weird to dree!

As ever,
S. McBride.

The John Grier Home,
Friday, likewise Saturday.

Dear Judy:

Singapore is still living in the carriage house, and receiving a daily carbolic-scented bath from Tammas Kehoe. I am hoping that some day, in the distant future, my darling will be fit to return.

You will be pleased to hear that I have instituted a new method of spending your money. We are henceforth to buy a part of our shoes and dry-goods and drug-store comestibles from local shops, at not quite such low prices as the wholesale jobbers give, but still at a discount, and the education that is being thrown in is worth the difference. The reason is this: I have made the discovery that half of my children know nothing of money or its purchasing power. They think that shoes and corn-meal and red-flannel petticoats and mutton stew and gingham shirts just float down from the blue sky.

Last week I dropped a new green dollar bill out of my purse, and an eight-year-old urchin picked it up and asked if he could keep that picture of a bird. (American eagle in the center.) That child had never seen a bill in his life! I began an investigation, and discovered that dozens of children in this asylum have never bought anything or have ever seen anybody buy anything. And we are planning to turn them out at sixteen into a world governed entirely by the purchasing power of dollars and cents! Good heavens! just think of it! They are not to lead sheltered lives with somebody eternally looking after them; they have got to know how to get the very most they can out of every penny they can manage to earn.

I pondered the question all one night, at intervals, and went to the village at nine o'clock the next morning. I held conferences with seven storekeepers; found four open-minded and helpful, two doubtful, and one actively stupid. I have started with the four—dry-goods, groceries, shoes, and stationery. In return for somewhat large orders from us, they are to turn themselves and their clerks into teachers for my children, who are to go to the stores, inspect the stocks, and do their own purchasing with real money.

For example, Jane needs a spool of blue sewing-silk and a yard of elastic; so two little girls, intrusted with a silver quarter, trot hand in hand to Mr. Meeker's. They match the silk with anxious care, and watch the clerk jealously while he measures the elastic, to make sure that he doesn't stretch it. Then they bring back six cents change, receive my thanks and praise, and retire to the ranks tingling with a sense of achievement.

Isn't it pathetic? Ordinary children of ten or twelve automatically know so many things that our little incubator chicks have never dreamed of. But I have a variety of plans on foot. Just give me time, and you will see. One of these days I'll be turning out some nearly normal youngsters.

Later.

I've an empty evening ahead, so I'll settle to some further gossip with you.

You remember the peanuts that Gordon Hallock sent? Well, I was so gracious when I thanked him that it incited him to fresh effort. He apparently went into a toy shop, and placed himself unreservedly in the hands of an enterprising clerk. Yesterday two husky expressmen deposited in our front hall a crate full of expensive furry animals built to be consumed by the children of the rich. They are not exactly what I should have purchased had I been the one to disburse such a fortune, but my babies find them very huggable. The chicks are now taking to bed with them lions and elephants and bears and giraffes. I don't know what the psychological effect will be. Do you suppose when they grow up they will all join the circus?

Oh, dear me, here is Miss Snaith, coming to pay a social call. Good-by.

S.

P.S. The prodigal has returned. He sends his respectful regards, and three wags of the tail.

THE JOHN GRIER HOME,
April 7.

My dear Judy:

I have just been reading a pamphlet on manual training for girls, and another on the proper diet for institutions—right proportions of proteids, fats, starches, etc. In these days of scientific charity, when every problem has been tabulated, you can run an institution by chart. I don't see how Mrs. Lippett could have made all the mistakes she did, assuming, of course, that she knew how to read. But there is one quite important branch of institutional work that has not been touched upon, and I myself am gathering data. Some day I shall issue a pamphlet on the "Management and Control of Trustees."

I must tell you the joke about my enemy—not the Hon. Cy, but my first, my original enemy. He has undertaken a new field of endeavor. He says quite soberly (everything he does is sober; he has never smiled yet) that he has been watching me closely since my arrival, and though I am untrained and foolish and flippant (sic), he doesn't think that I am really so superficial as I at first appeared. I have an almost masculine ability of grasping the whole of a question and going straight to the point.

Aren't men funny? When they want to pay you the greatest compliment in their power, they naïvely tell you that you have a masculine mind. There is one compliment, incidentally, that I shall never be paying him. I cannot honestly say that he has a quickness of perception almost feminine.

So, though Sandy quite plainly sees my faults, still, he thinks that some of them may be corrected; and he has determined to carry on my education from the point where the college dropped it. A person in my position ought to be well read in physiology, biology, psychology, sociology, and eugenics; she should know the hereditary effects of insanity, idiocy, and alcohol; should be able to administer the Binet test;[16] and should understand the nervous system of a frog. In pursuance whereof, he has placed at my disposal his own scientific library of four thousand volumes. He not only fetches in the books he wants me to read, but comes and asks questions to make sure I haven't skipped.

We devoted last week to the life and letters of the Jukes family.[17] Margaret, the mother of criminals, six generations ago, founded a prolific line, and her progeny, mostly in jail, now numbers some twelve hundred. Moral: watch the children with a bad heredity so carefully that none of them can ever have any excuse for growing up into Jukeses.

So now, as soon as we have finished our tea, Sandy and I get out the Doomsday Book, and pore over its pages in an anxious search for alcoholic parents. It's a cheerful little game to while away the twilight hour after the day's work is done.

Quelle vie! Come home fast and take me out of it. I'm wearying for the sight of you.

SALLIE.

J. G. H.,
Thursday morning.

My dear Pendleton Family:

I have received your letter, and I seize my pen to stop you. I don't wish to be relieved. I take it back. I change my mind. The person you are planning to send sounds like an exact twin of Miss Snaith. How can you ask me to turn over my darling children to a kind, but ineffectual, middle-aged lady without any chin? The very thought of it wrings a mother's heart.

Do you imagine that such a woman can carry on this work even temporarily? No! The manager of an institution like this has got to be young and husky and energetic and forceful and efficient and red-haired and sweet-tempered, like me. Of course I've been discontented—anybody would be with things in such a mess,—but it's what you socialists call a holy discontent. And do you think that I am going to abandon all of the beautiful reforms I have so painstakingly started? No! I am not to be moved from this spot until you find a superintendent superior to Sallie McBride.

That does not mean, though, that I am mortgaging myself forever. Just for the present, until things get on their feet. While the face-washing, airing, reconstructing period lasts, I honestly believe you chose the right person when you hit upon me. I *love* to plan improvements and order people about.

This is an awfully messy letter, but I'm dashing it off in three minutes in order to catch you before you definitely engage that pleasant, inefficient middle-aged person without a chin.

Please, kind lady and gentleman, don't do me out of me job! Let me stay a few months longer. Just gimme a chance to show what I'm good for, and I promise you won't never regret it.

S. McB.

                                                    J. G. H.,
                                        Thursday afternoon.

Dear Judy:

I've composed a poem—a pæan of victory.

                    Robin MacRae
                    Smiled to-day.

It's the truth!

                                                    S. McB.

THE JOHN GRIER HOME,
April 13.

Dear Judy:

I am gratified to learn that you were gratified to learn that I am going to stay. I hadn't realized it, but I am really getting sort of attached to orphans.

It's an awful disappointment that Jervis has business which will keep you South so much longer. I am bursting with talk, and it is such a laborious nuisance having to write everything I want to say.

Of course I am glad that we are to have the building remodeled, and I think all of your ideas good, but I have a few extra good ones myself. It will be nice to have the new gymnasium and sleeping-porches, but, oh, my soul does long for cottages! The more I look into the internal workings of an orphan-asylum, the more I realize that the only type of asylum that can compete with a private family is one on the cottage system. So long as the family is the unit of society, children should be hardened early to family life.

The problem that is keeping me awake at present is, What to do with the children while we are being made over? It is hard to live in a house and build it at the same time. How would it be if I rented a circus tent and pitched it on the lawn?

Also, when we plunge into our alterations, I want a few guest-rooms where our children can come back when ill or out of work. The great secret of our lasting influence in their lives will be our watchful care afterward. What a terribly *alone* feeling it must give a person not to have a family hovering in the background! With all my dozens of aunts and uncles and mothers and fathers and cousins and brothers and sisters, I can't visualize it. I'd be terrified and panting if I didn't have lots of cover to run to. And for these forlorn little mites, somehow or other the John Grier Home must supply their need. So, dear people, send me half a dozen guest-rooms, if you please.

Good-by, and I'm glad you didn't put in the other woman.

The very suggestion of somebody else taking over my own beautiful reforms before they were even started, stirred up all the opposition in me. I'm afraid I'm like Sandy—I canna think aught is dune richt except my ain hand is in't.

Yours, for the present,
SALLIE McBRIDE.

THE JOHN GRIER HOME,
Sunday.

Dear Gordon:

I know that I haven't written lately; you have a perfect right to grumble, but oh dear! oh dear! you can't imagine what a busy person an orphan-asylum superintendent is. And all the writing energy I possess has to be expended upon that voracious Judy Abbott Pendleton. If three days go by without a letter, she telegraphs to know if the asylum has burned; whereas, if you—nice man—go letterless, you simply send us a present to remind us of your existence. So, you see, it's distinctly to our advantage to slight you often.

You will probably be annoyed when I tell you that I have promised to stay on here. They finally did find a woman to take my place, but she wasn't at all the right type and would have answered only temporarily. And, my dear Gordon, it's true, when I faced saying good-by to this feverish planning and activity, Worcester somehow looked rather colorless. I couldn't bear to let my asylum go unless I was sure of substituting a life packed equally full of sensation.

I know the alternative you will suggest, but please don't—just now. I told you before that I must have a few months longer to make up my mind. And in the meantime I like the feeling that I'm of use in the world. There's something constructive and optimistic about working with children; that is, if you look at it from my cheerful point of view, and not from our Scotch doctor's. I've never seen anybody like that man; he's always pessimistic and morbid and down. It's best not to be too intelligent about insanity and dipsomania and all the other hereditary details. I am just about ignorant enough to be light-hearted and effective in a place like this.

The thought of all these little lives expanding in every direction eternally thrills me; there are so many possibilities in our child garden for every kind of flower. It has been planted rather promiscuously, to be sure, but though we undoubtedly shall gather a number of weeds, we are also hoping for some rare and beautiful blossoms. Am I not growing sentimental? It is due to hunger—and there goes the dinner-gong! We are going to have a delicious meal: roast beef and creamed carrots and beet greens, with rhubarb pie for dessert. Would you not like to dine with me? I should love to have you.

Most cordially yours,

S. McB.

Skimmed Milk
is served in the
Woodshed at 12 o'clock

P.S. You should see the number of poor homeless cats that these children want to adopt. We had four when I came, and they have all had kittens since. I haven't taken an exact census, but I think the institution possesses nineteen.

April 15.

My dear Judy:

You'd like to make another slight donation to the J. G. H. out of the excess of last month's allowance? *Bene!* Will you kindly have the following inserted in all low-class metropolitan dailies:

NOTICE!

To Parents Planning to Abandon their Children:

Please do it before they have reached their third year.

I can't think of any action on the part of abandoning parents that would help us more effectually. This having to root up evil before you begin planting good is slow, discouraging work.

We have one child here who has almost floored me; but I *will not* acknowledge myself beaten by a child of five. He alternates between sullen moroseness, when he won't speak a word, and the most violent outbursts of temper, when he smashes everything within reach. He has been here only three months, and in that time he has destroyed nearly every piece of bric-à-brac in the institution—not, by the way, a great loss to art.

A month or so before I came he pulled the table-cloth from the officers' table while the girl in charge was in the corridor sounding the gong. The soup had already been served. You can imagine the mess! Mrs. Lippett half killed the child on that occasion, but the killing did nothing to lessen the temper, which was handed on to me intact.

His father was Italian and his mother Irish; he has red hair and freckles from County Cork and the most beautiful brown eyes that ever came out of Naples. After the father was stabbed in a fight and the mother had died of alcoholism, the poor little chap by some chance or other got to us; I suspect that he be-

longs in the Catholic Protectory. As for his manners—oh dear!
oh dear! They are what you would expect. He kicks and bites
and swears. I have dubbed him Punch.[18]

Yesterday he was brought squirming and howling to my office, charged with having knocked down a little girl and robbed
her of her doll. Miss Snaith plumped him into a chair behind
me, and left him to grow quiet, while I went on with my writing. I was suddenly startled by an awful crash. He had pushed
that big green jardinière off the window-sill and broken it into
five hundred pieces. I jumped with a suddenness that swept the
ink-bottle to the floor, and when Punch saw that second catas-
trophe, he stopped roaring with rage and threw back his head
and roared with laughter. The child is *diabolical.*

I have determined to try a new method of discipline that I
don't believe in the whole of his forlorn little life he has ever experienced. I am going to see what praise and encouragement
and love will do. So, instead of scolding him about the jardinière, I assumed that it was an accident. I kissed him and told
him not to feel bad; that I didn't mind in the least. It shocked
him into being quiet; he simply held his breath and stared while
I wiped away his tears and sopped up the ink.

The child just now is the biggest problem that the J. G. H. affords. He needs the most patient, loving, individual care—a
proper mother and father, likewise some brothers and sisters
and a grandmother. But I can't place him in a respectable family until I make over his language and his propensity to break
things. I separated him from the other children, and kept him
in my room all the morning, Jane having removed to safe
heights all destructible *objets d'art.* Fortunately, he loves to
draw, and he sat on a rug for two hours, and occupied himself
with colored pencils. He was so surprised when I showed an interest in a red-and-green ferry-boat, with a yellow flag floating
from the mast, that he became quite profanely affable. Until
then I couldn't get a word out of him.

In the afternoon Dr. MacRae dropped in and admired the
ferry-boat, while Punch swelled with the pride of creation.
Then, as a reward for being such a good little boy, the doctor
took him out in his automobile on a visit to a country patient.

Punch was restored to the fold at five o'clock by a sadder and

wiser doctor. At a sedate country estate he had stoned the chickens, smashed a cold frame, and swung the pet Angora cat by its
tail. Then when the sweet old lady tried to make him be kind to
poor pussy, he told her to go to hell.

Our little Punch
goes
visiting

I can't bear to consider what some of these children have
seen and experienced. It will take years of sunshine and happiness and love to eradicate the dreadful memories that they have
stored up in the far-back corners of their little brains. And there
are so many children and so few of us that we can't hug them
enough; we simply haven't arms or laps to go around.

Mais parlons d'autres choses![19] Those awful questions of
heredity and environment that the doctor broods over so constantly are getting into my blood, too; and it's a vicious habit.
If a person is to be of any use in a place like this, she must see
nothing but good in the world. Optimism is the only wear for
a social worker.

"'T is the middle of night by the castle clock"—do you know

where that beautiful line of poetry comes from? "Cristabel,"[20] of English K. Mercy! how I hated that course! You, being an English shark, liked it; but I never understood a word that was said from the time I entered the class-room till I left it. However, the remark with which I opened this paragraph is true. It *is* the middle of night by the mantel-piece clock, so I'll wish you pleasant dreams.

Addio!

SALLIE.

Tuesday.

Dear Enemy:

You doctored the whole house, then stalked past my library with your nose in the air, while I was waiting tea with a plate of Scotch scones sitting on the trivet, ordered expressly for you as a peace-offering.

If you really hurt, I will read the Kallikak book;[21] but I must tell you that you are working me to death. It takes almost all of my energy to be an effective superintendent, and this university-extension course that you are conducting I find wearing. You remember how indignant you were one day last week because I confessed to having stayed up until one o'clock the night before? Well, my dear man, if I were to accomplish all the vicarious reading you require, I should sit up until morning every night.

However, bring it in. I usually manage half an hour of recreation after dinner, and though I had wanted to glance at Wells's latest novel,[22] I will amuse myself instead with your feeble-minded family.

Life of late is unco steep.

Obligingly yours,

S. McB.

THE JOHN GRIER HOME,
April 17.

Dear Gordon:

Thank you for the tulips, likewise the lilies of the valley. They are most becoming to my blue Persian bowls.

Have you ever heard of the Kallikaks? Get the book and read them up. They are a two-branch family in New Jersey, I think, though their real name and origin is artfully concealed. But, anyway,—and this is true,—six generations ago a young gentleman, called for convenience Martin Kallikak, got drunk one night and temporarily eloped with a feeble-minded bar-maid, thus founding a long line of feeble-minded Kallikaks,—drunkards, gamblers, prostitutes, horse thieves—a scourge to New Jersey and surrounding States.

Martin later straightened up, married a normal woman, and founded a second line of proper Kallikaks,—judges, doctors, farmers, professors, politicians,—a credit to their country. And there the two branches still are, flourishing side by side. You can see what a blessing it would have been to New Jersey if something drastic had happened to that feeble-minded bar-maid in her infancy.

It seems that feeble-mindedness is a very hereditary quality, and science isn't able to overcome it. No operation has been discovered for introducing brains into the head of a child who didn't start with them. And the child grows up with, say, a nine-year brain in a thirty-year body, and becomes an easy tool for any criminal he meets. Our prisons are one-third full of feeble-minded convicts. Society ought to segregate them on feeble-minded farms, where they can earn their living in peaceful menial pursuits, and not have children. Then in a generation or so we might be able to wipe them out.

Did you know all that? It's very necessary information for a politician to have. Get the book and read it, please; I'd send my copy only that it's borrowed.

It's also very necessary information for me to have. There are eleven of these chicks that I suspect a bit, and I am *sure* of Loretta Higgins. I have been trying for a month to introduce one or two basic ideas into that child's brain, and now I know what the trouble is: her head is filled with a sort of soft cheesy substance instead of brain.

I came up here to make over this asylum in such little details as fresh air and food and clothes and sunshine, but, heavens! you can see what problems I am facing. I've got to make over society first, so that it won't send me sub-normal children to work with. Excuse all this excited conversation; but I've just met up with the subject of feeble-mindedness, and it's appalling—and interesting. It is your business as a legislator to make laws that will remove it from the world. Please attend to this immediately.

And oblige,
S. McBRIDE,
SUP'T JOHN GRIER HOME.

Friday.

Dear Man of Science:

You didn't come to-day. Please don't skip us tomorrow. I have finished the Kallikak family and I am bursting with talk. Don't you think we ought to have a psychologist examine these children? We owe it to adopting parents not to saddle them with feeble-minded offspring.

You know, I'm tempted to ask you to prescribe arsenic for Loretta's cold. I've diagnosed her case; she's a Kallikak. Is it right to let her grow up and found a line of 378 feeble-minded people for society to care for? Oh dear! I do hate to poison the child, but what can I do?

S. McB.

Dear Gordon:

You aren't interested in feeble-minded people, and you are shocked because I am? Well, I am equally shocked because you are not. If you aren't interested in everything of the sort that there unfortunately is in this world, how can you make wise laws? You can't.

However, at your request, I will converse upon a less morbid subject. I've just bought fifty yards of blue and rose and green and corn-colored hair-ribbon as an Easter present for my fifty little daughters. I am also thinking of sending you an Easter present. How would a nice fluffy little kitten please you? I can offer any of the following patterns:—

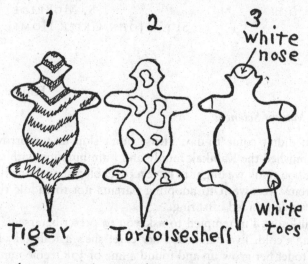

Number 3 comes in any color, gray, black, or yellow. If you will let me know which you would rather have, I will express it at once.

I would write a respectable letter, but it's tea-time and I see that a guest approaches.

Addio!

SALLIE.

P.S. Don't you know some one who would like to adopt a desirable baby boy with seventeen nice new teeth?

April 20.

My dear Judy:

One a penny, two a penny, hot cross buns! We've had a Good Friday present of ten dozen, given by Mrs. De Peyster Lambert, a high-church, stained-glass-window soul whom I met at a tea a few days ago. (Who says now that teas are a silly waste of time?) She asked me about my "precious little waifs," and said I was doing a noble work and would be rewarded. I saw buns in her eye, and sat down and talked to her for half an hour.

Now I shall go and thank her in person, and tell her with a great deal of affecting detail how much those buns were appreciated by my precious little waifs—omitting the account of how precious little Punch threw his bun at Miss Snaith and plastered her neatly in the eye. I think, with encouragement, Mrs. De Peyster Lambert can be developed into a cheerful giver.

Oh, I'm growing into the most shocking beggar! My family don't dare to visit me, because I demand *bakshish*[23] in such a brazen manner. I threatened to remove father from my calling-list unless he shipped immediately sixty-five pairs of overalls for my prospective gardeners. A notice from the freight office this morning asks me to remove two packing-cases consigned to them by the J. L. McBride Co. of Worcester; so I take it that father desires to continue my acquaintance. Jimmie hasn't sent us anything yet, and he's getting a huge salary. I write him frequently a pathetic list of our needs.

But Gordon Hallock has learned the way to a mother's heart. I was so pleasant about the peanuts and menagerie that now he sends a present of some sort every few days, and I spend my entire time composing thank-you letters that aren't exact copies of the ones I've sent before. Last week we received a dozen big scarlet balls. The nursery is *full* of them; you kick them before you as you walk. And yesterday there arrived a half-bushel of frogs and ducks and fishes to float in the bath-tubs.

Send, O best of trustees, the tubs in which to float them!

I am, as usual,

S. McBride.

                                                    Tuesday.

My dear Judy:

Spring must be lurking about somewhere; the birds are arriving from the South. Isn't it time you followed their example?

Society note from the *Bird o' Passage News:*
"Mr. and Mrs. First Robin have returned from a trip to Florida. It is hoped that Mr. and Mrs. Jervis Pendleton will arrive shortly."

Even up here in our dilatory Dutchess County the breeze smells green; it makes you want to be out and away, roaming the hills, or else down on your knees grubbing in the dirt. Isn't it funny what farmering instincts the budding spring awakens in even the most urban souls?

I have spent the morning making plans for little private gardens for every child over nine. The big potato-field is doomed. That is the only feasible spot for sixty-two private gardens. It is near enough to be watched from the north windows, and yet far enough away, so that their messing will not injure our highly prized landscape lawn. Also the earth is rich, and they have some chance of success. I don't want the poor little chicks to scratch all summer, and then not turn up any treasure in the

end. In order to furnish an incentive, I shall announce that the
institution will buy their produce and pay in real money, though
I foresee we shall be buried under a mountain of radishes.

I do so want to develop self-reliance and initiative in these
children, two sturdy qualities in which they are conspicuously
lacking (with the exception of Sadie Kate and a few other bad
ones). Children who have spirit enough to be bad I consider
very hopeful; it's those who are good just from inertia that are
discouraging.

The last few days have been spent mainly in charming the
devil out of Punch, an interesting task if I could devote my
whole time to it; but with one hundred and seven other little
devils to charm away, my attention is sorely deflected.

The awful thing about this life is that whatever I am doing,
the other things that I am not doing, but ought to be, keep tug-
ging at my skirts. There is no doubt but Punch's personal devil
needs the whole attention of a whole person,—preferably two
persons,—so that they could spell each other and get some rest.

Sadie Kate has just flown in from the nursery with news of a
scarlet gold-fish (Gordon's gift) swallowed by one of our babies.
Mercy! the number of calamities that can occur in an orphan-
asylum!

9 P.M.

My children are in bed, and I've just had a thought. Wouldn't
it be heavenly if the hibernating system prevailed among the human young? There would be some pleasure in running an asylum if one could just tuck the little darlings into bed the first of
October and keep them there until the twenty-second of April.

I'm yours, as ever,

SALLIE.

April 24.

Dear Jervis Pendleton, Esq.:

This is to supplement a night telegram which I sent you ten minutes ago. Fifty words not being enough to convey any idea of my emotions, I herewith add a thousand.

As you will know by the time you receive this, I have discharged the farmer, and he has refused to be discharged. Being twice the size of me, I can't lug him to the gate and chuck him out. He wants a notification from the president of the board of trustees written in vigorous language on official paper in typewriting. So, dear president of the board of trustees, kindly supply all of this at your earliest convenience.

Here follows the history of the case:

The winter season still being with us when I arrived and farming activities at a low ebb, I have heretofore paid little attention to Robert Sterry except to note on two occasions that his pig-pens needed cleaning; but to-day I sent for him to come and consult with me in regard to spring planting.

Sterry came, as requested, and seated himself at ease in my office with his hat upon his head. I suggested as tactfully as might be that he remove it, an entirely necessary request, as little orphan boys were in and out on errands, and "hats off in the house" is our first rule in masculine deportment.

Sterry complied with my request, and stiffened himself to be against whatever I might desire.

I proceeded to the subject in hand, namely, that the diet of the John Grier Home in the year to come is to consist less exclusively of potatoes. At which our farmer grunted in the manner of the Hon. Cyrus Wykoff, only it was a less ethereal and gentlemanly grunt than a trustee permits himself. I enumerated corn and beans and onions and peas and tomatoes and beets and carrots and turnips as desirable substitutes.

Sterry observed that if potatoes and cabbages was good enough for him, he guessed they was good enough for charity children.

I proceeded imperturbably to say that the two-acre potato-field was to be plowed and fertilized, and laid out into sixty individual gardens, the boys assisting in the work.

At that Sterry exploded. The two-acre field was the most fertile and valuable piece of earth on the whole place. He guessed if I was to break that up into play-gardens for the children to mess about in, I'd be hearing about it pretty danged quick from the board of trustees. That field was fitted for potatoes, it had always raised potatoes, and it was going to continue to raise them just as long as he had anything to say about it.

"You have nothing whatever to say about it," I amiably replied. "I have decided that the two-acre field is the best plot to use for the children's gardens, and you and the potatoes will have to give way."

Whereupon he rose in a storm of bucolic wrath, and said he'd be gol darned if he'd have a lot of these danged city brats interfering with his work.

I explained—very calmly for a red-haired person with Irish forebears—that this place was run for the exclusive benefit of these children; that the children were not here to be exploited for the benefit of the place, a philosophy which he did not grasp, though my fancy city language had a slightly dampening effect. I added that what I required in a farmer was the ability and patience to instruct the boys in gardening and simple out-door work; that I wished a man of large sympathies whose ex-ample would be an inspiring influence to these children of the city streets.

Sterry, pacing about like a caged woodchuck, launched into a tirade about silly Sunday-school notions, and, by a transition which I did not grasp, passed to a review of the general subject of woman's suffrage. I gathered that he is not in favor of the movement. I let him argue himself quiet, then I handed him a check for his wages, and told him to vacate the tenant house by twelve o'clock next Wednesday.

Sterry says he'll be danged if he will. (Excuse so many *dangeds*. It is the creature's only adjective.) He was engaged to work for this institution by the president of the board of trustees, and he will not move from that house until the president of the board of trustees tells him to go. I don't think poor Sterry realizes that since his arrival a new president has come to the throne.

Alors you have the story. I make no threats, but Sterry or McBride—take your choice, dear sir.

I am also about to write to the head of the Massachusetts Agricultural College,[24] at Amherst, asking him to recommend a good, practical man with a nice, efficient, cheerful wife, who will take the entire care of our modest domain of seventeen acres, and who will be a man with the right personality to place over our boys.

If we get the farming end of this institution into running shape, it ought to furnish not only beans and onions for the table, but education for our hands and brains.

I remain, sir,
Yours most truly,
S. McBRIDE,
Superintendent of the
John Grier Home.

P.S. I think that Sterry will probably come back some night and throw rocks through the windows. Shall I have them insured?

My dear Enemy:

You disappeared so quickly this afternoon that I had no chance to thank you, but the echoes of that discharge penetrated as far as my library. Also, I have viewed the debris. What on earth did you do to poor Sterry? Watching the purposeful set of your shoulders as you strode toward the carriage-house, I was filled with sudden compunction. I did not want the man murdered, merely reasoned with. I am afraid you were a little harsh.

However, your technic seems to have been effective. Report says that he has telephoned for a moving-wagon and that Mrs. Sterry is even now on her hands and knees ripping up the parlor carpet.

For this relief much thanks.

SALLIE McBRIDE.

April 26.

Dear Jervis:

Your vigorous telegram was, after all, not needed. Dr. Robin MacRae, who is a grand *pawky* mon when it comes to a fight, accomplished the business with beautiful directness. I was so bubbling with rage that immediately after writing to you I called up the doctor on the telephone, and rehearsed the whole business over again. Now, our Sandy, whatever his failings (and he has them), does have an uncommon supply of common sense. He knows how useful those gardens are going to be, and how worse than useless Sterry was. Also says he, "The superintendent's authority must be upheld." (That, incidentally, is beautiful, coming from him.) But anyway, those were his words. And he hung up the receiver, cranked up his car, and flew up here at lawless speed. He marched straight to Sterry, impelled by a fine Scotch rage, and he discharged the man with such vigor and precision, that the carriage-house window was shattered to fragments.

Since this morning at eleven, when Sterry's wagon-load of furniture rumbled out of the gates, a sweet peace has reigned over the J. G. H. A man from the village is helping us out while we hopefully await the farmer of our dreams.

I am sorry to have troubled you with our troubles. Tell Judy that she owes me a letter, and won't hear from me until she has paid it.

Your ob'd't servant,
S. McBride.

Dear Judy:

In my letter of yesterday to Jervis I forgotted (Punch's word) to convey to you our thanks for three tin bath-tubs. The sky-blue tub with poppies on the side adds a particularly bright note to the nursery. I do love presents for the babies that are too big to be swallowed.

You will be pleased to hear that our manual training is well under way. The carpenter-benches are being installed in the old primary room, and until our school-house gets its new addition, our primary class is meeting on the front porch, in accordance with Miss Matthews' able suggestion.

The girls' sewing-classes are also in progress. A circle of benches under the copper beech-tree accommodates the hand sewers, while the big girls take turns at our three machines. Just as soon as they gain some proficiency we will begin the glorious work of redressing the institution. I know you think I'm slow, but it's really a task to accomplish one hundred and eighty new frocks. And the girls will appreciate them so much more if they do the work themselves.

I may also report that our hygiene system has risen to a high level. Dr. MacRae has introduced morning and evening exer-

cises, and a glass of milk and a game of tag in the middle of
school hours. He has instituted a physiology class, and has separated the children into small groups, so that they may come to
his house, where he has a manikin that comes apart and shows
all its messy insides. They can now rattle off scientific truths
about their little digestions as fluently as Mother-Goose rhymes.
We are really becoming too intelligent for recognition. You would
never guess that we were orphans to hear us talk; we are quite
like Boston children.

2 P.M.

O Judy, such a calamity! Do you remember several weeks
ago I told you about placing out a nice little girl in a nice family home where I hoped she would be adopted? It was a kind
Christian family living in a pleasant country village, the foster-
father a deacon in the church. Hattie was a sweet, obedient,
housewifely little body, and it looked as though we had exactly fitted them to each other. My dear, she was returned this
morning for *stealing*. Scandal piled on scandal: *she had stolen
a communion-cup from church!*

Between her sobs and their accusations it took me half an
hour to gather the truth. It seems that the church they attend is
very modern and hygienic, like our doctor, and has introduced
individual communion-cups. Poor little Hattie had never heard
of communion in her life; in fact, she wasn't very used to church,
Sunday-school having always sufficed for her simple religious
needs. But in her new home she attended both, and one day, to
her pleased surprise, they served refreshments. But they skipped
her. She made no comment, however; she is used to being skipped.
But as they were starting home she saw that the little silver cup
had been casually left in the seat, and supposing that it was a
souvenir that you could take if you wished, she put it into her
pocket.

It came to light two days later as the most treasured ornament of her doll's-house. It seems that Hattie long ago saw a set
of doll's-dishes in a toy-shop window, and has ever since
dreamed of possessing a set of her own. The communion-cup
was not quite the same, but it answered. Now, if our family had

only had a little less religion and a little more sense, they would have returned the cup, perfectly unharmed, and have marched Hattie to the nearest toy-shop and bought her some dishes. But instead, they bundled the child and her belongings into the first train they could catch, and shoved her in at our front door, proclaiming loudly that she was a thief.

I am pleased to say that I gave that indignant deacon and his wife such a thorough scolding as I am sure they have never listened to from the pulpit; I borrowed some vigorous bits from Sandy's vocabulary, and sent them home quite humbled. As for poor little Hattie, here she is back again, after going out with such high hopes. It has an awfully bad moral effect on a child to be returned to the asylum in disgrace, especially when she wasn't aware of committing a crime. It gives her a feeling that the world is full of unknown pitfalls, and makes her afraid to take a step. I must bend all my energies now toward finding another set of parents for her, and ones that haven't grown so old and settled and good that they have entirely forgotten their own childhood.

Sunday.

I forgot to tell you that our new farmer is here, Turnfelt by name; and his wife is a love, yellow hair and dimples. If she were an orphan, I could place her in a minute. We can't let her go to waste. I have a beautiful plan of building an addition to the farmer's cottage, and establishing under her comfortable care a sort of brooding-house where we can place our new little chicks, to make sure they haven't anything contagious and to eliminate as much profanity as possible before turning them loose among our other perfect chicks.

How does this strike you? It is very necessary in an institution as full of noise and movement and stir as this to have some isolated spot where we can put cases needing individual attention. Some of our children have inherited nerves, and a period of quiet contemplation is indicated. Isn't my vocabulary pro-

fessional and scientific? Daily intercourse with Dr. Robin MacRae
is extremely educational.

Since Turnfelt came, you should see our pigs. They are so
clean and pink and unnatural that they don't recognize one another any more as they pass.

Our potato-field is also unrecognizable. It has been divided
with string and pegs into as many squares as a checker-board,
and every child has staked out a claim. Seed catalogues form
our only reading matter.

Noah has just returned from a trip to the village for the Sunday papers to amuse his leisure. Noah is a very cultivated person;
he not only reads perfectly, but he wears tortoise-shell-rimmed
spectacles while he does it. He also brought from the post-
office a letter from you, written Friday night. I am pained to
note that you do not care for "Gösta Berling"[25] and that Jervis
doesn't. The only comment I can make is, "What a shocking
lack of literary taste in the Pendleton family!"

Dr. MacRae has another doctor visiting him, a very melancholy gentleman who is at the head of a private psychopathic
institution, and thinks there's no good in life. But I suppose this
pessimistic view is natural if you eat three meals a day with a
tableful of melancholics. He goes up and down the world looking for signs of degeneracy, and finds them everywhere. I expected, after half an hour's conversation, that he would ask to

look down my throat to see if I had a cleft palate. Sandy's taste
in friends seems to resemble his taste in literature.

Gracious! this is a letter!

Good-by.
SALLIE.

Thursday, May 2.

Dear Judy:

Such a bewildering whirl of events! The J. G. H. is breathless.
Incidentally, I am on the way toward solving my problem of
what to do with the children while the carpenters and plumbers
and masons are here. Or, rather, my precious brother has solved
it for me.

This afternoon I went over my linen supply, and made the
shocking discovery that we have only sheets enough to change the
children's beds every two weeks, which, it appears, is our shiftless
custom. While I was still in the midst of my household gear, with
a bunch of keys at my girdle, looking like the chatelaine of a medieval château, who should be ushered in but Jimmie?

Being extremely occupied, I dropped a slanting kiss on his
nose, and sent him off to look over the place in charge of my
two oldest urchins. They collected six friends and organized a
base-ball game. Jimmie came back blown, but enthusiastic, and
consented to prolong his visit over the week-end, though after
the dinner I gave him he has decided to take his future meals at
the hotel. As we sat with our coffee before the fire, I confided
to him my anxiety as to what should be done with the chicks
while their new brooder is building. You know Jimmie. In one
half a minute his plan was formulated.

"Build an Adirondack camp on that little plateau up by the
wood-lot. You can make three open shacks, each holding eight
bunks, and move the twenty-four oldest boys out there for the
summer. It won't cost two cents."

"Yes," I objected, "but it will cost more than two cents to engage a man to look after them."

"Perfectly easy," said Jimmie, grandly. "I'll find you a college fellow who'll be glad to come during the vacation for his board and a mere pittance, only you'll have to set up more filling board than you gave me to-night."

Dr. MacRae dropped in about nine o'clock, after visiting the hospital ward. We've got three cases of whooping-cough, but all isolated, and no more coming. How those three got it is a mystery. It seems that there is a little bird that brings whooping-cough to orphan-asylums.

Jimmie fell upon him for backing in his camp scheme, and the doctor gave it enthusiastically. They seized pencil and paper and drew up plans; and before the evening was over, the last nail was hammered. Nothing would satisfy those two men but to go to the telephone at ten o'clock and rouse a poor carpenter from his sleep. He and some lumber are ordered for eight in the morning.

I finally got rid of them at ten-thirty, still talking uprights and joists and drainage and roof slants.

The excitement of Jimmie and coffee and all these building operations induced me to sit down immediately and write a letter to you; but I think, by your leave, I'll postpone further details to another time.

Yours ever,
SALLIE.

Saturday.

Dear Enemy:

Will you be after dining with us at seven to-night? It's a real dinner-party; we're going to have ice-cream.

My brother has discovered a promising young man to take charge of the boys,—maybe you know him,—Mr. Witherspoon, at the bank. I wish to introduce him to asylum circles by easy steps, so *please* don't mention insanity or epilepsy or alcoholism or any of your other favorite topics.

He is a gay young society leader, used to very fancy things to

eat. Do you suppose we can ever make him happy at the John
Grier Home?

Yours in evident haste,
SALLIE McBRIDE.

Sunday.

Dear Judy:

Jimmie was back at eight Friday morning, and the doctor at
a quarter past. They and the carpenter and our new farmer and
Noah and our two horses and our eight biggest boys have been
working ever since. Never were building operations set going
in faster time. I wish I had a dozen Jimmies on the place, though
I will say that my brother works faster if you catch him before
the first edge of his enthusiasm wears away. He would not be
much good at chiseling out a medieval cathedral.

He came back Saturday morning aglow with a new idea. He
had met at the hotel the night before a friend who belongs to
his hunting-club in Canada, and who is cashier of our First (and
only) National Bank.

"He's a bully good sport," said Jimmie, "and exactly the man
you want to camp out with those kids and lick 'em into shape.
He'll be willing to come for his board and forty dollars a month,
because he's engaged to a girl in Detroit and wants to save. I
told him the food was rotten, but if he kicked enough, you'd
probably get a new cook."

"What's his name?" said I, with guarded interest.

"He's got a peach of a name. It's Percy de Forest Witherspoon."

I nearly had hysterics. Imagine a Percy de Forest Witherspoon
in charge of those twenty-four wild little savages!

But you know Jimmie when he has an idea. He had already
invited Mr. Witherspoon to dine with me on Saturday evening,
and had ordered oysters and squabs and ice-cream from the village caterer to help out my veal. It ended by my giving a very
formal dinner-party, with Miss Matthews and Betsy and the
doctor included.

I almost asked the Hon. Cy and Miss Snaith. Ever since I have known those two, I have felt that there ought to be a romance between them. Never have I known two people who matched so perfectly. He's a widower with five children. Don't you suppose it might be arranged? If he had a wife to take up his attention, it might deflect him a little from us. I'd be getting rid of them both at one stroke. It's to be considered among our future improvements.

Anyway, we had our dinner. And during the course of the evening my anxiety grew, not as to whether Percy would do for us, but as to whether we should do for Percy. If I searched the world over, I never could find a young man more calculated to win the affection of those boys. You know, just by looking at him, that he does everything well, at least everything vigorous. His literary and artistic accomplishments I suspect a bit, but he rides and shoots and plays golf and foot-ball and sails a boat. He likes to sleep out of doors and he likes boys. He has always wanted to know some orphans; often read about 'em in books, he says, but never met any face to face. Percy does seem too good to be true.

Before they left, Jimmie and the doctor hunted up a lantern, and in their evening clothes conducted Mr. Witherspoon across a plowed field to inspect his future dwelling.

And such a Sunday as we passed! I had absolutely to forbid their carpentering. Those men would have put in a full day, quite irrespective of the damage done to one hundred and four little moral natures. As it is, they have just stood and looked at those shacks and handled their hammers, and thought about where they would drive the first nail to-morrow morning. The more I study men, the more I realize that they are nothing in the world but boys grown too big to be spankable.

I am awfully worried as to how to feed Mr. Witherspoon. He looks as though he had a frightfully healthy appetite, and he looks as though he couldn't swallow his dinner unless he had on evening clothes. I've made Betsy send home for a trunkful of evening gowns in order to keep up our social standing. One thing is fortunate: he takes his luncheon at the hotel, and I hear their luncheons are very filling.

216

Tell Jervis I am sorry he is not with us to drive a nail for the camp. Here comes the Hon. Cy up the path. Heaven save us!

Ever your unfortunate,

S. McB.

THE JOHN GRIER HOME,
May 8.

Dear Judy:

Our camp is finished, our energetic brother has gone, and our twenty-four boys have passed two healthful nights in the open. The three bark-covered shacks add a pleasant rustic touch to the grounds. They are like those we used to have in the Adirondacks, closed on three sides and open in the front, and one larger than the rest to allow a private pavilion for Mr. Percy Witherspoon. An adjacent hut, less exposed to the weather, affords extremely adequate bathing facilities, consisting of a faucet in the wall and three watering-cans. Each camp has a bath-master who stands on a stool and sprinkles each little shiverer as he trots under. Since our trustees *won't* give us enough bath-tubs, we have to use our wits.

The three camps have organized into three tribes of Indians, each with a chief of its own to answer for its conduct, Mr. Witherspoon high chief of all, and Dr. MacRae the medicine man. They dedicated their lodges Tuesday evening with appropriate tribal ceremonies; and though they politely invited me to attend, I decided that it was a purely masculine affair, so I declined to go, but sent refreshments, a very popular move. Betsy and I walked as far as the base-ball-field in the course of the evening, and caught a glimpse of the orgies. The braves were squatting in a circle about a big fire, each decorated with a blanket from his bed and a rakish band of feathers. (Our chickens seem very scant as to tail, but I have asked no unpleasant questions.) The doctor, with a Navajo blanket about his shoulders, was executing a war-dance, while Jimmie and Mr. Witherspoon beat on war-drums—two of our copper kettles, now permanently dented. Fancy Sandy! It's the first youthful glimmer I have ever caught in the man.

After ten o'clock, when the braves were safely stowed for the night, the three men came in and limply dropped into comfortable chairs in my library, with the air of having made martyrs of themselves in the great cause of charity. But they did not deceive me. They originated all that tomfoolery for their own individual delectation.

So far Mr. Percy Witherspoon appears fairly happy. He is presiding at one end of the officers' table under the special protection of Betsy, and I am told that he instils considerable life into that sedate assemblage. I have endeavored to run up their menu a trifle, and he accepts what is put before him with a perfectly good appetite, irrespective of the absence of such accustomed trifles as oysters and quail and soft-shell crabs.

There was no sign of a private sitting-room that I could put at this young man's disposal, but he himself has solved the difficulty by proposing to occupy our new laboratory. So he spends his evenings with a book and a pipe, comfortably stretched in the dentist's chair. There are not many society men who would be willing to spend their evenings so harmlessly. That girl in Detroit is a lucky young thing.

Mercy! An automobile full of people has just arrived to look over the institution, and Betsy, who usually does the honors, not here. I fly.

Addio!
SALLIE.

My dear Gordon:

This is not a letter,—I don't owe you one,—it's a receipt for sixty-five pairs of roller-skates.

Many thanks.
S. McB.

Friday.

Dear Enemy:

I hear that I missed a call to-day, but Jane delivered your message, together with the "Genetic Philosophy of Education."[26] She says that you will call in a few days for my opinion of the book. Is it to be a written or an oral examination?

And doesn't it ever occur to you that this education business is rather one-sided? It often strikes me that Dr. Robin MacRae's mental attitude would also be the better for some slight refurbishing. I will promise to read your book, provided you read one of mine. I am sending herewith the "Dolly Dialogues,"[27] and shall ask for an opinion in a day or so.

It's uphill work making a Scotch Presbyterian frivolous, but persistency accomplishes wonders.

S. McB.

May 13.

My dear, dear Judy:

Talk about floods in Ohio! Right here in Dutchess County we are the consistency of a wet sponge. Rain for five days, and everything wrong with this institution.

The babies have had croup, and we have been up o' nights with them. Cook has given notice, and there's a dead rat in the walls. Our three camps leaked, and in the early dawn, after the first cloud-burst, twenty-four bedraggled little Indians, wrapped in damp bedding, came shivering to the door and begged for admission. Since then every clothes-line, every stair-railing has been covered with wet and smelly blankets that steam, but won't dry. Mr. Percy de Forest Witherspoon has returned to the hotel to wait until the sun comes out.

After being cooped up for four days with no exercise to speak of, the children's badness is breaking out in red spots, like the measles. Betsy and I have thought of every form of active and innocent occupation that could be carried on in such a congested quarter as this: blind-man's-buff and pillow fights and hide-and-go-seek, gymnastics in the dining-room, and bean-bags in the school-room. (We broke two windows.) The boys played leap-frog up and down the hall, and jarred all the plaster in the building. We have cleaned energetically and furiously. All the woodwork has been washed, and all of the floors polished; but despite everything, we have a great deal of energy left, and we are getting to that point of nerves where we want to punch one another.

Sadie Kate has been acting like a little deil—do they have feminine deils? If not, Sadie Kate has originated the species. And this afternoon Loretta Higgins had—well, I don't know whether it was a sort of fit or just a temper. She lay down on the floor and howled for a solid hour, and when any one tried to approach her, she thrashed about like a little windmill and bit and kicked.

By the time the doctor came she had pretty well worn herself out. He picked her up, limp and drooping, and carried her to a cot in the hospital-room; and after she was asleep he came down to my library and asked to look at the archives.

Loretta is thirteen; in the three years she has been here she has had five of these outbreaks, and has been punished good and hard for them. The child's ancestral record is simple: "Mother died of alcoholic dementia, Bloomingdale Asylum.[28] Father unknown."

He studied the page long and frowningly and shook his head.

"With a heredity like that, is it right to punish the child for having a shattered nervous system?"

"It is not," said I, firmly. "We will mend her shattered nervous system."

"If we can."

"We'll feed her up on cod-liver oil and sunshine, and find a nice kind foster-mother who will take pity on the poor little—"

But then my voice trailed off into nothing as I pictured Loretta's face, with her hollow eyes and big nose and open mouth and no chin and stringy hair and sticking-out ears. No foster-mother in the world would love a child who looked like that.

"Why, oh, why," I wailed, "doesn't the good Lord send orphan children with blue eyes and curly hair and loving dispositions? I could place a million of that sort in kind homes, but no one wants Loretta."

"I'm afraid the good Lord doesn't have anything to do with bringing our Lorettas into the world. It is the devil who attends to them."

Poor Sandy! He gets awfully pessimistic about the future of the universe; but I don't wonder, with such a cheerless life as he leads. He looked to-day as though his own nervous system was shattered. He had been splashing about in the rain since five this morning, when he was called to a sick-baby case. I made him sit down and have some tea, and we had a nice, cheerful talk on drunkenness and idiocy and epilepsy and insanity. He dislikes alcoholic parents, but he ties himself into a knot over insane parents.

Privately, I don't believe there's one thing in heredity, provided you snatch the babies away before their eyes are opened. We've got the sunniest youngster here you ever saw; his mother and Aunt Ruth and Uncle Silas all died insane, but he is as placid and unexcitable as a cow.

Good-by, my dear. I am sorry this is not a more cheerful letter, though at this moment nothing unpleasant seems to be happening. It's eleven o'clock, and I have just stuck my head into the corridor, and all is quiet except for two banging shutters and leaking eaves. I promised Jane I would go to bed at ten.

Good night, and joy be wi' ye baith!

SALLIE.

P.S. There is one thing in the midst of all my troubles that I have to be grateful for: the Hon. Cy has been stricken with a lingering attack of grippe. In a burst of thankfulness I sent him a bunch of violets.

P.S. (2) We are having an epidemic of pink-eye.

May 16.

Good morning, my dear Judy!

Three days of sunshine, and the J. G. H. is smiling.

I am getting my immediate troubles nicely settled. Those beastly blankets have dried at last, and our camps have been made livable again. They are floored with wooden slats and roofed with tar-paper. (Mr. Witherspoon calls them chicken-coops.) We are digging a stone-lined ditch to convey any further cloud-bursts from the plateau on which they stand to the corn-field below. The Indians have resumed savage life, and their chief is back at his post.

The doctor and I have been giving Loretta Higgins's nerves our most careful consideration. We think that this barrack life, with its constant movement and stir, is too exciting, and we have decided that the best plan will be to board her out in a private family, where she will receive a great deal of individual attention.

The doctor, with his usual resourcefulness, has produced the family. They live next door to him and are very nice people; I have just returned from calling. The husband is foreman of the casting-room at the iron works, and the wife is a comfortable soul who shakes all over when she laughs. They live mostly in their kitchen in order to keep the parlor neat; but it is such a cheerful kitchen that I should like to live in it myself. She has potted begonias in the window and a nice purry tiger cat asleep on a braided rug in front of the stove. She bakes on Saturday—cookies and ginger-bread and doughnuts. I am planning to pay my weekly call upon Loretta every Saturday morning at eleven o'clock. Apparently I made as favorable an impression on Mrs. Wilson as she made on me. After I had gone, she confided to the doctor that she liked me because I was just as common as she was.

Loretta is to learn housework and have a little garden of her own, and particularly play out of doors in the sunshine. She is to go to bed early and be fed up on nice nourishing food, and they are to pet her and make her happy. All this for three dollars a week!

Why not find a hundred such families, and board out all the children? Then this building could be turned into an idiot-asylum, and I, not knowing anything about idiots, could conscientiously resign and go back home and live happily ever after.

Really, Judy, I am growing frightened. This asylum will get me if I stay long enough. I am becoming so interested in it that I can't think or talk or dream of anything else. You and Jervis have blasted all my prospects in life.

Suppose I should retire and marry and have a family; as families go nowadays, I couldn't hope for more than five or six children at the most, and all with the same heredity. But mercy! such a family appears perfectly insignificant and monotonous. You have institutionalized me.

Reproachfully yours,
SALLIE McBRIDE.

P.S. We have a child here whose father was lynched. Isn't that a piquant detail to have in one's history?

Tuesday.

Dearest Judy:

What shall we do? Mamie Prout does not like prunes. This antipathy to a cheap and healthful food-stuff is nothing but imagination, and ought not to be countenanced among the inmates of a well-managed institution. Mamie must be made to like prunes. So says our grammar teacher, who spends the noonday hour with us and overlooks the morals of our charges. About one o'clock to-day she marched Mamie to my office charged with the offense of refusing, *absolutely* refusing, to open her mouth and put in a prune. The child was plumped down on a stool to await punishment from me.

Now, as you know, I do not like bananas, and I should hate awfully to be forced to swallow them; so, by the same token, why should I force Mamie Prout to swallow prunes?

While I was pondering a course that would seem to uphold Miss Keller's authority, but would at the same time leave a loophole for Mamie, I was called to the telephone.

"Sit there until I come back," I said, and went out and closed the door.

The message was from a kind lady wishing to motor me to a committee meeting. I didn't tell you that I am organizing local interest in our behalf. The idle rich who possess estates in this neighborhood are beginning to drift out from town, and I am laying my plans to catch them before they are deflected by too many garden parties and tennis tournaments. They have never been of the slightest use to this asylum, and I think it's about time they woke up to a realization of our presence.

Returning at tea-time, I was waylaid in the hall by Dr. MacRae, who demanded some statistics from my office. I opened the door, and there sat Mamie Prout exactly where she had been left four hours before.

"Mamie darling!" I cried in horror. "You haven't been here all this time?"

"Yes, ma'am," said Mamie; "you told me to wait until you came back."

That poor patient little thing was fairly swaying with weariness, but she never uttered a whimper.

I will say for Sandy that he was *sweet*. He gathered her up in his arms and carried her to my library, and petted her and caressed her back to smiles. Jane brought the sewing-table and spread it before the fire, and while the doctor and I had tea, Mamie had her supper. I suppose, according to the theory of some educators, now, when she was thoroughly worn out and hungry, would have been the psychological moment to ply her with prunes. But you will be pleased to hear that I did nothing of the sort, and that the doctor for once upheld my unscientific principles. Mamie had the most wonderful supper of her life, embellished with strawberry jam from my private jar and peppermints from Sandy's pocket. We returned her to her mates happy and comforted, but still possessing that regrettable distaste for prunes.

Did you ever know anything more appalling than this soul-crushing unreasoning obedience which Mrs. Lippett so insistently fostered? It's the orphan-asylum attitude toward life, and somehow I must crush it out. Initiative, responsibility, curiosity, inventiveness, fight—oh dear! I wish the doctor had a serum for injecting all these useful virtues into an orphan's circulation.

Portrait of an

Obedient Child

Later.

I wish you'd come back to New York. I've appointed you press-agent for this institution, and we need some of your floweriest writing immediately. There are seven tots here crying to be adopted, and it's your business to advertise them.

Little Gertrude is cross-eyed, but dear and affectionate and generous. Can't you write her up so persuasively that some loving family will be willing to take her even if she isn't beautiful? Her eyes can be operated on when she's older; but if it were a cross disposition she had, no surgeon in the world could remove that. The child knows there is something missing, though she has never seen a live parent in her life. She holds up her arms persuasively to every person who passes. Put in all the pathos you are capable of, and see if you can't fetch her a mother and father.

Maybe you can get one of the New York papers to run a Sunday-feature article about a lot of different children. I'll send some photographs. You remember what a lot of responses that "Smiling Joe" picture brought for the Sea Breeze people? I can furnish equally taking portraits of Laughing Lou and Gurgling Gertrude and Kicking Karl if you will just add the literary touch.

And do find me some sports who are not afraid of heredity. This wanting every child to come from one of the first families of Virginia is getting tiresome.

> Yours, as usual,
> SALLIE.

Friday.

My dear, dear Judy:

Such an upheaval! I've discharged the cook and the housekeeper, and in delicate language conveyed the impression to our grammar teacher that she needn't come back next year. But, oh, if I could only discharge the Honorable Cy!

I must tell you what happened this morning. Our trustee, who has had a dangerous illness, is now dangerously well again, and dropped in to pay a neighborly call. Punch was occupying a rug on my library floor, virtuously engaged with building-blocks. I am separating him from the other kindergarten children, and trying the Montessori method[29] of a private rug and no nervous distraction. I was flattering myself that it was working well; his vocabulary of late has become almost prudish.

After half an hour's desultory visit, the Hon. Cy rose to go. As the door closed behind him (I am at least thankful the child waited for that), Punch raised his appealing brown eyes to mine and murmured, with a confiding smile:

"Gee! ain't he got de hell of a mug?"

If you know a kind Christian family where I can place out a sweet little five-year boy, please communicate at once with

S. McBride,
Sup't John Grier Home.

Dear Pendletons:

I've never known anything like you two snails. You've only just reached Washington, and I have had my suit-case packed for days, ready to spend a rejuvenating week-end *chez vous*. Please hurry! I've languished in this asylum atmosphere as long as is humanely possible. I shall gasp and die if I don't get a change.

Yours,
on the point of suffocation,
S. McB.

P.S. Drop a card to Gordon Hallock, telling him you are there. He will be charmed to put himself and the Capitol at your disposal. I know that Jervis doesn't like him, but Jervis ought to get over his baseless prejudices against politicians. Who knows? I may be entering politics myself some day.

My dear Judy:

We do receive the most amazing presents from our friends and benefactors. Listen to this. Last week Mr. Wilton J. Leverett (I quote from his card) ran over a broken bottle outside our gate, and came in to visit the institution while his chauffeur was mending the tire. Betsy showed him about. He took an intelligent interest in everything he saw, particularly our new camps. That is an exhibit which appeals to men. He ended by removing his coat, and playing base-ball with two tribes of Indians. After an hour and a half he suddenly looked at his watch, begged for a glass of water, and bowed himself off.

We had entirely forgotten the episode until this afternoon, when the expressman drove up to the door with a present for the John Grier Home from the chemical laboratories of Wilton J. Leverett. It was a barrel—well, anyway, a good sized keg—full of liquid green soap!

Did I tell you that the seeds for our garden came from Washington? A polite present from Gordon Hallock and the U.S. Government. As an example of what the past régime did not accomplish, Martin Schladerwitz, who has spent three years on this pseudo-farm, knew no more than to dig a grave two feet deep and bury his lettuce seeds!

Oh, you can't imagine the number of fields in which we need making over; but of course you, of all people, can imagine. Little by little I am getting my eyes wide open, and things that just looked funny to me at first, now—oh dear! It's very disillusionizing. Every funny thing that comes up seems to have a little tragedy wrapped inside it.

Just at present we are paying anxious attention to our manners—not orphan-asylum manners, but dancing-school manners. There is to be nothing Uriah Heepish about our attitude toward the world. The little girls make courtesies when they shake hands, and the boys remove caps and rise when a lady stands, and push in chairs at the table. (Tommy Woolsey shot

Dancing School Manners

Sadie Kate into her soup yesterday, to the glee of all observers except Sadie, who is an independent young damsel and doesn't care for these useless masculine attentions.) At first the boys were inclined to jeer, but after observing the politeness of their hero, Percy de Forest Witherspoon, they have come up to the mark like little gentlemen.

Punch is paying a call this morning. For the last half-hour, while I have been busily scratching away to you, he has been established in the window-seat, quietly and undestructively engaged with colored pencils. Betsy, *en passant,* just dropped a kiss upon his nose.

"Aw, gwan!" said Punch, blushing quite pink, and wiping off the caress with a fine show of masculine indifference. But I notice he has resumed work upon his red-and-green landscape with heightened ardor and an attempt at whistling. We'll succeed yet in conquering that young man's temper.

Tuesday.

The doctor is in a very grumbly mood to-day. He called just as the children were marching in to dinner, whereupon he

marched, too, and sampled their food, and, oh, my dear! the
potatoes were scorched! And such a clishmaclaver as that man
made! It is the first time the potatoes ever have been scorched,
and you know that scorching sometimes happens in the best of
families. But you would think from Sandy's language that the
cook had scorched them on purpose, in accordance with my
orders.

As I have told you before, I could do very nicely without Sandy.

Wednesday.

Yesterday being a wonderful sunny day, Betsy and I turned
our backs upon duty and motored to the very fancy home of
some friends of hers, where we had tea in an Italian garden.
Punch and Sadie Kate had been *such* good children all day that
at the last moment we telephoned for permission to include
them, too.

"Yes, indeed, do bring the little dears," was the enthusiastic
response.

But the choice of Punch and Sadie Kate was a mistake. We

ought to have taken Mamie Prout, who has demonstrated her ability to sit. I shall spare you the details of our visit; the climax was reached when Punch went gold-fishing in the bottom of the swimming-pool. Our host pulled him out by an agitated leg, and the child returned to the asylum swathed in that gentleman's rose-colored bath-robe.

What do you think? Dr. Robin MacRae, in a contrite mood for having been so intensely disagreeable yesterday, has just invited Betsy and me to take supper in his olive-green house next Sunday evening at seven o'clock in order to look at some microscopic slides. The entertainment, I believe, is to consist of a scarlet-fever culture, some alcoholic tissue, and a tubercular gland. These social attentions bore him excessively; but he realizes that if he is to have free scope in applying his theories to the institution he must be a little polite to its superintendent.

I have just read this letter over, and I must admit that it skips lightly from topic to topic. But though it may not contain news of any great moment, I trust you will realize that its writing has consumed every vacant minute during the last three days.

I am,

Most fully occupied,

SALLIE McBRIDE.

P.S. A blessed woman came this morning and said she would take a child for the summer—one of the sickest, weakest, neediest babies I could give her. She had just lost her husband, and wanted something *hard* to do. Isn't that really very touching?

Saturday afternoon.

Dear Judy and Jervis:

Brother Jimmie (we are very alliterative!), spurred on by sundry begging letters from me, has at last sent us a present; but he picked it out himself.

We have a monkey! His name is Java.

The children no longer hear the school-bell ring. On the day the creature came, this entire institution formed in line and

filed past and shook his paw. Poor Sing's nose is out of joint. I
have to *pay* to have him washed.

Sadie Kate is developing into my private secretary. I have her
answer the thank-you letters for the institution, and her literary
style is making a hit among our benefactors. She invariably
calls out a second gift. I had hitherto believed that the Kilcoyne
family sprang from the wild west of Ireland, but I begin to suspect that their source was nearer Blarney Castle. You can see
from the inclosed copy of the letter she sent to Jimmie what a
persuasive pen the young person has. I trust that, in this case at
least, it will not bear the fruit that she suggests.

Dear Mr. Jimie: We thank you very much for the lovly monkey you
give. We name him java because that's a warm iland across the
ocian where he was born up in a nest like a bird only big the doctor told us.

The first day he come every boy and girl shook his hand and
said good morning java his hand feels funny he holds so tite. I was
afraid to touch him but now I let him sit on my shoulder and put
his arms around my kneck if he wants to. He makes a funny noise
that sounds like swering and gets mad when his tale is puled.

We love him dearly and we love you two.

The next time you have to give a present, please send an elifant.
Well I guess Ill stop.

  Yours truly
  SADIE KATE KILCOYNE.

 Percy de Forest Witherspoon is still faithful to his little fol-
lowers, though I am so afraid he will get tired that I urge him
to take frequent vacations. He has not only been faithful him-

self, but has brought in recruits. He has large social connections
in the neighborhood, and last Saturday evening he introduced
two friends, nice men who sat around the camp-fire and swapped
hunting-stories.

One of them was just back from around the world, and told
hair-raising anecdotes of the head-hunters of Sarawak, a narrow pink country on the top of Borneo. My little braves pant
to grow up and get to Sarawak, and go out on the war-path after head-hunters. Every encyclopedia in this institution has been
consulted, and there isn't a boy here who cannot tell you the history, manners, climate, flora, and fungi of Borneo. I only wish
Mr. Witherspoon would introduce friends who had been head-
hunting in England, France, and Germany, countries not quite
so *chic* as Sarawak, but more useful for general culture.

We have a new cook, the fourth since my reign began. I haven't
bothered you with my cooking troubles, but institutions don't
escape any more than families. The last is a negro woman, a big,
fat, smiling, chocolate-colored creature from Souf Ca'lina. And
ever since she came on honey dew we've fed! Her name is—
what do you guess? *Sallie*, if you please. I suggested that she
change it.

"Sho, Miss, I's had dat name Sallie longer 'n you, an' I couldn't
get used nohow to answerin' up pert-like when you sings out
'Mollie!' Seems like Sallie just b'longs to me."

So "Sallie" she remains; but at least there is no danger of our
getting our letters mixed, for her last name is nothing so ple-
beian as McBride. It's Johnston-Washington, with a hyphen.

                                                           Sunday.

Our favorite game of late is finding pet names for Sandy. His
austere presence lends itself to caricature. We have just originated a new batch. The "Laird o' Cockpen"[30] is Percy's choice.

> The Laird o' Cockpen he's proud and he's great;
> His mind is ta'en up wi' the things of the state.

Miss Snaith disguestedly calls him "that man," and Betsy refers
to him (in his absence) as "Dr. Cod-Liver." My present favorite

is "Macphairson Clon Glocketty Angus McClan." But for real poetic feeling, Sadie Kate beats us all. She calls him "Mister Someday Soon." I don't believe that the doctor ever dropped into verse but once in his life, but every child in this institution knows that one poem by heart.

> Someday soon something nice is going to happen;
>   Be a good little girl and take this hint:
> Swallow with a smile your cod-liver ile,
>   And the first thing you know you will have a peppermint.

It's this evening that Betsy and I attend his supper-party, and I confess that we are looking forward to seeing the interior of his gloomy mansion with gleeful eagerness. He never talks about himself or his past or anybody connected with himself. He appears to be an isolated figure standing on a pedestal labeled S C I E N C E, without a glimmer of any ordinary affections or emotions or human frailties except temper. Betsy and I are simply eaten up with curiosity to know what sort of past he came out of; but just let us get inside his house, and to our detective senses it will tell its own story. So long as the portal was guarded by a fierce McGurk, we had despaired of ever effecting an entrance; but now, behold! The door has opened of its own accord.

                    To be continued.

                                        S. McB.

                                                        Monday.

Dear Judy:

We attended the doctor's supper-party last night, Betsy and Mr. Witherspoon and I. It turned out a passably cheerful occasion, though I will say that it began under heavy auspices.

His house on the inside is all that the outside promises; never in my life have I seen such an interior as that man's dining-room. The walls and carpets and lambrequins are a heavy dark green. A black-marble mantelpiece shelters a few smoking black coals. The furniture is as nearly black as furniture comes. The decorations are two steel engravings in shiny black frames— the "Monarch of the Glen," and the "Stag at Bay."[31]

We tried hard to be light and sparkling, but it was like eating supper in the family vault. Mrs. McGurk, in black alpaca with a black silk apron, clumped around the table, passing cold, heavy things to eat, with a step so firm that she rattled the silver in the sideboard drawers. Her nose was up, and her mouth was down. She clearly does not approve of the master's entertaining, and she wishes to discourage all guests from ever accepting again.

Sandy sort of dimly knows that there is something the matter with his house, and in order to brighten it up a bit in honor of his guests, he had purchased flowers—dozens of them—the most exquisite pink Killarney roses and red and yellow tulips. The McGurk had wedged them all together as tight as they would fit into a peacock-blue jardinière, and plumped it down in the center of the table. The thing was as big as a bushel-basket. Betsy and I nearly forgot our manners when we saw that centerpiece; but the doctor seemed so innocently pleased at having obtained a bright note in his dining-room that we suppressed our amusement and complimented him warmly upon his happy color scheme.

The moment supper was over, we hastened with relief to his own part of the house, where the McGurk's influence does not penetrate. No one in a cleaning capacity ever enters either his library or office or laboratory except Llewelyn, a short, wiry, bow-legged Welshman, who combines to a unique degree the qualities of chambermaid and chauffeur.

The library, though not the most cheerful room I have ever seen, still, for a man's house, is not so bad—books all around from floor to ceiling, with the overflow in piles on floor and table and mantelpiece; half a dozen abysmal leather chairs and a rug or so, with another black marble mantelpiece, but this time containing a crackling wood fire. By way of bric-à-brac, he has a stuffed pelican and a crane with a frog in its mouth, also a racoon sitting on a log, and a varnished tarpon. A faint suggestion of iodoform floats in the air.

The doctor made the coffee himself in a French machine, and we dismissed his housekeeper from our spirits. He really did do his best to be a thoughtful host and I have to report that the word "insanity" was not once mentioned. It seems that Sandy, in his moments of relaxation, is a fisherman; he and Percy began swapping stories of salmon and trout, and he finally got out his case of fishing-flies, and gallantly presented Betsy and me with a "silver doctor" and a "Jack Scott" out of which to make hat-pins. Then the conversation wandered to sport on the Scotch moors, and he told about one time when he was lost, and spent the night out in the heather. There is no doubt about it, Sandy's heart is in the highlands.

I am afraid that Betsy and I have wronged him. Though it is hard to relinquish the interesting idea, he may not, after all, have committed a crime. We are now leaning to the belief that he was crossed in love.

It's really horrid of me to make fun of poor Sandy, for, despite his stern bleakness of disposition, he's a pathetic figure of a man. Think of coming home after an anxious day's round to eat a solitary dinner in that grim dining-room!

Do you suppose it would cheer him up a little if I should send my company of artists to paint a frieze of rabbits around the wall?

With love, as usual,
SALLIE.

Dear Judy:

Aren't you ever coming back to New York? Please hurry! I need a new hat, and am desirous of shopping for it on Fifth Avenue, not on Water Street. Mrs. Gruby, our best milliner, does not believe in slavishly following Paris fashions; she originates her own styles. But three years ago, as a great concession to convention, she did make a tour of the New York shops, and is still creating models on the uplift of that visit.

Also, besides my own hat, I must buy 113 hats for my children, to say nothing of shoes and knickerbockers and shirts and hair-ribbons and stockings and garters. It's quite a task to keep a little family like mine decently clothed.

Did you get that bit letter I wrote you last week? You never

had the grace to mention it in yours of Thursday, and it was
seventeen pages long, and took me *days* to write.

Yours truly,
S. McBride.

P.S. Why don't you tell me some news about Gordon? Have
you seen him, and did he mention me? Is he running after any
of those pretty Southern girls that Washington is so full of? You
know that I want to hear. Why must you be so beastly uncommunicative?

Tuesday, 4:27 P.M.

Dear Judy:

Your telegram came two minutes ago by telephone.

Yes, thank you, I shall be delighted to arrive at 5:49 on
Thursday afternoon. And don't make any engagements for that
evening, please, as I intend to sit up until midnight talking John
Grier gossip with you and the president.

Friday and Saturday and Monday I shall have to devote to
shopping. Oh, yes, you're right; I already possess more clothes
than any jail-bird needs, but when spring comes, I *must* have
new plumage. As it is, I wear an evening gown every night just
to wear them out—no, not entirely that; to make myself believe
that I'm still an ordinary girl despite this extraordinary life that
you have pushed me into.

The Hon. Cy found me yesterday arrayed in a Nile-green
crape (Jane's creation, though it looked Parisian). He was quite
puzzled when he found I wasn't going to a ball. I invited him to
stay and dine with me, and he accepted! We got on very affably. He expands over his dinner. Food appears to agree with
him. If there's any Bernard Shaw[32] in New York just now, I believe that I might spare a couple of hours Saturday afternoon
for a matinée. G. B. S.'s dialogue would afford such a life-giving
contrast to the Hon. Cy's.

There's no use writing any more; I'll wait and talk.
Addio.

SALLIE.

P.S. Oh dear! just as I had begun to catch glimmerings of niceness in Sandy, he broke out again and was *abominable*. We unfortunately have five cases of measles in this institution, and the
man's manner suggests that Miss Snaith and I gave the measles
to the children on purpose to make him trouble. There are many
days when I should be willing to accept our doctor's resignation.

Wednesday.

Dear Enemy:

Your brief and dignified note of yesterday is at hand. I have
never known anybody whose literary style resembled so exactly his spoken word.

And you will be greatly obliged if I will drop my absurd fashion of calling you "Enemy"? I will drop my absurd fashion of
calling you Enemy just as soon as you drop your absurd fashion of getting angry and abusive and insulting the moment any
little thing goes wrong.

I am leaving to-morrow afternoon to spend four days in
New York.

Yours truly,
S. McBRIDE.

Chez THE PENDLETONS,
NEW YORK.

My dear Enemy:

I trust that this note will find you in a more affable frame of
mind than when I saw you last. I emphatically repeat that it
was not due to the carelessness of the superintendent of our in-

stitution that those two new cases of measles crept in, but rather to the unfortunate anatomy of our old-fashioned building, which does not permit of the proper isolation of contagious cases.

As you did not deign to visit us yesterday morning before I left, I could not offer any parting suggestions. I therefore write to ask that you cast your critical eye upon Mamie Prout. She is covered all over with little red spots which may be measles, though I am hoping not. Mamie spots very easily.

I return to prison life next Monday at six o'clock.

Yours truly,
S. McBride.

P.S. I trust you will pardon my mentioning it, but you are not the kind of doctor that I admire. I like them chubby and round and smiling.

THE JOHN GRIER HOME,
June 9.

Dear Judy:

You are an awful family for an impressionable young girl to visit. How can you expect me to come back and settle down contentedly to institution life after witnessing such a happy picture of domestic concord as the Pendleton household presents?

All the way back in the train, instead of occupying myself with the two novels, four magazines, and one box of chocolates that your husband thoughtfully provided, I spent the time in a mental review of the young men of my acquaintance to see if I couldn't discover one as nice as Jervis. I did! (A little nicer, I think.) From this day on he is the marked-down victim, the destined prey.

I shall hate to give up the asylum after getting so excited over it, but unless you are willing to move it to the capital, I don't see any alternative.

The train was awfully late. We sat and smoked on a siding

while two accommodations and a freight dashed past. I think we must have broken something, and had to tinker up our engine. The conductor was soothing, but uncommunicative.

It was 7:30 when I descended, the only passenger, at our insignificant station in the pitch darkness and *rain*, without an umbrella, and wearing that precious new hat. No Turnfelt to meet me; not even a station hack. To be sure, I hadn't telegraphed the exact time of my arrival, but, still, I did feel rather neglected. I had sort of vaguely expected all *one hundred and thirteen* to be drawn up by the platform, scattering flowers and singing songs of welcome. Just as I was telling the station man that I would watch his telegraph instrument while he ran across to the corner saloon and telephoned for a vehicle, there came whirling around the corner two big search-lights aimed straight at me. They stopped nine inches before running me down, and I heard Sandy's voice saying:

"Weel, weel, Miss Sallie McBride! I'm thinking it's ower time you came back to tak' the bit bairns off my hands."

That man had come three times to meet me on the off chance of the train's getting in some time. He tucked me and my new hat and bags and books and chocolates all in under his waterproof flap, and we splashed off. Really, I felt as if I was getting back home again, and quite sad at the thought of ever having to leave. Mentally, you see, I had already resigned and packed and gone. The mere idea that you are not in a place for the rest of your life gives you an awfully unstable feeling. That's why trial marriages would never work. You've got to feel you're in a thing irrevocably and forever in order to buckle down and really put your whole mind into making it a success.

It's astounding how much news can accrue in four days. Sandy just couldn't talk fast enough to tell me everything I wanted to hear. Among other items, I learned that Sadie Kate had spent two days in the infirmary, her malady being, according to the doctor's diagnosis, half a jar of gooseberry jam and Heaven knows how many doughnuts. Her work had been changed during my absence to dish-washing in the officers' pantry, and the juxtaposition of so many exotic luxuries was too much for her fragile virtue.

Also, our colored cook Sallie and our colored useful man

Noah have entered upon a war of extermination. The original trouble was over a little matter of kindling, augmented by a pail of hot water that Sallie threw out of the window with, for a woman, unusual accuracy of aim. You can see what a rare character the head of an orphan-asylum must have. She has to combine the qualities of a baby nurse and a police magistrate.

The doctor had told only the half when we reached the house, and as he had not yet dined, owing to meeting me three times, I begged him to accept the hospitality of the John Grier. I would get Betsy and Mr. Witherspoon, and we would hold an executive meeting, and settle all our neglected businesses.

Sandy accepted with flattering promptness. He likes to dine outside of the family vault.

But Betsy, I found, had dashed home to greet a visiting grandparent, and Percy was playing bridge in the village. It's seldom the young thing gets out of an evening, and I'm glad for him to have a little cheerful diversion.

So it ended in the doctor's and my dining tête-à-tête on a hastily improvised dinner—it was then close upon eight, and our normal dinner hour is 6:30,—but it was such an improvised dinner as I am sure Mrs. McGurk never served him. Sallie, wishing to impress me with her invaluableness, did her absolutely Southern best. And after dinner we had coffee before the fire in my comfortable blue library, while the wind howled outside and the shutters banged.

We passed a most cordial and intimate evening. For the first time since our acquaintance I struck a new note in the man. There really is something attractive about him when you once come to know him. But the process of knowing him requires time and tact. He's no' very gleg at the uptak. I've never seen such a tantalizingly inexplicable person. All the time I'm talking to him I feel as though behind his straight line of a mouth and his half-shut eyes there were banked fires smoldering inside. Are you sure he hasn't committed a crime? He does manage to convey the delicious feeling that he has.

And I must add that Sandy's not so bad a talker when he lets himself go. He has the entire volume of Scotch literature at his tongue's end.

"Little kens the auld wife as she sits by the fire what the wind is doing on Hurly-Burly-Swire," he observed as a specially fierce blast drove the rain against the window. That sounds pat, doesn't it? I haven't, though, the remotest idea what it means. And listen to this: between cups of coffee (he drinks far too much coffee for a sensible medical man) he casually let fall the news that his family knew the R. L. S.[33] family personally, and used to take supper at 17 Heriot Row! I tended him assiduously for the rest of the evening in a

> Did you once see Shelley plain,
> And did he stop and speak to you?[34]

frame of mind.

When I started this letter, I had no intention of filling it with a description of the recently excavated charms of Robin MacRae; it's just by way of remorseful apology. He was so nice and companionable last night that I have been going about to-day feeling conscience-smitten at the thought of how mercilessly I made fun of him to you and Jervis. I really didn't mean quite all of the impolite things that I said. About once a month the man is sweet and tractable and engaging.

Punch has just been paying a social call, and during the course of it, he lost three little toadlings an inch long. Sadie Kate recovered one of them from under the bookcase, but the other two hopped away; and I'm so afraid they've taken sanctuary in my bed! I do wish that mice and snakes and toads and angleworms were not so portable. You never know what is going on in a perfectly respectable-looking child's pocket.

I had a beautiful visit in Casa Pendleton. Don't forget your promise to return it soon.

Yours as ever,

SALLIE.

P.S. I left a pair of pale-blue bedroom slippers under the bed. Will you please have Mary wrap them up and mail them to me? And hold her hand while she writes the address. She spelt my name on the place-cards "Mackbird."

Tuesday.

Dear Enemy:

As I told you, I left an application for an accomplished nurse with the employment bureau of New York.

Wanted! A nurse maid with an ample lap suitable for the accommodation of seventeen babies at once.

She came this afternoon, and this is the fine figure of a woman that I drew!

We couldn't keep a baby from sliding off her lap unless we fastened him firmly with safety-pins.

Please give Sadie Kate the magazine. I'll read it to-night and return it to-morrow.

Was there ever a more docile and obedient pupil than

S. McBride?

Thursday.

My dear Judy:

I've been spending the last three days busily getting under way all those latest innovations that we planned in New York. Your word is law. A public cooky-jar has been established.

Also, the eighty play-boxes have been ordered. It is a wonderful idea, having a private box for each child, where he can store up his treasures. The ownership of a little personal property will help develop them into responsible citizens. I ought to have thought of it myself, but for some reason the idea didn't come. Poor Judy! You have inside knowledge of the longings of their little hearts that I shall never be able to achieve, not with all the sympathy I can muster.

We are doing our best to run this institution with as few discommoding rules as possible, but in regard to those play-boxes there is one point on which I shall have to be firm. The children may not keep in them mice or toads or angleworms.

I can't tell you how pleased I am that Betsy's salary is to be raised, and that we are to keep her permanently. But the Hon. Cy Wykoff deprecates the step. He has been making inquiries, and he finds that her people are perfectly able to take care of her without any salary.

"You don't furnish legal advice for nothing," say I to him. "Why should she furnish her trained services for nothing?"

"This is charitable work."

"Then work which is undertaken for your own good should be paid, but work which is undertaken for the public good should not be paid?"

"Fiddlesticks!" says he. "She's a woman, and her family ought to support her."

This opened up vistas of argument which I did not care to

enter with the Hon. Cy, so I asked him whether he thought it would be nicer to have a real lawn or hay on the slope that leads to the gate. He likes to be consulted, and I pamper him as much as possible in all unessential details. You see, I am following Sandy's canny advice: "Trustees are like fiddle-strings; they maunna be screwed ower tight. Humor the mon, but gang your ain gait." Oh, the tact that this asylum is teaching me! I should make a wonderful politician's wife.

Thursday night.

You will be interested to hear that I have temporarily placed out Punch with two charming spinsters who have long been tottering on the brink of a child. They finally came last week, and said they would like to try one for a month to see what the sensation felt like.

They wanted, of course, a pretty ornament, dressed in pink and white and descended from the *Mayflower.* I told them that any one could bring up a daughter of the *Mayflower* to be an ornament to society, but the real feat was to bring up a son of an Italian organ-grinder and an Irish washerwoman. And I offered Punch. That Neapolitan heredity of his, aristically speaking, may turn out a glorious mixture, if the right environment comes along to choke out all the weeds.

I put it to them as a sporting proposition, and they were game. They have agreed to take him for one month and concentrate upon his remaking all their years of conserved force, to the end that he may be fit for adoption in some moral family. They both have a sense of humor and *accomplishing* characters, or I should never have dared to propose it. And really I believe it's going to be the one way of taming our young fire-eater. They will furnish the affection and caresses and attention that in his whole abused little life he has never had.

They live in a fascinating old house with an Italian garden, and furnishings selected from the whole round world. It does seem like sacrilege to turn that destructive child loose in such a collection of treasures. But he hasn't broken anything here for more than a month, and I believe that the Italian in him will respond to all that beauty.

I warned them that they must not shrink from any profanity that might issue from his pretty baby lips.

He departed last night in a very fancy automobile, and maybe I wasn't glad to say good-by to our disreputable young man! He has absorbed just about half of my energy.

Friday.

The pendant arrived this morning. Many thanks! But you really ought not to have given me another; a hostess cannot be held accountable for all the things that careless guests lose in her house. It is far too pretty for my chain. I am thinking of having my nose pierced, Cingalese fashion, and wearing my new jewel where it will really show.

I must tell you that our Percy is putting some good constructive work into this asylum. He has founded the John Grier Bank, and has worked out all the details in a very professional and businesslike fashion, entirely incomprehensible to my non-mathematical mind. All of the older children possess properly printed check-books, and they are each to be paid five dollars a week for their services, such as going to school and accomplishing housework. They are then to pay the institution (by check) for their board and clothes, which will consume their five dollars. It looks like a vicious circle, but it's really very educative; they will comprehend the value of money before we dump them into a mercenary world. Those who are particularly good in lessons or work will receive an extra recompense. My head aches at the thought of the bookkeeping, but Percy waves that aside as a mere bagatelle. It is to be accomplished by our prize arithmeticians, and will train them for positions of trust. If Jervis hears of any opening for bank officials, let me know; I shall have a well-trained president, cashier, and paying-teller ready to be placed by this time next year.

Saturday.

Our doctor doesn't like to be called "Enemy." It hurts his feelings or his dignity or something of the sort; but since I will persist, despite his expostulations, he has finally retaliated with a nickname for me. He calls me "Miss Sally Lunn,"[35] and is in a glow of pride at having achieved such an imaginative flight.

He and I have invented a new pastime: he talks Scotch, and I answer in Irish. Our conversations run like this:

"Good afthernoon to ye, docther. An' how's yer health the day?"

"Verra weel, verra weel. And how gaes it wi' a' the bairns?"

"Shure, they're all av thim doin' foin."

"I'm gey glad to hear it. This saft weather is hard on folk. There's muckle sickness aboot the kintra."

"Hiven be praised it has not lighted here! But sit down, docther, an' make yersilf at home. Will ye be afther havin' a cup o' tay?"

"Hoot, woman! I would na hae you fash yoursel', but a wee drap tea winna coom amiss."

"Whist! It's no thruble at all."

You may not think this a very dizzying excursion into frivolity; but I assure you, for one of Sandy's dignity, it's positively riotous. The man has been in a heavenly temper ever since I came back; not a single cross word. I am beginning to think I may reform him as well as Punch.

This letter must be about long enough even for you; I've been writing it bit by bit for three days, whenever I happened to pass my desk.

Yours as ever,

SALLIE.

P.S. I don't think much of your vaunted prescription for hair tonic. Either the druggist didn't mix it right, or Jane didn't apply it with discretion. I stuck to the pillow this morning.

THE JOHN GRIER HOME,
Saturday.

Dear Gordon:

Your letter of Thursday is at hand, and extremely silly I consider it. Of course I am not trying to let you down easy; that isn't my way. If I let you down at all, it will be suddenly and with an awful bump. But I honestly didn't realize that it had been three weeks since I wrote. Please excuse!

Also, my dear sir, I have to bring you to account. You were in New York last week, and you never ran up to see us. You thought we wouldn't find it out, but we heard—and are insulted.

Would you like an outline of my day's activities? Wrote monthly report for trustees' meeting. Audited accounts. Entertained agent of State Charities Aid Association for luncheon. Supervised children's menus for next ten days. Dictated five letters to families who have our children. Visited our little feeble-minded Loretta Higgins (pardon the reference; I know you don't like me to mention the feeble-minded), who is being boarded out in a nice comfortable family, where she is learning to work. Came back to tea and a conference with the doctor about sending a child with tubercular glands to a sanatorium. Read an article on cottage *versus* congregate system for housing dependent children. (We do need cottages! I wish you'd send us a few for a Christmas present.) And now at nine o'clock I'm sleepily beginning a letter to you. Do you know many young society girls who can point to such a useful day as that?

Oh, I forgot to say that I stole ten minutes from my accounts this morning to install a new cook. Our Sallie Washington-Johnston, who cooked fit for the angels, had a dreadful, dreadful temper and terrorized poor Noah, our super-excellent furnace-man, to the point of giving notice. We couldn't spare Noah. He's more useful to the institution than its superintendent, and so Sallie Washington-Johnston is no more.

When I asked the new cook her name, she replied, "Ma name is Suzanne Estelle, but ma friends call me Pet." Pet cooked the dinner to-night, but I must say that she lacks Sallie's delicate touch. I am awfully disappointed that you didn't visit us while Sallie was still here. You would have taken away an exalted opinion of my housekeeping.

Drowsiness overcame me at that point, and it's now two days later.

Poor neglected Gordon! It has just occurred to me that you

never got thanked for the modeling-clay which came two weeks
ago, and it was such an unusually intelligent present that I should
have telegraphed my appreciation. When I opened the box and
saw all that nice messy putty stuff, I sat down on the spot and created a statue of Singapore. The children love it; and it is very
good to have the handicraft side of their training encouraged.

After a careful study of American history, I have determined
that nothing is so valuable to a future president as an early
obligatory unescapable performance of *chores*.

Therefore I have divided the daily work of this institution
into a hundred parcels, and the children rotate weekly through
a succession of unaccustomed tasks. Of course they do everything badly, for just as they learn how, they progress to something new. It would be infinitely easier for us to follow Mrs.
Lippett's immoral custom of keeping each child sentenced for
life to a well-learned routine; but when the temptation assails
me, I recall the dreary picture of Florence Henty, who polished
the brass door-knobs of this institution for seven years—and I
sternly shove the children on.

I get angry every time I think of Mrs. Lippett. She had exactly the point of view of a Tammany politician—no slightest
sense of service to society; her only interest in the John Grier
Home was to get a living out of it.

Wednesday.

What new branch of learning do you think I have introduced
into my asylum? Table manners!

I never had any idea that it was such a lot of trouble to teach
children how to eat and drink. Their favorite method is to put
their mouths down to their mugs and lap their milk like kittens.
Good manners are not merely snobbish ornaments, as Mrs. Lippett's régime appeared to believe; they mean self-discipline and
thought for others, and my children have got to learn them.

That woman never allowed them to talk at their meals, and
I am having the most dreadful time getting any conversation
out of them above a frightened whisper. So I have instituted the
custom of the entire staff, myself included, sitting with them at
the table, and directing the talk along cheerful and improving

lines. Also I have established a small, very strict training-table, where the little dears, in relays, undergo a week of steady badgering. Our uplifting table conversations run like this:

"Yes, Tom, Napoleon Bonaparte was a very great man—elbows off the table. He possessed a tremendous power of concentrating his mind on whatever he wanted to have; and that is the way to accomplish—don't snatch, Susan; ask politely for the bread, and Carrie will pass it to you.—But he was an example of the fact that selfish thought just for oneself, without considering the lives of others, will come to disaster in the—Tom! Keep your mouth shut when you chew—and after the battle of Waterloo—let Sadie's cooky alone—his fall was all the greater because—Sadie Kate, you may leave the table. It makes no difference what he did. Under no provocation does a lady slap a gentleman."

Two more days have passed; this is the same kind of meandering letter I write to Judy. At least, my dear man, you can't complain that I haven't been thinking about you this week! I know you hate to be told all about the asylum, but I can't help it, for it's all I know. I don't have five minutes a day to read the papers. The big outside world has dropped away. My interests all lie on the inside of this little iron inclosure.

I am at present,

S. McBride,
Superintendent of the
John Grier Home.

Thursday.

Dear Enemy:

"Time is but the stream I go a-fishing in." Hasn't that a very philosophical, detached, Lord of the Universe sound? It comes from Thoreau, whom I am assiduously reading at present. As you see, I have revolted against your literature and taken to my own again. The last two evenings have been devoted to "Walden,"[36] a book as far removed as possible from the problems of the dependent child.

Did you ever read old Henry David Thoreau? You really ought; I think you'd find him a congenial soul. Listen to this: "Society is commonly too cheap. We meet at very short intervals, not having had time to acquire any new value for each other. It would be better if there were but one habitation to a square mile, as where I live." A pleasant, expansive, neebor-like man he must have been! He minds me in some ways o'Sandy.

This is to tell you that we have a placing-out agent visiting us. She is about to dispose of four chicks, one of them Thomas Kehoe. What do you think? Ought we to risk it? The place she has in mind for him is a farm in a no-license portion of Connecticut, where he will work hard for his board, and live in the farmer's family. It sounds exactly the right thing, and we can't keep him here forever; he'll have to be turned out some day into a world full of whisky.

I'm sorry to tear you away from that cheerful work on "Dementia Precox," but I'd be most obliged if you'd drop in here toward eight o'clock for a conference with the agent.

I am, as usual,

S. McBRIDE.

June 17.

My dear Judy:

Betsy has perpetrated a most unconscionable trick upon a pair of adopting parents. They have traveled East from Ohio in their touring-car for the dual purpose of seeing the country and picking up a daughter. They appear to be the leading citizens of their town, whose name at the moment escapes me; but it's a very important town. It has electric lights and gas, and Mr. Leading Citizen owns the controlling interest in both plants. With a wave of his hand he could plunge that entire town into darkness; but fortunately he's a kind man, and won't do anything so harsh, not even if they fail to reëlect him mayor. He lives in a brick house with a slate roof and two towers, and has a deer and fountain and lots of nice shade-trees in the yard. (He carries its photograph in his pocket.) They are good-natured, generous, kind-hearted, smiling people, and a little fat; you can see what desirable parents they would make.

Well, we had exactly the daughter of their dreams, only, as they came without giving us notice, she was dressed in a flannellet nightgown, and her face was dirty. They looked Caroline over, and were not impressed; but they thanked us politely, and said they would bear her in mind. They wanted to visit the New York Orphanage before deciding. We knew well that, if they saw that superior assemblage of children, our poor little Caroline would never have a chance.

Then Betsy rose to the emergency. She graciously invited them to motor over to her house for tea that afternoon and inspect one of our little wards who would be visiting her baby niece. Mr. and Mrs. Leading Citizen do not know many people in the East, and they haven't been receiving the invitations that they feel are their due; so they were quite innocently pleased at the prospect of a little social diversion. The moment they had retired to the hotel for luncheon, Betsy called up her car, and rushed baby Caroline over to her house. She stuffed her into baby niece's best pink-and-white embroidered frock, borrowed a hat of Irish lace, some pink socks and white slippers, and set her picturesquely upon the green lawn under a spreading beech-tree. A white-aproned nurse (borrowed also from baby niece) plied her with bread and milk and gaily colored toys. By the time prospective parents arrived, our Caroline, full of food and contentment, greeted them with cooes of delight. From the moment their eyes fell upon her they were ravished with desire. Not a suspicion crossed their unobservant minds that this sweet little rosebud was the child of the morning. And so, a few formalities having been complied with, it really looks as though baby Caroline would live in the Towers and grow into a leading citizen.

I must really get to work, without any further delay, upon the burning question of new clothes for our girls.

With the highest esteem, I am,

    D'r Ma'am

       Y'r most ob'd't and h'mble serv't,

                    SAL. MCBRIDE.

June 19th.

My dearest Judy:

Listen to the grandest innovation of all, and one that will delight your heart.

NO MORE BLUE GINGHAM!

Feeling that this aristocratic neighborhood of country estates might contain valuable food for our asylum, I have of late been moving in the village social circles, and at a luncheon yesterday I dug out a beautiful and charming widow who wears delectable, flowing gowns that she designs herself. She confided to me that she would have loved to have been a dressmaker, if she had only been born with a needle in her mouth instead of a golden spoon. She says she never sees a pretty girl badly dressed but she longs to take her in hand and make her over. Did you ever hear anything so apropos? From the moment she opened her lips she was a marked man.

"I can show you fifty-nine badly dressed girls," said I to her, "and you have got to come back with me and plan their new clothes and make them beautiful."

She expostulated; but in vain. I led her out to her automobile, shoved her in, and murmured, "John Grier Home" to the chauffeur. The first inmate our eyes fell upon was Sadie Kate, just fresh, I judge, from hugging the molasses-barrel; and a shocking spectacle she was for any esthetically minded person. In addition to the stickiness, one stocking was coming down, her pinafore was buttoned crookedly, and she had lost a hair-ribbon. But—as always—completely at ease, she welcomed us with a cheery grin, and offered the lady a sticky paw.

"Now," said I, in triumph, "you see how much we need you. What can you do to make Sadie Kate beautiful."

"Wash her," said Mrs. Livermore.

Sadie Kate was marched to my bathroom. When the scrubbing was finished and the hair strained back and the stocking restored to seemly heights, I returned her for a second inspection—a perfectly normal little orphan. Mrs. Livermore turned her from side to side, and studied her long and earnestly.

Sadie Kate by nature is a beauty, a wild, dark, Gipsyish little colleen; she looks fresh from the wind-swept moors of Connemara. But, oh, we have managed to rob her of her birthright with this awful institution uniform!

After five minutes' silent contemplation, Mrs. Livermore raised her eyes to mine.

"Yes, my dear, you need me."

And then and there we formed our plans. She is to head the committee on C L O T H E S. She is to choose three friends to help her; and they, with the two dozen best sewers among the girls and our sewing-teacher and five sewing-machines, are going to make over the looks of this institution. And the charity is all on our side. We are supplying Mrs. Livermore with the profession that Providence robbed her of. Wasn't it clever of me to find her? I woke this morning at dawn and crowed!

A Study in Clothes

Lots more news,—I could run into a second volume,—but I am going to send this letter to town by Mr. Witherspoon, who, in a very high collar and the blackest of evening clothes, is on the point of departure for a barn dance at the country club. I

JEAN WEBSTER

told him to pick out the nicest girls he danced with to come and
tell stories to my children.

It is dreadful, the scheming person I am getting to be. All the
time I am talking to any one, I am silently thinking, "What use
can you be to my asylum?"

There is grave danger that this present superintendent will
become so interested in her job that she will never want to
leave. I sometimes picture her a white-haired old lady, pro-
pelled about the building in a wheeled chair, but still tena-
ciously superintending her fourth generation of orphans.

Please discharge her before that day!

Yours,

SALLIE.

Friday.

Dear Judy:

Yesterday morning, without the slightest warning, a station
hack drove up to the door and disgorged upon the steps two
men, two little boys, a baby girl, a rocking-horse, and a Teddy
bear, and then drove off!

The men were artists, and the little ones were children of another artist, dead three weeks ago. They had brought the mites
to us because they thought "John Grier" sounded solid and respectable, and not like a public institution. It had never entered
their unbusinesslike heads that any formality is necessary about
placing a child in an asylum.

I explained that we were full, but they seemed so stranded
and aghast, that I told them to sit down while I advised them
what to do. So the chicks were sent to the nursery, with a rec-
ommendation of bread and milk, while I listened to their history. Those artists had a fatally literary touch, or maybe it was
just the sound of the baby girl's laugh, but, anyway, before they
had finished, the babes were ours.

Never have I seen a sunnier creature than the little Allegra
(we don't often get such fancy names or such fancy children).

She is three years old, is lisping funny baby-talk and bubbling with laughter. The tragedy she has just emerged from has never touched her. But Don and Clifford, sturdy little lads of five and seven, are already solemn-eyed and frightened at the hardness of life.

Their mother was a kindergarten teacher who married an artist on a capital of enthusiasm and a few tubes of paint. His friends say that he had talent, but of course he had to throw it away to pay the milk-man. They lived in a haphazard fashion in a rickety old studio, cooking behind screens, the babies sleeping on shelves.

But there seems to have been a very happy side to it—a great deal of love and many friends, all more or less poor, but artistic and congenial and high-thinking. The little lads, in their gentleness and fineness, show that phase of their upbringing. They have an air which many of my children, despite all the good manners I can pour into them, will forever lack.

The mother died in the hospital a few days after Allegra's birth, and the father struggled on for two years, caring for his brood and painting like mad—advertisements, anything—to keep a roof over their heads.

He died in St. Vincent's three weeks ago,—over-work, worry, pneumonia. His friends rallied about the babies, sold such of the studio fittings as had escaped pawning, paid off the debts, and looked about for the best asylum they could find. And, Heaven save them! they hit upon us!

Well, I kept the two artists for luncheon,—nice creatures in soft hats and Windsor ties, and looking pretty frayed themselves,—and then started them back to New York with the promise that I would give the little family my most parental attention.

So here they are, one little mite in the nursery, two in the kindergarten-room, four big packing-cases full of canvases in the cellar, and a trunk in the store-room with the letters of their father and mother. And a look in their faces, an intangible spiritual *something*, that is their heritage.

I can't get them out of my mind. All night long I was planning for their future. The boys are easy; they have already been graduated from college, Mr. Pendleton assisting, and are pursuing honorable business careers. But Allegra I don't know about; I can't think what to wish for the child. Of course the normal thing to wish for any sweet little girl is that two kind foster-parents will come along to take the place of the real parents that Fate has robbed her of; but in this case it would be cruel to steal her away from her brothers. Their love for the baby is pitiful. You see, they have brought her up. The only time I ever hear them laugh is when she has done something funny. The poor little fellows miss their father horribly. I found Don, the five-year-old one, sobbing in his crib last night because he couldn't say good night to "daddy."

But Allegra is true to her name, the happiest young miss of three I have ever seen. The poor father managed well by her, and she, little ingrate, has already forgotten that she has lost him.

Whatever can I do with these little ones? I think and think and think about them. I can't place them out, and it does seem too awful to bring them up here; for as good as we are going to be when we get ourselves made over, still, after all, we are an institution, and our inmates are just little incubator chicks. They don't get the individual, fussy care that only an old hen can give.

There is a lot of interesting news that I might have been telling you, but my new little family has driven everything out of my mind.

Bairns are certain joy, but nae sma' care.

                                        Yours ever,

                                        SALLIE.

P.S. Don't forget that you are coming to visit me next week.

P.S. II. The doctor, who is ordinarily so scientific and unsentimental, has fallen in love with Allegra. He didn't so much as glance at her tonsils; he simply picked her up in his arms and hugged her. Oh, she is a little witch! Whatever is to become of her?

June 22.

My dear Judy:

I may report that you need no longer worry as to our inadequate fire protection. The doctor and Mr. Witherspoon have been giving the matter their gravest attention, and no game yet devised has proved so entertaining and destructive as our fire-drill.

The children all retire to their beds and plunge into alert slumber. Fire-alarm sounds. They spring up and into their shoes, snatch the top blanket from their beds, wrap it around their imaginary night-clothes, fall into line, and trot to the hall and stairs.

Our seventeen little tots in the nursery are each in charge of an Indian, and are bundled out, shrieking with delight. The remaining Indians, so long as there is no danger of the roof falling, devote themselves to salvage. On the occasion of our first drill, Percy in command, the contents of a dozen clothes-lockers were dumped into sheets and hurled out of the windows. I usurped dictatorship just in time to keep the pillows and mattresses from following. We spent hours resorting those clothes, while Percy and the doctor, having lost all interest, strolled up to the camp with their pipes.

Our future drills are to be a touch less realistic. However, I am pleased to tell you that, under the able direction of Fire-chief Witherspoon, we emptied the building in six minutes and twenty-eight seconds.

That baby Allegra has fairy blood in her veins. Never did this institution harbor such a child, barring one that Jervis and I know of. She has completely subjugated the doctor. Instead of going about his visits like a sober medical man, he comes down to my library hand and hand with Allegra, and for half an hour at a time crawls about on a rug, pretending he's a horse, while the bonnie wee lassie sits on his back and kicks.

You know, I am thinking of putting a card in the paper:

Characters neatly remodeled.

S. McBride.

Sandy dropped in two nights ago to have a bit of conversation with Betsy and me, and he was *frivolous*. He made three jokes, and he sat down at the piano and sang some old Scotch, "My luve's like a red, red rose," and "Come under my plaidie," and "Wha's at the window? Wha? Wha?" not in the least educational, and then danced a few steps of the strathspey!

I sat and beamed upon my handiwork, for it's true, I've done it all through my frivolous example and the books I've given him and the introductions of such lightsome companions as Jimmie and Percy and Gordon Hallock. If I have a few more months in which to work, I shall get the man human. He has given up purple ties, and at my tactful suggestion has adopted a suit of gray. You have no idea how it sets him off. He will be quite distinguished-looking as soon as I can make him stop carrying bulgy things in his pockets.

Good-by; and remember that we're expecting you on Friday.

SALLIE.

P.S. Here is a picture of Allegra, taken by Mr. Witherspoon. Isn't she a love? Her present clothes do not enhance her beauty, but in the course of a few weeks she will move into a pink smocked frock.

Wednesday, June 24, 10 A.M.

MRS. JERVIS PENDLETON.
Madam:

You letter is at hand, stating that you cannot visit me on Friday per promise, because you husband has business that keeps him in town. What clishmaclaver is this! Has it come to such a pass that you can't leave him for two days?

I did not let 113 babies interfere with my visit to you, and I see no reason why you should let one husband interfere with your visit to me. I shall meet the Berkshire express on Friday as agreed.

S. MCBRIDE.

June 30.

My *dear Judy:*

That was a very flying visit you paid us; but for all small favors we are grateful. I am awfully pleased that you were so delighted with the way things are going, and I can't wait for Jervis and the architect to get up here and really begin a fundamental ripping-up.

You know, I had the queerest feeling all the time that you were here. I can't make it seem true that you, my dear, wonderful Judy, were actually brought up in this institution, and know from the bitter inside what these little tots need. Sometimes the tragedy of your childhood fills me with an anger that makes me want to roll up my sleeves and fight the whole world and force it into making itself over into a place more fit for children to live in. That Scotch-Irish ancestry of mine seems to have deposited a tremendous amount of *fight* in my character.

If you had started me with a modern asylum, equipped with nice, clean, hygienic cottages and everything in running order, I couldn't have stood the monotony of its perfect clockwork. It's the sight of so many things crying to be done that makes it possible for me to stay. Sometimes, I must confess, I wake up in the morning and listen to these institution noises, and sniff this institution air, and long for the happy, care-free life that by rights is mine.

You, my dear witch, cast a spell over me, and I came; but often in the night watches your spell wears thin, and I start the day with the burning decision to run away from the John Grier Home. But I postpone starting until after breakfast. And as I issue into the corridor, one of these pathetic tots runs to meet me, and shyly slips a warm, crumpled little fist into my hand, and looks up with wide baby eyes, mutely asking for a little petting, and I snatch him up and hug him; and then, as I look over his shoulder at the other forlorn little mites, I long to take all 113 into my arms and love them into happiness. There is something hypnotic about this working with children. Struggle as you may, it gets you in the end.

Your visit seems to have left me in a broadly philosophical frame of mind; but I really have one or two bits of news that I might convey. The new frocks are marching along, and, oh, but they are going to be sweet! Mrs. Livermore was entranced with those parti-colored bales of cotton cloth you sent,—you should see our workroom, with it all scattered about,—and when I think of sixty little girls, attired in pink and blue and yellow and lavender, romping upon our lawn on a sunny day, I feel that we should have a supply of smoked eye-glasses to offer visitors. Of course you know that some of those brilliant fabrics are going to be very fadeable and impractical; but Mrs. Livermore is as bad as you—she doesn't give a hang. She'll make a second and a third set if necessary. DOWN WITH CHECKED GINGHAM!

I am glad you like our doctor. Of course we reserve the right to say anything about him we choose, but our feelings would be awfully hurt if anybody else should make fun of him.

He and I are still superintending each other's reading. Last week he appeared with Herbert Spencer's "System of Synthetic Philosophy"[37] for me to glance at; I gratefully accepted it, and gave him in return the "Diary of Marie Bashkirtseff."[38] Do you remember in college how we used to enrich our daily speech with quotations from Marie? Well, Sandy took her home and read her painstakingly and thoughtfully.

"Yes," he acknowledged to-day when he came to report, "it is a truthful record of a certain kind of morbid, egotistical personality that unfortunately does exist; but I can't understand why you care to read it; for, thank God! Sally Lunn, you and Bash haven't anything in common."

That's the nearest to a compliment he ever came, and I feel extremely flattered. As to poor Marie, he refers to her as "Bash" because he can't pronounce her name, and is too disdainful to try.

We have a child here, the daughter of a chorus-girl, and she is a conceited, selfish, vain, posing, morbid, lying little minx, but she has eyelashes! Sandy has taken the most violent dislike to that child; and since reading poor Marie's diary, he has found a new comprehensive adjective for summing up all of her distressing qualities. He calls her *bashy*, and dismisses her.

Good-by and come again.

SALLIE.

P.S. My children show a distressing tendency to draw out their entire bank-accounts to buy candy.

Tuesday night.

My dear Judy:

What do you think Sandy has done now? He has gone off on a pleasure-trip to that psychopathic institution whose head

alienist visited us a month or so ago. Did you ever know anything like the man? He is fascinated by insane people, and can't
let them alone.

When I asked for some parting medical instructions, he replied:
"Feed a cowld and hunger a colic and put nae faith in doctors."

With that advice, and a few bottles of cod-liver oil we are left
to our own devices. I feel very free and adventurous. Perhaps
you had better run up here again, as there's no telling what joyous upheaval I may accomplish when out from under Sandy's
dampening influence.

S.

THE JOHN GRIER HOME,
Friday.

Dear Enemy:

Here I stay lashed to the mast, while you run about the country disporting yourself with insane people. And just as I was
thinking that I had nicely cured you of this morbid predilection
for psychopathic institutions! It's very disappointing. You had
seemed almost human of late.

May I ask how long you are intending to stay? You had permission to go for two days, and you've already been away for
four. Charlie Martin fell out of a cherry-tree yesterday and cut
his head open, and we were driven to calling in a foreign doctor. Five stitches. Patient doing well. But we don't like to de-
pend on strangers. I wouldn't say a word if you were away on
legitimate business, but you know very well that, after associ-
ating with melancholics for a week, you will come back home
in a dreadful state of gloom, dead-sure that humanity is going
to the dogs; and upon me will fall the burden of getting you decently cheerful again.

Do leave those insane people to their delusions, and come
back to the John Grier Home, which needs you.

I am most fervent'
Your friend and servant,

S. McB.

P.S. Don't you admire that poetical ending? It was borrowed from Robert Burns, whose works I am reading assiduously as a compliment to a Scotch friend.

                                                            July 6.

Dear Judy:

That doctor man is still away. No word; just disappeared into space. I don't know whether he is ever coming back or not, but we seem to be running very happily without him.

I lunched yesterday *chez* the two kind ladies who have taken our Punch to their hearts. The young man seems to be very much at home. He took me by the hand, and did the honors of the garden, presenting me with the bluebell of my choice. At luncheon the English butler lifted him into his chair and tied on his bib with as much manner as though he were serving a prince of the blood. The butler has lately come from the household of the Earl of Durham, Punch from a cellar in Houston Street. It was a very uplifting spectacle.

My hostesses entertained me afterward with excerpts from their table conversations of the last two weeks. (I wonder the butler hasn't given notice; he looked like a respectable man.) If nothing more comes of it, at least Punch has furnished them with funny stories for the rest of their lives. One of them is even thinking of writing a book. "At least," says she, wiping hysterical tears from her eyes, "we have lived!"

The Hon. Cy dropped in at 6:30 last night, and found me in an evening gown, starting for a dinner at Mrs. Livermore's house. He mildly observed that Mrs. Lippett did not aspire to be a society-leader, but saved her energy for her work. You know I'm not vindictive, but I never look at that man without wishing he were at the bottom of the duck-pond, securely anchored to a rock. Otherwise he'd pop up and float.

Singapore respectfully salutes you, and is very glad that you can't see him as he now appears. A shocking calamity has befallen his good looks. Some bad child—and I don't think she's a boy—has clipped that poor beastie in spots, until he looks

like a mangy, moth-eaten checkerboard. No one can imagine
who did it. Sadie Kate is very handy with the scissors, but she
is also handy with an alibi! During the time when the clipping
presumably occurred, she was occupying a stool in the corner
of the school-room with her face to the wall, as twenty-eight
children can testify. However, it has become Sadie Kate's daily
duty to treat those spots with your hair tonic.

I am, as usual,

SALLIE.

P.S. This is a recent portrait of the Hon. Cy drawn from life.
The man, in some respects, is a fascinating talker; he makes
gestures with his nose.

Thursday evening.

Dear Judy:

Sandy is back after a ten-days' absence—no explanations,—
and plunged deep into gloom. He resents our amiable efforts to
cheer him up, and will have nothing to do with any of us except
baby Allegra. He took her to his house for supper to-night and
never brought her back until half-past seven, a scandalous hour
for a young miss of three. I don't know what to make of our
doctor; he grows more incomprehensible every day.

But Percy, now, is an open-minded, confiding young man. He has just been making a dinner-call (he is very punctilious in all social matters), and our entire conversation was devoted to the girl in Detroit. He is lonely and likes to talk about her; and the wonderful things he says! I hope that Miss Detroit is worthy of all this fine affection, but I'm afraid. He fetched out a leather case from the innermost recesses of his waistcoat and, reverently unwrapping two layers of tissue-paper, showed me the photograph of a silly little thing, all eyes and ear-rings and fuzzy hair. I did my best to appear congratulatory, by my heart shut up out of pity for the poor boy's future.

Isn't it funny how the nicest men often choose the worst wives, and the nicest women the worst husbands? Their very niceness, I suppose, makes them blind and unsuspicious.

You know, the most interesting pursuit in the world is studying character. I believe I was meant to be a novelist; people fascinate me—until I know them thoroughly. Percy and the doctor form a most engaging contrast. You always know at any moment what that nice young man is thinking about; he is written like a primer in big type and one-syllable words. But the doctor! He might as well be written in Chinese so far as legibility goes. You have heard of people with a dual nature; well, Sandy possesses a triple one. Usually he's scientific and as hard as granite, but occasionally I suspect him of being quite a sentimental person underneath his official casing. For days at a time he will be patient and kind and helpful, and I begin to like him; then without any warning an untamed wild man swells up from the innermost depths, and—oh, dear! the creature's impossible.

I always suspect that sometime in the past he has suffered a terrible hurt, and that he is still brooding over the memory of it. All the time he is talking you have the uncomfortable feeling that in the far back corners of his mind he is thinking something else. But this may be merely my romantic interpretation of an uncommonly bad temper. In any case, he's baffling.

We have been waiting for a week for a fine windy afternoon, and this is it. My children are enjoying "kite-day," a leaf taken from Japan. All of the big-enough boys and most of the girls

are spread over "Knowltop" (that high, rocky sheep-pasture which joins us on the east) flying kites made by themselves.

I had a dreadful time coaxing the crusty old gentleman who owns the estate into granting permission. He doesn't like orphans, he says, and if he once lets them get a start in his grounds, the place will be infested with them forever. You would think, to hear him talk, that orphans were a pernicious kind of beetle.

But after half an hour's persuasive talking on my part, he grudgingly made us free of his sheep-pasture for two hours, provided we didn't step foot into the cow-pasture over the lane, and came home promptly when our time was up. To insure the sanctity of his cow-pasture, Mr. Knowltop has sent his gardener and chauffeur and two grooms to patrol its boundaries while the flying is on. The children are still at it, and are having a wonderful adventure racing over that windy height and getting tangled up in one another's strings. When they come panting back they are to have a surprise in the shape of ginger cookies and lemonade.

These pitiful little youngsters with their old faces! It's a difficult task to make them young, but I believe I'm accomplishing it. And it really is fun to feel you're doing something positive for the good of the world. If I don't fight hard against it, you'll be accomplishing your purpose of turning me into a useful person. The social excitements of Worcester almost seem tame before the engrossing interest of 113 live, warm, wriggling little orphans.

Yours with love,
SALLIE.

P.S. I believe, to be accurate, that it's 107 children I possess this afternoon.

Dear Judy:

This being Sunday and a beautiful blossoming day, with a warm wind blowing, I sat at my window with the "Hygiene of the Nervous System" (Sandy's latest contribution to my mental needs) open in my lap, and my eyes on the prospect without. "Thank Heaven!" thought I, "that this institution was so commandingly placed that at least we can look out over the cast-iron wall which shuts us in."

I was feeling very cooped-up and imprisoned and like an orphan myself; so I decided that my own nervous system required fresh air and exercise and adventure. Straight before me ran that white ribbon of road that dips into the valley and up over

the hills on the other side. Ever since I came I have longed to
follow it to the top and find out what lies beyond those hills.
Poor Judy! I dare say that very same longing enveloped your
childhood. If any one of my little chicks ever stands by the window and looks across the valley to the hills and asks, "What's
over there?" I shall telephone for a motor-car.

But to-day my chicks were all piously engaged with their little souls, I the only wanderer at heart. I changed my silken Sunday gown for homespun, planning meanwhile a means to get to
the top of those hills.

Then I went to the telephone and brazenly called up 505.

"Good afternoon, Mrs. McGurk," said I, very sweet. "May
I be speaking with Dr. MacRae?"

"Howld the wire," said she, very short.

"Afternoon, Doctor," said I to him. "Have ye, by chance,
any dying patients who live on the top o' the hills beyant?"

"I have not, thank the Lord!"

"'Tis a pity," said I, disappointed. "And what are ye afther
doin' with yerself the day?"

"I am reading the 'Origin of Species.'"

"Shut it up; it's not fit for Sunday. And tell me now, is yer
moter-car iled and ready to go?"

"It is at your disposal. Are you wanting me to take some orphans for a ride?"

"Just one who's sufferin' from a nervous system. She's taken
a fixed idea that she must get to the top o' the hills."

"My car is a grand climber. In fifteen minutes—"

"Wait!" said I. "Bring with ye a frying-pan that's a decent
size for two. There's nothing in my kitchen smaller than a cart-
wheel. And ask Mrs. McGurk can ye stay out for supper."

So I packed in a basket a jar of bacon and some eggs and
muffins and ginger cookies, with hot coffee in the thermos-bottle,
and was waiting on the steps when Sandy chugged up with his
automobile and frying-pan.

We really had a beautiful adventure, and he enjoyed the sensation of running away exactly as much as I. Not once did I let
him mention insanity. I made him look at the wide stretches of
meadow and the lines of pollard willows backed by billowing

hills, and sniff the air, and listen to the cawing crows and the tin-
kle of cow-bells and the gurgling of the river. And we talked—
oh, about a million things far removed from our asylum. I made
him throw away the idea that he is a scientist, and pretend to be
a boy. You will scarcely credit the assertion, but he succeeded—
more or less. He did pull off one or two really boyish pranks.
Sandy is not yet out of his thirties, and, mercy! that is too early
to be grown up.

We camped on a bluff overlooking our view, gathered some
driftwood, built a fire, and cooked the *nicest* supper—a sprin-
kling of burnt stick in our fried eggs, but charcoal's healthy.
Then, when Sandy had finished his pipe and "the sun was setting in its wonted west," we packed up and coasted back home.

He says it was the nicest afternoon he has had in years, and,
poor deluded man of science, I actually believe it's true. His
olive-green home is so uncomfortable and dreary and uninspiring that I don't wonder he drowns his troubles in books. Just as
soon as I can find a nice comfortable house-mother to put in
charge, I am going to plot for the dismissal of Maggie McGurk,
though I foresee that she will be even harder than Sterry to pry
from her moorings.

Please don't draw the conclusion that I am becoming unduly
interested in our bad-tempered doctor, for I'm not. It's just that
he leads such a comfortless life that I sometimes long to pat
him on the head and tell him to cheer up; the world's full of
sunshine, and some of it's for him—just as I long to comfort my
hundred and seven orphans; so much and no more.

I am sure that I had some real news to tell you, but it has
completely gone out of my head. The rush of fresh air has made
me sleepy. It's half-past nine, and I bid you good night.

                                                                S.

P.S. Gordon Hallock has evaporated into thin air. Not a
word for three weeks; no candy or stuffed animals or tokimen-
toes of any description. What on earth do you suppose has become of that attentive young man?

July 13.

Dearest Judy:

Hark to the glad tidings!

This being the thirty-first day of Punch's month, I telephoned to his two patronesses, as nominated in the bond, to arrange for his return. I was met by an indignant refusal. Give up their sweet little volcano just as they are getting it trained not to belch forth fire? They are outraged that I can make such an ungrateful request. Punch has accepted their invitation to spend the summer.

The dressmaking is still going on; you should hear the machines whir and the tongues clatter in the sewing-room. Our most cowed, apathetic, spiritless little orphan cheers up and takes an interest in life when she hears that she is to possess three perfectly private dresses of her own, and each a different color, chosen by herself. And you should see how it encourages their sewing ability; even the little ten-year-olds are bursting into seamstresses. I wish I could devise an equally effective way to make them take an interest in cooking. But our kitchen is extremely uneducative; you know how hampering it is to one's enthusiasm to have to prepare a bushel of potatoes at once.

I think you've heard me mention that fact that I should like to divide up my kiddies into ten nice little families, with a nice comfortable house-mother over each? If we just had ten picturesque cottages to put them in, with flowers in the front yard and rabbits and kittens and puppies and chickens in the back, we should be a perfectly presentable institution, and wouldn't be ashamed to have these charity experts come visiting us.

Thursday.

I started this letter three days ago, was interrupted to talk to a potential philanthropist (fifty tickets to the circus), and have not had time to pick up my pen since. Betsy has been in Philadelphia for three days, being a bridesmaid for a miserable cousin.

I hope that no more of her family are thinking of getting married, for it's most upsetting to the J. G. H.

While there, she investigated a family who had applied for a child. Of course we haven't a proper investigating plant, but once in a while, when a family drops right into our arms, we do like to put the business through. As a usual thing, we work with the State Charities' Aid Association. They have a lot of trained agents traveling about the State, keeping in touch with families who are willing to take children, and with asylums that have them to give. Since they are willing to work for us, there is no slightest use in our going to the expense of peddling our own babies. And I do want to place out as many as are available, for I firmly believe that a private home is the best thing for the child, provided, of course, that we are very fussy about the character of the homes we choose. I don't require rich foster-parents, but I do require kind, loving, intelligent parents. This time I think Betsy has landed a gem of a family. The child is not yet delivered or the papers signed, and of course there is always danger that they may give a sudden flop, and splash back into the water.

Ask Jervis if he ever heard of J. F. Bretland of Philadelphia. He seems to move in financial circles. The first I ever heard of him was a letter addressed to the "Supt. John Grier Home, Dear Sir,"—a curt, typewritten, businesslike letter, from an *awfully* businesslike lawyer, saying that his wife had determined to adopt a baby girl of attractive appearance and good health between the ages of two and three years. The child must be an orphan of American stock, with unimpeachable heredity, and no relatives to interfere. Could I furnish one as required and oblige, yours truly, J. F. Bretland?

By way of reference he mentioned "Bradstreets." Did you ever hear of anything so funny? You would think he was opening a charge-account at a nursery, and enclosing an order from our seed catalogue.

We began our usual investigation by mailing a reference-blank to a clergyman in Germantown, where the J. F. B.'s reside.

Does he own any property?

Does he pay his bills?

Is he kind to animals?

Does he attend church?

Does he quarrel with his wife? And a dozen other impertinent questions.

We evidently picked a clergyman with a sense of humor. Instead of answering in laborious detail, he wrote up and down and across the sheet, "I wish they'd adopt me!"

This looked promising, so B. Kindred obligingly dashed out to Germantown as soon as the wedding breakfast was over. She is developing the most phenomenal detective instinct. In the course of a social call she can absorb from the chairs and tables a family's entire moral history.

She returned from Germantown bursting with enthusiastic details.

Mr. J. F. Bretland is a wealthy and influential citizen, cordially loved by his friends and deeply hated by his enemies (discharged employees, who do not hesitate to say that he is a *har-rd* man). He is a little shaky in his attendance at church, but his wife seems regular, and he gives money.

She is a charming, kindly, cultivated gentlewoman, just out of a sanatorium after a year of nervous prostration. The doctor says that what she needs is some strong interest in life, and advises adopting a child. She has always longed to do it, but her hard husband has stubbornly refused. But finally, as always, it is the gentle, persistent wife who has triumphed, and hard husband has been forced to give in. Waiving his own natural preference for a boy, he wrote, as above, the usual request for a blue-eyed girl.

Mrs. Bretland, with the firm intention of taking a child, has been reading up for years, and there is no detail of infant dietetics that she does not know. She has a sunny nursery, with a southwestern exposure, all ready. And a closet full of surreptitiously gathered dolls! She has made the clothes for them herself,—she showed them to Betsy with a greatest pride,—so you can understand the necessity for a girl.

She has just heard of an excellent English trained nurse that she can secure, but she isn't sure but that it would be better to start with a French nurse, so that the child can learn the language before her vocal cords are set. Also, she was extremely interested when she heard that Betsy was a college woman. She couldn't make up her mind whether to send the baby to college or not. What was Betsy's honest opinion? If the child were Betsy's own daughter, would Betsy send her to college?

All this would be funny if it weren't so pathetic; but really I can't get away from the picture of that poor lonely woman sewing those doll-clothes for the little unknown girl that she wasn't sure she could have. She lost her own two babies years ago, or, rather, she never had them; they were never alive.

You can see what a good home it's going to be. There's lots of love waiting for the little mite, and that is better than all the wealth which, in this case, goes along.

But the problem now is to find the child, and that isn't easy; the J. F. Bretlands are so abominably explicit in their requirements. I have just the baby boy to give them; but with that closetful of dolls, he is impossible. Little Florence won't do—one tenacious parent living. I've a wide variety of foreigners with liquid brown eyes—won't do at all. Mrs. Bretland is a blonde, and daughter must resemble her. I have several sweet little mites with unspeakable heredity, but the Bretlands want six generations of church-attending grandparents, with a colonial governor at the top. Also I have a darling little curly-headed girl (and curls are getting rarer and rarer), but illegitimate. And that seems to be an unsurmountable barrier in the eyes of adopting parents, though, as a matter of fact, it makes no slightest difference in the child. However, she won't do; the Bretlands hold out sternly for a marriage-certificate.

There remains just one child out of all these one hundred and seven that appears available. Our little Sophie's father and mother were killed in a rail-road accident, and the only reason she wasn't killed was because they had just left her in a hospital to get an abscess cut out of her throat. She comes from good common American stock, irreproachable and uninteresting in every way. She's a washed-out, spiritless, whiney little thing. The doctor has been pouring her full of his favorite cod-liver oil and spinach, but he can't get any cheerfulness into her.

However, individual love and care does accomplish wonders in institution children, and she may bloom into something rare and beautiful after a few months' transplanting. So I yesterday wrote a glowing account of her immaculate family history to J. F. Bretland, offering to deliver her in Germantown.

This morning I received a telegram from J. F. B. Not at all! He does not purpose to buy any daughter sight unseen. He will come and inspect the child in person at three o'clock on Wednesday next.

Oh dear, if he shouldn't like her! We are now bending all our energies toward enhancing that child's beauty—like a pup bound for the dog show. Do you think it would be awfully immoral if I rouged her cheeks a suspicion? She is too young to pick up the habit.

Heavens! what a letter! A million pages written without a break. You can see where my heart is. I'm as excited over little Sophie's settling in life as though she were my own darling daughter.

Respectful regards to the president.

SAL. McB.

Dear Gordon:

That was an obnoxious, beastly, low-down trick not to send me a cheering line for four weeks just because, in a period of abnormal stress, I once let you go for three. I had really begun to be worried for fear you'd tumbled into the Potomac. My chicks would miss you dreadfully; they love their Uncle Gordon. Please remember that you promised to send them a donkey.

Please also remember that I'm a busier person than you. It's a lot harder to run the John Grier Home than the House of Representatives. Besides, you have more efficient people to help.

This isn't a letter; it's an indignant remonstrance. I'll write to-morrow—or the next day.

S.

P.S. On reading your letter over again I am slightly mollified, but dinna think I believe a' your saft words. I ken weel ye only flatter when ye speak sae fair.

July 17.

Dear Judy:

I have a history to recount.

This, please remember, is Wednesday next. So at half-past two o'clock our little Sophie was bathed and brushed and clothed in fine linen, and put in charge of a trusty orphan, with anxious instructions to keep her clean.

At three-thirty to the minute—never have I known a human being so disconcertingly businesslike as J. F. Bretland—an automobile of expensive foreign design rolled up to the steps of this imposing château. A square-shouldered, square-jawed personage, with a chopped-off mustache and a manner that inclines one to hurry, presented himself three minutes later at my library door. He greeted me briskly as "Miss McKosh." I gently corrected him, and he changed to "Miss McKim." I indicated my most soothing arm-chair, and invited him to take some light refreshment after his journey. He accepted a glass of water (I admire a temperate parent), and evinced an impatient desire to be done with the business. So I rang the bell and ordered the little Sophie to be brought down.

"Hold on, Miss McGee!" said he to me. "I'd rather see her in her own environment. I will go with you to the playroom or corral or wherever you keep your youngsters."

So I led him to the nursery, where thirteen or fourteen mites in gingham rompers were tumbling about on mattresses on the floor. Sophie, alone in the glory of feminine petticoats, was ensconced in the blue-ginghamed arms of a very bored orphan. She was squirming and fighting to get down, and her feminine petticoats were tightly wound about her neck. I took her in my arms, smoothed her clothes, wiped her nose, and invited her to look at the gentleman.

That child's whole future hung upon five minutes of sunniness, and instead of a single smile, she *whined!*

Mr. Bretland shook her hand in a very gingerly fashion and chirruped to her as you might to a pup. Sophie took not the slightest notice of him, but turned her back, and buried her face in my neck. He shrugged his shoulders, supposed that they could take her on trial. She might suit his wife; he himself didn't want one, anyway. And we turned to go out.

Then who should come toddling straight across his path but that little sunbeam Allegra! Exactly in front of him she staggered, threw her arms about like a windmill, and plumped down on all fours. He hopped aside with great agility to avoid stepping on her, and then picked her up and set her on her feet. She clasped her arms about his leg, and looked up at him with a gurgling laugh.

"Daddy! Frow baby up!"

He is the first man, barring the doctor, whom the child has seen for weeks, and evidently he resembles somewhat her almost forgotten father.

J. F. Bretland picked her up and tossed her in the air as handily as though it were a daily occurrence, while she ecstatically shrieked her delight. Then when he showed signs of lowering her, she grasped his by an ear and a nose, and drummed a tattoo on his stomach with both feet. No one could ever accuse Allegra of lacking vitality!

J. F. disentangled himself from her endearments, and emerged, rumpled as to hair, but a firm-set jaw. He set her on her feet, but retained her little doubled-up fist.

"This is the kid for me," he said. "I don't believe I need look any further."

I explained that we couldn't separate little Allegra from her brothers; but the more I objected, the stubborner his jaw became. We went back to the library, and argued about it for half an hour.

He liked her heredity, he liked her looks, he liked her spirit, he liked *her.* If he was going to have a daughter foisted on him, he wanted one with some ginger. He'd be hanged if he'd take the other whimpering little thing. It wasn't natural. But if I gave

him Allegra, he would bring her up as his own child, and see
that she was provided for for the rest of her life. Did I have any
right to cut her out from all that just for a lot of sentimental
nonsense? The family was already broken up; the best I could
do for them now was to provide for them individually.

"Take all three," said I, quite brazenly.

But, no, he couldn't consider that; his wife was an invalid,
and one child was all that she could manage.

Well, I was in a dreadful quandary. It seemed such a chance
for the child, and yet it did seem so cruel to separate her from
those two adoring little brothers. I knew that if the Bretlands
adopted her legally, they would do their best to break all ties
with the past, and the child was still so tiny she would forget
her brothers as quickly as she had her father.

Then I thought about you, Judy, and of how bitter you have
always been because, when that family wanted to adopt you,
the asylum wouldn't let you go. You have always said that you
might have had a home, too, like other children, but that Mrs.
Lippett stole it away from you. Was I perhaps stealing little Allegra's home from her? With the two boys it would be different;
they could be educated and turned out to shift for themselves.
But to a girl a home like this would mean everything. Ever since
baby Allegra came to us, she has seemed to me just such another child as baby Judy must have been. She has ability and
spirit. We must somehow furnish her with opportunity. She,
too, deserves her share of the world's beauty and good—as
much as nature has fitted her to appreciate. And could any asylum ever give her that? I stood and thought and thought while
Mr. Bretland impatiently paced the floor.

"You have those boys down and let me talk to them," Mr.
Bretland insisted. "If they have a spark of generosity, they'll be
glad to let her go."

I sent for them, but my heart a solid lump of lead. They were
still missing their father; it seemed merciless to snatch away
that darling baby sister, too.

They came hand in hand, sturdy, fine little chaps, and stood
solemnly at attention, with big, wondering eyes fixed on the
strange gentleman.

"Come here, boys. I want to talk to you." He took each by a hand. "In the house I live in we haven't any little baby, so my wife and I decided to come here, where there are so many babies without fathers and mothers, and take one home to be ours. She will have a beautiful house to live in, and lots of toys to play with, and she will be happy all her life—much happier than she could ever be here. I know that you will be very glad to hear that I have chosen your little sister."

"And won't we ever see her any more?" asked Clifford.

"Oh, yes, sometimes."

Clifford looked from me to Mr. Bretland, and two big tears began rolling down his cheeks. He jerked his hand away and came and hurled himself into my arms.

"Don't let him have her! Please! Please! Send him away!"

"Take them all!" I begged.

But he's a hard man.

"I didn't come for an entire asylum," said he, shortly.

By this time Don was sobbing on the other side. And then who should inject himself into the hubbub but Dr. MacRae, with baby Allegra in his arms!

I introduced them, and explained. Mr. Bretland reached for the baby, and Sandy held her tight.

"Quite impossible," said Sandy, shortly. "Miss McBride will tell you that it's one of the rules of this institution never to separate a family."

"Miss McBride has already decided," said J. F. B., stiffly. "We have fully discussed the question."

"You must be mistaken," said Sandy, becoming his Scotchest, and turning to me. "You surely had no intention of performing any such cruelty as this?"

Here was the decision of Solomon all over again, with two of the stubbornest men that the good Lord ever made wresting poor little Allegra limb from limb.

I despatched the three chicks back to the nursery and returned to the fray. We argued loud and hotly, until finally J. F. B. echoed my own frequent query of the last five months: "Who is the head of this asylum, the superintendent or the visiting physician?"

I was furious with the doctor for placing me in such a position before that man, but I couldn't quarrel with him in public; so I had ultimately to tell Mr. Bretland, with finality and flatness, that Allegra was out of the question. Would he not reconsider Sophie?

No, he'd be darned if he'd reconsider Sophie. Allegra or nobody. He hoped that I realized that I had weakly allowed the child's entire future to be ruined. And with that parting shot he backed to the door. "Miss MacRae, Dr. McBride, good afternoon." He achieved two formal bows and withdrew.

And the moment the door closed Sandy and I fought it out. He said that any person who claimed to have any modern, humane views on the subject of child-care ought to be ashamed to have considered for even a moment the question of breaking up such a family; and I accused him of keeping her for the purely selfish reason that he was fond of the child and didn't wish to lose her. (And that, I believe, is the truth.) Oh, we had the battle of our career, and he finally took himself off with a stiffness and politeness that excelled J. F. B.'s.

Between the two of them I feel as limp as though I'd been run through our new mangling-machine. And then Betsy came home, and reviled me for throwing away the choicest family we have ever discovered!

So this is the end of our week of feverish activity; and both Sophie and Allegra are, after all, to be institution children. Oh dear! oh dear! Please remove Sandy from the staff, and send me, instead, a German, a Frenchman, a Chinaman, if you choose—anything but a Scotchman.

Yours wearily,
SALLIE.

P.S. I dare say that Sandy is also passing a busy evening in writing to have me removed. I won't object if you wish to do it. I am tired of institutions.

Dear Gordon:

You are a captious, caviling, carping, crabbed, contentious, cantankerous chap. Hoot mon! an' why shouldna I drap into Scotch gin I choose? An' I with a Mac in my name.

Of course the John Grier will be delighted to welcome you on Thursday next, not only for the donkey, but for your sweet sunny presence as well. I was planning to write you a mile-long letter to make up for past deficiencies, but wha's the use? I'll be seeing you the morn's morn, an' unco gude will be the sight o' you for sair een.

Dinna fash yoursel, Laddie, because o' my language. My forebears were from the Hielands.

MCBRIDE.

Dear Judy:

All's well with the John Grier—except for a broken tooth, a sprained wrist, a badly scratched knee, and one case of pink-eye. Betsy and I are being polite, but cool, toward the doctor. The annoying thing is that he is rather cool, too; and he seems to be under the impression that the drop in temperature is all on his side. He goes about his business in a scientific, impersonal way, entirely courteous, but somewhat detached.

However, the doctor is not disturbing us very extensively at present. We are about to receive a visit from a far more fascinating person than Sandy. The House of Representatives again rests from its labors, and Gordon enjoys a vacation, two days of which he is planning to spend at the Brantwood Inn.

I am delighted to hear that you have had enough seaside, and are considering our neighborhood for the rest of the summer. There are several spacious estates to be had within a few miles of the John Grier, and it will be a nice change for Jervis to come home only at week-ends. After a pleasantly occupied absence,

Red hair

S Mc B–
cramming
up on politics
as Gordon
is coming

you will each have some new ideas to add to the common stock.

I can't add any further philosophy just now on the subject of married life, having to refresh my memory on the Monroe Doctrine and one or two other political topics.

I am looking eagerly forward to August and three months with you.

As ever,
SALLIE.

Friday.

Dear Enemy:

It's very forgiving of me to invite you to dinner after that volcanic explosion of last week. However, please come. You remember our philanthropic friend, Mr. Hallock, who sent us the

peanuts and goldfish and other indigestible trifles? He will be
with us to-night, so this is your chance to turn the stream of his
benevolence into more hygienic channels.

We dine at seven.

As ever,
SALLIE McBRIDE.

Dear Enemy:

You should have lived in the days when each man inhabited
a separate cave on a separate mountain.

S. McBRIDE.

Friday, 6:30.

Dear Judy:

Gordon is here, and a reformed man so far as his attitude
toward my asylum goes. He has discovered the world-old truth
that the way to a mother's heart is through praise of her children, and he had nothing but praise for all 107 of mine. Even
in the case of Loretta Higgins he found something pleasant to
say; he thinks it nice that she isn't cross-eyed.

He went shopping with me in the village this afternoon, and
was very helpful about picking out hair-ribbons for a couple of
dozen little girls. He begged to choose Sadie Kate's himself, and
after many hesitations he hit upon orange satin for one braid
and emerald-green for the other.

While we were immersed in this business I became aware of
a neighboring customer, ostensibly engaged with hooks and
eyes, but straining every ear to listen to our nonsense.

She was so dressed up in a picture-hat, a spotted veil, a
feather boa, and a *nouveau art* parasol that I never dreamed
she was any acquaintance of mine till I happened to catch her
eye with a familiar malicious gleam in it. She bowed stiffly, and

disapprovingly; and I nodded back. Mrs. Maggie McGurk in her company clothes!

That is a pleasanter expression than she really has. Her smile is due to a slip of the pen.

Poor Mrs. McGurk can't understand any possible intellectual interest in a man. She suspects me of wanting to marry every single one that I meet. At first she thought I wanted to snatch away her doctor; but now, after seeing me with Gordon, she considers me a bigamous monster who wants them both.

Good-by; some guests approach.

11:30 P.M.

I have just been giving a dinner for Gordon, with Betsy and Mrs. Livermore and Mr. Witherspoon as guests. I graciously included the doctor, but he curtly declined on the ground that he wasn't in a social mood. Our Sandy does not let politeness interfere with truth!

There is no doubt about it, Gordon is the most presentable man that ever breathed. He is so good-looking and easy and

Mrs. McGurk

Red and green parrot

gracious and witty, and his manners are so impeccable—Oh, he would make a wonderfully decorative husband! But after all, I suppose you do live with a husband; you don't just show him off at dinners and teas.

He was exceptionally nice to-night. Betsy and Mrs. Livermore both fell in love with him—and I just a trifle. He entertained us with a speech in his best public manner, apropos of Java's welfare. We have been having a dreadful time finding a sleeping-place for that monkey, and Gordon proved with incontestable logic that, since he was presented to us by Jimmie, and Jimmie is Percy's friend, he should sleep with Percy. Gordon is a natural talker, and an audience affects him like champagne. He can argue with as much emotional earnestness on the subject of a monkey as on the greatest hero that ever bled for his country.

I felt tears coming to my eyes when he described Java's loneliness as he watched out the night in our furnace cellar, and pictured his brothers at play in the far-off tropical jungle.

A man who can talk like that has a future before him. I haven't a doubt but that I shall be voting for him for President in another twenty years.

We all had a beautiful time, and entirely forgot—for a space of three hours—that 107 orphans slumbered about us. Much as I love the little dears, it is pleasant to get away from them once in a while.

My guests left at ten, and it must be midnight by now. (This is the eighth day, and my clock has stopped again; Jane forgets to wind it as regularly as Friday comes around.) However, I know it's late; and as a woman, it's my duty to try for beauty sleep, especially with an eligible young suitor at hand.

I'll finish to-morrow. Good night.

Saturday.

Gordon spent this morning playing with my asylum and planning some intelligent presents to be sent later. He thinks that three neatly painted totem-poles would add to the attractiveness of our Indian camps. He is also going to make us a present of three dozen pink rompers for the babies. Pink is a color that is very popular with the superintendent of this asylum, who is deadly tired of blue! Our generous friend is likewise amusing himself with the idea of a couple of donkeys and saddles and a little red cart. Isn't it nice that Gordon's father provided for him so amply, and that he is such a charitably inclined young man? He is at present lunching with Percy at the hotel, and, I trust, imbibing fresh ideas in the field of philanthropy.

Perhaps you think I haven't enjoyed this interruption to the monotony of institution life! You can say all you please, my dear Mrs. Pendleton, about how well I am managing your asylum, but, just the same, it isn't natural for me to be so stationary. I very frequently need a change. That is why Gordon, with his bubbling optimism and boyish spirits, is so exhilarating, especially as a contrast to too much doctor.

Sunday morning.

I must tell you the end of Gordon's visit. His intention had been to leave at four, but in an evil moment I begged him to stay over till 9:30, and yesterday afternoon he and Singapore and I took a long 'cross-country walk, far out of sight of the towers of this asylum, and stopped at a pretty little roadside inn, where we had a satisfying supper of ham and eggs and cabbage. Sing stuffed so disgracefully that he has been languid ever since.

The walk and all was fun, and a very grateful change from this monotonous life I lead. It would have kept me pleasant and contented for weeks if something most unpleasant hadn't happened later. We had a beautiful, sunny, care-free afternoon, and I'm sorry to have had it spoiled. We came back very unromantically in the trolley-car, and reached the J. G. H. before nine, just in good time for him to run on to the station and catch his train. So I didn't ask him to come in, but politely wished him a pleasant journey at the porte-cochère.

A car was standing at the side of the drive, in the shadow of the house; I recognized it, and thought the doctor was inside with Mrs. Witherspoon. (They frequently spend their evenings together in the laboratory.) Well, Gordon, at the moment of parting, was seized with an unfortunate impulse to ask me to abandon the management of this asylum, and take over the management of a private house instead.

Did you ever know anything like the man? He had had the whole afternoon and miles of empty meadow in which to discuss the question, but instead he must choose our door-mat!

I don't know just what I did say: I tried to turn it off lightly and hurry him to his train. But he refused to be turned off lightly. He braced himself against a post and insisted upon arguing it out. I knew that he was missing his train, and that every window in this institution was open. A man never has the slightest thought of possible overhearers; it is always the woman who thinks of convention.

Being in a nervous twitter to get rid of him, I suppose I was pretty abrupt and tactless. He began to get angry, and then by some unlucky chance his eye fell on that car. He recognized it, too, and, being in a savage mood, he began making fun of the doctor. "Old Goggle-eyes" he called him, and "Scatchy!" and oh, the awfullest lot of unmannerly, silly things!

I was assuring him with convincing earnestness that I didn't care a rap about the doctor, that I thought he was just as funny and impossible as he could be, when suddenly the doctor rose out of his car and walked up to us.

I could have evaporated from the earth very comfortably at that moment!

Sandy was quite clearly angry, as well he might be, after the things he'd heard, but he was entirely cold and collected. Gordon was hot, and bursting with imaginary wrongs. I was aghast at this perfectly foolish and unnecessary muddle that had suddenly arisen out of nothing. Sandy apologized to me with unimpeachable politeness for inadvertently overhearing, and then turned to Gordon and stiffly invited him to get into his car and ride to the station.

I begged him not to go. I didn't wish to be the cause of any silly quarrel between them. But without paying the slightest attention to me, they climbed into the car, and whirled away, leaving me placidly standing on the door-mat.

I came in and went to bed, and lay awake for hours, expecting to hear—I don't know what kind of explosion. It is now eleven o'clock, and the doctor hasn't appeared. I don't know how on earth I shall meet him when he does. I fancy I shall hide in the clothes-closet.

Did you ever know anything as unnecessary and stupid as this whole situation? I suppose now I've quarreled with Gordon,—and I positively don't know over what,—and of course my relations with the doctor are going to be terribly awkward. I said horrid things about him,—you know the silly way I talk,—things I didn't mean in the least.

I wish it were yesterday at this time. I would make Gordon go at four.

SALLIE.

Sunday afternoon.

Dear Dr. MacRae:

That was a horrid, stupid, silly business last night. But by this time you must know me well enough to realize that I never mean the foolish things I say. My tongue has no slightest connection with my brain; it just runs along by itself. I must seem to you very ungrateful for all the help you have given me in this unaccustomed work and for the patience you have (occasionally) shown.

I do appreciate the fact that I could never have run this asylum by myself without your responsible presence in the background; and though once in a while, as you yourself must acknowledge, you have been pretty impatient and bad tempered and difficult, still I have never held it against you, and I really didn't mean any of the ill-mannered things I said last night. Please forgive me for being rude. I should hate very much to lose your friendship. And we are friends, are we not? I like to think so.

S. McB.

Dear Judy:

I am sure I haven't an idea whether or not the doctor and I
have made up our differences. I sent him a polite note of apology, which he received in abysmal silence. He didn't come near
us until this afternoon, and he hasn't by the blink of an eyelash
referred to our unfortunate contretemps. We talked exclusively
about an ichthyol salve that will remove eczema from a baby's
scalp; then, Sadie Kate being present, the conversation turned
to cats. It seems that the doctor's Maltese cat has four kittens,
and Sadie Kate will not be silenced until she has seen them. Before I knew what was happening I found myself making an engagement to take her to see those miserable kittens at four
o'clock to-morrow afternoon.

Whereupon the doctor, with an indifferently polite bow,
took himself off. And that apparently is the end.

Your Sunday note arrives, and I am delighted to hear that
you have taken the house. It will be beautiful having you for a
neighbor for so long. Our improvements ought to march along,
with you and the president at our elbow. But it does seem as
though you ought to get out here before August 7. Are you sure
the city air is good for you just now? I have never known so devoted a wife.

My respects to the president.

S. McB.

July 22.

Dear Judy:

Please listen to this!

At four o'clock I took Sadie Kate to the doctor's house to
look at those cats. But Freddy Howland just twenty minutes
before had fallen down-stairs, so the doctor was at the How-

land house occupying himself with Freddy's collar-bone. He
had left word for us to sit down and wait, that he would be
back shortly.

Mrs. McGurk ushered us into the library; and then, not to
leave us alone, came in herself on a pretense of polishing the
brass. I don't know what she thought we'd do! Run off with
the pelican perhaps.

I settled down to an article about the Chinese situation in the
Century,[39] and Sadie Kate roamed about at large examining
everything she found, like a curious little mongoose.

She commenced with his stuffed flamingo and wanted to
know what made it so tall and what made it so red. Did it always eat frogs, and had it hurt its other foot? She ticks off
questions with the steady persistency of an eight-day clock.

I buried myself in my article and left Mrs. McGurk to deal
with Sadie. Finally, after she had worked around the room, she
came to a portrait of a little girl occupying a leather frame in
the center of the doctor's writing desk—a child with a queer elf-
like beauty, resembling very strangely our little Allegra. This
photograph might have been a portrait of Allegra grown five
years older. I had noticed the picture the night we took supper
with the doctor, and had meant to ask which of his little patients she was. Happily I didn't!

"Who's that?" said Sadie Kate, pouncing upon it.

"It's the docthor's little gurrl."

"Where is she?"

"Shure, she's far away wit' her gran'ma."

"Where'd he get her?"

"His wife give her to him."

I emerged from my book with electric suddenness.

"His wife!" I cried.

The next instant I was furious with myself for having spoken, but I was so completely taken off my guard. Mrs. McGurk
straightened up and became volubly conversational at once.

"And didn't he never tell you about his wife? She went insane six years ago. It got so it weren't safe to keep her in the
house, and he had to put her away. It near killed him. I never
seen a lady more beautiful than her. I guess he didn't so much

as smile for a year. It's funny he never told you nothing, and you such a friend!"

"Naturally it's not a subject he cares to talk about," said I dryly, and I asked her what kind of brass polish she used.

Sadie Kate and I went out to the garage and hunted up the kittens ourselves; and we mercifully got away before the doctor came back.

But will you tell me what this means? Didn't Jervis know he was married? It's the queerest thing I ever heard. I do think, as the McGurk suggests, that Sandy might casually have dropped the information that he had a wife in an insane asylum.

But of course it must be a terrible tragedy and I suppose he can't bring himself to talk about it. I see now why he's so morbid over the question of heredity—I dare say he fears for the little girl. When I think of all the jokes I've made on the subject, I'm aghast at how I must have hurt him, and angry with myself and angry with him.

I feel as though I never wanted to see the man again. Mercy! did you ever know such a muddle as we are getting ourselves into?

Yours,

Sallie.

P.S. Tom McCoomb has pushed Mamie Prout into the box of mortar that the masons use. She's parboiled. I've sent for the doctor.

July 24.

My dear Madam:

I have a shocking scandal to report about the superintendent of the John Grier Home. Don't let it get into the newspapers, please. I can picture the spicy details of the investigation prior to her removal by the "Cruelty."

I was sitting in the sunshine by my open window this morning reading a sweet book on the Froebel theory[40] of child culture—

never lose your temper, always speak kindly to the little ones. Though they may appear bad, they are not so in reality. It is either that they are not feeling well or have nothing interesting to do. Never punish; simply deflect their attention. I was entertaining a very loving, uplifted attitude toward all this young life about me when my attention was attracted by a group of little boys beneath the window.

"Aw—John—don't hurt it!"

"Let it go!"

"Kill it quick!"

And above their remonstrances rose the agonized squealing of some animal in pain. I dropped Froebel and, running downstairs, burst upon them from the side door. They saw me coming, and scattered right and left, revealing Johnnie Cobden engaged in torturing a mouse. I will spare you the grisly details. I called to one of the boys to come and drown the creature quick! John I seized by the collar; and dragged him squirming and kicking in at the kitchen door. He is a big, hulking boy of thirteen, and he fought like a little tiger, holding on to posts and door-jambs as we passed. Ordinarily I doubt if I could have handled him, but that one sixteenth Irish that I possess was all on top, and I was fighting mad. We burst into the kitchen, and I hastily looked about for a means of chastisement. The pancake-turner was the first utensil that met my eye. I seized it and beat that child with all my strength, until I had reduced him to a cowering, whimpering mendicant for mercy, instead of the fighting little bully he had been four minutes before.

And then who should suddenly burst into the midst of this explosion but Dr. MacRae! His face was blank with astonishment. He strode over and took the pancake-turner out of my hand and set the boy on his feet. Johnnie got behind him and clung! I was so angry that I really couldn't talk; it was all I could do not to cry.

"Come, we will take him up to the office," was all the doctor said. And we marched out, Johnnie keeping as far from me as possible and limping conspicuously. We left him in the outer office, and went into my library and shut the door.

"What in the world has the child done?" he asked.

At that I simply laid my head down on the table and began to cry! I was utterly exhausted both emotionally and physically; it had taken all the strength I possessed to make the pancake-turner effective.

I sobbed out all the bloody details, and he told me not to think about it; the mouse was dead now. Then he got me some water to drink, and told me to keep on crying till I was tired; it would do me good. I am not sure that he didn't pat me on the head! Anyway, it was his best professional manner. I have watched him administer the same treatment a dozen times to hysterical orphans. And this was the first time in a week that we had spoken beyond the formality of "good morning"!

Well, as soon as I had got to the stage where I could sit up and laugh, intermittently dabbing my eyes with a wad of handkerchief, we began a review of Johnnie's case. The boy has a morbid heredity, and may be slightly defective, says Sandy. We must deal with the fact as we would with any other disease. Even normal boys are often cruel; a child's moral sense is undeveloped at thirteen.

Then he suggested that I bathe my eyes with hot water and resume my dignity. Which I did. And we had Johnnie in. He stood—by preference—through the entire interview. The doctor talked to him, oh, so sensibly and kindly and humanely! John put up the plea that the mouse was a pest and ought to be killed. The doctor replied that the welfare of the human race demanded the sacrifice of many animals for its own good, not for revenge, but that the sacrifice must be carried out with the least possible hurt to the animal. He explained about the mouse's nervous system, and how the poor little creature had no means of defense. It was a cowardly thing to hurt it wantonly. He told John to try to develop imagination enough to look at things from the other person's point of view, even if the other person was only a mouse. Then he went to the bookcase and took down my copy of Burns,[41] and told the boy what a great poet he was, and how all Scotchmen loved his memory.

"And this is what he wrote about a mouse," said Sandy, turning to the "Wee, sleekit, cow'rin, tim'rous beastie," which he read and explained to the lad as only a Scotchman could.

Johnnie departed penitent, and Sandy redirected his professional attention to me. He said I was tired and in need of a change. Why not go to the Adirondacks for a week? He and Betsy and Mr. Witherspoon would make themselves into a committee to run the asylum.

You know, that's exactly what I was longing to do! I need a shifting of ideas and some pine-scented air. My family opened the camp last week, and think I'm awful not to join them. They *won't* understand that when you accept a position like this you can't casually toss it aside whenever you feel like it. But for a few days I can easily manage. My asylum is wound up like an eight-day clock, and will run until a week from next Monday at 4 p.m., when my train will return me. Then I shall be comfortably settled again before you arrive, and with no errant fancies in my brain.

Meanwhile Master John is in a happily chastened frame of mind and body. And I rather suspect that Sandy's moralizing had the more force because it was preceded by my pancake-turner! But one thing I know—Suzanne Estelle is terrified whenever I step into her kitchen. I casually picked up the potato-masher this morning while I was commenting upon last night's over-salty soup, and she ran to cover behind the woodshed door.

To-morrow at nine I set out on my travels, after preparing the way with five telegrams. And, oh! you can't imagine how I'm looking forward to being a gay, care-free young thing again—to canoeing on the lake and tramping in the woods and dancing at the club-house. I was in a state of delirium all night long at the prospect. Really, I hadn't realized how mortally tired I had become of all this asylum scenery.

"What you need," said Sandy to me, "is to get away for a little and sow some wild oats."

That diagnosis was positively clairvoyant. I can't think of anything in the world I'd rather do than sow a few wild oats. I'll come back with fresh energy, ready to welcome you and a busy summer.

As ever,
SALLIE.

P.S. Jimmie and Gordon are both going to be up there. How I wish you could join us! A husband is very discommoding.

CAMP MCBRIDE,
July 29.

Dear Judy:

This is to tell you that the mountains are higher than usual, the woods greener, and the lake bluer.

People seem late about coming up this year; the Harrimans' camp is the only other one at our end of the lake that is open. The club-house is very scantily supplied with dancing-men, but we have as house guest an obliging young politician who likes to dance, so I am not discommoded by the general scarcity.

The affairs of the nation and the rearing of orphans are alike delegated to the background while we paddle among the lily-pads of this delectable lake. I look forward with reluctance to 7:56 next Monday morning, when I turn my back on the mountains. The awful thing about a vacation is that the moment it begins your happiness is already clouded by its approaching end.

I hear a voice on the veranda asking if Sallie is to be found within or without.

Addio!

S.

August 3.

Dear Judy:

Back at the John Grier, reshouldering the burdens of the coming generation. What should meet my eyes upon entering these grounds but John Cobden, of pancake-turner memory, wearing a badge upon his sleeve. I turned it to me and read "S. P. C. A."[42] in letters of gold! The doctor, during my absence, has formed a local branch of the Cruelty to Animals, and made Johnnie its president.

I hear that yesterday he stopped the workmen on the foundation for the new farm cottage and scolded them severely for whipping their horses up the incline! None of all this strikes any one but me as funny.

There's a lot of news, but with you due in four days, why bother to write? Just one delicious bit I am saving for the end. So hold your breath. You are going to receive a thrill on page 4. You should hear Sadie Kate squeal! Jane is cutting her hair. Instead of wearing it in two tight braids like this,

our little colleen will in the future look like this:

"Them pigtails got on my nerves," says Jane.

You can see how much more stylish and becoming the present coiffure is. I think somebody will be wanting to adopt her. Only Sadie Kate is such an independent, manly little creature; she is eminently fitted by nature to shift for herself. I must save adopting parents for the helpless ones.

You should see our new clothes! I can't wait for this assemblage of rosebuds to burst upon you. And you should have seen those blue ginghamed eyes brighten when the new frocks were actually given out—three for each girl, all different colors, and all perfectly private personal property, with the owner's indelible name inside the collar. Mrs. Lippett's lazy system of having each child draw from the wash a promiscuous dress each week, was an insult to feminine nature.

Sadie Kate is squealing like a baby pig. I must go to see if Jane has by mistake clipped off an ear.

Jane hasn't. Sadie's excellent ears are still intact. She is just squealing on principle; the way one does in a dentist's chair, under the belief that it is going to hurt the next instant.

I really can't think of anything else to write except my news,—so here it is,—and I hope you'll like it.

I am engaged to be married.

My love to you both.

S. McB.

THE JOHN GRIER HOME,
November 15.

Dear Judy:

Betsy and I are just back from a *giro* in our new motor-car. It undoubtedly does add to the pleasure of institution life. The car of its own accord turned up Long Ridge Road, and stopped before the gates of Shadywell. The chains were up, and the shutters battened down, and the place looked closed and gloomy and rain-soaked. It wore a sort of fall of the House of Usher[43] air, and didn't in the least resemble the cheerful house that used to greet me hospitably of an afternoon.

I hate to have our nice summer ended. It seems as though a section of my life was shut away behind me, and the unknown future was pressing awfully close. Positively, I'd like to postpone that wedding another six months, but I'm afraid poor Gordon would make too dreadful a fuss. Don't think I'm getting wobbly, for I'm not. It's just that somehow I need more time to think about it, and March is getting nearer every day. I know absolutely that I'm doing the most sensible thing. Everybody, man or woman, is the better for being nicely and appropriately and cheerfully married; but oh dear! oh dear! I do hate upheavals, and this is going to be such a world-without-end upheaval! Sometimes when the day's work is over, and I'm tired, I haven't the spirit to rise and meet it.

And now especially since you've bought Shadywell, and are going to be here every summer, I resent having to leave. Next year, when I'm far away, I'll be consumed with homesickness, thinking of all the busy, happy times at the John Grier, with you and Betsy and Percy and our grumbly Scotchman working away cheerfully without me. How can anything ever make up to a mother for the loss of 107 children?

I trust that Judy, Junior, stood the journey into town without upsetting her usual poise. I am sending her a bit giftie, made partly by myself and chiefly by Jane. But two rows, I must inform you, were done by the doctor. One only gradually plumbs the depths of Sandy's nature. After a ten-months' acquaintance with the man, I discover that he knows how to knit, an accomplishment he picked up in his boyhood from an old shepherd on the Scotch moors.

He dropped in three days ago and stayed for tea, really in almost his old friendly mood. But he has since stiffened up again to the same man of granite we knew all summer. I've given up trying to make him out. I suppose, however, that any one might be expected to be a bit down with a wife in an insane asylum. I wish he'd talk about it once. It's awful having such a shadow hovering in the background of your thoughts and never coming out into plain sight.

I know that this letter doesn't contain a word of the kind of news that you like to hear. But it's that beastly twilight hour of a damp November day, and I'm in a beastly uncheerful mood. I'm awfully afraid that I am developing into a temperamental person, and Heaven knows Gordon can supply all the temperament that one family needs! I don't know where we'll land if I don't preserve my sensibly stolid, cheerful nature.

Have you really decided to go South with Jervis? I appreciate your feeling (to a slight extent) about not wanting to be separated from a husband; but it does seem sort of hazardous to me to move so young a daughter to the tropics.

The children are playing blindman's-buff in the lower corridor. I think I'll have a romp with them, and try to be in a more affable mood before resuming my pen.

A bientôt!

SALLIE.

P.S. These November nights are pretty cold, and we are getting ready to move the camps indoors. Our Indians are very pampered young savages at present, with a double supply of blankets and hot-water bottles. I shall hate to see the camps go; they have done a lot for us. Our lads will be as tough as Canadian trappers when they come in.

November 20.

Dear Judy:

Your motherly solicitude is sweet, but I didn't mean what I said. Of course it's perfectly safe to convey Judy, Junior, to the temperately tropical lands that are washed by the Caribbean. She'll thrive as long as you don't set her absolutely on top of the equator. And your bungalow, shaded by palms and fanned by sea-breezes, with an ice-machine in the back yard and an English doctor across the bay, sounds made for the rearing of babies.

My objections were all due to the selfish fact that I and the John Grier are going to be lonely without you this winter. I really think it's entrancing to have a husband who engages in such picturesque pursuits as financing tropical railroads and developing asphalt lakes and rubber groves and mahogany forests. I wish that Gordon would take to life in those picturesque countries; I'd be more thrilled by the romantic possibilities of the future. Washington seems awfully commonplace compared with Honduras and Nicaragua and the islands of the Caribbean.

I'll be down to wave good-by.

Addio!

SALLIE.

November 24.

Dear Gordon:

Judy has gone back to town, and is sailing next week for Jamaica, where she is to make her headquarters while Jervis cruises about adjacent waters on these entertaining new ventures of his. Couldn't you engage in traffic in the South Seas? I think I'd feel pleasanter about leaving my asylum if you had something romantic and adventurous to offer instead. And think how beautiful you'd be in those white linen clothes! I really believe I might be able to stay in love with a man quite permanently if he always dressed in white.

You can't imagine how I miss Judy. Her absence leaves a dreadful hole in my afternoons. Can't you run up for a week-end soon? I think the sight of you would be very cheering, and I'm feeling awfully down of late. You know, my dear Gordon, I like you much better when you're right here before my eyes than when I merely think about you from a distance. I believe you must have a sort of hypnotic influence. Occasionally, after you've been away a long time, your spell wears a little thin; but when I see you, it all comes back. You've been away now a long, long time; so, please come fast and bewitch me over again!

S.

December 2.

Dear Judy:

Do you remember in college, when you and I used to plan our favorite futures, how we were forever turning our faces southward? And now to think it has really come true, and you are there, coasting around those tropical isles! Did you ever have such a thrill in the whole of your life, barring one or two connected with Jervis, as when you came up on deck in the early dawn and found yourself riding at anchor in the harbor of Kingston, with the water so blue and the palms so green and the beach so white?

I remember when I first woke in that harbor; I felt like a heroine of grand opera surrounded by untruly beautiful painted scenery. Nothing in my four trips to Europe ever thrilled me like the queer sights and tastes and smells of those three warm weeks seven years ago. And ever since, I've panted to get back. When I stop to think about it, I can hardly bring myself to swallow our unexciting meals; I wish to be dining on curries and tamales and mangos. Isn't it funny? You'd think I must have a dash of Creole or Spanish or some warm blood in me somewhere, but I'm nothing on earth but a chilly mixture of English and Irish and Scotch. Perhaps that is why I hear the South calling. "The palm dreams of the pine, and the pine of the palm."[44]

After seeing you off, I turned back to New York with an awful wander-thirst gnawing at my vitals. I, too, wanted to be starting off on my travels in a new blue hat and a new blue suit with a big bunch of violets in my hand. For five minutes I would cheerfully have said good-by forever to poor dear Gordon in return for the wide world to wander in. I suppose you are thinking they are not entirely incompatible—Gordon and the wide world—but I don't seem able to get your point of view about husbands. I see marriage as a man must, a good, sensible workaday institution; but awfully curbing to one's liberty. Somehow, after you're married forever, life has lost its feeling of adventure. There aren't any romantic possibilities waiting to surprise you around each corner.

The disgraceful truth is that one man doesn't seem quite enough for me. I like the variety of sensation that you get only from a variety of men. I'm afraid I've spent too flirtatious a youth, and it isn't easy for me to settle.

I seem to have a very wandering pen. To return: I saw you off, and took the ferry back to New York with a horribly empty feeling. After our intimate gossipy three months together, it seems a terrible task to tell you my troubles in tones that will reach to the bottom of the continent. My ferry slid right under the nose of your steamer, and I could see you and Jervis plainly leaning on the rail. I waved frantically, but you never blinked an eyelash. Your gaze was fixed in homesick contemplation upon the top of the Woolworth Building.

Back in New York, I took myself to a department store to accomplish a few trifles in the way of shopping. As I was entering through their revolving doors, who should be revolving in the other direction but Helen Brooks! We had a terrible time meeting, as I tried to go back out, and she tried to come back in; I thought we should revolve eternally. But we finally got back together and shook hands, and she obligingly helped me choose fifteen dozen pairs of stockings and fifty caps and sweaters and two hundred union suits, and then we gossiped all the way up to Fifty-second Street, where we had luncheon at the Women's University Club.

I always liked Helen. She's not spectacular, but steady and dependable. Will you ever forget the way she took hold of that senior pageant committee and whipped it into shape after Mildred had made such a mess of it? How would she do here as a successor to me? I am filled with jealousy at the thought of a successor, but I suppose I must face it.

"When did you last see Judy Abbott?" was Helen's first question.

"Fifteen minutes ago," said I. "She has just set sail for the Spanish main with a husband and daughter and nurse and maid and valet and dog."

"Has she a nice husband?"

"None better."

"And does she still like him?"

"Never saw a happier marriage."

It struck me that Helen looked a trifle bleak, and I suddenly remembered all that gossip that Marty Keene told us last summer; so I hastily changed the conversation to a perfectly safe subject like orphans.

But later she told me the whole story herself in as detached and impersonal a way as though she were discussing the characters in a book. She has been living alone in the city, hardly seeing any one, and she seemed low in spirits and glad to talk. Poor Helen appears to have made an awful mess of her life. I don't know any one who has covered so much ground in such a short space of time. Since her graduation she has been married, has had a baby and lost him, divorced her husband, quarreled with her family, and come to the city to earn her own living. She is reading manuscript for a publishing house.

There seems to have been no reason for her divorce from the ordinary point of view; the marriage just simply didn't work. They weren't friends. If he had been a woman, she wouldn't have wasted half an hour talking with him. If she had been a man, he would have said: "Glad to see you. How are you?" and gone on. And yet they *married*. Isn't it dreadful how blind this sex business can make people?

She was brought up on the theory that a woman's only legitimate profession is home-making. When she finished college, she was naturally eager to start on her career, and Henry presented himself. Her family scanned him closely, and found him perfect in every respect—good family, good morals, good financial position, good-looking. Helen was in love with him. She had a big wedding and lots of new clothes and dozens of embroidered towels. Everything looked propitious.

But as they began to get acquainted, they didn't like the same books or jokes or people or amusements. He was expansive and social and hilarious, and she wasn't. First they bored, and then they irritated, each other. Her orderliness made him impatient, and his disorderliness drove her wild. She would spend a day getting closets and bureau drawers in order, and in five minutes he would stir them into chaos. He would leave his clothes about for her to pick up, and his towels in a messy heap on the bathroom floor, and he never scrubbed out the tub. And she, on her side, was awfully unresponsive and irritating,—she realized it fully,—she got to the point where she wouldn't laugh at his jokes.

I suppose most old-fashioned, orthodox people would think it awful to break up a marriage on such innocent grounds. It seemed so to me at first; but as she went on piling up detail on detail, each trivial in itself, but making a mountainous total, I agreed with Helen that it was awful to keep it going. It wasn't really a marriage; it was a mistake.

So one morning at breakfast, when the subject of what they should do for the summer came up, she said quite casually that she thought she would go West and get a residence in some State where you could get a divorce for a respectable cause; and for the first time in months he agreed with her.

You can imagine the outraged feelings of her Victorian family. In all the seven generations of their sojourn in America they have never had anything like this to record in the family Bible. It all comes from sending her to college and letting her read such dreadful modern people as Ellen Key[45] and Bernard Shaw.

"If he had only got drunk and dragged me about by the hair," Helen wailed, "it would have been legitimate; but because we didn't actually throw things at each other, no one could see any reason for a divorce."

The pathetic part of the whole business is that both she and Henry were admirably fitted to make some one else happy. They just simply didn't match each other; and when two people don't match, all the ceremonies in the world can't marry them.

Saturday morning.

I meant to get this letter off two days ago; and here I am with volumes written, but nothing mailed.

We've just had one of those miserable deceiving nights—cold and frosty when you go to bed, and warm and lifeless when you wake in the dark, smothered under a mountain of blankets. By the time I had removed my own extra covers and plumped up my pillow and settled comfortably, I thought of those fourteen bundled-up babies in the fresh-air nursery. Their so-called night nurse sleeps like a top the whole night through. (Her name is next on the list to be expunged.) So I roused myself again, and made a little blanket-removing tour, and by the time I had finished I was forever awake. It is not often that I pass a *nuit blanche;* but when I do, I settle world problems. Isn't it funny how much keener your mind is when you are lying awake in the dark?

I began thinking about Helen Brooks, and I planned her whole life over again. I don't know why her miserable story has taken such a hold over me; it's a disheartening subject for an engaged girl to contemplate. I keep saying to myself, What if Gordon and I, when we really get acquainted, should change our minds about liking each other? The fear grips my heart and wrings it dry. But I am marrying him for no reason in the world except affection. I'm not particularly ambitious. Neither his position nor his money ever tempted me in the least; and certainly I am not doing it to find my life-work, for in order to marry I am having to give up the work that I love. I really do love this work; I go about planning and planning their baby futures, feeling that I'm constructing the nation. Whatever becomes of me in after life, I am sure I'll be more capable for having had this tremendous experience. And it *is* a tremendous experience, the nearness to humanity that an asylum brings. I am learning so many new things every day that when each Saturday night comes I look back on the Sallie of last Saturday night, amazed at her ignorance.

You know I am developing a funny old characteristic; I am getting to hate change. I don't like the prospect of having my life disrupted. I used to love the excitement of volcanoes, but now a high level plateau is my choice in landscape. I am very comfortable where I am; my desk and closet and bureau drawers are organized to suit me; and, oh, I dread unspeakably the thought of the upheaval that is going to happen to me next year! Please don't imagine that I don't care for Gordon quite as much as any man has a right to be cared for. It isn't that

I like him any the less, but I am getting to like orphans the more.

I just met our medical adviser a few minutes ago as he was emerging from the nursery—Allegra is the only person in the institution who is favored by his austere social attentions. He paused in passing to make a polite comment upon the sudden change in the weather, and to express the hope that I would remember him to Mrs. Pendleton when I wrote.

This is a miserable letter to send off on its travels, with scarcely a word of the kind of news that you like to hear. But our bare little orphan-asylum up in the hills must seem awfully far away from the palms and orange-groves and lizards and tarantulas that you are enjoying.

Have a good time, and don't forget the John Grier Home
and
SALLIE.

December 11.

Dear Judy:

Your Jamaica letter is here, and I'm glad to learn that Judy, Junior, enjoys traveling. Write me every detail about your house, and send some photographs, so I can see you in it. What fun it must be to have a boat of your own that chugs about those entertaining seas! Have you worn all of your eighteen white dresses yet? And aren't you glad now that I made you wait about buying a Panama hat till you reached Kingston?

We are running along here very much as usual without anything exciting to chronicle. You remember little Maybelle Fuller, don't you—the chorus girl's daughter whom our doctor doesn't like? We have placed her out. I tried to make the woman take Hattie Heaphy instead,—the quiet little one who stole the communion-cup,—but no, indeed! Maybelle's eyelashes won the day. After all, as poor Marie says, the chief thing is to be pretty. All else in life depends on that.

When I got home last week, after my dash to New York, I

made a brief speech to the children. I told them that I had just been seeing Aunt Judy off on a big ship, and I am embarrassed to have to report that the interest—at least on the part of the boys—immediately abandoned Aunt Judy and centered upon the ship. How many tons of coal did she burn a day? Was she long enough to reach from the carriage-house to the Indian camp? Were there any guns aboard, and if a privateer should attack her, could she hold her own? In case of a mutiny, could the captain shoot down anybody he chose, and wouldn't he be hanged when he got to shore? I had ignominiously to call upon Sandy to finish my speech. I realize that the best-equipped feminine mind in the world can't cope with the peculiar class of questions that originate in a thirteen-year boy's brain.

As a result of their seafaring interest, the doctor conceived the idea of inviting seven of the oldest and most alert lads to spend the day with him in New York and see with their own eyes an ocean-liner. They rose at five yesterday morning, caught the 7:30 train, and had the most wonderful adventure that has happened in all their seven lives. They visited one of the big liners (Sandy knows the Scotch engineer), and were conducted from the bottom of the hold to the top of the crow's-nest, and then had luncheon on board. And after luncheon they visited the aquarium and the top of the Singer Building, and took the subway up-town to spend an hour with the birds of America in their habitats. Sandy with great difficulty pried them away from the Natural History Museum in time to catch the 6:15 train. Dinner in the dining-car. They inquired with great particularity how much it was costing, and when they heard that it was the same, no matter how much you ate, they drew deep breaths and settled quietly and steadily to the task of not allowing their host to be cheated. The railroad made nothing on that party, and all the tables around stopped eating to stare. One traveler asked the doctor if it was a boarding-school he had in charge; so you can see how the manners and bearing of our lads have picked up. I don't wish to boast, but no one would ever have asked such a question concerning seven of Mrs. Lippett's youngsters. "Are they bound for a reformatory?" would have been the natural question after observing the table manners of her offspring.

My little band tumbled in toward ten o'clock, excitedly babbling a mess of statistics about reciprocating compound engines and water-tight bulkheads, devil-fish and sky-scrapers and birds of paradise. I thought I should never get them to bed. And, oh, but they had had a glorious day! I do wish I could manage breaks in the routine oftener. It gives them a new outlook on life and makes them more like normal children. Wasn't it really nice of Sandy? But you should have seen that man's behavior when I tried to thank him. He waved me aside in the middle of a sentence, and growlingly asked Miss Snaith if she couldn't economize a little on carbolic acid. The house smelt like a hospital.

I must tell you that Punch is back with us again, entirely renovated as to manners. I am looking for a family to adopt him. I had hoped those two intelligent spinsters would see their way to keeping him forever, but they want to travel, and they feel he's too consuming of their liberty. I inclose a sketch in colored chalk of your steamer, which he has just completed. There is some doubt as to the direction in which it is going; it looks as

though it might progress backward and end in Brooklyn. Owing to the loss of my blue pencil, our flag has had to adopt the Italian colors.

The three figures on the bridge are you and Jervis and the baby. I am pained to note that you carry your daughter by the back of her neck, as if she were a kitten. That is not the way we handle babies in the J. G. H. nursery. Please also note that the artist has given Jervis his full due in the matter of legs. When I asked Punch what had become of the captain, he said that the captain was inside, putting coal on the fire. Punch was terribly impressed, as well he might be, when he heard that your steamer burned three hundred wagon-loads a day, and he naturally supposed that all hands had been piped to the stoke-hole.

BOW! WOW!

That's a bark from Sing. I told him I was writing to you, and he responded instantly.

We both send love.

Yours,
SALLIE.

THE JOHN GRIER HOME,
Saturday,

Dear Enemy:

You were so terribly gruff last night when I tried to thank you for giving my boys such a wonderful day that I didn't have a chance to express half of the appreciation I felt.

What on earth is the matter with you, Sandy? You used to be a tolerably nice man—in spots, but these last three or four months you have only been nice to other people, never to me.

We have had from the first a long series of misunderstandings and foolish contretemps, but after each one we seemed to reach a solider basis of understanding, until I had thought our friendship was on a pretty firm foundation, capable of withstanding any reasonable shock.

And then came that unfortunate evening last June when you overheard some foolish impolitenesses, which I did not in the slightest degree mean; and from then on you faded into the distance. Really, I have felt terribly bad about it, and have wanted to apologize, but your manner has not been inviting of confidence. It isn't that I have any excuse or explanation to offer; I haven't. You know how foolish and silly I am on occasions, but you will just have to realize that though I'm flippant and foolish and trivial on top, I am pretty solid inside; and you've got to forgive the silly part. The Pendletons knew that long ago, or they wouldn't have sent me up here. I have tried hard to pull off an honest job, partly because I wanted to justify their judgment, partly because I was really interested in giving the poor little kiddies their share of happiness, but mostly, I actually believe, because I wanted to show you that your first derogatory opinion of me was ill founded. Won't you please expunge that unfortunate fifteen minutes at the porte-cochère last June, and remember instead the fifteen hours I spent reading the Kallikak Family?

I would like to feel that we're friends again.

SALLIE McBRIDE.

THE JOHN GRIER HOME,
Sunday.

Dear Dr. MacRae:

I am in receipt of your calling card with an eleven-word answer to my letter on the back. I didn't mean to annoy you by my attentions. What you think and how you behave are really matters of extreme indifference to me. Be just as impolite as you choose.

S. McB.

December 14.

Dear Judy:

Please pepper your letters with stamps, inside and out. I have thirty collectors in the family. Since you have taken to travel, every day about post-time an eager group gathers at the gate, waiting to snatch any letters of foreign design, and by the time the letters reach me they are almost in shreds through the tenacity of rival snatchers. Tell Jervis to send us some more of those purple pine-trees from Honduras; likewise some green parrots from Guatemala. I could use a pint of them!

Isn't it wonderful to have got these apathetic little things so enthusiastic? My children are getting to be almost like real children. B dormitory started a pillow-fight last night of its own accord; and though it was very wearing to our scant supply of linen, I stood by and beamed, and even tossed a pillow myself.

Last Saturday those two desirable friends of Percy's spent the whole afternoon playing with my boys. They brought up three rifles, and each man took the lead of a camp of Indians, and passed the afternoon in a bottle-shooting contest, with a prize for the winning camp. They brought the prize with them—an atrocious head of an Indian painted on leather. Dreadful taste; but the men thought it lovely, so I admired it with all the ardor I could assume.

When they had finished, I warmed them up with cookies and hot chocolate, and I really think the men enjoyed it as much as the boys; they undoubtedly enjoyed it more than I did. I couldn't help being in a feminine twitter all the time the firing was going on for fear somebody would shoot somebody else. But I know that I can't keep twenty-four Indians tied to my apron-strings, and I never could find in the whole wide world three nicer men to take an interest in them.

Just think of all that healthy, exuberant volunteer service going to waste under the asylum's nose! I suppose the neighbor-

hood is full of plenty more of it, and I am going to make it my business to dig it out.

What I want most are about eight nice, pretty, sensible young women to come up here one night a week, and sit before the fire and tell stories while the chicks pop corn. I do so want to contrive a little individual petting for my babies. You see, Judy, I am remembering your own childhood, and am trying hard to fill in the gaps.

The trustees' meeting last week went beautifully. The new women are most helpful, and only the nice men came. I am happy to announce that the Hon. Cy Wykoff is visiting his married daughter in Scranton. I wish she would invite father to live with her permanently.

                                                          Wednesday.

I am in the most childish temper with the doctor, and for no
very definite reason. He keeps along his even, unemotional way
without paying the slightest attention to anything or anybody. I
have swallowed more slights during these last few months than
in the whole of my life before, and I'm developing the most
shockingly revengeful nature. I spend all my spare time planning
situations in which he will be terribly hurt and in need of my
help, and in which I, with the utmost callousness, will shrug my
shoulders and turn away. I am growing into a person entirely
foreign to the sweet, sunny young thing you used to know.

                                                          Evening.

Do you realize that I am an authority on the care of dependent children? To-morrow I and other authorities visit officially
the Hebrew Sheltering Guardian Society's Orphan Asylum at
Pleasantville.[46] (All that's its name!) It's a terribly difficult and
roundabout journey from this point, involving a daybreak start
and two trains and an automobile; but if I'm to be an authority, I must live up to the title. I'm keen about looking over other
institutions and gleaning as many ideas as possible against our
own alterations next year. And this Pleasantville asylum is an
architectural model.

I acknowledge now, upon sober reflection, that we were wise
to postpone extensive building operations until next summer.
Of course I was disappointed, because it meant that I won't be
the center of the ripping-up, and I do so love to be the center of
ripping-ups! But, anyway, you'll take my advice, even though
I'm no longer an official head? The two building details we did
accomplish are very promising. Our new laundry grows better
and better; it has removed from us that steamy smell so dear to
asylums. The farmer's cottage will finally be ready for occu-
pancy next week. All it now lacks is a coat of paint and some
door-knobs.

But, oh dear! oh dear! another bubble has burst! Mrs. Turnfelt, for all her comfortable figure and sunny smile, hates to
have children messing about. They make her nervous. And as
for Turnfelt himself, though industrious and methodical and an
excellent gardener, still his mental processes are not quite what
I had hoped for. When he first came, I made him free of the library. He began at the case nearest the door, which contains
thirty-seven volumes of Pansy's works. Finally, after he had
spent four months on Pansy, I suggested a change, and sent him
home with "Huckleberry Finn." But he brought it back in a
few days, and shook his head. He says that after reading Pansy,
anything else seems tame. I am afraid I shall have to look about
for some one a little more up-and-coming. But at least, compared with Sterry, Turnfelt is a scholar!

And speaking of Sterry, he paid us a social call a few days
ago, in quite a chastened frame of mind. It seems that the "rich
city feller" whose estate he has been managing no longer needs
his services; and Sterry has graciously consented to return to us
and let the children have gardens if they wish. I kindly, but con-
vincingly, declined his offer.

                                           Friday.

I came back from Pleasantville last night with a heart full of
envy. Please, Mr. President, I want some gray stucco cottages,
with Luca della Robbia[47] figures baked into the front. They
have nearly 700 children there, and all sizable youngsters. Of
course that makes a very different problem from my hundred
and seven, ranging from babyhood up. But I borrowed from
their superintendent several very fancy ideas. I'm dividing my
chicks into big and little sisters and brothers, each big one to
have a little one to love and help and fight for. Big sister Sadie
Kate has to see that little sister Gladiola always has her hair
neatly combed and her stockings pulled up and knows her lessons and gets a touch of petting and her share of candy—very
pleasant for Gladiola, but especially developing for Sadie Kate.

Also I am going to start among our older children a limited
form of self-government such as we had in college. That will
help fit them to go out into the world and govern themselves

when they get there. This shoving children into the world at the age of sixteen seems terribly merciless. Five of my children are ready to be shoved, but I can't bring myself to do it. I keep remembering my own irresponsible silly young self, and wondering what would have happened to me had I been turned out to work at the age of sixteen!

I must leave you now to write an interesting letter to my politician in Washington, and it's hard work. What have I to say that will interest a politician? I can't do anything any more but babble about babies, and he wouldn't care if every baby was swept from the face of the earth. Oh, yes, he would, too! I'm afraid I'm slandering him. Babies—at least boy babies—grow into voters.

Good-by,
SALLIE.

Dearest Judy:

If you expect a cheerful letter from me this day, don't read this. The life of man is a wintry road. Fog, snow, rain, slush, drizzle, cold—such weather! such weather! And you in dear Jamaica with the sunshine and the orange-blossoms!

We've got whooping-cough, and you can hear us whoop when you get off the train two miles away. We don't know how we got it—just one of the pleasures of institution life. Cook has left,—in the night,—what the Scotch call a "moonlicht flitting." I don't know how she got her trunk away, but it's gone. The kitchen fire went with her. The pipes are frozen. The plumbers are here, and the kitchen floor is all ripped up. One of our horses has the spavin. And, to crown all, our cheery, resourceful Percy is down, down, down in the depths of despair. We have not been quite certain for three days past whether we could keep him from suicide. The girl in Detroit,—I knew she was a heartless little minx,—without so much as going through the formality of sending back his ring, has gone and married herself to a man and a couple of automobiles and a yacht. It is

the best thing that could ever have happened to Percy, but it
will be a long, long time before he realizes it.

We have our twenty-four Indians back in the house with us.
I was sorry to have to bring them in, but the shacks were
scarcely planned for winter quarters. I have stowed them away
very comfortably, however, thanks to the spacious iron veran-
das surrounding our new fire-escape. It was a happy idea of
Jervis's having them glassed in for sleeping-porches. The babies' sun-parlor is a wonderful addition to our nursery. We can
fairly see the little tots bloom under the influence of that extra
air and sunshine.

With the return of the Indians to civilized life, Percy's occupation was ended, and he was supposed to remove himself to the
hotel. But he didn't want to remove himself. He has got used to
orphans, he says, and he would miss not seeing them about. I
think the truth is that he is feeling so miserable over his wrecked
engagement that he is afraid to be alone; he needs something to
occupy every waking moment out of banking hours. And goodness knows we're glad enough to keep him! He has been wonderful with those youngsters, and they need a man's influence. But
what on earth to do with the man? As you discovered last summer, this spacious château does not contain a superabundance of
guest-rooms. He has finally fitted himself into the doctor's laboratory, and the medicines have moved themselves to a closet
down the hall. He and the doctor fixed it up between them, and
if they are willing to be mutually inconvenienced, I have no fault
to find.

Mercy! I've just looked at the calendar, and it's the eighteenth, with Christmas only a week away. However shall we
finish all our plans in a week? The chicks are making presents
for one another, and something like a thousand secrets have
been whispered in my ear.

Snow last night. The boys have spent the morning in the
woods, gathering evergreens and drawing them home on sleds;
and twenty girls are spending the afternoon in the laundry,
winding wreaths for the windows. I don't know how we are
going to do our washing this week. We were planning to keep
the Christmas-tree a secret, but fully fifty children have been

boosted up to the carriage-house window to take a peep at it, and I am afraid the news has spread among the remaining fifty.

At your insistence, we have sedulously fostered the Santa Claus myth, but it doesn't meet with much credence. "Why didn't he ever come before?" was Sadie Kate's skeptical question. But Santa Claus is undoubtedly coming this time. I asked the doctor, out of politeness, to play the chief rôle at our Christmas-tree; and being certain ahead of time that he was going to refuse. I had already engaged Percy as an understudy. But there is no counting on a Scotchman. Sandy accepted with unprecedented graciousness, and I had privately to unengage Percy!

                                                             Tuesday.

Isn't it funny, the way some inconsequential people have of pouring out whatever happens to be churning about in their minds at the moment? They seem to have no residue of small talk, and are never able to dismiss a crisis in order to discuss the weather.

This is apropos of a call I received to-day. A woman had come to deliver her sister's child—sister in a sanatorium for tuberculosis; we to keep the child until the mother is cured, though I fear, from what I hear, that will never be. But, anyway, all the arrangements had been made, and the woman had merely to hand in the little girl and retire. But having a couple of hours between trains, she intimated a desire to look about, so I showed her the kindergarten-rooms and the little crib that Lily will occupy, and our yellow dining-room, with its frieze of bunnies, in order that she might report as many cheerful details as possible to the poor mother. After this, as she seemed tired, I socially asked her to walk into my parlor and have a cup of tea. Doctor MacRae, being at hand and in a hungry mood (a rare state for him; he now condescends to a cup of tea with the officers of this institution about twice a month), came, too, and we had a little party.

The woman seemed to feel that the burden of entertainment rested upon her, and by way of making conversation, she told us that her husband had fallen in love with the girl who sold tickets at a moving-picture show (a painted, yellow-haired thing who chewed gum like a cow, was her description of the enchantress), and he spent all his money on the girl, and never came home except when he was drunk. Then he smashed the furniture something awful. An easel, with her mother's picture on it, that she had had since before she was married, he had thrown down just for the pleasure of hearing it crash. And finally she had just got too tired to live, so she drank a bottle of swamp-root because somebody had told her it was poison if you took it all at once. But it didn't kill her; it only made her sick. And he came back, and said he would choke her if she ever tried that on him again; so she guessed he must still care something for her. All this quite casually while she stirred her tea.

I tried to think of something to say, but it was a social exigency that left me dumb. But Sandy rose to the occasion like a gentleman. He talked to her beautifully and sanely, and sent her away actually uplifted. Our Sandy, when he tries, can be exceptionally nice, particularly to people who have no claim upon him. I suppose it is a matter of professional etiquette—part of a doctor's business to heal the spirit as well as the body. Most spirits appear to need it in this world. My caller has left me needing it. I have been wondering ever since what I should do if I married a man who deserted me for a chewing-gum girl, and who came home and smashed the bric-à-brac. I suppose, judging from the theaters this winter, that it is a thing that might happen to any one, particularly in the best society.

You ought to be thankful you've got Jervis. There is something awfully certain about a man like him. The longer I live, the surer I am that character is the only thing that counts. But how on earth can you ever tell? Men are so good at talking!

Good-by, and a merry Christmas to Jervis and both Judies.

S. McB.

P.S. It would be a pleasant attention if you would answer my letters a little more promptly.

JOHN GRIER HOME,
December 29.

Dear Judy:

Sadie Kate has spent the week composing a Christmas letter
to you, and it leaves nothing for me to tell. Oh, we've had a
wonderful time! Besides all the presents and games and fancy
things to eat, we have had hay-rides and skating-parties and
candy-pulls. I don't know whether these pampered little orphans will ever settle down again into normal children.

Many thanks for my six gifts. I like them all, particularly the
picture of Judy, Junior; the tooth adds a pleasant touch to her
smile.

You'll be glad to hear that I've placed out Hattie Heaphy in
a minister's family, and a dear family they are; they never
blinked an eyelash when I told them about the communion-
cup. They've given her to themselves for a Christmas present,
and she went off so happily, clinging to her new father's hand!

I won't write more now, because fifty children are writing
thank-you letters, and poor Aunt Judy will be buried beneath
her mail when this week's steamer gets in.

My love to the Pendletons.

S. McB.

P.S. Singapore sends his love to Togo, and is sorry he bit him
on the ear.

JOHN GRIER HOME,
December 30.

O, dear, Gordon, I have been reading the most upsetting book!
I tried to talk some French the other day, and not making out
very well, decided that I had better take my French in hand if I
didn't want to lose it entirely. That Scotch doctor of ours has

mercifully abandoned my scientific education, so I have a little time at my own disposal. By some unlucky chance I began with "Numa Roumestan," by Daudet.[48] It is a terribly disturbing book for a girl to read who is engaged to a politician. Read it, Gordon dear, and assiduously train your character away from Numa's. It's the story of a politician who is disquietingly fascinating (like you). Who is adored by all who know him (like you). Who has a most persuasive way of talking and makes wonderful speeches (again like you). He is worshiped by everybody, and they all say to his wife, "What a happy life you must lead, knowing so intimately that wonderful man!"

But he wasn't very wonderful when he came home to her— only when he had an audience and applause. He would drink with every casual acquaintance, and be gay and bubbling and expansive; and then return morose and sullen and down. "Joie de rue, douleur de maison," is the burden of the book.

I read it till twelve last night, and honestly I didn't sleep for being scared. I know you'll be angry, but really and truly, Gordon dear, there's just a touch too much truth in it for my entire amusement. I didn't mean even to refer again to that unhappy matter of August 20,—we talked it all out at the time,—but you know perfectly that you need a bit of watching. And I don't like the idea. I want to have a feeling of absolute confidence and stability about the man I marry. I never could live in a state of anxious waiting for him to come home.

Read "Numa" for yourself, and you'll see the woman's point of view. I'm not patient or meek or long-suffering in any way, and I'm a little afraid of what I'm capable of doing if I have the provocation. My heart has to be in a thing in order to make it work, and, oh, I do so want our marriage to work!

Please forgive me for writing all this. I don't mean that I really think you'll be a "joy of the street, and sorrow of the home." It's just that I didn't sleep last night, and I feel sort of hollow behind the eyes.

May the year that's coming bring good counsel and happiness and tranquillity to both of us!

As ever,

S.

January 1.

Dear Judy:

Something terribly sort of queer has happened, and positively I don't know whether it did happen or whether I dreamed it. I'll tell you from the beginning, and I think it might be as well if you burned this letter; it's not quite proper for Jervis's eyes.

You remember my telling you the case of Thomas Kehoe, whom we placed out last June? He had an alcoholic heredity on both sides, and as a baby seems to have been fattened on beer instead of milk. He entered the John Grier at the age of nine, and twice, according to his record in the Doomsday Book, he managed to get himself intoxicated, once on beer stolen from some workmen, and once (and thoroughly) on cooking brandy. You can see with what misgivings we placed him out; but we warned the family (hard-working temperate farming-people) and hoped for the best.

Yesterday the family telegraphed that they could keep him no longer. Would I please meet him on the six o'clock train? Turnfelt met the six o'clock train. No boy. I sent a night message telling of his non-arrival and asking for particulars.

I stayed up later than usual last night putting my desk in order and—sort of making up my mind to face the New Year. Toward twelve I suddenly realized that the hour was late and I was very tired. I had begun getting ready for bed when I was startled by a banging on the front door. I stuck my head out of the window and demanded who was there.

"Tommy Kehoe," said a very shaky voice.

I went down and opened the door, and the lad, sixteen years old, tumbled in, dead drunk. Thank Heaven! Percy Witherspoon was within call, and not away off in the Indian camp. I roused him, and together we conveyed Thomas to our guest-room, the only decently isolated spot in the building. Then I telephoned for the doctor, who, I am afraid, had already had a long day. He came, and we put in a pretty terrible night. It developed afterward that the boy had brought along with his luggage a bottle of liniment belonging to his employer. It was made half of alcohol and half of witch-hazel; and Thomas had refreshed his journey with this!

He was in such shape that positively I didn't think we'd pull him through—and I hoped we wouldn't. If I were a physician, I'd let such cases gently slip away for the good of society; but you should have seen Sandy work! That terrible life-saving instinct of his was aroused, and he fought with every inch of energy he possessed.

I made black coffee, and helped all I could, but the details were pretty messy, and I left the two men to deal with him alone and went back to my room. But I didn't attempt to go to bed; I was afraid they might be wanting me again. Toward four o'clock Sandy came to my library with word that the boy was asleep and that Percy had moved up a cot and would sleep in his room the rest of the night. Poor Sandy looked sort of ashen and haggard and done with life. As I looked at him, I thought about how desperately he worked to save others, and never saved himself, and about that dismal home of his, with never a touch of cheer, and the horrible tragedy in the background of his life. All the rancor I've been saving up seemed to vanish, and a wave of sympathy swept over me. I stretched my hand out to him; he stretched his out to me. And suddenly—I don't know—something electric happened. In another moment we were in each other's arms. He loosened my hands, and put me down in the big arm-chair. "My God! Sallie, do you think I'm made of iron?" he said and walked out. I went to sleep in the chair, and when I woke the sun was shining in my eyes and Jane was standing over me in amazed consternation.

This morning at eleven he came back, looked me coldly in the eye without so much as the flicker of an eyelash, and told me that Thomas was to have hot milk every two hours and that the spots in Maggie Peters's throat must be watched.

Here we are back on our old standing, and positively I don't know but what I dreamed that one minute in the night!

But it would be a piquant situation, wouldn't it, if Sandy and

I should discover that we were falling in love with each other, he with a perfectly good wife in the insane asylum and I with an outraged fiancé in Washington? I don't know but what the wisest thing for me to do is to resign at once and take myself home, where I can placidly settle down to a few months of embroidering "S McB" on table-cloths, like any other respectable engaged girl.

I repeat very firmly that this letter isn't for Jervis's consumption. Tear it into little pieces and scatter them in the Caribbean.

                                                              S.

                                                     January 3.

Dear Gordon:

You are right to be annoyed. I know I'm not a satisfactory love-letter writer. I have only to glance at the published correspondence of Elizabeth Barrett and Robert Browning[49] to realize that the warmth of my style is not up to standard. But you know already—you have known a long time—that I am not a very emotional person. I suppose I might write a lot of such things as: "Every waking moment you are in my thoughts." "My dear boy, I only live when you are near." But it wouldn't be absolutely true. You don't fill all my thoughts; 107 orphans do that. And I really am quite comfortably alive whether you are here or not. I have to be natural. You surely don't want me to pretend more desolation than I feel. But I do love to see you,—you know that perfectly,—and I am disappointed when you can't come. I fully appreciate all your charming qualities, but, my dear boy, I *can't* be sentimental on paper. I am always thinking about the hotel chambermaid who reads the letters you casually leave on your bureau. You needn't expostulate that you carry them next to your heart, for I know perfectly well that you don't.

Forgive me for that last letter if it hurt your feelings. Since I came to this asylum I am extremely touchy on the subject of drink; you would be, too, if you had seen what I have seen. Several of my chicks are the sad result of alcoholic parents, and they are never going to have a fair chance all their lives. You can't look about a place like this without "aye keeping up a terrible thinking."

You are right, I am afraid, about it's being a woman's trick to make a great show of forgiving a man, and then never letting him hear the end of it. Well, Gordon, I positively don't know what the word "forgiving" means. It can't include "forgetting," for that is a physiological process, and does not result from an act of the will. We all have a collection of memories that we would happily lose, but somehow those are just the ones that insist upon sticking. If "forgiving" means promising never to speak of a thing again, I can doubtless manage that. But it isn't always the wisest way to shut an unpleasant memory inside you. It grows and grows, and runs all through you like a poison.

Oh dear! I really didn't mean to be saying all this. I try to be the cheerful, care-free (and somewhat light-headed) Sallie you like best; but I've come in touch with a great deal of *realness* during this last year, and I'm afraid I've grown into a very different person from the girl you fell in love with. I'm no longer a gay young thing playing with life. I know it pretty thoroughly now, and that means that I can't be always laughing.

I know this is another beastly uncheerful letter,—as bad as the last, and maybe worse,—but if you knew what we've just been through! A boy—sixteen—of unspeakable heredity has nearly poisoned himself with a disgusting mixture of alcohol and witch-hazel. We have been working three days over him, and are just sure now that he is going to recuperate sufficiently to do it again! "It's a gude warld, but they're ill that's in 't."

Please excuse that Scotch—it slipped out. Please excuse everything.

                                                        SALLIE.

                                                        January 11.

Dear Judy:

I hope my two cablegrams didn't give you too terrible a shock. I would have waited to let the first news come by letter, with a chance for details, but I was so afraid you might hear it in some indirect way. The whole thing is dreadful enough, but no lives were lost, and only one serious accident. We can't help shuddering at the thought of how much worse it might have been, with over a hundred sleeping children in this fire-trap of a building. The new fire-escape was absolutely useless. The wind was blowing toward it, and the flames simply enveloped it. We saved them all by the center stairs—but I'll begin at the beginning, and tell the whole story.

It had rained all day Friday, thanks to a merciful Providence, and the roofs were thoroughly soaked. Toward night it began to freeze, and the rain turned to sleet. By ten o'clock, when I went to bed, the wind was blowing a terrible gale from the northwest, and everything loose about the building was banging and rattling. About two o'clock I suddenly started wide awake, with a bright light in my eyes. I jumped out of bed and ran to the window. The carriage-house was a mass of flames, and a shower of sparks was sweeping over our eastern wing. I ran to the bath-room and leaned out of the window. I could see that the roof over the nursery was already blazing in half a dozen places.

Well, my dear, my heart just simply didn't beat for as much as a minute. I thought of those seventeen babies up under that roof, and I couldn't swallow. I finally managed to get my shaking knees to work again, and I dashed back to the hall, grabbing my automobile coat as I ran.

I drummed on Betsy's and Miss Matthews' and Miss Snaith's doors, just as Mr. Witherspoon, who had also been wakened by the light, came tumbling upstairs three steps at a time, struggling into an overcoat as he ran.

"Get all the children down to the dining-room, babies first," I gasped. "I'll turn in the alarm."

He dashed on up to the third floor while I ran to the telephone—and oh, I thought I'd never get Central! She was sound asleep.

"The John Grier Home is burning! Turn in the fire-alarm and rouse the village. Give me 505," I said.

In one second I had the doctor. Maybe I wasn't glad to hear his cool, unexcited voice!

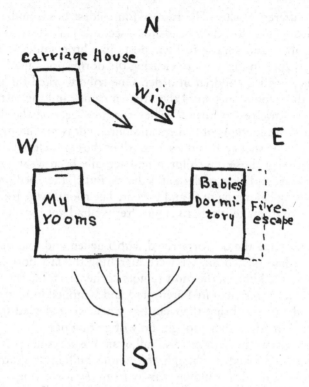

"We're on fire!" I cried. "Come quick, and bring all the men you can!"

"I'll be there in fifteen minutes. Fill the bath-tubs with water and put in blankets." And he hung up.

I dashed back to the hall. Betsy was ringing our fire-bell, and Percy had already routed out his Indian tribes in dormitories B and C.

Our first thought was not to stop the fire, but to get the children to a place of safety. We began in G, and went from crib to crib, snatching a baby and a blanket, and rushing them to the door, and handing them out to the Indians, who lugged them down-stairs. Both G and F were full of smoke, and the children so dead asleep that we couldn't rouse them to a walking state.

Many times during the next hour did I thank Providence—and Percy Witherspoon—for those vociferous fire-drills we have suffered weekly. The twenty-four oldest boys, under his direction, never lost their heads for a second. They divided into four tribes, and sprang to their posts like little soldiers. Two tribes helped in the work of clearing the dormitories and keeping the terrified children in order. One tribe worked the hose from the cupola tank until the firemen came, and the rest devoted themselves to salvage. They spread sheets on the floor, dumped the contents of lockers and bureau drawers into them, and bundled them down the stairs. All of the extra clothes were saved except those the children had actually been wearing the day before, and most of the staff's things. But clothes, bedding— everything belonging to G and F went. The rooms were too full of smoke to make it safe to enter after we had got out the last child.

By the time the doctor arrived with Luellen and two neighbors he had picked up, we were marching the last dormitory down to the kitchen, the most remote corner from the fire. The poor chicks were mainly barefooted and wrapped in blankets; we told them to bring their clothes when we wakened them, but in their fright they thought only of getting out.

By this time the halls were so full of smoke we could scarcely breathe. It looked as though the whole building would go, though the wind was blowing away from my west wing.

Another automobile full of retainers from Knowltop came up almost immediately, and they all fell to fighting the fire. The regular fire department didn't come for ten minutes after that. You see, they have only horses, and we are three miles out, and the roads pretty bad. It was a dreadful night, cold and sleety, and such a wind blowing that you could scarcely stand up. The men climbed out on the roof, and worked in their stocking-feet to keep from slipping off. They beat out the sparks with wet blankets, and chopped, and squirted that tankful of water, and behaved like heroes.

The doctor meanwhile took charge of the children. Our first thought was to get them away to a place of safety, for if the whole building should go, we couldn't march them out of doors into that awful wind, with only their night-clothes and blankets for protection. By this time several more automobiles full of men had come, and we requisitioned the cars.

Knowltop had providentially been opened for the week-end in order to entertain a house-party in honor of the old gentleman's sixty-seventh birthday. He was one of the first to arrive, and he put his entire place at our disposal. It was the nearest refuge, and we accepted it instantaneously. We bundled our twenty littlest tots into cars, and ran them down to the house. The guests, who were excitedly dressing in order to come to the fire, received the chicks and tucked them away into their own beds. This pretty well filled up all the available house room, but Mr. Reimer (Mr. Knowltop's family name) has just built a big stucco barn, with a garage hitched to it, all nicely heated, and ready for us.

After the babies were disposed of in the house, those helpful guests got to work and fixed the barn to receive the next older kiddies. They covered the floor with hay, and spread blankets and carriage robes over it, and bedded down thirty of the children in rows like little calves. Miss Matthews and a nurse went with them, administered hot milk all around, and within half an hour the tots were sleeping as peacefully as in their little cribs.

But meanwhile we at the house were having sensations. The doctor's first question upon arrival had been:

"You've counted the children? You know they're all here?"

"We've made certain that every dormitory was empty before we left it," I replied.

You see, they couldn't be counted in that confusion; twenty or so of the boys were still in the dormitories, working under Percy Witherspoon to save clothing and furniture, and the older girls were sorting over bushels of shoes and trying to fit them to the little ones, who were running about underfoot and wailing dismally.

Well, after we had loaded and despatched about seven carloads of children, the doctor suddenly called out:

"Where's Allegra?"

There was a horrified silence. No one had seen her. And then Miss Snaith stood up and *shrieked*. Betsy took her by the shoulders, and shook her into coherence.

It seems that she had thought Allegra was coming down with a cough, and in order to get her out of the cold, had moved her crib from the fresh-air nursery into the store-room—and then forgotten it.

Well, my dear, you know where the store-room is! We simply stared at one another with white faces. By this time the whole east wing was gutted and the third-floor stairs in flames. There didn't seem a chance that the child was still alive. The doctor was the first to move. He snatched up a wet blanket that was lying in a soppy pile on the floor of the hall and sprang for the stairs. We yelled to him to come back. It simply looked like suicide; but he kept on, and disappeared into the smoke. I dashed outside and shouted to the firemen on the roof. The store-room window was too little for a man to go through, and they hadn't opened it for fear of creating a draft.

I can't describe what happened in the next agonizing ten minutes. The third-floor stairs fell in with a crash and a burst of flame about five seconds after the doctor passed over them. We had given him up for lost when a shout went up from the crowd on the lawn, and he appeared for an instant at one of those dormer-windows in the attic, and called for the firemen to put up a ladder. Then he disappeared, and it seemed to us that they'd never get the ladder in place; but they finally did, and two men went up. The opening of the window had created a draft, and they were almost overpowered by the volume of smoke that burst out at the top. After an eternity the doctor appeared again with a white bundle in his arms. He passed it out to the men, and then he staggered back and dropped out of sight!

I don't know what happened for the next few minutes; I turned away and shut my eyes. Somehow or other they got him out and half-way down the ladder, and they let him slip. You see, he was unconscious from all the smoke he'd swallowed, and the ladder was slippery with ice and terribly wobbly. Anyway, when I looked again he was lying in a heap on the ground, with the crowd all running, and somebody yelling to give him air. They thought at first he was dead. But Dr. Metcalf from the village examined him, and said his leg was broken, and two ribs, and that aside from that he seemed whole. He was still unconscious when they put him on two of the baby mattresses that had been thrown out of the windows and laid him in the wagon that brought the ladders and started him home.

And the rest of us, left behind, kept right on with the work as though nothing had happened. The queer thing about a calamity like this is that there is so much to be done on every side that you don't have a moment to think, and you don't get any of your values straightened out until afterward. The doctor, without a moment's hesitation, had risked his life to save Allegra. It was the bravest thing I ever saw, and yet the whole business occupied only fifteen minutes out of that dreadful night. At the time, it was just an incident.

And he saved Allegra. She came out of that blanket with rumpled hair and a look of pleased surprise at the new game of peek-a-boo. She was smiling! The child's escape was little short of a miracle. The fire had started within three feet of her wall, but owing to the direction of the wind, it had worked away from her. If Miss Snaith had believed a little more in fresh air and had left the window open, the fire would have eaten back; but fortunately Miss Snaith does not believe in fresh air, and no such thing happened. If Allegra had gone, I never should have forgiven myself for not letting the Bretlands take her, and I know that Sandy wouldn't.

Despite all the loss, I can't be anything but happy when I think of the two horrible tragedies that have been averted; for seven minutes, while the doctor was penned in that blazing third floor, I lived through the agony of believing them both gone, and I start awake in the night trembling with horror.

But I'll try to tell you the rest. The firemen and the volunteers—particularly the chauffeur and stablemen from Knowltop—worked all night in an absolute frenzy. Our newest negro cook, who is a heroine in her own right, went out and started the laundry fire and made up a boilerful of coffee. It was her own idea. The non-combatants served it to the firemen when they relieved one another for a few minutes' rest, and it helped.

We got the remainder of the children off to various hospitable houses, except the older boys, who worked all night as well as any one. It was absolutely inspiring to see the way this entire township turned out and helped. People who haven't appeared to know that the asylum existed came in the middle of the night and put their whole houses at our disposal. They took the children in, gave them hot baths and hot soup, and tucked them into bed. And so far as I can make out, not one of my one hundred and seven chicks is any the worse for hopping about on drenched floors in their bare feet, not even the whooping-cough cases.

It was broad daylight before the fire was sufficiently under control to let us know just what we had saved. I will report that my wing is entirely intact, though a little smoky, and the main corridor is pretty nearly all right up to the center staircase; after that everything is charred and drenched. The east wing is a blackened, roofless shell. Your hated Ward F, dear Judy, is gone forever. I wish that you could obliterate it from your mind as absolutely as it is obliterated from the earth. Both in substance and in spirit the old John Grier is done for.

I must tell you something funny; I never saw so many funny things in my life as happened through that night. When everybody there was in extreme negligée, most of the men in pajamas and ulsters, and all of them without collars, the Hon. Cyrus Wykoff put in a tardy appearance, arrayed as for an afternoon tea. He wore a pearl scarf-pin and white spats! But he really was extremely helpful. He put his entire house at our disposal, and I turned over to him Miss Snaith in a state of hysterics, and her nerves so fully occupied him that he didn't get in our way the whole night through.

I can't write any more details now; I've never been so rushed in the whole of my life. I'll just assure you that there's no slightest reason for you to cut your trip short. Five trustees were on the spot early Saturday morning, and we are all working like mad to get affairs into some semblance of order. Our asylum at the present moment is scattered over the entire township; but don't be unduly anxious. We know where all the children are. None of them is permanently mislaid. I didn't know that perfect strangers could be so kind. My opinion of the human race has gone up.

I haven't seen the doctor. They telegraphed to New York for a surgeon, who set his leg. The break was pretty bad, and will take time; they don't think there are any internal injuries, though he is awfully battered up. As soon as we are allowed to see him I will send more detailed particulars. I really must stop if I am to catch to-morrow's steamer.

Good-by. Don't worry. There are a dozen silver linings to this cloud that I'll write about to-morrow.

SALLIE.

Good heavens! here comes an automobile with J. F. Bretland in it!

THE JOHN GRIER HOME,
January 14.

Dear Judy:

Listen to this! J. F. Bretland read about our fire in a New York paper (I will say that the metropolitan press made the most of details), and he posted up here in a twitter of anxiety. His first question as he tumbled across our blackened threshold was, "Is Allegra safe?"

"Yes," said I.

"Thank God!" he cried, and dropped into a chair. "This is no place for children," he said severely, "and I have come to take her home. I want the boys, too," he added hastily before I had a chance to speak. "My wife and I have talked it over, and we have decided that since we are going to the trouble of starting a nursery, we might as well run it for three as for one."

I led him up to my library, where our little family had been domiciled since the fire, and ten minutes later, when I was called down to confer with the trustees, I left J. F. Bretland with his new daughter on his knee and a son leaning against each arm, the proudest father in the United States.

So, you see, our fire accomplished one thing: those three children are settled for life. It is almost worth the loss.

But I don't believe I told you how the fire started. There are so many things I haven't told you that my arm aches at the thought of writing them all. Sterry, we have since discovered, was spending the week-end as our guest. After a bibulous evening passed at "Jack's Place," he returned to our carriage-house, climbed in through a window, lighted a candle, made himself comfortable, and dropped asleep. He must have forgotten to put out the candle; anyway, the fire happened, and Sterry just escaped with his life. He is now in the town hospital, bathed in sweet-oil, and painfully regretting his share in our troubles.

I am pleased to learn that our insurance was pretty adequate, so the money loss won't be so tremendous, after all. As for other kinds of loss, there aren't any! Actually, nothing but gain so far as I can make out, barring, of course, our poor smashed-up doctor. Everybody has been wonderful; I didn't know that so much charity and kindness existed in the human race. Did I ever say anything against trustees? I take it back. Four of them posted up from New York the morning after the fire, and all of the local people have been wonderful. Even the Hon. Cy has been so occupied in remarking the morals of the five orphans quartered upon him that he hasn't caused any trouble at all.

The fire occurred early Saturday morning, and Sunday the ministers in all the churches called for volunteers to accept in their houses one or two children as guests for three weeks, until the asylum could get its plant into working order again.

It was inspiring to see the response. Every child was disposed of within half an hour. And consider what that means for the future: every one of those families is going to take a personal interest in this asylum from now on. Also, consider what it means for the children. They are finding out how a real family lives, and this is the first time that dozens of them have ever crossed the threshold of a private house.

As for more permanent plans to take us through the winter, listen to all this. The country club has a caddies' club-house which they don't use in winter and which they have politely put at our disposal. It joins our land on the back, and we are fitting it up for fourteen children, with Miss Matthews in charge. Our dining-room and kitchen still being intact, they will come here for meals and school, returning home at night all the better for half a mile walk. "The Pavilion on the Links" we are calling it.

Then that nice motherly Mrs. Wilson, next door to the doctor's,—she who has been so efficient with our little Loretta,—has agreed to take in five more at four dollars a week each. I am leaving with her some of the most promising older girls who have shown house-keeping instincts, and would like to learn cooking on a decently small scale. Mrs. Wilson and her husband are such a wonderful couple, thrifty and industrious and simple and loving, I think it would do the girls good to observe them. A training class in wifehood!

I told you about the Knowltop people on the east of us, who took in forty-seven youngsters the night of the fire, and how their entire house-party turned themselves into emergency nurse-maids? We relieved them of thirty-six the next day, but they still have eleven. Did I ever call Mr. Knowltop a crusty old curmudgeon? I take it back. I beg his pardon. He's a sweet lamb. Now, in the time of our need, what do you think that blessed man has done? He has fitted up an empty tenant house on the estate for our babies, has himself engaged an English trained baby-nurse to take charge, and furnishes them with the superior milk from his own model dairy. He says he has been wondering for years what to do with that milk. He can't afford to sell it, because he loses four cents on every quart!

The twelve older girls from dormitory A I am putting into the farmer's new cottage; the poor Turnfelts, who had occupied it just two days, are being shoved on into the village. But they wouldn't be any good in looking after the children, and I need their room. Three or four of these girls have been returned from foster-homes as intractable, and they require pretty efficient supervision. So what do you think I've done? Telegraphed to Helen Brooks to chuck the publishers and take charge of my girls instead. You know she will be wonderful with them. She accepted provisionally. Poor Helen has had enough of this irrevocable contract business; she wants everything in life to be on trial!

For the older boys something particularly nice has happened; we have received a gift of gratitude from J. F. Bretland. He went down to thank the doctor for Allegra; they had a long talk about the needs of the institution, and J. F. B. came back and gave me a check for $3000 to build the Indian camps on a substantial scale. He and Percy and the village architect have drawn up plans, and in two weeks, we hope, the tribes will move into winter quarters.

What does it matter if my one hundred and seven children have been burned out, since they live in such a kind-hearted world as this?

Friday.

I suppose you are wondering why I don't vouchsafe some details about the doctor's condition. I can't give any first-hand information, since he won't see me. However, he has seen everybody except me—Betsy, Allegra, Mrs. Livermore, Mr. Bretland, Percy, various trustees; they all report that he is progressing as comfortably as could be expected with two broken ribs and a fractured fibula. That, I believe, is the professional name of the particular leg bone he broke. He doesn't like to have a fuss made over him, and he won't pose gracefully as a hero. I myself, as grateful head of this institution, called on several different occasions to present my official thanks, but I was invariably met at the door with word that he was sleeping and did not wish to be disturbed. The first two times I believed Mrs. McGurk; after that—well, I know our doctor! So when it came time to send our little maid to prattle her unconscious good-bys to the man who had saved her life, I despatched her in charge of Betsy.

I haven't an idea what is the matter with the man. He was friendly enough last week, but now, if I want an opinion from him, I have to send Percy to extract it. I do think that he might see me as the superintendent of the asylum, even if he doesn't wish our acquaintance to be on a personal basis. There is no doubt about it, our Sandy is Scotch!

Later.

It is going to require a fortune in stamps to get this letter to Jamaica, but I do want you to know all the news, and we have never had so many exhilarating things happen since 1876, when we were founded. This fire has given us such a shock that we are going to be more alive for years to come. I believe that every institution ought to be burned to the ground every twenty-five years in order to get rid of old-fashioned equipment and obsolete ideas. I am superlatively glad now that we didn't spend Jervis's money last summer; it would have been intensively tragic to have had that burn. I don't mind so much about John Grier's, since he made it in a patent medicine which, I hear, contained opium.

As to the remnant of us that the fire left behind, it is already boarded up and covered with tar-paper, and we are living along quite comfortably in our portion of a house. It affords sufficient room for the staff and the children's dining-room and kitchen, and more permanent plans can be made later.

Do you perceive what has happened to us? The good Lord has heard my prayer, and the John Grier Home is a cottage institution!

I am,

The busiest person north of the equator,

S. McBride.

The John Grier Home,
January 16.

Dear Gordon:

Please, please behave yourself, and don't make things harder than they are. It's absolutely out of the question for me to give up the asylum this instant. You ought to realize that I can't abandon my chicks just when they are so terribly in need of me. Neither am I ready to drop this blasted philanthropy. (You can see how your language looks in my handwriting!)

You have no cause to worry. I am not overworking. I am enjoying it; never was so busy and happy in my life. The papers made the fire out much more lurid than it really was. The picture of me leaping from the roof with a baby under each arm was overdrawn. One or two of the children have sore throats, and our poor doctor is in a plaster cast; but we're all alive, thank Heaven! and are going to pull through without permanent scars.

I can't write details now; I'm simply rushed to death. And don't come—please! Later, when things have settled just a little,

you and I must have a talk about you and me, but I want time
to think about it first.

                                                                    S.

                                                      January 21.

Dear Judy:

   Helen Brooks is taking hold of those fourteen fractious girls
in a most masterly fashion. The job is quite the toughest I had
to offer, and she likes it. I think she is going to be a valuable addition to our staff.

   And I forgot to tell you about Punch. When the fire occurred,
the two nice women who kept him all summer were on the point
of catching a train for California—and they simply tucked him
under their arms, along with their luggage, and carried him off.
So Punch spends the winter in Pasadena, and I rather fancy he
is theirs for good. Do you wonder that I am in an exalted mood
over all these happenings?

                                                      Later.

   Poor bereaved Percy has just been spending the evening with
me, because I am supposed to understand his troubles. Why
must I be supposed to understand everybody's troubles? It's awfully wearing to be pouring out sympathy from an empty heart.
The poor boy at present is pretty low, but I rather suspect—
with Betsy's aid—that he will pull through. He is just on the
edge of falling in love with Betsy, but he doesn't know it. He's
in the stage now where he's sort of enjoying his troubles; he
feels himself a tragic hero, a man who has suffered deeply. But
I notice that when Betsy is about, he offers cheerful assistance
in whatever work is toward.

   Gordon telegraphed to-day that he is coming to-morrow. I
am dreading the interview, for I know we are going to have an
altercation. He wrote the day after the fire and begged me to
"chuck the asylum" and get married immediately, and now he's
coming to argue it out. I can't make him understand that a job
involving the happiness of one hundred or so children can't be

chucked with such charming insouciance. I tried my best to keep him away, but, like the rest of his sex, he's stubborn. Oh dear, I don't know what's ahead of us! I wish I could glance into next year for a moment.

The doctor is still in his plaster cast, but I hear is doing well, after a grumbly fashion. He is able to sit up a little every day and to receive a carefully selected list of visitors. Mrs. McGurk sorts them out at the door, and repudiates the ones she doesn't like.

Good-by. I'd write some more, but I'm so sleepy that my eyes are shutting on me. (The idiom is Sadie Kate's.) I must go to bed and get some sleep against the one hundred and seven troubles of to-morrow.

With love to the Pendletons,

S. McB.

January 22.

Dear Judy:

This letter has nothing to do with the John Grier Home. It's merely from Sallie McBride.

Do you remember when we read Huxley's letters[50] our senior year? That book contained a phrase which has stuck in my memory ever since: "There is always a Cape Horn in one's life that one either weathers or wrecks oneself on." It's terribly true; and the trouble is that you can't always recognize your Cape Horn when you see it. The sailing is sometimes pretty foggy, and you're wrecked before you know it.

I've been realizing of late that I have reached the Cape Horn of my own life. I entered upon my engagement to Gordon honestly and hopefully, but little by little I've grown doubtful of the outcome. The girl he loves is not the *me* I want to be. It's the *me* I've been trying to grow away from all this last year. I'm not sure she ever really existed. Gordon just imagined she did. Anyway, she doesn't exist any more, and the only fair course both to him and to myself was to end it.

We no longer have any interests in common; we are not

friends. He doesn't comprehend it; he thinks that I am making it up, that all I have to do is to take an interest in his life, and everything will turn out happily. Of course I do take an interest when he's with me. I talk about the things he wants to talk about, and he doesn't know that there's a whole part of me— the biggest part of me—that simply doesn't meet him at any point. I pretend when I am with him. I am not myself, and if we were to live together in constant daily intercourse, I'd have to keep on pretending all my life. He wants me to watch his face and smile when he smiles and frown when he frowns. He can't realize that I'm an individual just as much as he is.

I have social accomplishments. I dress well, I'm spectacular, I would be an ideal hostess in a politician's household—and that's why he likes me.

Anyway, I suddenly saw with awful distinctness that if I kept on I'd be in a few years where Helen Brooks is. She's a far better model of married life for me to contemplate just this moment than you, dear Judy. I think that such a spectacle as you and Jervis are a menace to society. You look so happy and peaceful and companionable that you induce a defenseless on-looker to rush off and snap up the first man she meets—and he's always the wrong man.

Anyway, Gordon and I have quarreled definitely and finally. I should rather have ended without a quarrel, but considering his temperament,—and mine, too, I must confess,—we had to go off in a big smoky explosion. He came yesterday afternoon, after I'd written him not to come, and we went walking over Knowltop. For three and a half hours we paced back and forth over that windy moor and discussed ourselves to the bottom-most recesses of our beings. No one can ever say the break came through misunderstanding each other!

It ended by Gordon's going, never to return. As I stood there at the end and watched him drop out of sight over the brow of the hill, and realized that I was free and alone and my own master, well, Judy, such a sense of joyous relief, of freedom, swept over me! I can't tell you; I don't believe any happily married person could ever realize how wonderfully, beautifully *alone* I felt. I wanted to throw my arms out and embrace the

whole waiting world that belonged suddenly to me. Oh, it is
such a relief to have it settled! I faced the truth the night of the
fire when I saw the old John Grier go, and realized that a new
John Grier would be built in its place and that I wouldn't be
here to do it. A horrible jealousy clutched at my heart. I
couldn't give it up, and during those agonizing moments while
I thought we had lost our doctor, I realized what his life meant,
and how much more significant than Gordon's. And I knew
then that I couldn't desert him; I had to go on and carry out all
of the plans we made together.

I don't seem to be telling you anything but a mess of words,
I am so full of such a mess of crowding emotions; I want to talk
and talk and talk myself into coherence. But, anyway, I stood
alone in the winter twilight, and I took a deep breath of clear
cold air, and I felt beautifully, wonderfully, electrically free; and
then I ran and leaped and skipped down the hill and across the
pastures toward our iron confines, and I sang to myself. Oh, it
was a scandalous proceeding, when, according to all precedent,
I should have gone trailing home with a broken wing. I never
gave one thought to poor Gordon, who was carrying a broken,
bruised, betrayed heart to the railroad station.

As I entered the house I was greeted by the joyous clatter of
the children trooping to their supper. They were suddenly *mine,*
and lately, as my doom became more and more imminent, they
had seemed fading away into little strangers. I seized the three
nearest and hugged them hard. I have suddenly found such new
life and exuberance, I feel as though I had been released from
prison and were free. I feel,—oh, I'll stop,—I just want you to
know the truth. Don't show Jervis this letter, but tell him what's
in it in a decently subdued and mournful fashion.

It's midnight now, and I'm going to try to go to sleep. It's
wonderful not to be going to marry some one you don't want
to marry. I'm glad of all these children's needs, I'm glad of Helen
Brooks, and, yes, of the fire, and everything that has made me
see clearly. There's never been a divorce in my family, and they
would have hated it.

I know I'm horribly egotistical and selfish; I ought to be
thinking of poor Gordon's broken heart. But really it would

just be a pose if I pretended to be very sorrowful. He'll find
some one else with just as conspicuous hair as mine, who will
make just as effective a hostess, and who won't be bothered by
any of these damned modern ideas about public service and
woman's mission and all the rest of the tomfoolery the modern
generation of women is addicted to. (I paraphrase, and soften
our young man's heartbroken utterances.)

Good-by, dear people. How I wish I could stand with you on
your beach and look across the blue, blue sea! I salute the
Spanish main.

Addio!

SALLIE.

January 27.

Dear Dr. MacRae:

I wonder if this note will be so fortunate as to find you
awake? Perhaps you are not aware that I have called four times
to offer thanks and consolation in my best bed-side manner? I
am touched by the news that Mrs. McGurk's time is entirely
occupied in taking in flowers and jelly and chicken broth, do-
nated by the adoring ladies of the parish to the ungracious hero
in a plaster cast. I know that you find a cap of home-spun more
comfortable than a halo, but I really do think that you might
have regarded me in a different light from the hysterical ladies
in question. You and I used to be friends (intermittently), and
though there are one or two details in our past intercourse that
might better be expunged, still I don't see why we should let
them upset our entire relationship. Can't we be sensible and expunge them?

The fire has brought out such a lot of unexpected kindliness
and charity, I wish it might bring out a little from you. You see,
Sandy, I know you well. You may pose to the world as being
gruff and curt and ungracious and scientific and inhuman and
S C O T C H, but you can't fool me. My newly trained psy-

chological eye has been upon you for ten months, and I have
applied the Binet test. You are really kind and sympathetic and
wise and forgiving and big, so please be at home the next time
I come to see you, and we will perform a surgical operation
upon Time and amputate five months.

Do you remember the Sunday afternoon we ran away, and
what a nice time we had? It is now the day after that.

SALLIE McBRIDE.

P.S. If I condescend to call upon you again, please condescend to see me, for I assure you I won't try more than once!
Also, I assure you that I won't drip tears on your counterpane
or try to kiss your hand, as I hear one admiring lady did.

The Dochther is ashleep and I can't be lettin' ye oop.

THE JOHN GRIER HOME,
Thursday.

Dear Enemy:

You see, I'm feeling very friendly toward you this moment.
When I call you "MacRae" I don't like you, and when I call
you "Enemy" I do.

Sadie Kate delivered your note (as an after-thought). And it's
a very creditable production for a left-handed man; I thought
at first glance it was from Punch.

You may expect me to-morrow at four, and mind you're
awake! I'm glad that you think we're friends. Really, I feel that

I've got back something quite precious which I had carelessly
mislaid.

                                                       S. McB.

P.S. Java caught cold the night of the fire and he has the
toothache. He sits and holds his cheek like a poor little kiddie.

                                          Thursday, January 29.

Dear Judy:

Those must have been ten terribly incoherent pages I dashed
off to you last week. Did you respect my command to destroy
that letter? I should not care to have it appear in my collected
correspondence. I know that my state of mind is disgraceful,
shocking, scandalous, but one really can't help the way one
feels. It is usually considered a pleasant sensation to be engaged, but, oh, it is nothing compared with the wonderful un-
trammeled, joyous, free sensation of being unengaged! I have
had terribly unstable feeling these last few months, and now at
last I am settled. No one ever looked forward to spinsterhood
more thankfully than I.

Our fire, I have come to believe, was providential. It was sent
from heaven to clear the way for a new John Grier. We are already deep in plans for cottages. I favor gray stucco, Betsy
leans to brick, and Percy, half-timber. I don't know what our
poor doctor would prefer; olive green with a mansard roof appears to be his taste.

With ten different kitchens to practise in, won't our children
learn how to cook! I am already looking about for ten loving
house mothers to put in charge. I think, in fact, I'll search for
eleven, in order to have one for Sandy. He's as pathetically in
need of a little mothering as any of the chicks. It must be pretty
dispiriting to come home every night to the ministrations of
Mrs. McGur-rk.

How I do not like that woman! She has with complacent
firmness told me four different times that the dochther was

ashleep and not wantin' to be disturbed. I haven't set eyes on
him yet, and I have just about finished being polite. However, I
waive judgment until to-morrow at four, when I am to pay a
short, unexciting call of half an hour. He made the appoint-
ment himself, and if she tells me again that he is ashleep, I shall
give her a gentle push and tip her over (she's very fat and unstable) and, planting a foot firmly on her stomach, pursue my
way tranquilly in and up. Luellen, formerly chauffeur, chambermaid, and gardener, is now also trained nurse. I am eager to
see how he looks in a white cap and apron.

The mail has just come, with a letter from Mrs. Bretland,
telling how happy they are to have the children. She inclosed
their first photograph—all packed in a governess cart, with
Clifford proudly holding the reins, and a groom at the pony's
head. How is that for three late inmates of the John Grier
Home? It's all very inspiring when I think of their futures, but
a trifle sad when I remember their poor father, and how he
worked himself to death for those three chicks who are going
to forget him. The Bretlands will do their best to accomplish
that. They are jealous of any outside influence and want to
make the babies wholly theirs. After all, I think the natural way
is best—for each family to produce its own children, and keep
them.

Friday.

I saw the doctor to-day. He's a pathetic sight, consisting
mostly of bandages. Somehow or other we got our misunderstandings all made up. Isn't it dreadful the way two human beings, both endowed with fair powers of speech, can manage to
convey nothing of their psychological processes to each other?
I haven't understood his mental attitude from the first, and he
even yet doesn't understand mine. This grim reticence that we
Northern people struggle so hard to maintain! I don't know after all but that the excitable Southern safety-valve method is
the best.

But, Judy, such a dreadful thing—do you remember last year
when he visited that psychopathic institution, and stayed ten
days, and I made such a silly fuss about it? Oh, my dear, the im-

possible things I do! He went to attend his wife's funeral. She died there in the institution. Mrs. McGurk knew it all the time, and might have added it to the rest of her news, but she didn't.

He told me all about her, very sweetly. The poor man for years and years has undergone a terrible strain, and I fancy her death is a blessed relief. He confesses that he knew at the time of his marriage that he ought not to marry her, he knew all about her nervous instability; but he thought, being a doctor, that he could overcome it, and she was beautiful! He gave up his city practice and came to the country on her account. And then after the little girl's birth she went all to pieces, and he had to "put her away," to use Mrs. McGurk's phrase. The child is six now, a sweet, lovely thing to look at, but, I judge from what he said, quite abnormal. He has a trained nurse with her always. Just think of all that tragedy looming over our poor patient good doctor, for he is patient, despite being the most impatient man that ever lived!

Thank Jervis for his letter. He's a dear man, and I'm glad to see him getting his deserts. What fun we are going to have when you get back to Shadywell, and we lay our plans for a new John Grier! I feel as though I had spent this past year learning, and am now just ready to begin. We'll turn this into the nicest orphan-asylum that ever lived. I'm so absurdly happy at the prospect that I start in the morning with a spring, and go about my various businesses singing inside.

The John Grier Home sends its blessings to the two best friends it ever had!

Addio!

SALLIE.

THE JOHN GRIER HOME,
Saturday at half-past six in the morning!

My dearest Enemy:

"Some day soon something nice is going to happen."

Weren't you surprised when you woke up this morning and remembered the truth? I was! I couldn't think for about two minutes what made me so happy.

It's not light yet, but I'm wide awake and excited and having to write to you. I shall despatch this note by the first to-be-trusted little orphan who appears, and it will go up on your breakfast tray along with your oatmeal.

I shall follow *very promptly* at four o'clock this afternoon. Do you think Mrs. McGurk will ever countenance the scandal if I stay two hours, and no orphan for a chaperon?

It was in all good faith, Sandy, that I promised not to kiss your hand or drip tears on the counterpane, but I'm afraid I did both—or worse! Positively, I didn't suspect how much I cared for you till I crossed the threshold and saw you propped up against the pillows, all covered with bandages, and your hair singed off. You are a sight! If I love you now, when fully one third of you is plaster of Paris and surgical dressing, you can imagine how I'm going to love you when it's all you!

But my dear, dear Robin, what a foolish man you are! How should I ever have dreamed all those months that you were caring for me when you acted so abominably S C O T C H? With most men, behavior like yours would not be considered a mark of affection. I wish you had just given me a glimmering of an idea of the truth, and maybe you would have saved us both a few heartaches.

But we mustn't be looking back; we must look forward and be grateful. The two happiest things in life are going to be ours, a *friendly* marriage and work that we love.

Yesterday, after leaving you, I walked back to the asylum sort of dazed. I wanted to get by myself and *think,* but instead of being by myself, I had to have Betsy and Percy and Mrs. Livermore for dinner (already invited) and then go down and talk to the children. Friday night—social evening. They had a lot of new records for the victrola, given by Mrs. Livermore, and I had to sit politely and listen to them. And, my dear— you'll think this funny—the last thing they played was "John Anderson, my joe John,"[51] and suddenly I found myself crying! I had to snatch up the nearest orphan and hug her hard, with my head buried in her shoulder, to keep them all from seeing.

> John Anderson, my joe John,
> We clamb the hill thegither,
> And monie a canty day, John,
> We've had wi' ane anither;
> Now we maun totter down, John,
> But hand in hand we'll go,
> And sleep thegither at the foot,
> John Anderson, my joe.

I wonder, when we are old and bent and tottery, can you and I look back, with no regrets, on monie a canty day we've had wi' ane anither? It's nice to look forward to, isn't it—a life of work and play and little daily adventures side by side with somebody

you love? I'm not afraid of the future any more. I don't mind
growing old with you, Sandy. "Time is but the stream I go
a-fishing in."

The reason I've grown to love these orphans is because they
need me so, and that's the reason—at least one of the reasons—
I've grown to love you. You're a pathetic figure of a man, my
dear, and since you won't make yourself comfortable, you must
be *made* comfortable.

We'll build a house on the hillside just beyond the asylum—
how does a yellow Italian villa strike you, or preferably a pink
one? Anyway, it won't be green. And it won't have a mansard
roof. And we'll have a big cheerful living-room, all fireplace
and windows and view, and no McGURK. Poor old thing!
won't she be in a temper and cook you a dreadful dinner when
she hears the news! But we won't tell her for a long, long
time—or anybody else. It's too scandalous a proceeding right
on top of my own broken engagement. I wrote to Judy last
night, and with unprecedented self-control I never let fall so
much as a hint. I'm growing Scotch mysel'!

Perhaps I didn't tell you the exact truth, Sandy, when I said I
hadn't known how much I cared. I think it came to me the
night the John Grier burned. When you were up under the
blazing roof, and for the half hour that followed, when we
didn't know whether or not you would live, I can't tell you
what agonies I went through. It seemed to me, if you did go,
that I would never get over it all my life; that somehow to have
let the best friend I ever had pass away with a dreadful chasm
of misunderstanding between us—well—I couldn't wait for the
moment when I should be allowed to see you and talk out all
that I have been shutting inside me for five months. And then—
you know that you gave strict orders to keep me out; and it
hurt me dreadfully. How should I suspect that you really
wanted to see me more than any of the others, and that it was
just that terrible Scotch moral sense that was holding you
back? You are a very good actor, Sandy. But, my dear, if ever in
our lives again we have the tiniest little cloud of a misunderstanding, let's promise not to shut it up inside ourselves, but to
talk.

Last night, after they all got off,—early, I am pleased to say, since the chicks no longer live at home,—I came up-stairs and finished my letter to Judy, and then I looked at the telephone and struggled with temptation. I wanted to call up 505 and say good night to you. But I didn't dare. I'm still quite respectably bashful! So, as the next best thing to talking to you, I got out Burns and read him for an hour. I dropped asleep with all those Scotch love-songs running in my head, and here I am at day-break writing them to you.

Good-by, Robin lad, I lo'e you weel.

                                               SALLIE.

THE END

Explanatory Notes

Thanks to my research assistant, Adena Spingarn, Princeton '03, who helped with the introduction and the preparation of these notes and also consulted the Webster archive at Vassar.

DADDY-LONG-LEGS

1. *Michael Angelo:* Michelangelo (1475–1564) was an Italian painter, sculptor, and poet.
2. *Maurice Maeterlinck:* Successful dramatist and poet (1862–1949), known as the "Belgian Shakespeare."
3. *Second Punic war:* One of the wars between Rome and Carthage in the third and second centuries B.C.E. over control of Sicily. Specifically, the second, lasting from 218 to 201 B.C.E., was called the "Hannibalic War," which ended in the complete triumph of Rome.
4. *Three Musketeers:* 1844 novel by French writer Alexandre Dumas (1802–1870).
5. *Mother Goose . . . Rudyard Kipling: Mother Goose* is the traditional designation for a body of nursery rhymes, some dating back to the seventeenth or early eighteenth century. Although this is most likely the work Judy means by "Mother Goose," the term was also popularized by French author Charles Perrault (1628–1703) in the subtitle of his 1697 fairy tale collection, *Stories and Tales from the Past: Tales of Mother Goose,* which included his now standard versions of stories such as "Cinderella" and "Blue Beard." *David Copperfield* is the 1849 novel by the English writer Charles Dickens (1812–1870). *Ivanhoe* is the 1819 novel by Scottish poet and novelist Walter Scott (1771–1832). *The Life and Adventures of Robinson Crusoe* (1719) is a novel by English novelist and journalist Daniel Defoe (1660–1731). *Jane Eyre* is

the 1847 novel by English novelist Charlotte Brontë (1816–1855); see also note 41, below. *Alice's Adventures in Wonderland* (1865) is a fantasy novel by Lewis Carroll (Charles Lutwidge Dodgson, 1832–1898). Rudyard Kipling (1865–1936) was a British author born in Bombay who merged the east and the west in his stories and poems.

6. *Henry the Eighth:* Henry VIII (1491–1547) ruled England from 1509–1547 and was married six times.

7. *Shelley:* Percy Bysshe Shelley (1792–1822) was an English Romantic poet.

8. *Robert Louis Stevenson:* Scottish-born author (1850–1894).

9. *George Eliot:* Pen name for English novelist Mary Ann Evans (1819–1880).

10. *Mona Lisa:* Painting—and one of the most recognizable images in the world—by Italian artist Leonardo da Vinci (1452–1519).

11. *Sherlock Holmes:* Detective protagonist in a number of popular novels and stories by Scottish-born writer Arthur Conan Doyle (1859–1930).

12. *Tennyson's poems:* Alfred, Lord Tennyson (1809–1892), was the poet laureate of England.

13. *Vanity Fair:* 1848 novel of the Napoleonic Wars by English novelist William Makepeace Thackeray (1811–1863).

14. *Plain Tales:* Rudyard Kipling's 1887 collection of short stories about India.

15. *Little Women:* Beloved 1868 novel about four spunky sisters by American author Louisa May Alcott (1832–1888).

16. *pickled limes:* An item from *Little Women*. Made with limes and salt, they are exchanged among the schoolgirls as a symbolic measure of friendship.

17. *Matthew Arnold's poems:* Arnold (1822–1888) was an English poet and critic.

18. *Judge not that ye be not judged:* Matthew 7:1.

19. *Richard Feverel: The Ordeal of Richard Feverel* (1859) by British novelist and poet George Meredith (1823–1909). The novel tells the story of a proud, opinionated father who tries to turn his son into a perfect state of manhood through a repressive system of education.

20. *Emerson's "Essays":* Ralph Waldo Emerson (1803–1882), American poet and essayist, wrote a series of essays based on lectures he gave during the 1840s.

21. *Lockhart's "Life of Scott":* John Gibson Lockhart (1794–1854), Scottish writer and editor, was Walter Scott's son-in-law. His multivolume biography of Scott was considered one of the most impressive life histories in the English language.

22. *Gibbon's "Roman Empire"*: English historian Edward Gibbon (1737–1794) wrote a multi-volume history of the Roman Empire, *The Decline and Fall of the Roman Empire* (1776–1788).

23. *Benvenuto's Cellini's "Life"*: Cellini (1500–1571), Italian artist, metalsmith, and sculptor, wrote an autobiography of his romantic adventures.

24. *Livy*: Roman historian (59 B.C.E.–C.E. 17).

25. *De Senectute . . . De Amicitia*: Works by Roman orator and politician Marcus Tullus Cicero (106–43 B.C.E.).

26. *Wuthering Heights*: English novelist Emily Brontë (1818–1848) wrote this 1847 novel, a saga of two Yorkshire families and a passionate love story.

27. *Heathcliffe*: Heathcliff was the Byronic and darkly glamorous hero of *Wuthering Heights*.

28. *pie-plant*: The old-fashioned name for rhubarb.

29. *I asked no other thing . . .* : From Emily Dickinson's poem "Part One: Life." Webster and her classmates studied this poem at Vassar, well in advance of Dickinson's critical acclaim as a major American poet.

30. *The Portrait of a Lady*: 1881 novel by American-born writer Henry James (1843–1916).

31. *Cher Daddy-Jambes-Longes . . .* : Judy makes several mistakes in French, and invents her own hybrid Franglais in this letter. Translation of the letter:

Dear Daddy-Long-Legs,
    You are a brick!
    I am very glad about the farm because I've never been on a farm in my life and I'd hate to return to the John Grier home, and wash dishes all summer. There would be a risk of something terrible happening there, because I have lost my former humility. I'm afraid that I would just break out someday and smash every cup and saucer in the house.
    Pardon the brevity and the writing-paper. I cannot send more news of me because I am in French class and I'm afraid the professor is going to call on me right away.
    He did!
    Goodbye,
    I love you very much,
    Judy

32. *Jamais je ne t'oublierai*: I will never forget you.

33. *Marcelle waves*: A deep artificial wave in the hair, named after Marcel Grateau, who invented the method.

34. *Lesbia in Catullus*: Roman lyric poet Catullus (87–?54 B.C.E.) fell

in love with a woman named Clodia, who appears in his poetry as "Lesbia."

35. *Doric columns . . . Ionic:* From Greek architecture, a Doric column has a fluted shaft and plain capital, while an Ionic column is characterized by scroll shapes on either side of the capital.

36. *William Shakespeare:* English dramatist and poet (1564–1616).

37. *Marie Bashkirtseff's journal:* The melodramatic diary of the Russian artist and writer Marie Constantinova Bashkirtseff (1860–1884), who began it when she was thirteen. Her account of the struggles of women artists inspired many women readers.

38. *William the Conqueror . . . 1492 . . . Columbus discovered America . . . 1066:* William, Duke of Normandy (?1028–1087), invaded England in 1066 and took the English throne as William I. Christopher Columbus (1451–1506), Italian navigator, set sail in 1492 on a westward voyage from Spain bound for Asia and instead found America.

39. *Hamlet:* Play by William Shakespeare written in about 1601. Contrary to Judy's Ophelia, the character in the play is rejected by Hamlet, prince of Denmark, and goes mad.

40. *As You Like It:* Play by Shakespeare from about 1600.

41. *Jane Eyre:* Charlotte Brontë's 1847 novel, about a gifted and intense orphan girl who seeks independence as a governess and defies class expectations to find love with her rakish master, Rochester, has obvious parallels to Judy's life.

42. *Lowood Institute:* The charitable school young Jane attends unhappily in *Jane Eyre.*

43. *set of Stevenson:* The works of Scottish author Robert Louis Stevenson (1850–1894).

44. *South Seas:* In ailing health, Robert Louis Stevenson sailed from London for New York with his wife in 1887 and never set foot in Europe again.

45. *Treasure Island:* Stevenson's 1883 adventure novel of a young boy's voyage with pirates.

46. *violet cream:* A kind of candy.

47. *Life and Letters of Thomas Huxley:* Leonard Huxley wrote and edited this 1900 biography of his English biologist father, Thomas Henry Huxley (1825–1895).

48. *archaeopteryx:* The oldest known fossil bird, of the late Jurassic period. It has wings and feathers like a bird, but teeth and a bony tail like a reptile.

49. *stereognathus:* Middle Jurassic mammal.

50. *Plato:* Greek philosopher (?428–348 B.C.E.).

51. *It's the one touch of nature . . . :* From Shakespeare's *Troilus and Cressida.*

52. *Fabian:* A member or supporter of the Fabian Society, an organization of British intellectuals aiming at a gradual rather than revolutionary achievement of socialism. In May 1898, Sidney and Beatrice Webb, two of the founders of the Fabian Society, spoke at Vassar on "The Scope of Democracy in England."

53. *Wordsworth's "Tinturn Abbey":* Poem by English Romantic poet William Wordsworth (1770–1850) about memory and the past, part of his *Lyrical Ballads* collection.

54. *Byron, Keats:* English Romantic poets Lord Byron (George Gordon Byron, 1788–1824) and John Keats (1795–1821).

55. *Locksley Hall:* 1842 poem by Alfred, Lord Tennyson.

56. *aniline dyes:* A synthetic dye made from a colorless oily liquid.

57. *recherché:* Exclusive.

58. *figurez vous:* Can you imagine?

59. *C'est drôle ça n'est pas?:* That's funny, isn't it? (Judy's French is still ungrammatical).

60. *Are women citizens? I don't suppose they are:* The Nineteenth Amendment to the U.S. Constitution, granting American women the right to vote, was not ratified until 1920, eight years after the first publication of *Daddy-Long-Legs.*

61. *Schopenhauer:* Arthur Schopenhauer (1788–1860), anti-Enlightenment German philosopher whose chief work emphasized the central role of blind, irrational human will as the creative, primary factor in understanding.

62. *Sam'l Pepys:* Samuel Pepys (1633–1703), seventeenth-century English naval administrator and lively diarist of contemporary life. Like many readers of Pepys' diary, Judy can't resist imitating his style.

63. *Rousseau:* Jean Jacques Rousseau (1712–1778), Swiss-born French philosopher and author of *The Social Contract.* Rousseau had five children with a servant girl and placed them in an orphan asylum.

64. *Anthony Trollope's mother:* Frances Milton Trollope (1779–1863) was a prolific novelist and travel writer.

DEAR ENEMY

1. *single tax:* A system by which revenue is derived from a tax on one thing, usually land.

2. *It's up wi' the bonnets o' McBride and MacRae!*: Sallie is parody-
   ing a famous ballad by Sir Walter Scott about the Highlands mili-
   tary hero John Graham, Viscount Dundee, known as "Bonnie
   Dundee," who died at the Battle of Killiekrakie. Sallie thus indi-
   cates that she is going to do battle with Dr. MacRae. The chorus
   of the Scott ballad goes:

   > Come fill up my cup, come fill up my can,
   > Come saddle my horses, and call out my men.
   > Come open the West Port, and let us gae free,
   > For it's up wi' the bonnets o' Bonnie Dundee!

3. *C'est à rire!*: It's laughable!
4. *Where did you come from . . .*: Inexact quotation of "Baby," a
   poem by George MacDonald (1824–1905), which reads

   > "Where did you come from, Baby Dear?
   > Out of the everywhere, into the here."

5. *There may be heaven . . .*: A rewriting of the last two lines of
   Robert Browning's (1812–1889) poem "Time's Revenges,"
   which reads "There may be heaven; there must be hell;/Mean-
   time, there is our earth here—well!"
6. *Altman & Co.*: New York City department store founded in 1865.
7. *Muckle-mouthed Meg*: In a legend described by Sir Walter Scott
   in *Border Antiquities,* "Muckle-Mouthed Meg" was the "ill-
   favoured daughter" of a baron who forced a young man to
   choose between marrying her and hanging. "Muckle-mouthed"
   means having a very large mouth.
8. *felon*: Infection of the fingertip, often caused by a splinter.
9. *samp*: Porridge made of coarsely ground maize.
10. *model institution at Hastings*: The Graham-Windham Home for
    orphans and foster children, part of the oldest nonsectarian child
    welfare agency in the United States, was in Hastings-on-Hudson,
    New York. It is now the Graham School. Thanks to Janet Murphy,
    reference librarian at the Hastings Public Library for this informa-
    tion.
11. *Vive la bagatelle!*: Long live small talk!
12. *Soyez tranquille*: Stay calm.
13. *Vere de Vere*: A reference to "Lady Clara Vere de Vere," a poem
    by Alfred, Lord Tennyson. The Vere family was a noted English
    family reaching back to the eleventh century.

14. *Uriah Heepish:* Uriah Heep was a hypocritical character in Charles Dickens' 1849 novel *David Copperfield.*

15. *Now follows the dim horror . . . :* Lines from "Bob Polter," a ballad by Gilbert and Sullivan.

16. *Binet test:* A test used to measure intelligence, especially of children, developed by French psychologists.

17. *Jukes family:* Pseudonym for a family from Ulster County, in upstate New York, with a large percentage of criminals, studied by psychologists to determine why people engage in undesirable and antisocial behavior, in order to facilitate crime prevention and correction.

18. *Punch:* The puppet character Punch, in seaside British Punch-and-Judy shows, or Italian commedia dell'arte, is a likable rogue who fights with his wife and bullies his child. His violence is a cartoon-like fantasy of rebellion against civilized morality.

19. *Mais parlons d'autres choses!:* But let us talk of other things!

20. *Cristabel:* A ballad by English Romantic poet Samuel Taylor Coleridge (1772–1834).

21. *Kallikak book:* The Kallikak family was the subject of a best-selling 1912 study by Henry Goddard, *The Kallikak Family: A Study in The Heredity of Feeble-mindedness,* which argued that genetic transmission caused mental deficiency.

22. *Wells's latest novel:* H. G. Wells was a prolific and popular novelist, but this might be *The Wife of Sir Isaac Harmon* (1914).

23. *bakshish:* In some Oriental countries, a small sum of money given as gratuity or as alms.

24. *Massachusetts Agricultural College:* The University of Massachusetts was founded in 1863 as a land grant institution in Amherst, and became a leading center for agricultural research and instruction.

25. *Gösta Berling:* 1891 novel by Nobel Prize–winning Swedish writer Selma Lagerlöf (1858–1940) about twelve cavaliers led by a charming renegade priest named Gösta Berling.

26. *Genetic Philosophy of Education:* Probably refers to a work by David J. Hill, *Genetic Philosophy,* which argues that truth is not to be made, but to be discovered through recurrence and order.

27. *Dolly Dialogues:* A light novel by the British novelist Anthony Hope (1863–1933).

28. *Bloomingdale Asylum:* Opened in 1821, a place of "moral treatment" for the care of the insane.

29. *Montessori method:* An educational method founded by Dr. Maria Montessori (1870–1952). Rather than "teaching" a child, the Montessori environment was designed to stimulate the child's interest in learning with little or no adult intervention.

30. *The Laird o' Cockpen:* Popular melody by Carolina Oliphant, Lady Nairne (1766–1845).

31. *Monarch of the Glen ... Stag at Bay:* Two mid-nineteenth-century oil paintings of majestic stags by English painter Sir Edwin Henry Landseer (1802–1873). His brother Thomas engraved many of his paintings.

32. *Bernard Shaw:* George Bernard Shaw (1856–1950), Dublin-born playwright, critic, Socialist, satirist, and wit. Perhaps his most famous play was *Pygmalion,* which was first produced in 1914.

33. *R.L.S.:* Scottish essayist, novelist, and poet Robert Louis Stevenson (1850–1894).

34. *Did you once see Shelley plain ... :* The first lines of Robert Browning's poem "Memorabilia."

35. *Sally Lunn:* A rich round bread bun.

36. *Thoreau ... Walden: Walden* is the 1854 record of the two years that American naturalist and writer Henry David Thoreau (1817–1862) spent in an isolated hut he constructed on Walden Pond.

37. *Herbert Spencer's "System of Synthetic Philosophy":* Spencer (1820–1903) was an English philosopher of the great scientific movement of the second half of the nineteenth century. His *Synthetic Philosophy* proposed an inscrutable power called the unknowable and presented progress as the supreme law of the univer~e.

38. *Diary of ... arie Bashkirtseff:* The journal of Russian artist and writer Marie Constantinova Bashkirtseff (1860–1884). See also *Daddy-Long-Legs* note 37.

39. *Century: The Century: A Popular Quarterly,* was a New York magazine that published illustrated articles on history and politics, as well as fiction. The issue of May–October 1914 had several articles on China.

40. *Froebel theory:* Friedrich Wilhelm August Froebel (1782–1852), a German philosopher and educational reformer, invented the concept of "kindergarten" in his *The Education of Man* (1826), arguing for the necessity of play as an important educational and developmental tool.

41. *Burns:* Robert Burns (1759–1796), the great Scottish poet, wrote "To a Mouse, on Turning Her Up in Her Nest with the Plough" (1785): "Wee, sleekit, cow'rin, tim'rous beastie, / O, what a panic's in thy breastie!"

42. *S.P.C.A.:* Society for the Prevention of Cruelty to Animals, the first humane society in America, founded in 1866, which still exists today.

43. *House of Usher:* "The Fall of the House of Usher," a famous gothic story of a doomed family by American poet, fiction writer, and critic Edgar Allan Poe (1809–1849).

44. *The palm dreams of the pine . . . :* "The Palm and the Pine," adapted from Heine, was a poem by the American writer Sidney Lanier.

45. *Ellen Key:* Swedish-born author (1849–1926) of *The Century of the Child* (1900), an argument that the central work of society should be aimed at molding children into great men.

46. *Hebrew Sheltering Guardian Society's Orphan Asylum at Pleasantville:* Society founded in 1879 to care for destitute children, orphaned or not. Rather than housing all the children under one roof, the school opened in 1912 with 25 cottages and a school built on 175 acres of field and woods. House mothers were assigned to the 480 children in an effort to give the children personalized attention.

47. *Luca della Robbia:* Italian sculptor (1400–1482). The della Robbia family of sculptors and ceramists created glazed terracotta figures on many buildings in Florence.

48. *Numa Roumestan:* 1881 novel by French novelist Alphonse Daudet (1840–1897).

49. *published correspondence of Elizabeth Barrett and Robert Browning:* English poet Elizabeth Barrett married English poet Robert Browning in 1846 after a secret courtship. Their letters during their two-year courtship were published after their deaths and became models of romantic writing.

50. *Huxley's letters:* Thomas Henry Huxley (1825–1895) was an English biologist. See also *Daddy-Long-Legs* note 47.

51. *"John Anderson, my joe John":* Poem by Robert Burns, which celebrates a long and happy marriage.